First published in Great Britain in 2017 through Blurb by BookWright

Copyright © Andrew Henley 2017

The moral right of Andrew Henley to be identified as the author of this work has been asserted in accordance with the Copyright, Designs and Patents Act, 1988.

All rights reserved. No part of this publication may be reproduced or transmitted in any form or by any means, electronic or mechanical, including photocopy, recording, or any information storage and retrieval system, without permission in writing from the author.

This book is a work of fiction. Names, characters, businesses, organizations, places and events are either a product of the author's imagination or are used fictitiously. Any resemblance to actual persons, living or dead, events or locales is entirely coincidental.

BLACK HOLE HEARTBEAT

Andrew Henley

A woman of fire, reborn from ashes

ABOUT THE AUTHOR

Andrew Henley studied Creative Writing at Nottingham University and currently lives in North East England, where he teaches English, watches movies and shouts about the news

He is an independent author

More information is available online at
https://andrewhenleyauthor.wixsite.com/andrewhenleyauthor

Black Hole Heartbeat is his debut novel

For my parents, who always allowed me to write; and to the Hermitage Creative Writing Club, for reminding me why I do.

'Sometimes it feels like the whole damn galaxy is trying to kill me'
'It should have picked an easier fight'
- **Shepard and Liara, Mass Effect 2**

Elizabeth

Elizabeth Ranger's heart was full of fire, her head was full of fury, and her ship was full of loot. As she stepped out onto the blustery terrain of Green 3, the wind swept her cropped red hair across her face. Her crew followed her out.

"I still say there's plenty of treasure for us back in the Known Systems. We didn't need to come to The Barely Charted," Forr said.

Forr was a Krei, wide set with pale skin. Below average size in his species, Forr stood at seven foot.

Brack, a Torfus male with glistening scarlet scales, nudged past Forr to stand alongside Elizabeth.

"Live a little, dear."

"The Barely Charted system one," Elizabeth reminded them, "Only carries a mild punishment."

"Electroshock. Mild to me and Brack, and even a Human wouldn't be hurt too badly. But Lavell's a Jahlder. They've died from electroshock before," Forr said.

Lavell looked up from picking flowers around the Victory Pearl's ramp.

"You worry too much. Firstly, we won't get caught. Secondly, they'd give me water punishment over electroshock to avoid anymore Jahlder/electro bad press. Third, we can hardly call ourselves explorers if we don't explore."

Explorers was generous. They were thieves.

"Steal from The Barely Charted has always been on my list," Elizabeth said.

"That damn list of yours," Brack smirked.

"Fourthly, thank you for worrying."

Lavell stuffed one of the flowers into her robe. She stood on tiptoes to peck Forr's cheek. Her long white hair brushed against the fur on his shoulder.

Completing the crew alongside them was another Human named Olivia. She did not join in the conversation.

The temple of Allke stood in front of them, low sun casting long shadows over them. A pyramid of crumbling stone. Elizabeth would bet it hadn't had a visitor in decades.

Forr ran his thick fingers down the hinge, "Explosives?"

"The whole thing could fall," Brack said.

"I don't see you coming up with any ideas," Olivia said.

When Elizabeth had heard Olivia was saving up for a place in Russia's Human Only colony, she had invited her to join the crew to change her mind. It was not going well.

"Couldn't we like, set up the explosives so they just blow the doors off?"

"Wind might be about to do that for us," Elizabeth said, turning her shoulder against the gust.

No one else replied.

Elizabeth's hair blew into her mouth. She spat it out and looked up at the temple. There had to be a way inside. They would find it.

"Window," she said, pointing upwards.

"Probably too high," Brack said after a glance.

"I could climb it. Couldn't I, Ranger? I used to be the best climber back when we were kids!" Olivia said.

"I don't think this is *quite* the same, Liv dear," Brack told her.

"Don't call me dear, and don't call me Liv!"

"Lavell!" Elizabeth shouted over the noise.

If smashing or blasting things didn't work, Lavell normally had a solution.

"Working on it," Lavell shouted back.

She was already kneeling by the keyhole, sliding a pin inside. Metal teeth crawled out from the pin like the legs of an insect uncoiling. They slotted into the shape of the lock. As Lavell turned the pin, the teeth pushed against the stone, rotating until the pin spun full circle. The door eased open with a wailing creak.

"You know, I gave you those bracelets for a reason. You people really have to learn that there is more to life than brute force," Lavell said.

Elizabeth had her back to the temple, looking out across the dry plains of Green 3. The gardens had died. The grass was frail and strawlike. She pushed her hair back behind her ear. The wind immediately dragged it across her cheeks again. Clumps of dirt slapped off the long tail of her blue leather jacket. She swept the jacket back behind her holster and tightened her fingers around her white pistol's grip. Dust swirled around the dark boots on her feet. In Green 3's low sun, her shadow extended further than the rest.

Brack tried to pull the door. The stone squeaked but the door barely moved. Forr pushed him aside and yanked it open with two strong tugs.

"After you, of course," Brack said, stepping aside for Forr.

"After me, actually," Elizabeth said.

"Who else, dear?" Brack said, planting a kiss on her face.

Elizabeth stepped into the pitch black. The sun through the widow was a candle in a cave. She could feel and fumble further than she could see.

"Let's just grab what we can and leave," Olivia said.

"If you don't want to be here, go home," Elizabeth said.

"I'm only here so I can go home."

Lavell clicked her bracelet to lightbeam and a laser of illumination pierced the darkness. It landed on Brack, shimmering off the red scales of his neck and reflecting off his metal armour. The rest of them followed suit and slashed into the black with their lightbeams. All of them, except Olivia.

"You okay there?" Elizabeth asked.

Olivia twisted the dials on her bracelet back and forth. The clicking sound grew louder as her fingers became frustrated. She gave up with a scream screeched through clenched teeth.

"When are you gonna fix this for me?" she demanded.
"When you ask me nicely," Lavell told her.
"Why don't you fuck off, you Jahlder bitch?"
"She can't hear you," Elizabeth said, "Lavell's adapted her translation implant to turn all known curse words into static."

Lavell

Her light beam found a painting on the wall. The frame was cracked, bottom border sagging down. She brushed a clump of faded red feathers aside to see the art. There were two shadowy figures, each of them appearing to hide from –
Her panels started to glow. The white stripes down her pink body started to tingle. There was something here to absorb. She reached out to touch the painting and felt the knowledge flow.

Music poured into Lavell, drowning her in songs. She learnt of Green 3's old name – Gohdet – and of the Gods they worshipped. She became soaked in the dust the people left behind.
"This is just creepy," Olivia said, turning her back.
Lavell started to spasm. She could feel her muscles at war.
Elizabeth's voice was faint, "Something's wrong..."

The stories Lavell watched unfold became twisted and distorted, out of sequence. She felt herself breathing heavily, skin moist. The secrets that filled her expanded and shriveled. Every new thought attacked her mind. This was different. It would not let her stop.

She saw fire, and felt her body start to burn...

"Lavell. Lavell!"
Forr was leaning over her. His face stretched and danced. Voices were just sounds.
"What happened?" she asked woozily.
Forr scooped her up in his strong arms and squeezed her to his chest. She roped her arms around his wide shoulders, lacing through the fur that climbed the back of his neck.
"Don't worry. I'm okay," she whispered in his ear.
He put her down gently, a hint of a smile cracking his giant face.

"Next time you want to learn, maybe just read a book, huh?"
The new Human... Olivia?
"Why don't you shut up? She could've died," Elizabeth said. There was no mistaking her voice.
"We *all* could've died. We shouldn't be here, there's lots to steal in Paxet System."

Olivia and Elizabeth were about to fight. She thought... Things were still blurred.

"We're not here for cash like you. We're treasure hunters."

"Oh don't give me your poetry, you and your space freaks steal for cash like everybody else."

They stepped closer. Their blurred figures stepped through each other like ghosts.

"*Thieves* steal for cash. We're treasure hunters. All we want is treasure."

Elizabeth punctuated every short burst with a jab to Olivia's chest plate. Her finger slammed straight through Olivia's fading ghost.

"Jab me with your finger one more time and I'll break it."

"Try and break my finger and I'll snap your arm off and give it to you as a backscratcher."

Elizabeth's eyes did not blink, even as her red hair fell across them. The ghosts disappeared and clarity returned.

Lavell broke the silence.

"We shouldn't be here."

"What did you see?" Forr asked her.

"Fire. It wasn't like normal, it was... like a warning. Something wants us to leave."

Forr nodded.

"We should leave," he said.

A lightbeam shone across the argument. They all followed it to an ornate door. Lavell's eyes ran down the beam to its owner. Brack.

"On the other hand..." he said.

"Open it," Elizabeth said.

"Lavell said we go back," Forr said, turning harsh.

"I say we go forward. We didn't come this far to turn back because of a ghost story," Elizabeth said.

Lavell did not object. Elizabeth Ranger had saved her life on multiple occasions, not least getting her away from the Jahlder in the first place. Lavell owed her one.

5

Elizabeth

Elizabeth turned the handle. Her fingers wrapped around the thick loop, unable to meet. More dust blew up from the floor as the door's gilded base scratched against stone. Forr stepped into Elizabeth's path.
"Lavell saw fire. We should leave."
Elizabeth strained her neck to look Forr in the eye. His stare was made of polished pebbles.
"She doesn't see dreams. What just happened wasn't normal."
"All the more reason to leave," Forr said, the thick skin of his face tensing around his dark eyes.
Elizabeth tried to push him aside. He rocked slightly to the left then returned to centre.
"Elizabeth's right," Lavell said, "It wasn't like usual. We should just ignore it."
Forr turned to Lavell, face solid and jaw tensed. His chin was like a fist. She gave him a small nod and he stepped aside.
"We don't stay long," he said.

She pulled the door further with heaving effort. It latched into a shallow trough with an echoing thunk. Elizabeth swept her blue jacket back behind her holster. She drew her pistol and held her finger softly on the trigger. Elizabeth was a traditionalist. Her cartridge was packed bullets. They had torn through anything she had come across just as well as the twitching purple energy favoured by Lavell, Forr and Brack.

Elizabeth's skin turned cold, like plunging into ice water. Forr turned to Lavell.
"Anything new?"
The markings on her skin remained pale.
"Nothing."
"Minds on the job people. Guns out and eyes open," Elizabeth said.
They readied their guns to an off key symphony of metal and plastic. They kept their lightbeams low. Unknown creatures lurked in the shadows on abandoned planets.

Elizabeth's lightbeam sat on the tips of her toes, moving forward with each slow step. The floor was paved with crystal, her light dancing across the azure tiles. She swirled the lightbeam in semi-circle. The reflection glinting off the tiles turned amber, emerald, ruby.
"Looks like some sort of mosaic," she said.
Brack was already on bended knee, sliding the knife out of his bracelet. He pried the blade into the floor and eked out one of the small tiles, holding it to his eye.
"What we got?"
"Just coloured glass. Worthless," he said, tossing it away.
It skidded across the floor, a hollow clack with every bounce.

Lavell and Forr were huddled in the corner, examining a statue. They were speaking in whispers.

"Worth anything?" Elizabeth asked without looking over.
"It's not made of anything precious. I doubt it's worth very much. Heavy too."
"Leave it then."

Olivia was standing in the doorway, unwilling to step inside the cold dark.
"Is there any point in me even being here?"
"No," Brack replied.
"I know you're new to this, but nobody comes up to you and hands you the treasure. You have to hunt for it. Clue's in the name," Elizabeth said.
"My light don't work."
"Lavell..." Elizabeth said.
Olivia had been a good pickpocket on Earth, but she wasn't cut out for this line of work. This mission was her first and last.

Lavell took hold of Olivia's bracelet. She tightened the secure holds on Olivia's wiring, using a foldaway knife as a makeshift screwdriver.
"Try it now," she said.
Olivia flicked the switch on her bracelet and the lightbeam hazed into life.
"Fixed," Olivia said. Blunt and ungrateful.
Lavell still had her by the wrist.
"I'll let you when you say thank you."
"Let go, you little pink dwarf!"
Olivia snatched her hand away, sending her lightbeam into the rafters.

There was a terrible guttural screech. A thousand black tongues squawked from a thousand beaks.
"Run!"
Awful red wings descended on them.
"Now look what you did!" Olivia screamed at Lavell.
She pushed Lavell further inside and tried to draw her gun. She fumbled. Lavell was quicker on the draw, gunning down a blood red bird that dove at Olivia. The creatures were rapui, deadly birds with claws like razors and beaks strong enough to bite through metal.

The room exploded with purple light as Brack and Forr sent a barrage of energy blasts into the swooping pack. One landed on Forr, claws sinking into his armour. There was a shower of feathers, and the bird fell limp, claws still stuck into the chest plate. The bird dangled like a pendulum, dripping blood and mangled feathers.

Elizabeth's hands were on her weapon, but she had fired no shots. The rapui were her second priority. Just before Olivia's lightbeam had awoken the creatures, it had found a glint. When she heard the first bloodlust scream of the rapui, she turned her lightbeam off and rolled into the shadows. The rest of them could handle rapui. At least, she knew Forr, Brack and Lavell could. She wasn't so sure about Olivia.

Dropping into a crawl, Elizabeth shuffled forward. She did not look back at the birds.

Her hand stubbed against flat stone and felt the hard outline of steps. She hunched over as she climbed. At the top, her hands reached out expecting to grab something. They swiped at the air and felt nothing.

She was so close. One flash of her lightbeam. That was all it would take. But that was all the rapui would need. She shone it quickly. Polished metal. Jewels. It was beautiful. Behind her, the birds cackled and swooped as one, dive bombing for her. She lifted the glass box around the treasure and swung it for the swarm. It smashed in her hands, shattering in a burst of blood and feathers.

She fired her pistol into the flock. Half of them retreated. The rest continued to drive at Elizabeth, moving at a fantastic speed. Their cawing was a shrill howl. Feathers sprayed off their backs. Talons tensed forward. She ran, still firing. Blood spurted, spraying across Elizabeth's face as sodden organs landed in her hair.

Lavell was holding her position at the door. Olivia was still clumsily figuring out her gun. It was loaded with an empty clip. A new one had to be found and inserted with shaking hands. Elizabeth sprinted and caught up to Brack and Forr, showering shots as she ran. A dead rapui still hung from Forr. Elizabeth yanked its mangled leg out and threw it at the rapui swarm, sending them skittering sideways.

Lavell grabbed the gun and clip from Olivia's nervous fingers and rammed them together, tossing the loaded pistol back to Olivia. She didn't catch it.
"There, it's there!" Lavell shouted, pointing her lightbeam.
Elizabeth picked the pistol up midstride and forced it into Olivia's arms.

A rapui had landed on Lavell's back, shredding her clothes and skin. Her shout of pain was unbearable as the jagged claws burst through her. The lightbeam convulsed away.

Forr fired relentlessly at the bird, stomping on the feathered corpses at his feet to reach Lavell. A wet pulp of feathers and offal stuck to his legs. It smelled sick and rotten. He grabbed the bird attacking her and snapped its neck cleanly. A cracking pop echoed.

He gently peeled the rigid talons from Lavell's back. One toe broke off, staying pierced through her back. The sound was like a candy cane breaking, loud and hollow. He flung the bird aside and lifted Lavell into his arms.

"Everybody out of here!" Elizabeth roared.
Olivia ran immediately, followed by Forr carrying Lavell. Brack backed off in line with Elizabeth as she kept firing. There were fifty dead birds on the floor, maybe more, but they had barely made a dent in the rapui army.

As she and Brack shoved the doors closed, Elizabeth's lightbeam shone back to the podium.

Forr

Forr cradled Lavell's small frame into his arms, keeping her close against his chest. Hot blood dripped down his huge hands, staining the skin turquoise.
"We need to hurry."

The winds were growing stronger, tearing branches from trees. Forr huddled over to shelter Lavell as Elizabeth raced ahead to open the doors. By the time he reached her, the door was high enough for him to duck under. He carried Lavell frantically to the Med Bay and lay her gently on the table.
"You'll be okay, okay? We'll fix this," he said, laying a soft hand on her cheek.

He should've made her wear armour. He had warned her about the fabric robes on her back. She wouldn't have listened. She told him it helped her move quicker, but Forr knew the real reason. Elizabeth Ranger strolled into battle protected by only a long blue leather jacket. And from the moment Lavell joined up, she wanted to be Elizabeth Ranger more than anything.

But she was *not* Elizabeth. When he first met Elizabeth she had stuck her gun in his face. By the time the sun set that night they were laughing and sharing drinks. Lavell was the last to join. They'd found her when they were defending a Jahlder colony from a Krei attack. She was picking flowers on the outskirts, unaware that they were even under seige. She had cried and begged Elizabeth to take her with them.

The Krei viewed the Jahlder as gnats to be crushed under their heel. Forr had left his Excha homeworld before he was conscripted and had never seen a Jahlder before. Never seen anything as gorgeous as her pure white hair, or her candy pink skin and intriguing markings. They had broken each other's myths of their species. Even befriending her was illegal for someone like him. And falling in love... Still, he if concerned himself with the illegalities of his activities, he never would have become a treasure hunter.

"My pact..." he whispered in her ear.
Pact were small, rabbit like creatures. They were reared for meat on Excha, though he didn't tell Lavell that. He had given her the nickname when he washed his fur in front of her, making her his talanacti. His life partner. He remembered the cool water flowing down his back, cleansing him.

Brack handed him a flask and a set of pills.

"For her pain," he said.

She knocked the pills onto the floor. She must have aggravated her wounds by moving, letting out another desperate scream. It hurt Forr to hear it.

"Please, my pact," he said.

"My lion... I need to stay awake," she said, "I can help Ranger. I can tell her what do to do."

"I could use her help," Elizabeth said.

"Help? She needs a hospital Elizabeth!" Brack said.

"We might not make it back to Known Systems in time.

If Lavell was to be saved, she would have to be saved here.

"Isn't there a doctor?" Olivia said.

Forr hadn't noticed her was there. His flat nose widened, and his dark eyes gave no shine.

"Lavell was the doctor."

Elizabeth grabbed a pair of scissors and cut down the back of Lavell's robes. The wounds were worse than he feared. Rapui claws her long and sharp. They either punctured something vital and you died, or they missed anything important and you lived. But this one hadn't gotten hold of Lavell properly. Maybe it was her small size. Maybe the loose flowing fabric of her robes. It had swiped and scratched at Lavell's skin, tearing it to shreds. The snapped off claw was the biggest problem. If not removed delicately, it could puncture something on the way out and give Lavell the instant death the rapui were famed for.

Elizabeth

"How many cuts are on my back?" Lavell asked.
Elizabeth answered honestly, "Hundreds."
Forr put his head in his hands desperately.
"I mean real ones. The kind that need to be stitched up."
Elizabeth looked over Lavell's ruined flesh. The blood was flowing slower, drying over her in a violet glaze.
"Five."
"That's not too many," Lavell said.
"One of them still has the talon in it."
"We'll get to that later. Firstoooooowww!"
A stifled cry of agony interrupted her.
"First, look in the bottom cupboard in the left corner. See a bottle of pills?"
Brack held it out to her.
"Muslatron?" Elizabeth read out.
"That's them. Take two."
She handed them over.
"Not me!" Lavell said, "*You* take them. They'll keep your hands steady."
Elizabeth took four and washed them down with a gulp.
"I wouldn't count on sleeping much for the next two days," Lavell said.
Two days? Elizabeth couldn't think about that now.
"What do I need to do?"
"Look in the third drawer down on that trolley. It has thread for stitches in it."
Elizabeth writhed open the drawer. Her frantic hands searched blindly. Sweat ran into her eyes. Surgery was not in her wheelhouse.

Her hands found a coil.
"Give it here," Lavell said.
Elizabeth passed the needle to Lavell.
"That's too thick. It's for Krei skin and it'll just rip me openooo... open worse. Third drawer. A plastic bag with a pink seal. Do you see it?"
She looked again, forcing herself to slow down.
"Yeah."
"Gimmie."
"I haven't threaded it –"
"I'll be quicker. Give it here."
Elizabeth had never heard Lavell demand anything before. She passed Lavell the bag of thread and a new needle and waited for instruction.

Lavell's hands were trembling. Elizabeth watched the wet, raw muscles twitching beneath the flayed skin. The sinews dancing, tense. Her fingers were vibrating. Threading a needle in those conditions was impossible. Her focus was so intense she managed it in seconds.

The needle was back in Elizabeth's hands. So was the pressure. Lavell was too sacred to piss her pants without permission when they met. Now Elizabeth was the one standing behind, not daring to move until Lavell told her to.
"All right, how big is the biggest cut? Ignorrrrrrr... Ignoring the one with the claw."
Elizabeth measured with her fingers. She held her thumb and forefinger apart and leant forward to show Lavell. Forr's mighty hand grasped of Lavell's like a small and fragile bird. It was enough to make her heart break.
"That'll take eight stitches, each about a thumbwidth apart. You remember what I taught youuuuuuu, right?"
Elizabeth nodded, lying. Lavell had given them all basic first aid training. She had largely been ignored. Elizabeth hoped it would all come back to her.

Her hands shook above the valleys of Lavell's skin. Four Muslatron had not been enough. Elizabeth Ranger was not a woman squeamish to violence. The barrel of her gun had fired through brains, eyes and... other places. But piercing Lavell's skin with the needle, even to heal her, made her nauseous.
"I'm already in pain. A little more won't huuuuuuuurt. You have to do this, Elizabeth."
Elizabeth took a deep, focussing breath and got to work. The needle poked through the skin cleanly. Elizabeth's hand moved to secure the first stitch. Muscle memory of Lavell's lessons. She had no idea what she was doing, but her hands seemed to, and they were working quickly.

"Okay, four done," she said.
Sweat was gathering on her forehead. Brack swabbed it with a moist towel. The feeling was a blissful cool.
"Just the talon left," she said.
Her body was nervous, but her hands were steady.
"Take the pills now," Forr said, "Elizabeth can finish from here."
His voice was begging, eyes desperate.
"No. Not until it's over."
"What do I do?" Elizabeth said.
It was not a question she was used to asking.
"See the edges of the talon? The serrations?"
"Yeah."
"If myaaaaaah... head's north, are the serrations pointing north and south, or east west?"
Elizabeth moved her head closer to Lavell's body, picking up the stale scent of dried blood.
"They're diagonal!"
Her voice was louder and more helpless than she'd intended. She felt foolish.
"That's okay. Turn it until they're east and west."
"Turn it? Lavell, it'll break off!" Brack said.
"Just do it."
Elizabeth reached her the talon. Her hands started to tremble.
"I can't... I need a tweezer or something."
She couldn't stand to touch it.

"Get her a set of tweezers Forr!" Lavell yelled.

He grabbed a set from one of the trolleys and thrust them at Elizabeth. Once she had them in her hands, she was shaking again. Lavell had taught her nothing like this.

As lightly as she could manage, Elizabeth gripped the talon in between the thin tongs of the tweezers. Her heart was hammering on her ribcage. She felt her knees failing. She had to grit her teeth and force her body to strengthen. Gently, she rotated the talon around. There was a horrible moment where it caught flesh. Elizabeth was sure it was going to splinter and slice down into Lavell's wound. She held her breath and kept it twisting, unable to do anything else. Lavell gave a muted cry as the talon fought back, cutting a fresh rip in the open wound. Blood leaking out her jagged back. The new cut gave it space to manoeuvre. Eventually, Elizabeth had the serrations pointing out at east and west.

"It's done."

"Put your finger in front of the talon and pull it towards you, slowly but firmly. Understand?"

"Got it."

"Don't stop. No matter how much I scream, don't stop."

"Take the pills. Please!" Forr's voice cracked.

He thrust the pills and flask at her face. Water sloshed out from the flask's cap, landing on the floor with a splash.

"Soon, my lion," she said.

"She'll be fine, Forr. Don't worry," Brack said, placing an arm on his friend's shoulder.

As Elizabeth removed the talon, Lavell screeched with her eyes squeezed tight and her fists clenched shut.

"Is it out?" she gasped.

"It's done. You can sleep now," Elizabeth said.

Forr handed her the pills. She took them gratefully, craning her neck up to funnel them into her mouth. She washed the pills down with a long drink. The pills were strong and sleep came quickly. Her arms sagged limp before she could hand the flash back. It fell to the floor with a metallic crash. If she had taken them before Elizabeth had started, she might never have woken up.

"I'll stay with her," Forr said.

Elizabeth nodded. She went over to the sink to wash her hands clean, scrubbing away the blood. It had soaked into her fingerprints. Brack's hand on Forr's shoulder squeezed tight.

"Keep her safe, big guy," he said.

"I'm sorry, Forr," Elizabeth said, "We should've left."

Forr stroked Lavell's white hair and smiled, "If she remembers tonight and how the great Elizabeth Ranger was hanging on her every word, she'll think that rapui attack was the best thing that ever happened to her."

~*~

Elizabeth returned to her quarters. She sat at her desk, picking feathers off her pistol. Her thoughts were interrupted by a tapping at the doorframe.
"You did well," Brack said behind her.
"Thanks," Elizabeth said.
She did not look up at him.
"I mean it."
Brack walked further into the room.
"You just saved Lavell's life."

He kissed her gently. His skin was firmer than human flesh, with ridged scales that tickled Elizabeth's soft lips like stubble.
"What're you kissing me like that for?" she said.
"Nobody expects you to save our lives, you know."
She turned away from him.
"We expect you to fill them with vigour, excitement and riches," he continued, "With magnificent stories. And you deliver. We're all rich because of you, but more than that –"
Elizabeth cut across him, "I'm going back."
"You know, I was in the middle of a rather complementary speech about you," Brack said.
He was a master of faked offence, but Elizabeth suspected a double bluff.
"I can't wait to hear it. When I get back."
"You know we can't go back. Not now the rapui are awake."
"There's something in that temple. Something strange, and I need to find out what. Rapui or no rapui."
"But no rapui would be better," Brack said.
"I could use the bubble shield."
"It's still just a prototype."
"You know Lavell's a perfectionist with her inventions. If it's at the prototype stage now, that means it'll be okay for a short burst."
He laid his hand on hers. His palm was soft and fleshy.
"I don't get it, Elizabeth dear. You've never been this interested before."
"You know what I do for we living, right?"
"But you've always been more interested in the *hunting* than the *treasure* part. What makes this one so different? The Barely Charted?"
"Maybe I feel like this will be the one that got away."
She couldn't explain it.
"I don't want you getting hurt."
His voice turned tender. His hand rose to caress her cheek. They were warm. Elizabeth moved her hands to his back, one sliding up into the flexible spines on his head. She moved to kiss him, then jerked to the side and slammed him down on the desk in front of her. A pile of his books toppled. Holding him down, she wretched a set of handcuffs from her pockets.
"Why do you have handcuffs!"
"Never know when I'll need a hostage," she smirked.
He was strong, but the element of surprise gave her the edge. She slotted Brack's

hand inside one and her desk leg into the other. It was solid titanium, and bolted to the floor. He was not getting out easily.

"I'm sorry, but I have to," Elizabeth said.

"Wait!" Brack shouted.

She stopped and turned.

"If you're going to risk your life, you could at least give me a kiss goodbye," he said.

Elizabeth smiled and crouched down by him. She grabbed the sides of his face and pulled him to her lips. The ridges of the scales were jagged against her hands.

"See, wouldn't you rather stay here?" Brack said.

"I'll be back soon. Don't move."

"Pin um," he said.

"I love you too."

Elizabeth had deliberately disabled that phrase from her translator. It sounded more beautiful in Brack's native tongue.

Elizabeth walked through the Mess Hall. Olivia was sat there, slamming a knife into the table. She picked it up by the hilt and crashed it back down. Blood was running down her thumb.

"Where are you going?" Olivia said.

"You almost killed Lavell."

She averted her gaze from Elizabeth's hard stare.

"It's my fault," Elizabeth said, "I never should have brought you along."

Elizabeth pounded her fist against a blue button on the wall, opening the exit.

"Where are you going?"

Elizabeth stepped out onto the hard soil of Green 3.

"Whoever names these places might want to come up with something new."

Olivia followed her outside. She grabbed Elizabeth's arm to yank her back. Her hair was sprayed about in tangled tufts, face a dark scowl.

"Hey! Don't walk away from me!"

Elizabeth dragged her arm from Olivia's grip.

"As soon as we're back in the Known Systems, I'm dropping you off."

"It's so easy for you, isn't it?"

"I don't have time for this, Olivia."

"You got out, so fuck the rest of us, right? Elizabeth Ranger, queen of the galaxy, breaking into palaces while I'm fistfighting for a loaf of bread!"

"You honestly think I had no one else to call? You think I needed you for this job? You're here as a favour, and you nearly got one of my crew killed."

Olivia looked at the ground and kicked the dust.

"Please, Elizabeth. I need something. Wherever you're going, let me come with you. Just the two of us. How it should be."

"Well…"

Elizabeth swung her arm at Olivia, elbow into forehead.

"Nah,"

The strike was measured. Olivia would be awake in a couple of hours. She dragged her body over to the steps of the Victory Pearl, shielding her from the debris that blustered across the plains. Elizabeth turned to the temple, red hair blowing in the storm.

With a grunt of high pitched friction, the temple door scraped against the stone floor. Elizabeth had her gun readied, finger wrapped around the trigger. She waited for the red swarm.

She crept up to the door. Peeking through the cracks, she could see no trace of the birds. Sleeping back in the rafters. She would need to be silent.

Her lightbeam lit up the temple floor. It was a sea of red feathered corpses. Mangled bodies drowned in thick, rancid blood. Bony rapui talons poked up like snorkels. Elizabeth made her way through the ocean. *Crack*. Her foot found bone. It echoed around and the tall walls ominously. Elizabeth froze. The blood in her veins turned to icy shards. She waited. No attack came.

Her feet slid through the ooze of blood and raw meat. She was afraid to lift them. The rapui would not sleep through another broken bone. At the steps, she crouched over and brushed the shards of broken glass aside before climbing. The disc shone in front of her. She pressed the shield button on her bracelet. Lavell's prototype. An orange panel flashed in front of her with a crackling fizz. The rapui heard. Their eyes blinked open, bright. They dove for her as she reached out and grabbed it.

Her hands started to sear. A charred stench clogged her nostrils. Bones were melting. Muscles were tearing. Organs were swelling.

She felt herself burst.

Ana

The smell of molten flesh was barbaric. How could anyone have survived this? It didn't stink of meat. It was more like ash. Crisp, smoky and rotten. No question, this would be her biggest job yet.
"This isn't even the worst of it. Heart needs repaired too."
A woman had a tight grip around Ana's bicep. She half expected to be handcuffed to the bed, despite the money they were paying her.

~*~

The skin crackled as Ana cut through it. The blackness crumbled away from her scalpel. Inside, there was barely anything left of the heart. It was pumping, but only with a whimper. Most doctors would declare her dead and wait for the remnants of life to trickle out of her. But Ana was not most doctors. The woman next to her leaned over the wreckage.
"How do you rate her chances?"
"I'll save her," Ana said firmly.
"Save her? This one needs resurrecting."

~*~

Sam. The woman's name was Sam. Not the woman on the table, the other woman. The one with the guns and the strong thighs and the long lashes. With the plump brown lips and the short dark hair. There was a softness to her stoic face, a sweet pout when she studied Ana working.

The woman on the table was Elizabeth, but Ana didn't care much about that. She was just a patient who needed saving. The only reason she knew about Elizabeth at all was because she loved to listen to Sam. Loved to watch her face fill with passion. Days, weeks and months passed as she kept watch over Elizabeth, making sure she was healing on schedule.

~*~

It was a new procedure. Ana used stem cells to regrow Elizabeth's skin piece by piece. Once each raw, pink strip was ready, a special skin knitting salve of Ana's own design was sprayed on the blackened body. The new skin was laid on top and Elizabeth healed, scarlessly.

Sam kissed her on the cheek.
"Any progress?"
"Just what you can see."
"Don't work too late tonight. Okay?"

~*~

The heart was much more difficult.

An artificial heart was keeping Elizabeth alive, but it would not cope with the increased heartrate once she woke up. Ana's three previous attempts to grow a working heart had failed.

Sam handed Ana's notebook back to her.
"Did he make any more changes?"
"He suggested this," Sam said.
She handed Ana a set of wires in a glass jar.
"He can't be serious," Ana said.
Sam just shrugged.
"Says it'll give the artificial heart more power."
"I don't know…"

Sam put her hand at the small of Ana's back and pulled her close.
"Hey, you're the genius. I'm just the muscle."
Sam's breath was hot as she kissed Ana's neck. Ana's eyes never left the jar of cogs and springs.
"I guess we could try."

Elizabeth

Elizabeth's skull felt as if a grenade had just detonated inside of it. Her eyes flickered open slowly, eyelashes flailing like an insect on its back. Thin film kept her eyelids together. Bright light stabbed at her brain. Everything was white or polished metal. Everywhere a shining ray of light to hurt her. There were two figures over in the corner, nothing more than colourless shapes.

"She's waking up," one of them said.

They were both Humans, both women. One of them was dressed in a dark green uniform without a badge or marking, with twin pistols in hip holsters and another gun on her back. Her short dark hair sat under a beret. A woman prepared for violence. Elizabeth grabbed at her own thigh, grasping for her gun. She felt only a plastic smock and cool skin. The second woman wore a white uniform. No guns. She had loose blonde curls and bold red lipstick. Thick black eyeliner winged away from her blue eyes. They both wore bracelets like Lavell's.

Elizabeth tried to sit up but the blonde woman rushed forward, pushing her back down. She aimed a small torch into her pupil. Elizabeth winced away from the light. The first woman slapped the other's hand away.

"All these machines you've got plugged in and you need to shine that damn thing in her eyes as soon as she's awake? She been out for three years, you don't think she'll take a little while to adjust?"

"Three years?" Elizabeth said quietly. The words floated out of her.

She sunk back onto the bed, body numb.

"Break it to her gently, you said Sam," the blonde woman said, arms folded.

Years away from Earth – and three years asleep, apparently – had dulled her ear for accents, but there was no mistaking the hard Russian edge '*you zed Zam*' in the blonde woman's voice. She looked young, early twenties maybe. Sam was more like Elizabeth's age, around thirty.

"Bad news is bad news any way it's broken," Sam said. She forced a smile.

Sam sat down on the bed. Elizabeth's eyes never left Sam's pistol. She considered reaching for it, but this woman looked like she'd be match for her. With rusty reflexes, it was a race she would lose.

"Yeah, three years," Sam said, "Healing a burst heart takes time."

"Burst?"

"Your heart popped like a water balloon. Never seen anything like it."

"You did that?" Elizabeth said.

"Not me. Ana," Sam said, nodding at the nurse.

"Anastasia Yukishnov," Ana said, holding her hand out for Elizabeth to shake.

"I'll stick with Ana."

"I also had to repair several broken bones, regrow your organs and replace your charred skin."

"What happened to me?" Elizabeth asked.

They looked at each other. They remained silent.

"Go make the call," Sam said.

Sam looped her hand around the back of Ana's head, gently pulling her down until her forehead met Sam's dark lips. The kiss made a small sound.
"You two are together?" Elizabeth asked.
Ana's body jerked around, face hard. Pursed lips and tensed eyebrows.
"All across the galaxy, humans fall in love with creatures of green and red and purple, and people still can't tolerate lesbians?"
Sam was smiling.
"I've got nothing against it. I see something pretty, I fuck it," Elizabeth said, "You two just seem like a strange match."
"You've figured that out in the five minutes you've known us?"
"Sounds like I've known you for three years."
Ana's face flushed red as she turned to the door in another jerky movement.

Sam let out a chuckle, "You've got a read on her already, haven't you?"
"For someone who spent three years saving my life, she doesn't seem like she likes me very much."
"Don't take it personally."
Elizabeth became aware of long red strands falling in front of her eyes. She glanced at her shoulder and saw a stream of ginger locks flowing down it.
"Nobody thought to give me a haircut?"
"Ana's given you plenty. But she thought you looked better like this."
Elizabeth sat up and tossed her hair behind her back with irritation. Her skin itched. Her teeth were dirty. She wiped at her lips and looked at her fingers. They were red. Blood. No, worse than blood. Lipstick. Ana again. Elizabeth rubbed her forearm across her mouth, smearing the lipstick away into a waxy streak.
"So where am I?" Elizabeth said.
"A hospital."
"I figured that. Where? Earth?"
"Your heart burst in The Barely Charted, and you didn't die. Aren't you curious why not?"
"I was working my way up to it."
Her long hair was scratching her neck. She shook it away.
"There's somebody very keen to meet you."
"Why get me to ask if you're only offering half answers?"
"It burnt you, didn't it?" Sam asked. Her voice was full of admiration, mystique.
"Seriously. What happened?"

Suddenly, the room turned red. An alarm blared before Elizabeth could ask anymore. Sam jumped off the bed and drew both pistols from her hip holsters. Elizabeth snatched the rifle from Sam's back. Sam turned, teeth bared like an angry dog.
"Seriously?" Ranger said.
Sam gave a curt nod.
"I want it back after."
Elizabeth looked down at her thigh where her gun would be.
"Yeah, I want mine back too."

They kept low, creeping to the exit. Ana ran back into the room. Her knee crashed into Elizabeth's forehead. Elizabeth pressed her palm against the pain.
"Seriously?!"
"Goddamn ripegs!" Sam said.
Ripegs. Pointless little pirates. They were like pimples. Weak and pathetic on their own, hideously irritating in a large group.
"There's more of them this time. Too many!" Ana said.
"Why are ripegs attacking a hospital?" Elizabeth asked.
"Never been too many before. This time won't be any different."
"Right," Ana said, nodding quickly, "What should I do?"
Elizabeth stood up, hand still on her forehead.
"Listen, little girl. This isn't some comic book where the Russian nurse is a highly trained assassin. Leave the fighting to the women and find us a way out of this hospital."
Ana's eyeballed Elizabeth, then looked beyond her for Sam's opinion.
"We'll need a ship, Ana."
Ana's eyes moved back to Elizabeth.
"I'm a doctor, not a nurse," Ana said as she left.

Sam and Elizabeth stood either side of the doorframe. Sam leaned out just in time to be sledgehammered by an explosion. Her body shot back into Elizabeth's, sending them both flying down the hallway. Orange flames spat out thick smoke.

Sam sent a flurry of shots while Elizabeth slid for cover. Part of the wall had collapsed inwards, leaving a mound of rubble to hide behind. Elizabeth examined the chamber to see how many shots she had, but saw only a canister of purple energy.
"You don't use bullets?"
"Unlimited ammo," Sam said.
"I guess so."
Now wasn't the time to explain that canisters *weren't* actually unlimited, as the less stored in the canister the weaker the shots were. Not to mention they took four hours to restore naturally.

Her head moved up quickly. Three quick shots. Pewpewpew. The muted whimper of energy shots. All three of them hit ripegs in the chest. They kept moving as if they were fly bites.
"Bullet's would've torn them open," Elizabeth said.
"Best we can hope for is to slow them down," Sam said.
Elizabeth ducked behind the cover again and stared down the corridor.
"An exit," she pointed, "Come on, Ana's gonna be waiting with our ship!"
"You go," Sam breathed.
Fear had taken her voice away.
"What are you waiting for? Come on!" Elizabeth said.
She grabbed Sam by the midriff and pulled her. Sam let out a ferocious groan, but did not move. Sam looked down at her feet, Elizabeth's eyes following. Sam's right leg was twisted and bloody, her foot chewed up and swallowed by the pile of rubble.

Elizabeth gripped the stone, jutting edges cutting into her finger as she tried to lift it. No movement.
"You can still get out of here. Go!" Sam shouted, pushing Elizabeth away.
There was a glint of acceptance in Sam's eyes. Maybe Elizabeth only wanted to see it.

Sweat soaked through the armpits of Sam's shirt.
"You aren't supposed to feel wounds like this... The adrenaline's supposed to..."
Her hand trembled as it raised the gun to her mouth. She bit down on the barrel. A burst of purple ricocheted off her tooth, ripping her bottom lip in half as it left her mouth. More blood. More burning torture.
"Bullet's would've tore me open," she mumbled weakly through a bloody pulp.
Elizabeth raised her own gun and placed it gently against the back of Sam's head.
"I'll make it quick," she promised.

~*~

Elizabeth reached the exit. The door was locked. The only key she had on her was a full speed shoulder charge. It did the trick, splintering the wood away from the hinges. The exit did not take her outside as she had expected. She was inside a glass tube, with arrows pointing to the Shuttle Bay, Living Quarters and Kitchen. Shuttle Bay was the obvious choice.

This was no hospital. This was a space station. Why would patients fly out to hospital when there were hundreds on every populated planet?

Ana

Ana waited by the shuttle for Sam and Elizabeth to arrive. Goddamn ripegs. The attacks had been getting worse. If they had just waited one more day... The plan was to move as soon as Elizabeth woke up anyway.

Elizabeth ran into the shuttle bay, tripping as her bare feet hit the steel floor. Ana took her by the elbow and picked her up.
"I can give you some salve for that when you're on board," Ana said.
She led Elizabeth over to their ship.
"Where's Sam? Is that her rifle?"
Elizabeth dropped it and turned pale as a cooked apple.
"Ana..." the rest of her words died on her.

Ana didn't need them. Tears pooled in her eyes, murky with black mascara. She shook her head violently, and the gloomy streams overflowed down her cheeks.
"She was brave," Elizabeth said.
A fitting epitaph, but no comfort.
"So much for the great Elizabeth Ranger," Ana said.
Ana shoved Elizabeth in the chest. Elizabeth stumbled back and hit her head off the floor. She got to her feet and ran at Ana, grabbing her collar and forcing her against the wall.
"You woke me up and brought me a ship. You're done. Tell me why I shouldn't throw you out and leave you here to die?"
Ana pulled out a derringer pistol and pressed it up under Ranger's chin.
"Because I read a lot of comics," she said.
"That's a little girl's weapon."
Ana kept her gun pressed into Elizabeth. She tried to stop her hand from quaking. Elizabeth let her drop.
"You drive. I'll man the turrets," Elizabeth said.
"We don't have any. It's an ambulance."

Elizabeth hovered near Ana as she flew. Her eyes were jittery, clambering across the controls. She moved either side of Ana, leaning over. A hand stretched out, feeling the buttons.
"That salve I mentioned is in a clear glass jar in that cupboard," Ana said, pointing.
Elizabeth straightened up quickly. She wandered away from the control panel.
"Got it."
"And your stuff's in that room."
"Stuff?"

23

Elizabeth

Elizabeth stepped into the next room of the shuttle. The jar slipped through surprised fingers. Her blue leather jacket floated there, limp on a peg. Haunted by a three year old ghost, it swayed as the ship turned. Her black boots were waiting for her in the corner, her cargo trousers folded up on a bench, white pistol lying on top. Ana had even left out a clean vest, bra and underwear for her. She picked up the gun and checked the chamber. Empty.

She needed a shower. She threw on the bra, vest and underwear. Her hand hesitated on the jacket. The leather was cool in her hand. She picked it up and the ghost washed away, exorcised. It was like slipping on old skin.

She sat down and her skinned knee stung. The pain felt like guilt against the memory of Sam's foot. Bones crushed to powder. The salve on the floor was a translucent pile of goop with curled fangs of broken glass poking out from it. She dipped her hand in, scooping a glob onto her fingertips. She massaged it against her knees until the hurt turned numb.

She wiped her hands down her thighs, trailing clear slugs of salve on her skin. The trousers stuck to the wetness of the salve as she tugged them up her legs. Her empty gun slotted perfectly into the empty holster at her hip. Having her weapon within reach again felt good. She sat down on the bench and pulled on the socks. Pink nail varnish glowed through the white fabric. Finally, she grabbed her boots and pushed her feet inside, lacing them up tight. Her toes wriggled into their familiar grooves. Her hair fell down across her face and she blew it away. It would be chopped short at her first opportunity.

She was dressed like Elizabeth Ranger again. Memories flowed back into her. She moved back to the flight deck and watched Ana fly, recognizing the buttons and dials. Her long hair fell into her eye line and she flicked it away. When she looked back to the control panel, it seemed distant again. Her hair would have to go to.

The shuttle rocked as the ripegs fired at them. Ana swerved away from the barrage of missiles, hands frantic at the wheel.
"These guys don't quit, huh?" Elizabeth said.
Ana didn't answer. Her fist hit a green button and the ship jolted forward. The ripegs couldn't get close.
"I thought this was an ambulance?"
"It is," Ana said, "Most of the time."

Elizabeth saw white shooting beams off in the distance. A meteor shower zipping through space. Ana's hands yanked the wheel into a hard starboard, diving straight towards the rapid rocks. Ana squirmed their ship through the onrushing storm. The ripeg vessels did not even attempt it. Ranger watched the sweat beading on Ana's forehead, the blur of the wheel handle as Ana worked it this way and that. An atomic blonde comic book heroine after all.

The rest of the journey was silent.

~*~

They came to a space station. It was a glass dome, perfectly round. No imperfections. Elizabeth left the ambulance and looked around at the cosmos. Nebulas swam through the darkness, the black eternity speckled with starlight.
"This is so cool!" Elizabeth said.
"There's a desk through there," Ana said, pointing.

The next room was just a beautiful. The glass walls were sprayed with interstellar rainbows of beautiful planets. A desk and a set of chairs sat in the centre. Elizabeth dragged a chair around. She rested her feet on the desk.
"You got anything to drink? I could really use one," she said.
"I don't drink."
"Really? Well, guess I'm one to judge. I'm three years sober."
Ana sat the other side of the desk. She leaned forward and knocked Elizabeth's feet to the floor.
"This isn't yours. Don't put your feet on it."
Ana reached under the desk and slammed a bottle of vodka down onto it.
"Sam always planned to open this when you woke up," she said.
"I only knew her for ten minutes, but I liked her. I wish I knew her better," Elizabeth said.
Ana poured two glasses. She slid one across to Elizabeth.
"Today feels like a good day to start drinking," Ana said, downing the glass in one.
She screwed up her face from the taste.
"Why do people even drink this?"
"Mainly to forget," Elizabeth said, taking a sip.
"I knew she'd end up getting herself killed. I shouldn't blame you. But there was nothing you could've done?"
Elizabeth never trusted anything anyone said before they said 'but'.
"Nothing."
Ana thought for a minute.
"Was it at least quick?"
Elizabeth remembered blood from knee to ankle, foot disappearing down the throat of the rubble. The energy bolt off her tooth, mouth seeping red.
"Instant," she said.
"We survived three years without you," Ana told her. The words were spat from her lips.
Elizabeth didn't know what to say, so she took another drink.

She let Ana talk for a while. She learned that they were on the edges of the Known Systems, and that ripeg attacks had been regular, but minor. The result of a custom-built station in a system stricken by poverty.

"If you live in the sewer, you're gonna get bitten by rats," Elizabeth said.

Elizabeth had been the only patient, Ana and Sam the only crew. Someone named West had a war chest to bring Elizabeth back to life. Though Ana didn't say it, Elizabeth knew it had to be connected to the treasure on Allke. West had a mission for her, one that would be explained soon.

"I don't work for anyone," Elizabeth said.

"You owe this man your life."

"I owe *you* my life, and I would've shot you if you hadn't pulled a gun on me."

"You wouldn't," Ana said.

It wasn't a question. Ana's voice was resolute. Elizabeth wasn't sure what to make of her pretty blonde resurrector.

~*~

They drank more.

"Do you like your makeup?" Ana asked, "I did it while you were asleep. I figured you wouldn't want to wake up naked."

"I mean... makeup's not really my thing."

"I figured you'd be an autumn. With the red hair and all," Ana said.

Elizabeth finished her drink.

"So where's my crew?"

"Your crew?"

"Brack? Forr? Lavell?"

"Oh. Forr and Lavell have been quite successful. They have a broadcast show that tops the ratings on six different planets, including Earth."

"I'm gonna bet not Excha or Herso," Elizabeth said.

"The Krei aren't very happy that one of their own has achieved fame with a Jahlder. You've gained quite a bit of posthumous fame yourself. Is it true you once killed someone by clicking your fingers?"

Elizabeth remembered. They had been meeting a Shrook warlord. Lavell had tuned the chandelier lock mechanism to release at the sound of a Human's clicked fingers. When the little rodent had taken them hostage in gravity barriers, she'd sent it crashing down with a single click. Wait. Posthumous?

"They think I'm dead?"

"Everybody does. Technically, until about an hour ago you were. Krei scare me. They're like beasts, aren't they? Not as bad as Ang, though."

"How come your wearing her bracelet?"

Elizabeth pointed at the slender metal loop around her wrist.

"Lavell sold the patent to the Turanga marketplace. Anyone who's anyone wears one. Your original survived your injury. I think it's waiting on the ship."

"Brack," Elizabeth pushed, "Where's Brack?"

"On Karno, last I heard."

"Karno? Loose slots and looser women. It doesn't sound like Brack."

"You've been gone three years, remember."

There was a knock at the door. A man entered. Poorly fit jeans and blue polo shirt that tried to hide the swell of a pot belly.
"You West?" Elizabeth asked.
Ana burst into a fit of girlish giggles. The man's jaw tensed.
"Eddie Donovan. I'm the pilot," he said.
He held out a hand for Elizabeth to shake. The skin was hard and sweating.
"Couldn't you fly?" Elizabeth said, turning to Ana.
"I have other responsibilities."
"Besides," Donovan added, "Miss. Yukishnov is not qualified to fly a ship of this complexity or magnitude. I can wrap a bandage but it don't make me a doctor."
"Magnitude? How big we talking?" Elizabeth asked.
Donovan just smiled.

He led them back down the tube to the shuttle bay. The new ship dwarfed the ambulance they had flew here in. It had a long sleek body, with wings that fanned darkly into points. Like a shark diving, fins spread. A name was printed against the side in caligraphy.
'Minerva'
"Minerva?" Elizabeth asked.
"Minerva was the Roman goddess of –"
"Wisdom. Yeah, I know," Elizabeth cut across Ana, "I mean, why the name?"
"Rome was the greatest civilization in Human history."
"Until it burnt itself to the ground. This is my ship, right?"
"That's what we've been told," Donovan said.
"I don't have a ship named after any Roman gods. This is now the Victory Pearl. We'll get to painting the name soon, but as of now, her name's changed."
"Never liked Minerva anyway," Donovan said.
"Her name is Minerva," Ana said firmly.
"Nope."
Elizabeth climbed aboard.

The ship was huge inside. She felt like a blood cell in a vein. Donovan and Ana directed her around, but there were too many rooms, too many floors to remember. She felt a sadness, not having to duck through small corridors. Doors that slid open with a whoosh. No litter to kick aside. It was soulless.
"Something wrong?" Ana asked.
Difficult questions were like bullets. Better to dodge them than catch them.
"Hell of a lot bigger than the old Victory Pearl."
"Bigger bedrooms, a gym... this ain't the whole nine yards. We've got twelve yards," Donovan said, "Hangar's my favourite."
"Why's that?" Elizabeth asked.
"Grav-lock floors, anti airlock tech... You can open the shutters and stare right out into space."
"And you don't suffocate?"
"Impossible to suffocate anywhere on this ship, ma'am."
"Your bedroom's up there," Ana pointed, "The fridge is stocked with snacks and

27

mineral water."
"I tried to convince 'em you'd want something stronger," Donovan said.

They walked her to her room. A golden box, the treasure from her first ever hunt, sat on her desk. Its touch was cold and familiar, the grooves like the wrinkles on an uncle's hands.
"You saved this from the Victory Pearl..."
Her fingers traced the gilding.
"From the first hospital. It was the only thing you had with you."
The walls were clean and without damp. The bed was bigger, plumper than her original. Pillows were arranged neatly on top of it. They had even left her a full coin purse. It felt like she was being fattened up.
"Say, who flies when you're asleep?" she asked.
"Autopilot can handle to day to day. Or night to night, I guess. Anything more complicated and you'll need me. But don't worry. I'm a light sleeper."

Ana led her out of the bedroom. Donovan turned off for the flight deck.
"West wanted to speak to you as soon as you were on board. I'll take you to the com room."
They walked to the heart of the ship. Ana pulled her eyelid open and pressed her eyeball flat against a biometric scanner. Elizabeth turned away in disgust.
"What's wrong with you?"
"I just... hate eyes,"
The doors did not open.
"Broken?"
"You have to push them," Ana said, eyebrow raised.
Elizabeth shoved the door aside.

There was a microphone at a desk in the middle. A light hung over it, offering a dim glow.
Hello, Miss Ranger
The voice was thick with mythos. Heavy. Wise.
"There a com screen in here I'm supposed to be seeing?" Elizabeth asked.
"There's not," Ana told her.
Ana stayed back, lingering in the shadows.
"So you're the guy who kept me alive?"
Anastasia Yukishnov kept you alive
"Why'd you tell her to?"
I needed your skills
She felt like a teddy bear in a child's hand, being made to dance. She'd never understood why children played with bears. Bears had sharp teeth and long claws. Bears killed.
"I've just lost three years. Humans don't live as long as a lot of other species; time's kinda of the essence for me."
The treasure you found in Allke is not a shield
Elizabeth clicked her tongue.

"Tick-tock."

It's part of a key. I need you to recover its other fragments, then bring them to me

"You don't need me specifically for that."

Your reputation is exemplary

So she would not get an answer today.

"How are you paying me?"

Your life

"You got any plans to collect on that?"

I invested well. You will be compensated for your efforts

Elizabeth rocked back on her heel.

"Any leads?"

Querius Loslou is the leading mind on relics of this nature. He should be your first port of call

"I know Querius. He still work with Jemsa?"

A step ahead already. Your reputation is proving correct

"Just one more question. Why should I do any of this?"

Elizabeth heard Ana step forward, out of the shadows.

Remember this. Without my intervention, your heart would not be beating. Act wisely

She turned and left the com room. She heard metal scraping on the floor behind her as Ana pulled the doors to a close.

Elizabeth headed for the flight deck. Ana followed.

Donovan looked up as she entered, "Where we headed first?"

"Karno," Elizabeth said.

"Karno? Well, I guess that's as good a place as any to catch up on three years of lost livin'. Mind if I ask why?"

"According to Ana, it's Brack Harganagan's last known location."

"According to Ana?" Donovan said, "According to anyone who ever reads the news. Harganagan owns Glevla, the second biggest casino on the whole planet."

Elizabeth glared at Ana sharply.

"You let me think he was rotting away under a table somewhere."

"All I said was Karno. Whatever judgement you made about that filthy little planet is your business."

"Anyway," Donovan said, "I can get us there no trouble, only we're taking supplies on board now. Be a few hours. I know you've been out for three years, but I'd recommend some shut eye."

Ana

Ana sat at her desk rubbing a nail file over her fingers. A photograph of Sam faced her. It had been Ana's birthday. Sam was wearing a paper hat that had been taken off and screwed up the moment the picture was taken. She was beautiful. But Sam was gone now. She would have to look after herself. Last night, she went to the armoury and picked out an assault rifle and fitted herself for protective armour. She had not slept.

Ana was the one who would have to go with Elizabeth into the field now. She bubbled with nausea. Donovan appeared at the door.
"Are we nearly there?" she asked.
"Yeah. I'm gonna com Elizabeth soon and tell her to head down. I just wanted to…"
He turned away.
"What is it?"
"I've been thinking on how to say this all night, and I still can't get a word out. I'm awful sorry about Sam, Miss."
"How did you…"
"When she didn't show up, I figured something was wrong. And your room's pretty close to my room. I heard you pacing round last night. Heard you crying."
Ana flushed red.
"I'm not trying to embarrass you or upset you none. What I'm really trying to say is, you need someone to talk to, you got one."
Ana felt her eyes well. Donovan handed her a tissue.
"Thank you, Eddie."
"Only my mother calls me Eddie. It's Donovan."
She smiled and handed the tissue back.
"That's all I came to say. You'd best get down now, I'll radio for Elizabeth."
"Don't you want to know what happened?"
"None of my business. We're in a dangerous line of work, Ana. But you ever feel like tellin', you know where to find me."

Donovan was a good man. But right now Sam was a black hole. All of her love was disappearing, turning dark. Anything Sam had ever seen or touched or talked about was being pulled into the void. Ana could fall in with it. Dissolve herself with the pain. Suffocate. Without Sam there was no more air to breathe.

She hurried down to the armoury. She had chosen a full body carbon fibre shell, sturdy but not too bulky. It was white, with a silvery pearlescent sheen that gleamed. She took her combat bracelet off as she dressed, then snapped it back on top of the armour. Med supplies packed. The new assault rifle slung over her shoulder. Her derringer fit in a hidden holster.

Elizabeth swept into the room, blue leather jacket swaying around her boots. She had cut her hair short. Jagged red across her fringe, length mismatched. Tugging at the collar, Elizabeth's eyes rolled up and down Ana's battle gear.
"That carbon fibre?" Elizabeth asked.
Ana nodded yes.
"Good choice. Most rookies pick armour that's far too big for them."
Ana mumbled her thanks.
"But you won't need a weapon that big today. Too conspicuous. Stick with your derringer."

~*~

In the shuttle bay, a green scaled Torfus leant against the shuttle's doors.
"Who are you?" Elizabeth asked.
"This is Roka, our shuttle pilot," Ana said.
He waved hello nonchalantly.
"Is Mogg with you?" Ana asked him.
"Yeah, we both came aboard last night. Think he's down in the kitchen."
"Who's Mogg?" Elizabeth asked.
"He's...," Ana faltered and turned to Roka, "What would you say he is?"
"Damn nuisance. Nah, he's okay. Pretty much you need a job doing, Mogg'll do it. Engineering, cooking, hell the guy can even fly a little. Not the most sociable though."
"That doesn't bother me any," Elizabeth said as she climbed aboard.

Ana did not speak for the shuttle ride. Elizabeth made light conversation with Roka but their words were a haze. Her first time into the field. She wanted to throw up. Sam had made it look so easy. Elizabeth couldn't protect the greatest woman Ana had ever known. Why should she trust her with her own life?
"Here we are," Roka said.
He took a magazine out and pressed the door release. The landing pad had more a hundred shuttles in it, easily. A cavalcade, sharp and curved, large and small.

Ana followed Ranger closely, her eyes twitching as she scanned the filth they had descended into. A Torfus woman was bent over one of the shuttles, eyes watering as a Torfus male thrust into her from behind. Ana had heard that Torfus men had scales everywhere. *Everywhere.* She wondered how Elizabeth managed to stand it. Swerving her vision away from the couple, she noticed Elizabeth was already several paces ahead. Right hand inside the lapel of her jacket, fingers no doubt coiled around her pistol. Ana squeezed the barrel of her derringer even harder and quickened her pace to catch up.
"Put that away," Elizabeth said as Ana reached her.
"What?"
"The gun. Hide it."
Ana did as she was told.

She peeked down at Elizabeth's hand. It wasn't holding the pistol, but was poised just above it, ready for a quick draw.

Ana could still hear the vile, pleasured grunts of the Torfus couple as she stepped into the marketplace. A few steps in and the noise disappeared, drowned out by the packed footsteps and shouts of bartering. A group of Krei thundered past them, knocking Ana to the dirty ground.

Ana watched the Krei stampede away with a disgusted click of her tongue. Elizabeth offered her hand. She swept her hands down her thighs to brush away the dirt, glaring as the furry backs disappeared into the crowd. The sizzle of cooked meat wafted through the market, carrying scents of ginger, garlic and garghot. She could hear the bubbling fizz of grease in frying pans, the metallic tinkling of coins in pockets. Every step had to be jostled for. She would wear bruises as her evidence tomorrow. Elizabeth's body was liquid, flowing through the mesh of crowds with ease.

Elizabeth

Elizabeth slid through the crowd and looked back with a sigh. Ana bounced off the bodies. Elizabeth grabbed her arm and dragged her towards a stall selling lasrell, a flightless bird around the size of a sparrow that tasted like smoked bacon. Elizabeth bought two. Most places still preferred to take coin, even with the availability of biometric transfer and scan cards. Elizabeth always liked to physically hand her cash over, the feel of the metal leaving her hands in exchange for goods.

The lasrell was served on wooden sticks, clear juices running down them as the Human woman handed them over. Elizabeth bit into one, teeth crackling the crispy skin and causing more sweet juice to burst from the meat. She handed the other one to Ana, who took it with recoil as the grease dribbled over her fingers.
"What is it?" Ana asked, face still gurning.
"Lasrell. You've never had it before?"
Lasrell was among the most common meat in the galaxy, along with pokku, grerwen and cow. Ana sniffed at the golden brown. Elizabeth devoured hers in four hungry bites, pushing the meat to the corners of her mouth to make room for more.
"Have you ever eaten any food not from Earth?" Elizabeth asked, tossing her stick over her shoulder.
"I just like the taste of Earth food."
Elizabeth shrugged and continued on through the crowd, wiping her mouth clean with her cuff. Ana did not look disappointed when a passerby knocked hers to the ground.

Eventually, they were standing at Glevla's feet. It was trident shaped, the east and west wings curving upwards like the horns of an upturned ram's skull. The central pillar as the sharp face, a jagged pyramid. It stabbed into the cloudy orange sky. Blades of light shimmered across countless windows.

Gnarled fingers squirmed their way up Elizabeth's hand, their skin warted and monstrously dry.
"Can I interest you ladies in some fine, hand crafted Shrook jewellery?"
He held open his coat to show his merchandise. Smiling with bared yellow teeth. The gems were glass and their chains were tarnished.
"Get lost."
He moved onto Ana. He snaked up her arm and lingered.
"We're fine," Ana said, pulling her arm away from him sharply.
"Very well. Enjoy your day."
His voice was practised niceness, trying too hard and fooling no one.
Elizabeth grabbed his fur by the chunk, yanking his head back.
"What's in your hand?" she said.
"Nuthin'."
The false politeness shriveled into an angry rasp. Elizabeth pushed her gun against the side of his face. No more kidding around. She thumbed back the hammer, the

locking click pounding in the Shrook's ear.

"Fine," he spat out in defeat.

He opened his fist, dropping a bracelet into Elizabeth's hand. Ana looked down at her wrist, unaware it had even gone.

"You're not gonna kill me over a cheap watch, are ya?" he said, eyes wide on her. No question asked of a stranger with a gun to your head was ever entirely rhetorical.

"No," she said, letting him go, "But this isn't a cheap watch."

She smashed the gun across his nose, knocking him to his knees. The point of her elbow sent him the rest of the way down. A kick to the stomach sent him rolling away as he oozed blood.

"You give thieves a bad name."

Ana pulled Elizabeth away, as if afraid she might not relent.

"Wasn't that a little extreme?"

Elizabeth snapped her gun back in its holster.

"He stole from you."

The doorman standing outside Glevla was an Ang.

"I hate the Ang," Ana said, cowering.

"Everyone hates the Ang. No one stops and thinks that they're basically slaves though. You ever spoke to one?"

"Why would I want to? They took those Torfus hostage."

"Now they're stuck as the goons in a world they can't understand."

A century ago, a group of Torfus crash landed on the Ang homeworld. The Ang had never met aliens before. The crew had been kept captive until they agreed to build a space fleet for the Ang.

The doorman was wide set with thick skin so yellow it looked noxious, Horns curled out from his forehead and collarbones. Three eyes, fat and round as roaches. The Ang tilted slightly, looking beyond them to the bleeding pile of Shrook. Then he looked Elizabeth in the eye and stepped aside, holding the door open.

Ana

Brass horns blared high tempo jazz as they entered Glevla, interrupted by the whisper of rapid shuffling and boisterous hollers. Glitzy lightbulbs swarmed overhead. The carpet was a deep red. Crowds encircled them. It stank of polish and spilled drinks.

A Torfus waitress sashayed past them. She winked and blew a sultry kiss. Ana ducked away from it and knocked into a Krei sitting nearby. The impact jerked his hand down, sending three slot reels spinning. Each of them stopped on glittery red cherries. The machine whistled as it started to spit out coins.
"Sorry," Ana said, stumbling away.
The Krei was scooping up his winnings, laughing too much to hear.
"Don't apologise," another voice said.
It wrapped its hand around Ana's hips and pulled her close. It belonged to a grey haired Human in a white suit. He held up a coin in front of Ana's face.
"Kiss it," he demanded softly.
Ana's eyes darted to the side, searching for Elizabeth. She could not find her. Ana's eyes snapped back to the coin. A grimy fingerprint stained it. She planted a quick dry kiss. The man smiled, rolling it into the bandit's slot. His hand was climbed up her body like moss. She froze like a stone.
"Lady Luck is not a myth," he told her, "Pull."
He offered her the bauble on the chrome shaft. It glistened with the sweat of previous contestants. Ana tugged the arm down quickly. Cherry. Cherry. The man's hand slid back down to her hip, cupping her through the armour. Lightning bolt. His hold weakened and Ana twisted away, ready to run for Elizabeth. He caught her hand in a vicelike squeeze.
"I'm s... sorry," she said, stammering as her lip quivered.
He raised her hand to his lips and kissed it.
"Thank you for trying."
He tossed her away with a cackle, and only then did Ana remember her concealed derringer.

She ran through the wailing noise until she was free of the crowds. She skirted around the edges of the carnage, keeping her hand against the cold wall. Eventually, she found Elizabeth leaning there impatiently.
"You get lost?"
Elizabeth didn't wait for an answer, continuing her march towards the elevator.

Elizabeth

Her fist pounded the elevator call button and the doors opened. Inside was a column of white buttons. All but the top three were labelled, offering stops at rooms dedicated to popular card games or themed bars and restaurants. Elizabeth pushed the highest button. It had to be Brack's.
"To access this floor, please state your name and business," an electronic voice commanded.
Elizabeth quickly pressed cancel.
"Don't you think he'd let you in?" Ana said.
"I don't want him to know I'm here. Not until he sees me."
"You don't seem like a woman big on surprises."
"If he doesn't see me until I see him, he can't fake anything."
"We need to do something."
"Maybe this wasn't such a good idea," Elizabeth said.
She felt herself sweating. Ana pushed the button again and eased Elizabeth away.
"To access this floor, please state your name and business."
"Turanga package for a Brack Harganagan," Ana said.
The top button illuminated, and the elevator began to whoosh upwards.
"How the hell did you know that'd work?" Elizabeth asked.
"Please. Do you know anyone in the universe who doesn't order from Turanga?"

The elevator reached the top with a chime. Brack was standing by a desk wearing dark trousers with cream pinstripes. The scarlet scales of his naked torso gleamed. He was writing in a little black book, not looking up at them. It was all so unfair. The Torfus had a lifespan of nearly four hundred years. Brack couldn't have spent three of them pouring life back into her? Instead Ana had spent three years of her much shorter life dragging her back from the fiery claws of death. Brack's life had just... gone on.

Ana coughed to get his attention, but his eyes remained fixed on the pad.
"You said you had a package?"
Brack looked up. The black book fell to the floor and his jaw hung slack.
"Did you miss me?" she said.
A genuine question.
"I had no idea. I thought..."
Brack squeezed her body tightly, and the rest of his words were lost.

Elizabeth stepped back. Brack released her and smiled broadly.
"I should've known death was something you'd just shrug off."
"Guess so."
Their words were like gears grinding. The cogs used to whir so easily.
"I still can't believe you're here," he said.
Brack reached out and touched her face. He didn't need to say a word. The unfamiliar scratch of his fingers, from hands she once called home, told her he had

changed.

"I need you for a mission," she said. A reason to keep him around.

Brack wandered over to his desk. Elizabeth followed him, trying to uncover details of his last three years. There was a framed picture on his desk. In the glare of the lights she could only make out Brack kissing... someone. Her? She picked it up and the light disappeared. It was a Torfus woman, a stranger to her. Her red scales were fanned out, away from her body like a bloodied Christmas tree.

"Who's this?" she asked, holding up the picture to Brack.

"Her name's Isoline."

He spoke with a fondness that scratched at her.

"What's she like?" Elizabeth asked, tone firm and flat.

"Ice did forty years in the military with distinction in combat, and served an extra ten. She'd be a valuable addition to your dangerous, important mission."

Brack took the frame from Elizabeth's hand. It slipped through her fingers like sand. He set it down with tenderness.

"That's not what I meant," Elizabeth said.

Ice?

"Besides, that's not for you to decide," Ana told Brack.

Her arms were folded, one leg cocked. She was a tense animal. Brack ran his eyes over her coolly then looked back at Elizabeth.

"Elizabeth dear, who is this woman?"

"I'm the woman who saved her life," Ana said.

Her accent cut razor sharp.

"Stole her, you mean."

"I wouldn't be here without her, Brack."

"I dragged you from that temple. I flew you to the Known Systems!"

"She doesn't need to hear it," Ana said.

"The doctors told me you were dead!"

"They couldn't have saved me. Ana did," Elizabeth said.

"I was lied to!" Brack said.

"For a greater good," Ana said.

"And what's that?" Brack asked.

"I..." Ana hesitated.

"You don't know, do you? You're just a lackey."

"A lackey? No one could've done what I did!"

Elizabet was on a torture rack, Ana at one end and Brack at the other. They were each trying pull her closer, each only succeeding ripping her in half.

"Enough!" Ranger yelled.

She pounded her fist on the table. The picture of Brack and Isoline fell over, glass frame fracturing.

"You can argue over who saved me more all you like. The fact that I'm here means I'm in charge. Both of you! Get back to the shuttle! Now!" Elizabeth spun on her heels and walked back into the elevator.

~★~

She thumped her fist against the door of the shuttle with three rhythmic bangs. Roka opened it and she stepped aboard.
"Helluva place you've got here," Roka told Brack.
"It pays the bills," Brack said, then immediately followed with, "Excuse me."
He disappeared into the bathroom.
"When you gotta go..." Roka said.

Elizabeth took a seat. Her body touched down on Ana's warm hand and she lurched forward again. Ana had taken off her stuffy leg armour, sitting on the bench barelegged in breezy white shorts. Her face was cherry red embarrassed.
"Sorry."

She sat down across from Ana and ran her hand through her auburn hair. Her nails scraped her scalp. She felt her own skin hot and flushed too. The silence was crippling. She had to say something. Ana must've been thinking the same thing.
"I didn't know you were stolen from the hospital," Ana said.
"Do you think it was Sam?"
Elizabeth noticed Ana look down and catch her breath.
"It saved me," she added.
"Sam was already on the station when I was shuttled in," Ana said, "All she said was she was charged with protecting you. I don't think anyone knew you were there, but we were in a dangerous sector. I guess you know that already though."

With a hiss of air, the bathroom door opened.
"I've called Isoline and told her to meet us on your ship," Brack said.
Elizabeth felt her fingers clench into a fist. Had it not been Brack, he would've been sprayed across the floor. She settled for forcing him against the wall.
"*My* ship. Exactly. I didn't give the okay for that," she said.
Her face tensed. She heard herself snarl. Brack looked back at her calmly. He rested his hands on her arms, but made no attempt to free himself.
"I meant no offense, dear. But if you need me, you'll need her."
"What if I don't want her there?"
"You heard her record."
"I don't care about her record."
Brack touched her wrists and eased her away
"Back in the day we were a rag tag outfit. The best rag tag outfit there was, but none of us had any training. None of us knew tactics, strategies. Isoline knows all that. If you didn't want the best, you wouldn't have asked me."
Why did she ask him? Why not eighty-six him right now?

"How will she meet us on the ship? You don't even know its co-ordinates," Ana said.
Brack held up his wrist and a metallic loop slipped down his arm, tangling in his scales. It looked like the one Lavell had designed for them, only more chic and slim line.

"You got a new one?" Elizabeth said.

"Millions of us did. Do you know her and Forr are celebrities now?" Brack said.

"I heard. Does it still have the knife?" Elizabeth asked, looking down at the chunkier bangle around her own wrist.

"They're fully customizable now, I'm sure the knife is available as an accessory, but mine doesn't include it. I don't need one."

"Knife's the only thing I ever used," Elizabeth said.

"Yes, I'm familiar with your wanton brutality Elizabeth," Brack chuckled.

Elizabeth kept her eyes on her bracelet and did not laugh.

The jaws of the Victory Pearl's hangar stretched wide as Roka steered them back aboard.

"They rebuilt the Victory Pearl?" Brack said.

Elizabeth noticed the black lettering etched onto the fin. The curled letters of *Minerva* had been replaced with harsh, sharp characters.

"Recently christened. Used to be the Minerva," Elizabeth said.

A Krei stood waiting as they left the shuttle.

"You must be Mogg," Elizabeth said.

"Must be."

His fur was shorter and darker than Forr's. He was around seven and a half foot, but slim.

"You painted the ship's new name already?" Roka said.

"Unlike you, I actually *do* my work."

"Hey, I do my work," Roka said, "It's just unlike you, I don't need to do fifteen different jobs to earn my keep."

"Anyway," Mogg said, turning back to Elizabeth, "Dinner'll be served in the Mess Hall in about two hours. If you and Ana prefer, I can send your meals up to your quarters."

"Separate quarters," Elizabeth added, glancing at Brack.

"Aren't I allowed to eat in my room?" Brack asked.

"You have not yet been assigned quarters," Mogg told him, condescendingly polite.

"Give him one of the free doubles. He'll be expecting company," Elizabeth said.

Her lips popped on the 'p' of 'company'. She spat it out with disdain.

"But not tonight, so I'm happy to eat in the Mess Hall. I suspect it's gotten bigger since I last saw it," Brack said cheerfully, appearing not to notice her tone.

"We'll all be in the Mess. I want to discuss our mission to Mispeck tomorrow. Ask Donovan to sit with us too," Elizabeth said.

~*~

Elizabeth was the first to arrive. She had changed into a different vest and had applied a roll on deodorant, though that was as far as her dinner preparations went. Ana walked in next, wearing a black dress that glittered. Her lips were red and full, eyeliner thick and dark. Her short nails had been repainted in pink and she wore her blonde hair in loose flowing curls. She looked very pretty. As she sat down with a

smile, Elizabeth caught the scent of her perfume over the smell of roasting meat wafting in from the kitchen.
"You look nice," Ana said.
Elizabeth looked down at her blue leather coat.
"I feel a little overdressed."
She saw Ana's smile leak out.

Brack arrived shortly after. Instead of washing themselves with water, Torfus groomed themselves by coating their scales in a cleansing, sweet smelling wax. His sheen glinted as he walked towards their table.
"Any idea what's on the menu tonight? I remember Lavell would just cook something we'd killed," Brack said.
Ana made a horrified noise, inhaling sharply.
"He means animals, not people," Elizabeth said.
"Tonight's dish is roast beef with potatoes grown on the Human colony Pax," Mogg shouted from the kitchen.

Roka arrived and sat at the end of the table. He was chewing loudly, mouth open.
"Are you already eating?" Elizabeth said.
He swallowed in a gulp.
"Just a little snack. Mogg isn't exactly known for his generous portions."
Mogg shouted from the kitchen again, "Mr Donovan has asked me to tell you that he will be arriving presently. He thanks you for this honour, and apologizes for his lateness. All his words."
"Never heard Donovan talk like that before," Roka said.
He took a snack bar out of his pocket and had another bite.

Donovan walked with his chest puffed out in a black tuxedo and bowtie, smiling like he wanted to show off his teeth.
"A tuxedo?" Elizabeth said.
Roka laughed loudly, not covering his mouth as he sprayed crumbs. Donovan ignored him.
"I've been invited to dine at the Captain's Table. I'm just a lowly pilot, ma'am."
"Captain's Table?" Elizabeth repeated.
"I reckon so. You run this ship, don't you? That makes you Captain. Miss Yukishnov here's your deputy."
"What does that make me?" Brack asked.
"Don't know. Never seen you before."

Mogg brought the food over. It was the first real meal she had eaten since she woke up.
"These are small portions to you, Roka?" she said.
The beef was medium rare, just the right amount of chewy, and the potatoes were served mashed, soaking up the thick gravy. She ate fast.

Elizabeth was the first finished. She watched the others. Brack's dining habits had not changed. He had only a small piece of steak left. Ana used as little of the gravy as possible, being exceedingly careful not to spill any onto her dress. Roka didn't eat at all, just played with his food. He caught Elizabeth watching him.

"Full," he said.

Donovan was the most interesting, cutting his steak up into very small pieces, taking small mouthfuls and swallowing before taking another. She suspected he was on his best behavior. He noticed her looking and sat up straight, adjusting his grip on the fork to what he must have assumed was the more proper way to hold cutlery, though damned if Elizabeth knew them.

Once he was done, Donovan dabbed this mouth with his napkin.

"I take it you didn't just ask me here for my company?"

"I want to talk about Mispeck."

"Going after Querius next?" Donovan asked.

"He should be fine. But Jemsa's unpredictable. We need a plan."

Brack almost choked on his water, "*Jemsa?* When you said Mispeck I assumed you were planning a routine trip to the Valley."

"The Valley is the base of operations for two of the most notorious gangs in the galaxy. Hardly routine," Ana said, pushing away her plate. She had eaten less than half.

"It's still safer than going anywhere near Jemsa Buiteke."

"Excuse my ignorance, but who is this Jemsa Buiteke?" Donovan asked.

"Querius' boss. She's a museum curator. Enqer, it's called. Always gave us a fair price for our wares," Elizabeth said.

"The last time we met she put a gun to my head," Brack said.

"I also remember she put her hand down your pants."

"And I have no desire to relive either incident."

"She's paranoid," Elizabeth said, "Thinks someone is out to kill her."

"Do you think she's right?" Ana asked.

"It doesn't matter. She believes it, and that's why I want you both in there with me. We go in as a three, watch each other's backs. If everything goes smoothly we just pick up Querius and leave."

"If not?" Ana said.

"Well, that's why there's three of us," Brack said.

"Where do I come in?" Donovan said.

"Jemsa's rich enough to have an armada, and if she decides *we're* the ones who've been sent to kill her, I don't want my getaway vehicle to be some tin can she could bring down with a water pistol."

"We've got sharp-fighters in the hangar," Roka said.

"Really?" Elizabeth said.

"Don't like to use them. They attract ripegs."

"Stick with just bringing the Pearl in close then."

"What's the surrounding area like?"

"I don't know. Rocks? Some plants. The planet's surface is red clay," Elizabeth said.

Donovan bit down on his lip. He was trying to be patient.

"Any buildings nearby? Mountains? Tall trees, stuff like that?"
"Nothing like that for miles," Elizabeth said.
"Then I can take you to the front door."

They finished their meal and said their goodnights. Brack and Donovan stayed behind, exchanging war stories, but Elizabeth just wanted to get back to her quarters. She knew it was only a matter of time before tales of the battlefield became tales of the bedroom, and soon after tales of the bedroom would come tales of the heart. Those types of stories used to be her favourites, and the best part was she shared them all with Brack. Now her name had been erased, replaced with Isoline. She had lost him and she hadn't even been able to fight.

Ana caught up to her, shoes clicking against the floor, echoing in the silence.
"I was supposed to say this when you woke up, but then everything happened, so I'll say it now. Welcome back to life."
There was a muffled noise behind her. Elizabeth turned to see mascara oilslicks down Ana's face as she sobbed.
"You okay?"
Elizabeth touched Ana's shoulder tentatively. Ana smothered her face in her hands and took a deep breath.
"Sorry. Sam always wanted to say that."
"She'd be proud of you, y'know," Elizabeth said.
Ana looked at her through her fingers. A rabbit staring through reeds.
"I've lost people before," Elizabeth said, "People leave their shards in you. First it stings, but you're numb, so it doesn't really hit you. Then your heart pumps it round your body and it slices you to pieces. Sooner or later, it cuts through you and bursts out. Then you gotta decide if you're gonna heal, or you're gonna let it kill you."
Elizabeth put an arm around her shoulder and squeezed.
"You're getting sliced right now. Hurts like hell, but it gets better."
Ana nodded. Elizabeth stayed with her until the tears dried.

~*~

They gathered in the cockpit the next morning. Elizabeth was in her blue jacket with her gun strapped to her thigh. Ana wore the white carbon fibre armour. This time Elizabeth had okayed the assault rifle. Brack was covered up in a black body shell. A long barreled machine gun hung from his hips like a broadsword at the hand of a knight. Three spare energy canisters were clipped onto his belt. Donovan had swapped his tuxedo for a blue polo and traded his well-behaved bites of steak for furious focus, unafraid to push any of them out of his way if they strayed into his path of vision.
"I'll put Roka and Mogg on the door when you leave," Donovan said.
The landing was smoother than a pool hall hustler.
"Thanks. Hopefully we won't need them," Elizabeth said.
She patted Donovan on the shoulder and the three of them headed out.

Elizabeth jumped out onto Mispeck's soft surface. Two Ang outside Jemsa's museum stood to attention, readying their weapons.

"Who go there?" one of them cried out in a growl.

"Elizabeth Ranger. I'm here to talk to Querius."

"Nobody tell me," the same one said.

They both had their guns pointed at Elizabeth, but she could see their hands were shaking. Knees unsteady. They were mere ornaments to Jemsa, a cannon fodder warning system to alert her of an attack.

"Just say the word," Brack said, hand hovering above his gun.

"What word? Kill the innocent guards of our host?"

The Ang who had not yet spoken pushed one of his sharp fingers against his ear. He nodded, listening, then stepped aside.

"Go to Fol Buiteke first. Querius after."

Fol. The Torfus word for Mrs, another phrase Elizabeth had removed from her translation implant. She made a mental note to reinstall the Human English phrase when she got back to the ship.

The walk to Enquer was straight and barren. Elizabeth had always gotten on well with Jemsa, but that was three years ago. Back then the paved strip was decorated with outdoor exhibits, statues of gold and stone. She wondered if they had all been moved inside, or if they had been damaged by Jemsa gunning down would-be intruders. A deep, bullet sized rut by the side of the path gave her the answer. Enquer itself was a large dome, perfectly round with pink sunlight bathing its milky marble surface. The door opened inward as they approached. Jemsa was stood in the middle of a curling staircase, two hands on a big pistol. Elizabeth could make out the black yawning muzzle of the gun more than she could make out Jemsa's face.

"In! Quickly!" Jemsa shouted.

They hurried inside and the Ang slammed the door behind them.

"We'll be safe in my office," Jemsa said.

She ran up the stairs and Elizabeth was forced to follow. The hallway and stairs were full of armed Ang, a different one watching guard over her every step.

Jemsa kicked the door closed before Elizabeth reached it. She pushed it open. The mouth of Jemsa's gun greeted her, wide open and ready to bite. One green eye, wild and bloodshot, peeked out. She was curled up on a chair, rocking slightly back and forth. Behind Jemsa, the desk had been swallowed by a confetti of loose paper and open files. More files sprouted out of drawers and cabinets like weeds.

"We don't want any trouble. I was told you were expecting us," Elizabeth said, stepping into the room slowly.

"No trouble? That Human girl's got a cannon on her back!" Jemsa said from behind the gun.

Jemsa used to speak like she knew secrets about everyone in the room. It was a voice that could bring down empires. Now it was the mewling of a skittish kitten.

"People who want trouble hide their weapons. People who want trouble lie. We won't shoot as long as no one shoots us first. Put the gun down, Jemsa. We're friends, remember?"

She lowered the gun only as far as her chin, keeping it pointed at Elizabeth's stomach. It would be a painful way to die if Jemsa got an itch. Elizabeth took another cautious step forward.

"I heard you were dead," Jemsa said.

"Pretty close to it for three years."

With a sudden jerk of her arm, Jemsa's aim switched from Elizabeth's midriff to Brack's face.

"I nearly shot you once," she told him.

"Yes, you did," he said.

"Braaaack," Jemsa said.

She formed the sound slowly and deliberately, like a child learning a word for the first time.

"Yes, that's me," Brack said, hand moving towards his weapon.

He had a lightning draw, but his weapon was long and heavy. Jemsa's was already pointed at him. The odds were against him, if it came to it.

"Why didn't I shoot you?" she asked.

Elizabeth wasn't sure if this was a test or if Jemsa had forgotten.

"You told me I was too pretty for a bullet hole in the face. Then you grabbed my crotch."

She nodded, as if satisfied.

Then, with an even faster jolt, she turned the gun to Ana.

"Get her out of here! Get her out of here!" she shouted.

The fright knocked Ana back against the wall, sending a pile of files crashing to the floor.

"I don't like her! Get her out!"

Jemsa seemed to have forgotten she was even holding a gun, legs flailing chaotically beneath her as she slammed her elbows off her chair.

"Go, Ana!" Elizabeth shouted.

"Go and get Querius, dear. We'll meet you outside as soon as we can leave," Brack said, helping her to her feet and pushing her through the door.

Jemsa covered her face with her hands. Gun pointed at the ceiling, still looped around one of her fingers.

"Everything's okay, Jemsa. She's gone," Elizabeth said, softening her voice to a whisper.

Jemsa lowered her hands timidly, peeking out through gaps in her slender red fingers. She looked at them both closely, her face not understanding.

"Elizabeth? Brack?"

This Jemsa was a spectre. A demon to gnaw at memories. A dark cloud that cast a heavy shadow. The real Jemsa was gone.

"Yeah. We're here to get Querius for our mission, remember?"

Clearly she did not, but she bobbed her head back and forwards anyway.

"Can I get you a drink?"

Jemsa handed Brack and Elizabeth a glass each of red wine and sat back in her chair, crossing one leg over the other. A wry grin grew on her thin lips. Elizabeth took a small sip. Brack did not drink at all. Jemsa was how Elizabeth had remembered her, regaling them with stories in a voice thick with glamour. No matter how much Jemsa laughed and smiled and entertained, Elizabeth could not forget the withered creature that was inside the chrysalis, cowering behind the gun with manic eyes.

"How can she be like this?" she said to Brack quietly.

"Torfus brains are different. No one knows much about how they work or why they break down."

Jemsa told them a story of how she had acquired a set of emerald rings, each marked with the symbol of love from different worlds. Like of the stories Jemsa told, it was full of action, adventure and ended with rich, loud laughter. Then her laughter subsided. She started the exact same story again. Elizabeth grew anxious, a lead weight dropping inside of her and she prepared herself to draw her gun quickly.

Suddenly, a fist hammered against the door.

Ana

Ana snatched the door closed. Jemsa's eerie screech still stung her ears, echoing. *Get her out of here! I don't like her!* The words were hauntingly childish. At their meal last night, Elizabeth and Brack spoke of Jemsa Buiteke as a fearsome woman, admiration filling their voices. It was tragic that her mind had rotted into insanity so quickly.

The hard faced Ang guards had deserted the spiral staircase. Without them, the whole place felt dead. Ana walked through the museum with trepidation. Her eyes darted everywhere. Where had the Ang gone?

She kept her eyes moving and her hands on her gun. She wished Sam had showed her how to shoot it.

She reached the bottom of the stairs and turned right. A golden artefact twinkled and caught her eye. She stepped closer. Grime gathered in the corner of the glass casing. Inside was a figurine of a Krei soldier mounted on a four legged animal she did not recognize. It vaguely resembled a horse, but its skin was rougher and its nose was flatter, with long teeth poking out of its gums. The Krei's eyes were royal blue sapphires, clear and bright. Ana wondered if Elizabeth was the one who brought it here. She wanted to experience the rush of owning a piece of history, the way Elizabeth had. She continued down the hall, eyes breathing in the jeweled goblets and dusty leather bound books, crisp pages yellowed with age.

Her footsteps echoed through the hollow hall. Eventually she reached a door with 'Querius Loslou' written on the door in thick black lettering. She rapped on the door lightly and got no answer. She knocked again, louder. Still no response. She twisted the handle and eased the door open. The hinges creaked.
"Hello?" she said, stepping inside.
A concrete fist greeted her chin. She slumped to the floor with all the grace of a bagful of hammers.

~*~

An angry woodpecker jabbed inside her skull. She could feel blood, cold and congealed, running from her nose. Her arms and ankles were bound with thick, coarse rope. Her gun was at her feet, tantalizingly close.
"What –"
Another blow from the solid stone fist cut her off.

It opened another gash on her face. Molten blood flowed down her skin. The woodpecker got angrier. She looked up at her captors. They were Ang, five of them. All with sharp horns and bulbous warts splattered across their ugly yellow skin.

"Please! Let me go!"

"No talk," one of them said.

He loomed over Ana, his acrid breath stale and sour, choking her. His eyes were dead, shineless stones. He kept them on her as he pressed his gun against the head of the Jahlder next to her. Querius Loslou, she presumed. His white hair was erratic, shooting off in all directions. His beige eyes were very small and scared.

"Last chance. Where bomb?"

"I have told you, time and again. I don't know what bomb you mean!"

The Ang crashed the gun into Ana's cheek. She was already in so much pain she scarcely felt it. Turning numb. As she looked up, she only saw three Ang. The gun rammed against her face and she looked back down, shaking inside the rope.

"Tell us! We shoot assistant!"

"I'm not his assistant. I don't know what you want with me!" Ana said.

She burst into a sobbing wail. The Ang's eyes ignited. He let out a roar of fury. Ana could see his black teeth, the mucus green syrup that dripped from them.

"No talk! I say no talk!"

He switched on the energy canister on his gun's chamber. It started to crackle and fizz with purple as he readied his finger to squeeze the trigger...

Rusalka

Ana, Querius and the Ang were not the only ones in the lab.

High up on the steel beams, hidden in the darkness, Rusalka was watching. She was an Umbra, a race that had been a part of the galaxy long before even the Jahlder. They had shaped history; the hands above the puppet strings, the silent blade in the shadows. Rusalka channeled those centuries of evolution to remain undetected here. Her body was covered in a sensitive blonde fur, giving her a constant radar on everybody in the room. Her sharp ears could hear an ant cough and her bright eyes could see him politely raise a hand to cover his mouth. Quickly, silently, her long legs carried her over the beam, cape fluttering behind her. She heard one of the Ang talking.
"Where bomb?"
She smiled with satisfaction. Her whisper had blossomed into fruit, and it was ripe. She hung from the beam, toes curled under it in a strong grip. Wrapping her cape of velvet all around her, she plunged into the invisibility of darkness. One Ang was standing with the two hostages, the other four stood in two groups of two.

She let go of the beam and landed lightly, body turning in mid-air. She touched down on all fours then sprang upright. A floating feather becoming a viper. She drew twin knives, curved like cutlasses. The razz of metal as the blades unsheathed sang harmonies in her finely tuned ear. It would be silent to the Ang. Skulking up to the closest pair with muted footsteps, she kept a watchful eye on the other three. Her cape flitted as she leapt into the air, cleaving the head of the first Ang open with the blade in her right hand. Her left slit the neck of the second. She caught them both as they fell. The oily sludge of black blood coated her hands in wet warmth. She wiped them dry on the fur of her stomach and jumped up onto the wall again, limbs moving swiftly to climb the flat surface.

The next pair of Ang were standing directly under a bright light. As slow and as dumb as the Ang were, it was foolish to attack them head on with no shadows to swim through. She took a moment to prepare a new plan then bolted along the beams again, her body a blur. The light protecting the Ang had a metallic lampshade, swathing the surroundings in its glow. Rusalka pounced at the wire, grabbing it high to avoid swinging the bulb wildly. It shook from side to side gently, but the Ang were too stupid to notice. She slid down the wire and rested on the lampshade. It was burning hot, but she was able to flatten her feet and withstand it, soaking the warmth up against her splayed pads of flesh. The telltale click of an energy canister being loaded exploded in her ears. She would have to move fast. Her long shadow stretched on the floor in front of the Ang. She drove down on them, twisting her body so her feet wrapped around both of their necks. They were strangled before they hit the ground. Their gasping moans of terror altered the one Ang left and Rusalka heard the loud buzz and pop of his canister. Ready to fire. Lightning quick, Rusalka whipped one of her blades towards him, impaling the back of his head, right in the centre.

Ana

Ana screamed as the curved blade burst through the Ang's face, splitting his nose open. His eyes rolled up lifelessly as he flopped to his knees at her feet. Dark blood sprayed against her. She sniveled to get her voice back.
"Who's there?"
The horrible blood trickled into her mouth. It tasted like ink, twice as thick.
"Stranger? Could we be untied?" Querius called out.
A figure walked towards them, cape flowing behind nimble footsteps. She slid her knife out from the dead Ang's head with a wet and meaty scrape. She was... Umbra? Ana had never seen one before.
"Who are you?" Ana said.
The Umbra used the bloodied knife to cut the ropes that tied Ana and Querius to their chairs, wiped it clean against her fur, then sheathed it.
"Rusalka," she said, offering her hand for Ana to shake, "You can stop crying now, sweetie."
Ana looked down at the tangled fur of Rusalka's wrist, mangy with dried clumps of flesh. There were deep scores, old scars, raking down from her shoulder to her chest. Ana took her hand, shook it once then withdrew, rubbing her hand dry on her leg afterwards.
"Do you know what this bomb is they were so desperate to locate?" Querius asked.
The corners of Rusalka's lips curled upwards, dimpling her pale cheeks.
"I'm responsible for that. I heard that Jemsa's personal guard were planning on assassinating her and stealing her artefacts, so I started a few rumours that a bomb was set to detonate upon her death, blowing up the entire museum. I hoped that would dissuade them, but seems they figured out that the smartest person in the building must know something about it. I am sorry, if they hurt you," Rusalka said.
"Nothing too bad. Though I am looking forward to getting away from this place. I assume that's why you're here?" Querius said, turning to Ana.

Ana ignored him and picked her gun up. What had she walked into? She was a *doctor*. With a few deep breaths, she was halfway to composed.
"How long were you hiding there?" she asked Rusalka.
"A while."
"Why didn't you step in sooner?" Ana demanded.
Ana's finger tensed on the trigger. Before she even knew what her hand was doing, Rusalka slapped the flat side of the knife against the gun. It sprawled loose on the floor.
"I was waiting to see how painfully they deserved to die."
"Very painfully, I hope."
Ana felt the cut on her cheek.
"Rather quick, actually. Your injuries will heal within a day, and they did not torture you or cause you any serious pain."
"No pain? How would you like to be tied up and beaten?"

Ana looked at her close and saw deep gashes gathered around her neck.

"I guess I should be grateful," Ana said, "If it wasn't for you they might have killed us."

"You can thank me by inviting me on this mission of yours. I've been meaning to make more friends," Rusalka said.

"So you *are* the one who was sent to collect me?" Querlus asked.

"Yes. Anastasia Yukishnov. Miss Ranger will brief you once we make it back to the ship."

"And me? You know I'll be able to sneak onto your ship whether you grant me permission or not," Rusalka said.

"I'm sure Elizabeth will have use for you," Ana told her.

They left the room and walked back down the hallway. It felt much shorter now, without the threat of a hundred Ang emerging to attack her. One of the display boxes showcased a selection of rings, all emeralds engraved with the symbol for love from different races in the galaxy. A heart for Human. Three connected circles, a gollak, for Krei. A spiral inside a square, pin to, for Torfus. A few more that Ana did not recognize. Rusalka peered inside and pressed her hand to the glass. Razor sharp claws sprung from her fingertips, and she ran one of them around the glass in a circle.

"Why wouldn't you just kill Jemsa yourself if you wanted her things?" Ana said.

"I don't kill people who don't deserve it. But I don't mind stealing from them," Rusalka replied, stuffing the rings into the pocket of her leather shorts.

They climbed the stairs to Jemsa's office. Ana's weary fist knocked on the door.

Elizabeth

Elizabeth peeled the door open. Ana's face was crimson with welts, her right cheek swelling up over her eye.
"My God, are you okay?" Elizabeth said.
She raised her hand to Ana's cheek, easing apart the red crust of scabbing. Blood oozed down the skin.
"Let's go," Ana said, leaning away.
"Leaving so soon?" Jemsa said.
"Until next time," Brack said.
Jemsa stood and kindly showed them to the door. Once they were out she slammed it with a pained scream.
"Don't come back!" she screeched through the wood.
"She's very sick," Querius reassured them as Jemsa continued wailing.

"I kept some of that salve you gave me," Elizabeth said.
She took out a small pot and rubbed the gel along the bleeding slit in Ana's face. Dried flecks of blood crumbled to the floor. Their eyes caught other for a second before Elizabeth tore hers away, distracted by a creature lurking beyond in the darkness.

"Who are you?" Elizabeth asked, ripping her gun from her holster. She aimed it into the shadows.
There was a gust of wind and the sound of the air tearing. The figure disappeared. Eyes darted everywhere, clueless. Instinctively, Elizabeth spun and pointed her gun directly at where the woman was now standing. It was an Umbra. She could see her face, moving towards her slowly, grinning with no weapon drawn. Her light fur was clotted in dark patches.
"You are good," the Umbra said.
"And who are you?"
"Rusalka. Pleased to meet you."
"Elizabeth Ranger," she said, snapping her gun back into her holster.
"What are you doing here?" Elizabeth asked.
"Protecting Jemsa Buiteke. A woman once so imposing should not be murdered by dimwitted brutes like the Ang. But maybe my true reason for being here is to join you. You're here to recruit Querius. Recruit me too."
"You don't offer what he does," Elizabet told her.
"Nobody offers what I do."
"If you're so concerned about Jemsa's wellbeing, shouldn't you stay here?" Brack said.
Rusalka readjusted her cape with an amused smirk.
"The Ang will no longer be a problem, I assure you."

Querius put his hand on Elizabeth's shoulder and spoke up.
"This has been enough excitement for one day. This woman saved me, Miss Ranger,

and your friend's life too. You do not know me very well, but if my word means anything to you I implore you. Allow her to join your crew, just as you have allowed me."

Elizabeth looked Ruslaka up and down.

"Welcome to the party, I guess."

Rusalka reached behind her back and produced three purple energy canisters.

"You can have these back now," she said, throwing them to Brack.

Brack's embarrassed hands felt the nothingness on his belt. He hurriedly scooped them up and clipped them back into place as Rusalka gave a wink.

"Seriously?" Elizabeth said.

~*~

Donovan was waiting at the entrance to the Victory Pearl as they left Enquer. Rusalka bounded past him, disappearing into the ship.

"Who was that, Captain?"

"Her name's Rusalka. Apparently she saved Ana's life."

Ana covered her face.

"Where's she goin'? She don't even know where the quarters are," Donovan said.

"Give her an hour and she'll know the layout of this ship better than anyone else on board."

"Could I possibly be shown to mine? I fear I need to lie down," Querius said.

"I'll take you," Donovan said, slapping a friendly hand on Querius' back.

"Thank you," he said, struggling for breath.

"Once you're up to it I can show you your research centre too."

"What happened to sending Roka and Mogg?" Elizabeth asked.

"When they heard it was clear, they both decided they had better things to do. Oh, and Captain? There's someone waiting to see you in the Mess Hall. Torfus woman. Said she was sent our co-ordinates."

"Isoline," Brack and Elizabeth said together.

Brack's voice was light and hopeful. Elizabeth's was velvet dark.

They walked into the ship, Ana dragging behind them. The swelling had disappeared under the coolness of the salve, and her skin had knitted together again, scabbing over the cut.

"I'm going for a lie down..." she said.

Elizabeth pushed open the door to the Mess Hall. Isoline was sat on a table, legs dangling with casual superiority. Her body glistened, ruby red. A sapphire sash sat across her scales. Elizabeth recognized it immediately. Brack had taken it for his personal stash from a raid on Desrang. Golden bangles laced their way up both her arms. Part of Brack's score on Maxxley.

Brack barged Elizabeth out of the way and ran up to Isoline. She wrapped her legs around him like pincers. Her spines punctured his flesh. Elizabeth had heard of that happening before with Torfus males who chose a mate with such attractively sharp

53

scales. She thought of the old Torfus phrase, *how sensual it was, to bleed for your lover*. They kissed, scarlet scales dovetailing violently. Elizabeth coughed pointedly. Their lips parted. Isoline's tongue slithered back into her mouth.
"I'm sorry if our display of affection offended you," Isoline said insincerely, "We have not seen each other in almost ten days."
"Try three years."
The words left Elizabeth's lips before she could bite them back.
"Brack told me about that terrible tragedy. But friends and lovers are different."
Isoline's hot eyes fixed on her. Elizabeth stared back until Isoline relented.

Brack

Brack strolled down the hall to his cabin, hand clamped to her waist while she draped her arm across the back of his shoulders. He could feel the sharpness of her scales sinking into his skin. His footsteps to the bedroom quickened. Once they were inside with the door locked, Isoline stripped. Her eyes never left his. Her skirt was made of woven aluminum fibre, not tearing as he slid it down the serrations of her legs. He slipped it off her feet and tossed it aside. She pulled him towards her.
"Were you happy to see Elizabeth again?" she said.
"I thought she was dead. It's all very confusing."
Isoline's hand caressed Brack's chin, then fingers dragged him close.
"But you don't love her, do you?" she said.
"I don't love her."
"You love me."
"I love you," Brack said, staring into Isoline's rich eyes.
"Good."

Isoline threw him onto the bed. She stood over him. He sat up to kiss her but she pushed him back down. With her hand around his throat, she started to kiss and bite. He writhed beneath her. She pulled him close and her hips rammed into him. He gripped her waist as she moved, so tight the blood burst from his palms.

Querius

Querius Loslou took out a handkerchief and blotted the sweat away from his forehead. The Ang had been far kinder to him than they had been to Ana. Possibly, they feared any assault on his frail body would kill him. The day had still been too much for him. Jemsa was no longer the elegant beauty she had been when they first met, and this relic sounded like a truly once in a lifetime find.

He took a sorrowful look out his window as Mispeck was swallowed by the stars. Watching the last morsel of that beautiful red planet disappear, he loaded up his com channel.
"Finally found time to call me?"
"Please dear, the day I've had..."
"I don't want to hear about whatever nonsense you've half invented today, Querius. Have you finally left that horrendous woman?"
"It was never like that, dear."
"I don't see why you couldn't have left years ago. Or why you can't come home to me."
"I told you, we need the currency. That's why I stayed with Jemsa all those years."
"Yeah, *that's* the reason, I'm sure."
"It was one kiss, dear. And a long time ago."
"One kiss that I know of, you mean. Look, how long is this excursion of yours going to take?"
"I promise I'll be back as soon as I can. I –"
The voice on the other end hung up.

A knock came at his door. A Krei was standing there.
"Hey. Having a game of cards tonight. You in?"
Querius looked up wearily. He thought for a moment, then nodded.

Rusalka

Rusalka elongated her back as she walked around the Victory Pearl. She had found a loose ceiling tile in the ship's gym, and had slept two hours up inside the cavern it led to, alone with the pipes and the heat and the darkness. The sleep came easy, but she always awoke with a stiffness which needed to be stretched away.

The corridors had an eerie beauty in the late violet shadows. She scanned the room. There were thirteen hiding places. Not that she planned on assassinating any of her crewmates. She... stopped. Footsteps behind her. Not innocent. She could feel the stealth in them, the potential for violence.

Rusalka spun. A defensive elbow blocked the incoming red scaled fist. Her other hand scraped down the attacker's face, peeling away diamonds of scarlet. Isoline, the Torfus woman. She swept Rusalka's legs away. Rusalka landed in a cartwheel and was back upright instantly. Isoline took a battle stance. Her jewelry jangled. Rusalka never trusted anyone who dressed well. What was the motive for this assault? Rusalka grabbed both her knives from her back and twirled them threateningly, daring Isoline to come again. Another attack would spell her death.

"What are your reasons for attacking me?" Rusalka said, angling her blades so the dim light bounced at Isoline's eyes.
Isoline's only answer was a lurch forward. Rusalka dropped her shoulder. Isoline landed on her front in a heap. Her flip onto her back was too slow. Rusalka had both curved blades at her throat.

Isoline stared into her eyes and let out a rich, dark cackle, "I had heard of your prowess in hand to hand combat, and I needed to see for myself. Sheathe your weapons. This was all fun and games."
Rusalka did as she was told, placing her blades back into their metal pockets strapped to her back. As Isoline got her feet, smiling, Rusalka grabbed her neck.
"The next game you play with me will be your last," she said.
Isoline continued to smile until Rusalka let her go.

Elizabeth

Elizabeth sat her desk staring out at the universe. She had not slept last night. Fourth night in a row. She just lay in bed until her brain blacked out. Then the light came back and time had passed a little. It was morning now, or at least it felt like it.

Until Querius discovered whatever he was being paid to discover, she and the Victory Pearl were simply floating. The stars she could see were not like the stars from the old Victory Pearl. Before she flew to untouched worlds, and the stars were bright and pure. Now they were in the hub of galactic activity, the stars tainted and dulled by the flurry of passing ships. They were like the mothers of the rebel daughter stars Elizabeth used to gaze upon. Wiser, kinder, and less fun.

The stars were just specks of light to her, inconsequential as dust. And what did that make her? She was one woman, drifting along. Surrounded by people, but with no one. Her own emptiness attacked her, pulling her inwards so she might disappear. She needed to leave the room, so she stood. But she had nowhere to go, so she sat back down. She ran her fingers through her hair and listened to her heart beating inside its cavern.

Her thoughts chattered, a brain full of windup teeth. She needed to silence them. She headed for the gym. She did press-ups until her shoulders burned, sit-ups until her stomach muscles screamed and ran until her legs ached. Slowly, the chattering stopped.

Ana

Ana's bed felt too big. There was a life missing from it. Galaxies couldn't have filled the hole. She thought about what Elizabeth had said, about the shards. She felt for her pulse. Gradually, the bloodflow kissed her fingertips. She wanted to claw the shards out and throw away the pain. But the memories were part of them. The joy and the kisses and the smiles... they were full of shards now too.

Elizabeth was very like Sam.

Ana found herself walking to Elizabeth's room. She knocked.
"Come in!" Elizabeth hollered.
Ana pushed the door. Water dripped down Elizabeth's red hair, running over her body. Tiny auburn curls sprouted from her legs. She was naked. Ana covered her eyes and looked away.
"I sorry! I thought you said come in."
"I did."
"I could come back..." Ana said, hand still over her face.
"Ana, you've seen me without my skin."
She took Ana's hand and eased it away from her eyes.
"There's nothing to do here," Elizabeth sighed. She slumped down on the bed.
"Nothing's interesting to you unless it's shooting at you."
Elizabeth gestured for Ana to join her. Ana threw a towel over Elizabeth and sat down on the edge of the bed. She folded her arms across her chest, shifting them uncomfortably.
"I just wanted to say thanks. If you hadn't applied that salve right away the swelling would have lasted for a week," Ana said.
"You should be thanking our new Umbra crewmate."
"I will. Once I find her. Hardly seen her these few days she's been aboard."
A nervous hiccup of laughter followed the sentence out of Ana's mouth.
"It's the same type you told me to use on my knees. That's the only reason I was carrying it," Elizabeth said.

She sat forward, her hand reaching out to lift Ana's blonde curls clear of her face. Ana's skin prickled with electricity.
"It *has* healed pretty quickly," Elizabeth said, inspecting the cut, "I'm glad I can recognize you again. I wish I could say the same for some other people."
Her red locks swaying softly as she spoke.
Brack. She meant Brack. Before she could even process the thought, her hand rose and tossed Elizabeth's hair over her ear.
"Was that annoying you?" Elizabeth asked with a smile.
Sudden waves of embarrassment, guilt and confusion crashed into her. Ana was a rock in a toxic sea.

"I'm kidding. It's terrible, isn't it?" Elizabeth said, pulling on her jagged locks.
"I could give you a haircut, if you..."

A siren started to blare. Elizabeth leapt up and grabbed her bracelet.
"What's the situation, Donovan?"
"We have picked up an emergency transmission from Rassek. Some Krei are attacking a village. Vires."
"We're not a lifeboat. What's our concern?"
"The message is from Lavell and Forr."
"Goddammit Donovan!" Elizabeth shouted.
She punched at the bedframe leaving a knuckle shaped dent.
"Should I not have told you about them, Cap?"
"You should have opened with that!"
Elizabeth got ready in a blur, grabbing her gun last. She ran to the elevator and slapped the button for the hangar. Not knowing what else to do, Ana followed.

The elevator stopped a floor early. When doors opened Brack hurried inside.
"I was with Donovan. We have to go and get them," he said.
No hint of a question.
"I know."
Brack handed Elizabeth a gun.
"Told you before. Two pistols is flashy and inconvenient."
"Extra firepower," he said.
"Ugh. It's an energy pistol too."
"I'll have you know that's the first energy enabled pistol Winchester ever made."
Ana wanted the walls to eat her.

After an age, the elevator stopped at the hangar. Roka was leaning out of the shuttle, his hand grabbing the roof.
"You carry a gun, Roka?" Elizabeth shouted to him.
"Sure do," he said, twisting his body to show her the plastic holster on his leg, "It's a Human weapon, made in –"
"Bullets?"
"Course."
Elizabeth tore the holster from him and removed the gun. She handed Roka the first energy Winchester ever made.
"I assume you know about the transmission," Ranger said, climbing into the shuttle.
"Quickest shuttle's only got room for me plus two."
Ana shrank away.

They burst from hangar and left her there, staring out at the stars. Ana slouched against the wall, waiting for the elevator to come and collect her. Her ears hurt from the shrieking siren. Her brain was an ambiguous fiasco. When the doors finally let her in, she pressed the button with a weary thumb, ready to crawl back into bed.

As she shuffled back to her cabin, Rusalka appeared by her side. She flicked a deck of cards between her hands, the thin cardboard rasping together.
"Want to play a game?" Rusalka said.
This animal that lurked in the shadows. She had been spying.
"How much did you see?" Ana said.
"How much did I see of what?" Rusalka asked.
She cut the deck four times with elaborate twists of her fingers.
"Me in Elizabeth's bedroom."
The rasping stopped. Rusalka held the cards still. She looked up.
"You were in bed with Elizabeth?"
Her eyes widened, lips sneaking up into a hungry grin.
"It wasn't like that," Ana said.
Rusalka grabbed hold of Ana's arm.
"I want you to tell me everything. Come with me, I know a place."
And suddenly they were running.

They reached the gym.
"I don't understand. You want to jog while we talk?" Ana asked.
"You need to learn to look."
Rusalka stood on her tiptoes to ease one of the ceiling tiles away, then jumped through the hole with a powerful leap. Leaning back through the opening, she thrust her hand down to Ana.
"I'll pull you up."

Ana's stomach scraped against the lip of the tiles as Rusalka heaved her up. Dust clung to her. Rusalka led her, ducking under pipes until they came to an opening. They sat down. Rusalka shuffled the cards again, dealing them five cards each from a Human deck.
"I'll let you win," Rusalka said, "or at least, I'll not cheat."
"What are we playing?" Ana said.
"Poker."
"I don't know the rules."
"Okay. Do you know blackjack? Gin? Three card brag?"
"I know snap. Kind of," Ana said.
Rusalka gathered up the cards with an amused sweep and stuffed them back into her pocket.
"Why don't you just tell me what happened. So, you're in bed with Elizabeth."
"Not exactly."
"You either were or you weren't. There is no grey area," Rusalka said.
"We weren't naked under the covers, but it wasn't like nothing happened either. There was a..."
Ana searched for the word to describe it exactly.
"A moment."
"Did you kiss her?"
Ana blushed.

"I mean, there's Sam..."
"Who's Sam?" Rusalka asked.
"We were together. But she died."
"How long has it been?"
"Just over a week," Ana said.
Rusalka nodded.
"Okay. But sweetie, Humans can't wait around like Umbra or Torfus. You don't have the time. You're still here..."
"It's not that easy. I don't... I don't know what I want."
"Let's pin that for now. What happened with Elizabeth?"
"I brushed her hair out of her face."
"Ooh. How dirty."
The sarcasm practically dripped from the corner of Rusalka's sharp lips.
"It was more than that. She talked about how she didn't recognize Brack anymore, like I was the only one she could trust."
"And you still didn't kiss her?"
"Why do you care?" Ana said, surprised at her own aggressiveness.
"Friends share things, or so I've heard."
"Is that why you're here? To make friends?"
"I can't steal from anyone when I'm by myself," Rusalka said, holding up a diamond stud. Ana felt her own bare ear, shocked but smiling as Rusalka handed it back.
"Have you always travelled alone?" Ana asked, slotting the stud back through her lobe.
"I had a partner," Rusalka said.
Her tone was wistful. Airy.
"What happened?"
"That's not a question you ask in my line of work."

Rusalka turned away. Ana wondered if she should leave. She stood and Rusalka spun quickly.
"Listen to me," Rusalka said, grabbing her, "Life is short, especially for Humans. The minute Elizabeth gets back from this rescue, grab her by her thick red hair, pull her close and kiss her until she can't breathe."
"I can't."
"Won't isn't can't," Rusalka said.
"Sam..."
"She's gone. Too many people make the mistake of never forgetting."
"She's going with Brack, to save Forr and Lavell. It'll be just like the old days."
"Trust me. Nothing interesting is going to happen on that mission."

Elizabeth

A grenade burst at Elizabeth's feet showering dirt up over her. The blast sent her stumbling to her knees. Brack reached out a hand to help her up. One of the Krei aimed square at his back. A coward's shot, but it would do the job. She pulled him down into the dirt. The gutless bullets whizzed safely beyond them into the dim battlefield mist. As Brack collapsed onto her, Elizabeth raised her gun and fired through the Krei's neck. He clutched a desperate hand to his gaping throat and fell to ground, gurgling.

Brack rolled with her. They fell into a shallow trench, bodies close together and warm. He smiled awkwardly. She pushed him aside. Elizabeth peered over the muddy parapet. The Krei had taken over a small village, holed up inside two of the houses. A single figures taskforce. They weren't military. The two houses were poor choices. One had a large window facing out at Elizabeth and Brack, the glass already broken. Sharp fangs hung on. The other building had only a splintered door guarding it. Neither could be held for very long.

Elizabeth only needed one glance. Forr and Lavell would have taken refuge in the east side tower. It was the most defensible building, strong walls and the advantage of height. She could see from the path of destruction that the Krei had not considered it yet. Starting from the most westerly point of the settlement, the Krei ransacked houses and buildings in a chaos. Beams were ablaze in bloody red on the piles of rubble that used to be homes. Corpses of the Jahlder innocents lay in undignified, painful positions, their purple blood draining away into the mud. One of them was mewling weakly nearby. Dead in every sense but the one that mattered. Elizabeth drew her gun and ended the Jahlder's misery with kindness.

One of the Krei leaned out of the window to see them. A careless look. Elizabeth shot but only caught his shoulder. He flopped over the window frame, bleeding down the stonework. Brack's rifle was more in tune with long range shots, taking out one of the others right between the eyes. The bolt of energy expanded as it pierced his skull, spraying wet and pulpy strips of face all over his dead comrade.

The gaping window continued to spit out blind bullets. Elizabeth climbed out of the trench, keeping low. She reached the protection of a wall. The three others had collapsed, but this one stood firm. There was a tang in the wind. Barbequed shrimp, only heavier and smokier. Elizabeth's stomach reeled with nausea. Jahlder burning. She retched, then composed herself.
"Two buildings," Elizabeth said.
"You take that one," they both said, both pointing to the same building.
They were out of sync. Brack laughed. Elizabeth just shook her head.
"I'll take it," she said.

Sprinting out from her cover, she drove towards the first house. Each footstep sent out a bullet from one of her twin pistols. She hurdled through the shattered window, leaping over the glass daggers that clung to the frame. There was only one Krei left, lying against the wall, defeated. The rest had been killed as she had surged over. Glass teeth were splintered in his neck. The wounds glistened darkly, juices running down his arm. There was a deep slash down his chest. His gun was on the far side of the room. He lacked the strength to even crawl for it. The corpses all wore armour, but this one had his chest plate in his hands. She wondered if he'd taken it off to treat his injuries, or just get a better look at them. He was defenseless. So were the Jahlder Elizabeth could smell.

She kicked him over. He fell hard on his wound. His yelp cracked with fear.
"Why are you here?" Elizabeth said sternly.
He struggled to speak, mumbling and eventually coughing out, "Fo...Forr."
Elizabeth stamped down on his black seeping mess and he gave another pathetic cry.
"Why?" she demanded.
"Died! His father... died!"
Not good enough. She twisted her heel. He started to sob and blubber at her feet.
"You're burning a village in his honour? In Forr's honour?"
"Forr... Please... I..."
"Who sent you?"
Another twist. The sobs worsened.
"Please... please... It's my first..."
She would get no more out of him. A shot through the neck stopped the crying and Elizabeth nudged him over with her toes. She wiped the bloodied sole of her boots dry on his fur. He was a bad soldier, but she could tolerate that. Some people weren't meant to hold guns. But killing innocents, burning them alive... He deserved no respect. He deserved her hatred, but she wouldn't waste it on him. As her boots were clean, Brack entered the hut and the Krei was flushed from her mind.

"There were only two of them in the second building. One of them threw a grenade but it bounced off the door and landed back inside. Fools," Brack said with a chuckle.
"They're here for Forr."
Brack looked around thoughtfully.
"Why? He left years ago."
"Something about his dad?"
"His father... wait. You don't think Brack's a Harkrak, do you?"
"I have no idea what that even is," Elizabeth said.
"It's like a King, but also like a prisoner, really. Lots of rules. Never leave Excha is a big one."
"Why hunt him down though? He could be dead for all they know. Forr doesn't have any contact with Excha."
"Considering their hatred for the Jahlder, don't start a broadcast show with your Jahlder wife is probably an implied rule," Brack said.

"How do you know all that? The Harkrak stuff?" Elizabeth asked.

"All Torfus learn the traditions of the Krei. They're the most likely species to attack us."
"What do you know about Humans?"
"Only what you've told me really. The Torfus don't consider your species very important, I'm afraid. We know a lot more about the Jahlder, but that's more because of the Krei's long standing feud with them than the importance of the Jahlder themselves."
Elizabeth looked down at the dead Krei beneath her, his fur tufted with congealed blood, cold salvia drooling from his mouth.

They left the building and continued through the settlement towards the tower. Elizabeth pinched her nose tight, the sickening smell of Jahlder flesh crisping still in the air. She suspected it always would be. Long after the flames were extinguished, the houses would be rebuilt. The Jahlder would return to Vires. They were not a sentimental race. Land suitable for housing and education would not be wasted on something as ballast as a memorial. Life in the village would go back to normal. But that thick, burnt smell, meat sticking to a grill, would remain forever.

At the tower, Elizabeth figured knocking was worth a shot. No answer. She knelt down on the soft earth and pushed her eye to the keyhole. The lock was a standard metal key rather than electric code. She pulled a pin from her bracelet and slotted it into the lock. She rotated it slowly, teeth uncoiling to unlock the door. Lavell was always much faster, but Elizabeth made it her business to be at least second best at everything her crew could do. She thought back to Lavell's surgery, the needle trembling in her fingers. The meek and sweet Lavell refusing medication for her pain. Seething out stern instructions. Elizabeth wondered if Lavell had changed. She felt strangely like a mother who had missed her child grow up.
"I thought Lavell wasn't allowed to sell her lock picking accessory. Illegality and all that," Brack said.
"This is my original one," Elizabeth said, "I didn't buy it off Turanga."
"You know, for a moment there I forgot –"
Elizabeth's bracelet beeped, its task complete.
"Forgot what?" Elizabeth pushed him.
"Nothing. Ignore me."
That I was dead for three years. How could he just forget?

The shadows cast the room in grey. Thin, miserly patches of light were splashed across the hallway, a broken jigsaw of illumination. That was all she saw before a lunge from the side sent her crashing to the floor. She spun with her attacker, throwing punches. Her fists hit only air. At the wall the rolling stopped. A feeble circle of light illuminating the assailant's face. Pink flesh and huge white eyes.
"Lavell?"
"Elizabeth?" the voice broke in disbelief.
Elizabeth shone her bracelet torch on Lavell, and saw the knife held an inch from her throat. Lavell pulled the cool metal safely back from Elizabeth's skin and stabbed it into the floorboards. Lavell dove forwards and held Elizabeth tightly, lovingly. She

noticed the stiff carbon fibre plating on Lavell's back. The loose fabric had been replaced after the rapui attack.
"I thought you were dead," Lavell said, face pressed close to Elizabeth's chest.
She could feel her wet breath, her hot tears.
"I've been getting that a lot recently."
Lavell chuckled.
"It's safe, Forr. We know her."
Forr's deep baritone came from the darkness, "We know both of them."
Elizabeth looked around and saw the barrel of Forr's gun pushed playfully into Brack's cheek, Brack with his back against the wall, arms out in mock surrender.

Forr

Forr slung the weapon over his shoulder and shook Brack's hand. Lavell ran and hugged him. The four of them back together. It had been too long.

"Does this mean you're finished with that Isoline lady?"

"I'm still with Isoline."

There was a silent moment full of disappointment. Lavell gave him a knowing look.

"She's back on the ship," Elizabeth said.

"You invited her on a hunt? Before us?" Lavell said.

"She's got more training than each of us combined. She had to be there," Brack said.

"I don't recall inviting her at all. Brack did, and this hunt is different."

"A hunt's a hunt," Forr said.

"We're only here because we heard your distress signal," Elizabeth said.

Forr spat on the floor, a thick wad of phlegm.

"Those Krei were cowards, sent here to die. And they couldn't even do it with honour, they had to slaughter innocent men and women on their way out. I won't go. I won't disown Lavell"

Forr squeezed Lavell's hand tenderly. She reached up to kiss his cheek.

"I know."

"So you're a Harkrak? You kept that quiet," Brack said.

Forr felt his stomach flood with rocks.

"I'm not a Harkrak. My father is. Was. They cut me out of the family, and now..."

He sank his fist into the wall.

"Shh. It's okay, my lion," Lavell said.

Lavell put her arm around him and turned to Elizabeth.

"You're only because of the signal? You don't want us?" Lavell asked.

"You're broadcast stars now, I hear. Maybe you've settled down. I didn't want to force you to get back in the game," Elizabeth said.

Disappointment stained another silent moment.

"Of course, the invitation's always there if you wanted to get the band back together."

Lavell nodded in immediate agreement. She looked up at Forr.

"So what's the prize in this hunt?" Forr said.

"I can explain it better back on the Victory Pearl. Basically, the thing I found in Allke has other bits that fit into it. And someone wants us to find them."

"Good enough for me."

"Speaking of Allke, I never got the chance to thank you for saving me," Lavell said.
"You never thanked me when I watched your back on any other hunts and I never thanked you. We just did it."

Forr took a long key off a hook at his waist and opened a hidden door. Jahlder children came spilling out, bodies trembling fearfully.
"Have the bad men gone?" one of them asked.
The child barely came to the knees of his massive legs. Forr bent down to his eye level and lay a soft hand on his back.
"Yes. This lady came and made them go away."
The child stared at Elizabeth with moist eyes.
"And my parents? Did she help them too?"
Forr swallowed the little boy up in his huge arms and rocked him gently.
"Everything will be okay, Mallo," he said.
Forr put the child down and gathered the rest together, guiding them to the door. All the time, whispering in their ears that everything would be okay.
"We can take them back to the ship for now, find a safe place for them later," Elizabeth said.
"Thank you."
She radioed two names he didn't recognize and arranged for shuttles.

The village smelled rancid, a cloying smell of smoke. Forr prayed the children would not understand the smell. He knew Lavell would not be so lucky. She coughed with sickness, all too aware that she was breathing in her own people.
"Keep looking at me, little ones. You'll be safe soon," she told them.
They walked the long way around the settlement, avoiding the carnage. Saving the children from walking through the rubble of their own homes.

"Seven," Forr said, "There's only seven!"
He had been performing a head count every few steps to keep watch on the children.
"Are you sure?" Lavell said, double checking.
"Mallo!" Forr cried out.
"Where is he? Why weren't you watching?"
"I was! I don't know what happened!"
The children slipped into bawling panic. Lavell knelt down and put her arms around as many as she could manage.
"Don't worry, we'll find him," she reassured them.

Their howls quietened, but their sobbing did not stop.

"He can't have gotten very far," Brack said.

"There," Elizabeth said, pointing.

Forr turned and saw the small boy running back towards one of the houses, one that was still alight. His white hair bounced behind him in carefree swings.

"Mallo!" Forr screamed. The boy did not turn around.

Forr sprinted after him. By the time he caught up, he was close enough to feel the flame's intense heat.

"It's not safe, Mallo. We have to leave."

He gripped the boy's shoulders.

"Someone's still alive. A girl," Mallo said.

The absorbsion panels on Mallo's face were thin, still not fully grown. Forr could see them flickering with a white glow.

"You know that?" Forr said, gently tapping the boy's panels.

"I saw it. She's trapped under something. Screaming. I wanted to help her."

"That's very brave, Mallo," Forr said, staring directly into his big eyes, "But you have to go back to Lavell now. Don't worry about the girl, I'll get her."

He pushed Mallo back towards the rest of the children and continued his run towards the burning house. The fire crackled. It gnawed at the wood. Above it all, he could hear a desperate whisper for help from a voice too hoarse to shout.

"I'll save you!"

"In here!" the voice shouted back.

It sounded like it scratched at her throat enough to make her bleed.

Forr stepped over the crumbling rubble, the cries guiding him. He could hear a whistling noise, shrill and imminent. There was a beam blocking his path, too heavy to lift. With an almighty grunt, he pushed it aside, just high enough to crawl under. He finally saw the girl. He understood the whistling. She was trapped underneath a large gas boiler. Tongues of orange and red already starting to lick up the metal dome. It was about to blow. He gripped the boiler, hands searing. Every time he raised the boiler an inch, his hands sunk back down. The trapped girl wriggled forward each time, but he was getting weaker. The whistling was getting louder. Now just a continuous screaming. The tongues grew longer and thicker, starting to spit. He did not have much time. With a heroic effort, the girl forced herself forward once more. The harsh edge of the metal ripped the skin from her calf. Forr only had time to look down at the purple gushing from her leg when the whistling became an explosion, and the world turned white.

Ana

"So I've got three aces. That's a good hand, right?" Ana said.
Rusalka placed her hand softly on her arm, "This is one of those games where it's best to keep your cards secret, sweetie."
"But it's good, right?"

Donovan's voice came through Ana's bracelet.
"Ana? Elizabeth's demanding to see you when she lands."
"Demanding?"
"I believe her exact words were 'ASAP, urgent, whatever the fuck you need to say to make sure she's waiting'. Sure sounds like a demand to me."
Rusalka shuffled the deck.
"Well well," she said.
"You think it's good news?"
"She said urgent. People only rush good news, they put bad news off until they absolutely have to."
"What do you think she wants?" Ana said.
"If you haven't figured that out yet, maybe you're not what she needs."
"It won't mean –"
"I've lost count of the times I've returned from a heist, pulse racing, and all I want is to be devoured. You understand, Ana? De-vou-red," Rusalka syllabized.
"I'm not ready. I mean, Sam..."
Rusalka waved her protests away.
"You don't want to get stuck."
"What do you mean?"
"Wear something pretty. And if I were you I wouldn't bother with any underwear, unless you have a pair you don't mind getting ripped."

Ana scrambled back under the pipes. Her elbow caught hot metal, scalding her skin. She jumped down the hole and landed heavily. Clambering to her feet, she continued running until she was back into her quarters. She was a mess. Sweat was leaking down her forehead. Her makeup was streaked and her hair was glued in her skin in wet clumps. Her light blue shirt was bunched up into her armpits, moist circles stained to navy.
She forced her way out of her clothes and hurried towards the shower. As soon as she felt clean enough, she turned the taps off and activated the UV dryers. They were bad for the skin, but she didn't use them all that often and besides, now was an emergency. She stepped out of the shower hastily, wet foot sliding on the floor. She gripped the towel rail to keep her balance.

Her hair was dribbling down. Ana yanked her styling tongs from their holder, the plastic buckling under the strain. She cursed as she threaded her wet locks into the prongs. Water steamed away and she unfurled immaculate golden curls. She moved around her head in this fashion, growing more impatient with the few seconds it took her hair to transform itself each time. Once her hair was finally ready she flung opened her wardrobe doors.

Wear something pretty.
Rusalka was ridiculous. She would not debase herself like that. She picked out a simple green dress and put it on. She looked at herself in the mirror. She had worn this dress for Sam. But Sam was gone now. And Ana was so alone. Was it really wrong that she wanted to be held?

"Shuttle's approaching," Donovan told her through the bracelet.
Ana snatched open her makeup drawer and applied it in a hurry. The cold wax of the lipstick rode up onto her skin, the dusting on her eyelids layered too thickly.
"Coming into dock."
"I get it!" Ana shouted, stuffing her brushes and creams back into their drawer.
She took a long, deep breath, buckled the straps of her high heels and walked towards the elevator.

The shuttle slid into its berth as Ana left the elevator. The shuttle door creaked open, and Elizabeth stepped out. Her face was a thunderstorm. Her jacket was torn, a huge slice splitting up the back.
"Ana!" she hollered.
Ana ran forward and noticed the second shuttle coming into dock. Mogg got out with Brack, carrying out a stretcher.
"Why are you dressed like that? Didn't you get my message?" Elizabeth said. The words were sharp, impatient creatures.
"I just –"
"Get in your scrubs. Now. I need you to perform surgery."
"Surgery?"
She was a fool.
"Forr. His hand got blown off."
"His hand? Elizabeth, I can't –"
"You fixed me. A heart's more complicated than a hand."
"Out of the way!" Mogg shouted, carrying the unconscious Krei past them.
"Your heart was still there, Elizabeth. What I did was a glorified wound stitching. I can't regrow his hand."
Elizabeth put both her hands on Ana's shoulders and stared sincerely into her.
"I need you do this, Ana."
"I can stop the bleeding and make sure the wound's not infected. Other than that he'll have to adjust to life with one hand."
Elizabeth looked down at the floor, hands still on Ana's shoulders. Ana felt the fingers clutch harder.
"Just make sure he's alright."

Quickly, she followed Mogg. Her footsteps wobbled down the corridor. These were the wrong shoes to be rushed to surgery in. Alongside Mogg and Brack, there was a Jahlder woman. The Jahlder thumped her fist down on the Forr hard.
"Why! Why couldn't you just leave her?" it screamed.
She glanced up at Ana in horror.
"I didn't mean that," she whispered.
"I need to get by," Ana said.

In the changing room, Ana left her dress where it fell. She took a blue plastic smock from the locker. Her flaws inflated in the mirror. The hairs that encircled her belly button became coarse and black. Her skin blotchy. She was uncomfortable, but she knew it was unethical – not to mention downright humiliating – to delay surgery to fetch panties. The rubber shoe covers were not designed to protect high heels, so she slotted them over her bare feet.

Forr was waiting on the operating table when she stepped into the theatre. She stretched cream latex gloves over her hands. As the plastic snapped onto her skin, the outside world was compartmentalized. Whatever Ana was crying over or worried about or excited for, Dr Yukishnov simply didn't care. It had always been this way. She took a needle loaded with ferlomine and inserted it into Forr's neck. It would keep him asleep. His injury had been wrapped in thick bandages, darkened to purple. As she uncoiled them they cracked, stiff with dried blood. A rotten smell of rancid fruit. After Ang blood, Krei blood was just about the worst in the galaxy. Ana held her breath and removed the bandages from Forr's arm. She wondered why they were so desperate to spill it when it smelled so foul.

The bleeding had stopped. The stump was caked in congealed scabs, slashed with smaller cuts. Amputations sometimes had a way of taking of themselves, the body admitting defeat and shriveling up its blood flow. The Krei evolved in warfare. Their bodies were better than most at surviving adversary.

Ana detected the vaguely putrid aroma of infection. She cleaned it with an antibacterial solution. Along with a course of tablets for the next few days, it would be fine. If Ana had not caught it now, she might have ended up back in scrubs next week to perform a much more serious operation.

She couldn't grow his hand back though. Empathetic eyes surveyed her own hand, wondering what life would be like without it. It was rare for her to put herself in patient's place, to imagine the consequences of their condition. She could not remember ever doing it before. But Elizabeth had spoken so desperately. How important this Krei must be to her. There was nothing she could do. She could not rebuild his hand. No one could.

Lavell

Lavell sat with Forr for a while after Ana had finished. Both her small hands were wrapped around his remaining one. His flesh was dry and heavy. She looked at the vase by his bed. A single yellow flower sat inside it. She knew he would be happy to see she had continued her tradition when he woke up. A new flower from every planet they visited.

The children chattered, wondering what had happened to Forr's other hand, when he would wake up, where they were going... Their questions only distressed her. Roka came to fly them to Samane, another Jahlder territory nearby. She had kissed each of their foreheads, white lied that she would see them all again and waved their shuttle off. When Roka's shuttle disappeared into the darkness of space, decided not to return to Forr's side. Instead, she snuck into Querius' laboratory.

The door had been left open. He was fully absorbed in his work, muttering to himself. Lavell was surprised at the amount of cursing she heard, the static blockers in the translator distorting the words. She crawled underneath his workbench, periodically peeping up to grab parts she needed.

She reached for a soldering iron and felt some resistance. She glanced up. Querius' hand rested on it. He had not noticed Lavell's attempts to wedge it free, but she did not dare risk another. Querius was holding up a scale close to his eye, examining it through a strange glass gadget. Hours seemed to pass. Lavell's legs started to ache. He brought the scale closer, then moved it further away. He brought it closer once more, squinting until his eyes were barely there. He shouted, but all Lavell heard was static. She let out a shocked gasp, but it was drowned out by the rattle as Querius tossed the glass gadget aside. He leapt around the lab happily, leaving the soldering iron free. She gathered up the rest of her supplies and stole out.

She carried the things to her own workstation and spilled them across her table. She didn't know exactly what the glass lens Querius had worn did, but she knew she could use it now. She made the shape from memory, knowing contours by heart. Her memory was nothing special by Jahlder standards, but that still meant around 200 hours photographic. The whistle and scream. Sometimes it was a curse.

When her invention was complete, she attached wire to the internal hinges, fixing brain monitoring electrodes to their ends. She slotted her own hand inside, giggling at the sheer size of it, her fingers wiggling freely through the wide spaces. Still snickering softly, Lavell scooped up her creation and wrapped the wires around and around.

Lavell returned to Forr's bedside. He was still asleep. She anointed his forehead will a cool towel and he jolted up. He had only been resting his eyes. The real awakening had been missed. She felt guilty, leaving him. He had woken up alone. She knew he would not bear her the grudge once he saw why.
"My pact," he said, his voice happy, dry and sore.
"My lion. I have a present for you."
She planted a tender kiss on his forehead. He turned, and saw the flowers.
"It's just what I wanted. How did you know?"
"That's not your present, silly."
She held his stump lovingly, without fear or pity, and placed her device on the end of it. She uncoiled the wires and stuck each of them on Forr's head.
"What's this?" he said.
"Try and move it."
He looked at the chunk of metal on his arm, his face awash with confusion. He lifted his arm and the contraption moved with it.
"No, *move* it. Think about moving it," she said.
He stared at it hard, brow furrowed and focused. They leapt up as the fingers formed a fist.
"It's not as dexterous as a real hand, but I'll improve on it."

He started to weep, slim tears rolling down his huge face.
"It's perfect," he said, carefully lifting a metal finger to wipe them away.

Elizabeth

The gym was hot. Elizabeth drove six rapid jabs into the punch bag. Sweat poured down her face. It ran through her eyelashes, the salt stinging. Next was the treadmill, so fast it began to whine. She couldn't bring herself to go and see Forr.

An inquisitive voice came from behind her, "Miss Ranger?"
She looked around and saw Querius, fingers tented curiously. His white hair was bushy and unkempt, like a bird's nest perched on his head. At first, Elizabeth had assumed it was a result of his ordeal. She saw now it was just his eccentric personality.
"What is it?" she said.
"Yes, well. I realize you have just returned from your mission, and one of your friends is joining us with a rather severe injury. Quite bad. In another way, rather good. It's all relative."
"Relative? In what way is Forr losing his hand good?"
She wiped her forehead dry with her arm and faced him fully, hands on hips.
"No, that's bad. Obviously. But it's only his hand. Had any of the rest of you been in his position, you may not have survived. The Krei are tough. He will heal. Adapt. Rather good that if one of you was involved in a close range explosion, it was the one most likely to survive. But I am digressing. I have not yet even begun what I came here to say, so it is less a digression than simple small talk."
She stepped closer to him, face firm.
"Why're you here?"
He bent away from her before answering.
"Breakthrough. Fascinating find. Still struggling to come to grips with its origin. Follows no know mythos or anthropological culture. At least, none known to me, although most are known to me so that I do not know is actually somewhat of a discovery in itself."
"But you have found something?"
Elizabeth had met people like Querius before, who built jungles around their point. Dense green leaves that needed to be hacked down.
"Scales were stuck to it. Black. Strange. Again, unknown to me."
"So you came to tell me you found nothing?"
He chuckled.
"I don't intend to bore you with the details, Miss Ranger. Essentially I found a stone particle within the fibres of the scale that suggests it is extremely old. Eons. It's a magnificent finding. I still need to trace the location, but I thought it would be best to notify you now."
"Consider me notified."
"I hope I have not offended you with my logical dissection of your friend's accident. I sincerely hope he is okay."

~*~

Back in her cabin, she fell asleep almost instantly. Her body collapsed on top of the covers, skin swathed in sweat. She turned over and saw Ana lying in bed with her, naked. Her elbow was on the pillow, hand cradling her chin. Exquisite curls flowed down onto the bed, the glimmering blonde.

"What are you doing here?" Elizabeth said.
Ana smiled to herself, "You invited me, silly. Didn't she?"
Ana spoke beyond Elizabeth. She turned over to see Brack's sharp scales shining.
"She invited both of us," Brack said, "I think she's a little greedy."
"But we don't mind," Ana said. Her soft hands ran through Elizabeth's hair.
Ana tugged slightly. Just the right amount of force to electrify her. Ana pushed her into a hard kiss with Brack. Too hard. Elizabeth felt the hot magma of blood run down her face. Brack's scales popped her lips like pink balloons. Ana laughed and pulled her away. Before she could catch her breath, Ana had her forward again, spraying a blood firework. Brack grinned unwholesomely, razor fangs dripping scarlet. Ana flipped her over so they were face to face. Ana had the same sharp grin, except her teeth were a pure clean white. She lunged and bit through Elizabeth's tongue. A copper tang filled her throat. Fingers laced their way through Elizabeth's hair, nails digging into the scalp. Fresh, wet blood. She touched her scalp and her fingers ran red. Brack's hand scored her back, carving a deep wound down her spine. Ana clawed her legs until the skin fell off in tatters. Elizabeth felt no pain.

Ana and Brack held her down, bloody hands pinning her shoulders. The bed swelled. Elizabeth a tiny island, floating on an ocean of sheets. The hands on her disappeared into smoke. They were circling above her like carrion birds, twisted spectres. Spitting out rich deep pantomime cackles from their diabolical smiles. Isoline appeared, standing over her, hands on hips. As Isoline touched her, Elizabeth's own body started to evaporate...

The bed was drenched wet. Sweat dripped onto the floor. Elizabeth touched her back, her scalp, her legs. Everything was fine. She ran to the bathroom and splashed icy water on her face. Her cheeks were pale and hollow. She ran her tongue across her teeth and tasted her own dry breath. She threw on some clothes and headed for the flight deck.

Her skin was sticky. She turned away from the dark window and knocked on Donovan's cabin. Her fist hit the metal with impatience. He opened the door groggily, eyes half shut. He had a pistol pointed at her, his grip loose.
"Captain? There some kind of emergency?"
"Put that down before you hurt someone. There's no emergency."
"Okay," he gave her a wary look, up and down, "You wanna come in?"

Donovan's room was cramped and bare. No decorations aside from a small mirror on his desk. He sat down on the bed and tossed the pistol aside. He kicked a chair closer for Elizabeth.
"You see everything on the ship, right?" she asked.

"Everything and nothing. Cameras are everywhere, but I don't watch people masturbate or nothin'"
"What? God, no! That's not what I'm saying."
"I didn't mean to offend you, Captain. It was Roka's first question, is all."
"But it's not my question. You understand that?"
"Of course, Captain. Sorry."
"I want to know about Brack and Isoline. They got a twin room?"
"You gave 'em it."
"Have they slept together yet?"
"They're both asleep right now," Donovan said.
"I mean, have they had sex."
Silence hung heavy.

Finally, Donovan spoke.
"I'm not sure that's an ethical question."
"It's my ship, Donovan."
"Cap, I –"
"Has he fucked her yet!"
Elizabeth's fist crashed into the mirror, shattering the glass into a mosaic of eyes, teeth and red hair.
"Look, I don't watch the cameras. I'm not a creep. But I got up to go to the can last night, and I heard 'em. I mean…"
His voice faded out. Elizabeth seethed at her distorted reflection. The horrible, monstrous form of herself.
"Sorry, I…"
Donovan laid his hand on Elizabeth's.
"It's okay. Lot happened in three years, right?"
Elizabeth nodded. Next to her, the fractured creature nodded too.

Ana

Ana sat at her desk, tearing pieces from a cupcake. She wiped the frosting from her fingertips as West's voice came through her com bracelet.
Miss Yukishnov. I need to speak to Miss Ranger
"I thought her bracelet was set up receive messages from you?"
Bring her to the room. And you should remain present
"Are you going to tell her about the surgery?"
Bring her, Miss Yukishnov

Still eating the cupcake, Ana rushed to Elizabeth's quarters. She found her in the gym instead, pounding a punching bag. She waved her over. Elizabeth dried her face on a towel. There were deep bags under her eyes. Ana explained that West needed to see her.

"Where'd you get the cake?" Elizabeth said.
"Rusalka gave it to me. I think she swiped it from the kitchen."
"Oh. I didn't realize you two got along so well," Elizabeth said.
Ana waited to see if Elizabeth said any more. She didn't.
"She's not very good at making friends. Neither am I. We don't expect normal behavior from each other, because we don't know what normal behavior is."

They reached the central chamber. Ana pressed her eye to the reader and Elizabeth turned away. Ana pushed the door open then stepped back. She gestured for Elizabeth to continue forwards.
"I'm only here to observe," she said, "It's you he wants to speak to."
The voice poured into the room again.
Hello again Miss Ranger
"This about the thing Querius found?"
We'll get to that. I understand you have added more to the crew roster than I was expecting. Characters of ill repute
"Their repute is no more ill than mine," Elizabeth said.
Ana hated the chill of this room. She hoped West would keep it short.
A thief with a penchant for grandeur and your old squad. Two broadcast stars igniting inter species conflict and another who has brought along his paramour; the highest ranking Torfus ever to resign her post in the military, an incident which occurred in mysterious circumstances. It is not the low key affair I was hoping for
"Mysterious circumstances?"
"They're a necessary part of the team."
They shall have to prove they are
"And if they don't?"
Her voice echoed around the chamber. Cold and damp and full of shadows.

In any case, another addition is required. Someone with the expertise to make sense of Loslou's findings

"You telling me we need an expert to help our expert?"

Querius Loslou is a virtuoso in interpreting ancient artefacts, but what he has discovered requires someone well versed in lesser known species. Cryptozoology

"I take it you have someone in mind?" Elizabeth said.

Uhkira. He has a small base on Blue 2

"The Barely Charted?"

That should give you some idea of what kind of Krei he is. He won't be expecting you

"What's that supposed to mean?" Elizabeth said.

No answer.

She turned to Ana.

"I think that's all we'll get," Ana said.

Elizabeth left the room quickly. She wouldn't look Ana in the eye.

"Is something wrong?" Ana asked.

"Let's just get this mission sorted."

They reached the flight deck. Donovan swiveled around in his chair.

"Any news, Captain?"

"We're heading to The Barely Charted."

"Nice. Anywhere special?"

"Blue 2," Ana said.

"Travel to The Barely Charted is forbidden," Mogg told them.

Ana hadn't noticed he was there. He had a screwdriver in his hand, leant over one of the control stations.

"You're no fun, you know that?" Donovan said.

"Any idea on an ETA Donovan?" Elizabeth said, ignoring Mogg.

"We're on the outskirts now. With warp drive we'll be there by the time you reach the hangar, if you walk slowly."

"Slowly it is."

They headed for the armoury.

"Get ready," Elizabeth told her.

Ana attached her white body plates and tucked her first aid supplies away.

"Should I take the derringer or the assault rifle for this one?" she asked, holding each of them up.

"Why do you even have that derringer? It won't do any damage," Elizabeth said without looking up.

"Sam gave it to me."

Elizabeth turned around, "It's cute. But assault rifle should be your go to from now on."

There was a knock on the armoury door, a playful melody.
"Come in, Lavell," Elizabeth shouted.
Lavell handed her a bracelet.
"This a new design?"
"I suppose they would be, to you. I've made some improvements, mainly to the com link function."
Another knock at the door. Hard and demanding.
"A captain's work is never done. I've told we're to call you that now. Captain Ranger," Lavell said with a teasing smirk.
"Call me captain and I'll blast you out of the airlock," Elizabeth said, smiling.

Elizabeth opened the door. Isoline was stood there.
"We should come on this mission," Isoline told her.
"We?" Ana asked.
"Brack and I."
"What makes you so sure?" Elizabeth said.
"This is not a simple treasure hunt, digging for metal in a pile of dirt. Uhkira's lair will be heavily guarded. The presence of one as highly training as myself will only aid the mission, won't it?"
Elizabeth stared at Isoline for a moment.
"Fine. Get suited up then meet us in the hangar."
Isoline nodded and walked away with long strides.
"Am I still coming?" Ana asked.
Elizabeth looked at her, eyes widening, like she was half asleep.
"Yeah."

Brack

Isoline kissed Brack as they walked from the elevator. He followed her over to the shuttle and saw Ana sitting there. Her blonde hair shone. Colours caked her face. She did not look like a woman built for action. He reminded him of Olivia, and that made him uneasy.
"Have you been on many missions like this, Ana?" he asked.
"Are you sure a crew of four is the right choice?" Isoline said before Ana could answer.
Elizabeth leaned out of the shuttle.
"Rather too many than too few."
Isoline pulled Brack close and the conversation seemed to fade. He did not feel aware of Elizabeth or Ana's presence as he stared into Isoline's eyes. As far as he was aware, the shuttle ride took place in gentle silence.

~*~

"Entering Blue 2's atmosphere. I've got the co-ordinates but he's got surface to air turrets" Roka called through to them.
"Play it safe. He's not expecting us. Let's keep it that way," Elizabeth said.
"Play it safe? That doesn't sound like Elizabeth Ranger," Brack said.
He laughed. Elizabeth did not.

The shuttle skittered across the gravel. They stepped out onto the planet's surface, the rocky ground a hostile grey. Almost black. Slabs of slate climbed around them in a dark valley of impregnable peaks and shadowy caverns.
"The co-ordinates are on the bracelet, but I'm not sure you'll need them," Roka said, closing the doors.
Uhkira's stone laboratory, lined with an array of huge steel cannons, sat at the end of a valley. Light glinted from the metal impressively.

Brack picked up one of the smaller stones at his feet and lobbed it through the air, along the road to Uhkira.
"What are you doing?" Ana asked.
"You'll see."
The rock landed without ceremony.
"What?"
A blast of fire rose and the ground split open, showering dirt and rock.
"Mines. We'll have to be careful."
Brack toggled the buttons on his bracelet. Several tiny drones uncoiled themselves. A swarm of metallic butterflies creaked as they scanned the dark road ahead. Their tails shone red, casting a crimson hue. Five vertical lines erupted from the ground stop sign poles.
"That's where the mines are," he said.
"Remember when this thing was just a torch?" Elizabeth said.

They teetered around the mines, watchful eyes steady on the red. The silence was tense.
"It was originally your intention to only bring three on his expedition, was it not? Elizabeth?"
"Let's just concentrate on getting through here safely," Elizabeth said without

looking back.
"A team of four offers less stealth. Four also raises the odds of one of us blowing a mine and alerting any security to the position of the other three."
Ana glared at Isoline, craning her neck to look around Brack.
"Do you disagree, Miss Yukishnov?" Isoline said.
"I'm not going back."
"You feel you have a greater value to the mission than someone else present?"
"I'm deputy captain," Ana said.
"Oh. In that case, humblest apologies," Isoline said, smiling.
"Ice, play nice dear," Brack said.

Ana stumbled, slipping on the flat black rocks. Her face shot towards a red light. Elizabeth grabbed her, one hand tucked into a crevice, and rocked her back to safety. *That* was the Elizabeth Ranger he knew. Isoline turned back to smirk.
"Be careful," Elizabeth said, "And no more talk. From any of you."

The rest of the way, the only sound the scratching of the rocks, spitting and sparking. He watched Ana, constantly looking back, unsure of herself. A liability, just like Olivia.

As the minefield ended, their road curved. There were two towers either side of Uhkira's main base, each pronged with lighting rods and a winding staircase around its outside. He watched Ana shiver.
"Cold, Miss Yukishnov?" Isoline asked.

A crashed shuttle smouldered in front of them. The blaze had died of exhaustion some time ago. All that was left was weak grey smoke.
"Looks like someone tried take the easy route," Brack said.
The ship was half buried in a pile of stones, its twisted rear poking up like a stuck rabbit. Lights scored along the ship's base were cracked and frazzled, bulbs extinguished.
"It's a recent crash," Brack said.
Elizabeth wiped the stone dust away from the buckled door.
"KNF?" she said, reading the letters painted on the door aloud.
"Society for the Eradication of Genetic Experimentation," Brack told her.
"That's not the right letters."
"Alien translators," Brack said, tapping the side of his head, "They're iffy."

A rasping cry came down the pathway.
"Who goes there?"
It was the voice of a man who liked his desk just so. Elizabeth signaled for them to remain quiet. They followed it and beyond another curve was an encampment of soldiers. They sat on footlockers, playing chess and eating berries. The man who had called to them was a Krei. As he saw them approach, he fumbled his firearm, fat fingers dropping it at his feet. He scooped it off the ground and pointed it at each of them in turn, swinging it wildly through the air. His armour was neon orange, a poor choice of camouflage against a dark landscape.
"Identify yourself! On behalf of the Society for the Eradication of Genetic Experimentation, I *demand* that you identify yourselves!"
Isoline rushed forward. She charged into the Krei and dislodged the weapon from his light grip. She caught the gun as he fell. Her foot slammed down onto his cheek to clamp him into place. Isoline pressed the gun through his lips, cracking

the muzzle against his teeth. She pulled the trigger. The hammer made an echoing click. Nothing else happened.
"Isnolow," the Krei mumbled around the gun.
"What?" Isoline asked, ripping the gun from his mouth.
"It's not loaded," he told her, his voice beginning to squeak.
"Why on earth do you carry it?" Brack asked him.

"Everybody calm down," Elizabeth said, pulling Isoline back and freeing the man. He stood quickly, as if there was still a scrap of dignity to be recovered in getting to his feet promptly.
"The planet is in a forbidden area of The Barely Charted. If you do not show me your identification I have authority to place you under governmental holding!"
"I think that ship has sailed, dear," Brack said.
Isoline drew her pistol and jabbed the Krei in the eye. He recoiled backwards, holding the watering socket.
"I must see identification!" he continued.
Isoline flicked a switch on the pistol and it unfolded out into a long range rifle, slithering closer to the injured Krei like a viper.
"Give it a rest, Gorgax!" one of the soldiers shouted.
The rest of them continued with their game, barely glancing over. Gorgax convulsed and collapsed as a bolt of green hit his back.
"Muscle relaxant. He'll be fine in a few hours," the soldier said.

She took off her helmet to reveal herself a Human woman, dark hair held in a loose bun. She put her hand out to Isoline, who holstered her weapon but did not accept the handshake. Elizabeth stepped in and took the hand. She said her name was Toni.
"Gorgax takes his work seriously, but the truth is we're all desk jockeys. The only reason no one's killed Gorgax in a mutiny yet is because none of us have the stomach for it. Our task was to come here and survey Uhkira's defenses before they sent in a real team. But Gorgax ordered our pilot to fly too close. Now we're stranded. Gorgax somehow got it in his head that we should be the ones to attack Uhkira, then he wasted all his bullets firing into the air to order us around. Are you the real task force? Here to rescue us?"
"Not exact -"
"Yeah, we are. Do you know a way in?" Elizabeth said, cutting across Brack's honesty.
"Fraid not," Toni turned to Isoline, "Oh, by the way, your gun? Coolest thing I've ever seen."
"This gun has seen things that would haunt you. Things that would leave you a hollowed out husk, unable to think a coherent thought," Isoline told her coldly.
Toni shrunk away from Isoline's icy stare. Brack's skin prickled.
"Have you found anything at all?" Elizabeth asked.
"This cave here will keep you dry when it starts to rain, and there's some bushes up that hillside that have edible berries on them. Other than that, we've learned less than bupkis."

Brack glanced where Toni pointed. A cluster of gnarled roots and branches that grew impossibly out of harsh, bare rock. The twisted vines were thick with thorns. Red berries, glossy and ripe, drooping down from their stems.

"Look out!" Elizabeth shouted.

One of the soldiers ran towards them, a Human with deranged eyes. His arms swung in chaotic windmills. Every step was a stumble that kept him skidding forwards. A green swoosh inside his coiled fist. A grenade with a pulled pin. Brack saw it too late.

His eyes were locked shut. Brack heard the explosion but felt nothing. He opened his eyelids. A huge engery field sheltered him. He never seen anything like it. Chunks of organ meat slipped down the dome, streaking blood. Isoline had her hand splayed, creating the protective barrier.
"How are you doing that?"
"What do you think the military trained me in? Needlework?"
She lowered her hand and the field faded.
Brack looked around urgently.
"Elizabeth!" he shouted.
"I need to..." Isoline slipped onto him woozily.

He shook away from her, eyes desperate around the dark wasteland.
"Elizabeth!" he screamed until his voice was hoarse.
The nearby cave had collapsed into rubble, a single orange leg, shattered and sticking out. It twitched lifelessly with the might of a dying insect.
"She's gone, Brack," Isoline said, pulling him close.
He cried against her, sobs echoing into the silence.

Elizabeth

Cold. Dark. Her eyes rattled, unable to settle in the pitch black. Wet rock chilled her skin. Numbness crawled her spine.
"Are you okay?"
The ringing in her ears quietened. Ana, calling to her.
"What happened?" Elizabeth asked.
She dragged herself to her feet.
"We're sealed inside the cave," Ana said.
"Cave?"
Elizabeth's brain was a thick soup.
"I pulled you to safety when the grenade went off."
The green through the air. The sound and the force.
"I... remember," she said.
She noticed Ana's arm, the armour broken. Red with blood.
"The tremor from the blast caused an avalanche."
"Brack?" Elizabeth asked.
Ana looked away from her, "I couldn't save everyone."
Elizabeth's blood froze. She hollowed out for a moment. All she could hear, all she could feel, was the empty thudding of her heart.

She ran both hands through her hair. A grenade at close quarters. People didn't survive that. It didn't matter. Unless they could get out, they would not survive long.
She tried to roll one of the smaller stones aside. It would not budge.
"A little help?"
Ana scurried over but her efforts added nothing.
"Maybe we can go this way?" Ana said, pointing further into the cave, "It might be a tunnel."
"Shh," Elizabeth said, holding up her hand for silence.
There was a faint whisper.
"I hear it too," Ana said quietly.
They crept around the shadows.
"It's louder near you," Ana said.
Elizabeth walked in slowly collapsing circles around the cave, but the volume never changed.
"I can't figure it out."
Ana leaned into Elizabeth.
"I think it's coming from you," she said.

Elizabeth patted herself down. What sort of macabre cave dweller had latched onto her skin? She lifted her left hand to inspect her cheek and the whisper started to scream static. Her bracelet. The speaker was hanging limp by a single frayed wire, the grille shattered.
"I think someone's trying to communicate with us. It's Brack, it has to be! Let me see your bracelet!" Elizabeth said.

"It's broken," Ana said, holding up the smashed shards of evidence.
Elizabeth carefully wrapped the distressed wire around the drum of the speaker and pressed it back inside.
"Hello? Brack?"
"Elizabeth!" Brack's voice shouted back.
"You're alive! Look, me and Ana are trapped in the cave and we can't –"
"Elizabeth!" Brack shouted over her.
"Yeah, I'm here, I'm here. But I'm stuck. Listen, you need to –"
"Elizabeth!"
A desperate wail.
Isoline's voice came through the speaker, "We have to go, Brack."
"We can't leave her. I don't see her or Ana anywhere."
"They're gone."
Isoline spoke with finality.
"We're in here!" Elizabeth shouted into the speaker.
"They can't hear you," Ana said.
"We'll be okay. We have each other, don't we?" Isoline said.
"Turn it off," Ana told her, placing her arm around Elizabeth.
"Yeah, we do," Brack said, the sadness suddenly washing away from his voice.
"We'll get through this. Pin um," Isoline said.
"Pin um," Brack replied.
Pin um. It sounded more beautiful in its original tongue. Now the words were molten barbed wire wrapped tight around her heart.
"Turn it off," Ana said again.

She reached across Elizabeth to flick the com link switch. Elizabeth shrugged her off with an elbow to the ribs. Elizabeth smashed her wrist off the rocks, splintering her bracelet into a fine electrical spray of frazzled fragments.
"There! You happy now!" Elizabeth yelled.
"Elizabeth, I –"
The rest of Ana's words were muffled. Their lips met in a hot and violent kiss.
"Elizabeth, are you sure about…"
"Shut up."
She pressed Ana up against the cave wall.

Ana

Her thoughts turned white. Elizabeth's hands were firm on her hips, slamming off the clasps on her armour. Ana felt the wet warmth of lips on her neck as Elizabeth nuzzled against her, quickly fumbling to undress her. Her body was weak, absorbing Elizabeth's every touch. Her legs felt liquid. Elizabeth moved down her body, soft lips tickling the fair skin of her stomach. Ana sunk against the wall. Elizabeth spun her like a ragdoll.

Ana was down to her underwear now, black lace. It shone like gossamer. Elizabeth still wearing the long blue jacket. She kissed Ana hard, the cold leather against Ana's hot skin. Ana tried to kiss back but Elizabeth was too fast. Too forceful. She was consuming her, biting into Ana's plump lips like they were ripe berries. Elizabeth moved vampirically onto her ear and began to suckle at the lobe. Ana tingled. Then the teeth sunk in.

Elizabeth slid her hand under the lacey sheen. Ana slipped back against the wet stone. Waves rippled through her. Elizabeth took Ana's hand and guided her. Soft sighs were enough to keep Ana's rhythm.

The waves crashed stronger as Elizabeth's touch quickened, quickened, hardened. Ana responded, Elizabeth biting down on her neck as the satisfaction swelled. Elizabeth sank against her. Ana gently slid down until they were lying on the ground, the stone icy cold on Ana's naked back, the burning heat of Elizabeth's body on top of her. Ana's chest rose and fell breathlessly. She pressed her palm to the damp rock, soaking the chill into her fiery skin.

Rusalka was right. Human life was short.

Elizabeth

The congealed blood, thick on Ana's arm, dragged against her skin. She thought of that old Torfus phrase. *How sensual it was, to bleed for you lover.* She had forgotten how good it felt with Human women.
"That was..." Ana said.
"I know," Elizabeth said, handing Ana her armour.
"What now?"
"We escape, I guess."
She kissed Ana again, then rolled off her.

Elizabeth walked further into the damp shadows. With both of their bracelets in smithereens, there was no torch to guide them. Instead they felt their way, hands gripping cold rocks. The distance caught her eye. Dim, distorted droplets of light. It was leaking in from somewhere.

The roof of the cavern sloped down. There was another blockage, a single boulder. Light seeped in through a crescent. Elizabeth pushed, but her hand only scraped up the rough surface, scratching a layer of skin off her palm. Wincing, she charged at the rock with her shoulder and bounced off.
"Come here," Ana said.
She took Elizabeth's skinned hand and opened it up slowly. Elizabeth seethed as skin stretched. Ana removed a glass vial of salve from her armour and gently massaged it into Elizabeth's skin.
"Those pockets are for bullets, you know," Elizabeth said.
"I'm a doctor, remember? You do the killing. I heal."
A strange kind of cold burn. The pain floated away. Ana took a coil of bandage from another slot and wrapped layers around Elizabeth's hand. The first sheet of thin fabric drank up the salve. The next pulled the bandage taut and bound the injury.

"We still need to figure out how we're going to move this rock," Elizabeth said.
"I've got an idea," Ana said.
She sat on the floor with her back to the boulder and strained. It eked forward half an inch.
"It's working! Help me!"
Her hand fluttered like an excited moth, gesturing for Elizabeth to join her.
She sat down and pressed her back straight against the boulder.
Ana timed them in.
"One, two three!"
The huge stone scraped and light started to flow.

Suddenly the rock fell away completely. It tipped and landed with a metal crash. Elizabeth leaned out over the edge. There was an iron staircase grafted onto the rock beneath them. Each step dented with a bang as the boulder rolled down. Her eyes climbed the staircase. A set of doors. Uhkira. It had to be. They had stumbled onto his secret entrance.

Elizabeth jumped down onto the steps. The doors themselves were thick glass, the key pad a mass of steel welded to the wall. It had a palm reader in the shape of a Krei hand and several worn buttons. By the time Ana caught up, she had figured it out.
"You've got more of that salve, right?"
"Another two vials," Ana said, "Why? Is your hand hurting still?"
"No. But my leg might be soon."
"Your leg?"
Elizabeth took a step back and booted the door, her foot crashing through the glass panel. Her trousers ripped to shreds, but her skin remained unscathed.
"False alarm."

Uhkira's base sweltered, a labyrinth of exposed pipes. Thick moss grew over the heavy bolts, slimy green fingers squirming over the metal. Elizabeth drew her gun and held it close to her chest.
"I don't know what we're gonna find in here, so watch your back," she said to Ana.
She heard Ana slap the rifle barrel down into her hand. The pipes. They could be full of coolant, or something explosive. She didn't trust Ana's naïve hands at the trigger.
"If anything happens, *don't* shoot," Elizabeth said.

The pipes led to a series of glass tanks that stretched from floor to ceiling. The first few were empty, nothing but limp rubber coils curled up on the floor like dead snakes. But the tanks began to fill, first with just a thick blue jelly, then with creatures suspended in the goo. The rubber tubes wrapped over their shoulders and fastened to hulking metal collars around their throats. Elizabeth stepped towards the first one cautiously. An Ang with swirling arcs of stitched up scars. Elizabeth rapped on the glass with her knuckles. No reaction from the Ang. She moved her index finger in front of the glistening black eyes. He did not track her movement.
"Is he dead?" Elizabeth asked.
Ana had pushed herself against the back wall, as far from the Ang as she could get. She eased forward and read the chart by the tube.
"Yes and no."
"That's not a question where that answer applies."
"If it was my patient, I'd pull the plug. But it's technically not dead."
"Let's keep moving," Elizabeth said.

There were more Ang, some stripped of their horns, others with one or both arms cut away to nubs. A Jahlder whose white absorbsion panels had been sliced away, scabs slashed over her naked body. A Torfus with scales ripped off, balding like a diseased chicken. Then the Humans. Bloody holes where the eyes should be. Deep red lines up the torso, the healed wounds of repeated vivisection. Mouths cut open, tongues lolling forward. But the worst were the Krei. Knowing Uhkira had experimented on his own kind.

One of them sagged forward, nose pressed against the glass. His forehead had been sliced open, the top of this skull flopping down loosely.
"What do you think he does here?" Ana said.
"Science. His twisted version of it."
"He can't think this is science," Ana said, turning away from the glass tanks.
"Nobody thinks they're evil. They all think it's for the greater good," Elizabeth said.

Elizabeth kept her head down. Too disgusted to glance at the half beings. Even the floor was sickening, spotted with blood. It clung to her soles with every footstep. Finally the parade of creatures stopped.

They came to a table sealed in a glass box. Ana doubled up and vomited. It spilled across the floor with a foul smell.
"You okay?" Elizabeth asked her.
"I'm a doctor. This shouldn't upset me."
Elizabeth rubbed down her back.
"I'm glad it does."
Ana looked up, skin ghostly pale and speckled with sweat.
"We can't work with this man. We have to kill him."
She held Ana in her arms, blonde curls lacing through her fingers.
"I know. We will."

A Jahlder was strapped to the bench with stiff leather cuffs. His skin had been peeled back and stretched flat across the heavy wooden table, held in place with sharp pins, red baubles shimmering at their ends. His flesh was pulled so thin it was almost transparent. His organs were splayed and slowly rotting. Maggots swarmed them. The mission had disintegrated into mulch. This was now an assassination.

Elizabeth led Ana away. To their left, the laboratory continued to unfold. A big expanse of concrete and steel. But to their right was a door. It was a simple wooden door. A closed door is an indescribable mystery. Elizabeth gravitated towards it, compelled by its ordinariness in a place that claimed to push the boundaries of extra-ordinariness. She twisted the handle and pushed. Inside was a cramped room, bookcases of either side with yellowed pages spilling out. She picked up one of the pages from the floor. It was crumpling with damp, crinkled brown. A picture of a Torfus woman was attached with a paperclip. Needles were impaled through each of her bright eyes. Her mouth was twisted in agony. She had been alive when Uhkira had done this to her. Elizabeth tossed the report aside.

She walked towards a large oak desk, stepping over Uhkira's catalogue of crimes. There was a picture framed on the desk, the photo inside creased with the ridges of fold marks. It was two Krei, smiling in front of a water fountain. She assumed the male was Uhkira, but his awkwardly happy smile could not belong to the same man who committed these atrocities. His arm was at her waist.

More pages were scattered across his desk. The only picture was an Ang that wore a shock collar but looked otherwise unharmed. Several crescents of brown marked the pages. There was a green china mug resting on the table. The contents had fermented into mould, thick and white and bubbling. How long since Uhkira had been here? Maybe Gorgax's shuttle had spooked him enough to make him flee.

There was single note in the middle of the table, untouched by the rest. A handwritten scribble on a torn out page. Like a magnet, it repelled everything around it. Elizabeth picked it up but could not make sense of the scrawl.
"What's that?" Ana said.
"I don't understand it," Elizabeth said, handing it to Ana.
She smoothed it out against the wall, ironing out the crinkles with her hand. Her eyes scanned across the messy inkblots.
"Translators won't work on handwritten notes," Ana said.
"It'll be the ravings of a mad man."
"If you are reading this, I am most likely dead. I apologize for the mess, and no doubt the odour," Ana said, reading aloud with slow deliberation.
"You can read it?"
"I learned all the major languages when I was growing up. It was policy."
"Where'd you grow up?" Elizabeth asked.
Ana peered closer to the note.
"I have been diagnosed with groklidders disease and do not have long left."
"What's that?"
"Sort of like Krei lukemia. Nothing like it medically, but it kills you just as cruelly."
"No more than he deserved."
"There was a woman I knew once, and I wish I could donate her some token from my dying moments. But I confess her name has long since been lost to me. No matter. History will remember me as a villain, but someone will arrive one day and become a hero on the back of my work, and for that I thank them. The code is 626."
"What code?"
"That's all it says," Ana said.
Ana handed the note back to Elizabeth. She scrunched it into a ball inside her fist, tempted to boot Uhkira's dying thoughts to the other side of the room. After a moment, she simply dropped it to the floor.

~*~

Columns of shelves were stacked high, mason jars filled with the same blue liquid. Floating chunks of lobotomized brain sat in them. As they weaved through them a chemical stench started to sting Elizabeth's nostrils. Her nose began to burn. She followed the scent and found Uhkira lying on the floor, decorated with broken glass. Slimy organ meat flopped across his grey chest like dead fish. The blue jelly dripped down his rigor mortised body, cold stare fixed on the ceiling. Next to him, traced in dark blood from his cut fingers, were three basic shapes. The first was the same as the third. Elizabeth could guess what it said.
"That 626?" she asked Ana.
Ana nodded, fingers pinched tight around her small nose.

"Whatever's in there must mean a lot to him," Elizabeth said.
They left him there and journeyed deeper.
"Do we really want to find something that means so much to this monster?"
"Maybe it's alive. Maybe we can help it."
There was a scuffed corner of brass protruding from beneath one of the shelves. A trapdoor. Something else to scratch off her bucket list.

She started to push the shelves away. Ana helped her and it tipped over, shattering the glass. The trapdoor creaked as Elizabeth lifted it. At halfway, it fell backwards on its wailing hinges. Inside was a dark chute. Horizontal poles were bolted onto the rear wall. They were twice as thick as Elizabeth's arm. Whatever was down there was big. Gripping around the bars was impossible. Elizabeth jammed her wrists up underneath the steps and started to descend.

There was a clash of fist against iron bars from the darkness. A creature begging to be freed. A single lightbulb dripped down from a stem of exposed wire, illuminating nothing.
"Master?" a voice called out.
It was a deep voice, scratchy and dry. A voice that could belong to a great leader. But instead it was submissive, kotowed. A voice of doubt. Elizabeth followed the sound. A hulking figure was crouched in a cage, hiding in the shadows.
"You are not my master," it said, covering its face.
"No," Elizabeth said, "I'm not."
Pistol drawn, Elizabeth examined the lock.
"No code," she said.
One bullet later, it fell open with a hard clang. The creature shuffled back, afraid of its freedom.
"What are you doing? We don't even know what it is," Ana said.
"It's a slave. And we're freeing it."

Elizabeth knelt down and offered her hand into the cage. It hovered there, in silence, in darkness. A gentle grasp smothered it. Holding on, the creature edged forward, face gradually emerging in the light. Yellow skin, three black eyes. It was an Ang.
"Where is my master?" it asked.
There was a spiked collar tight around its neck, sparking purple with energy. He stooped to exit the cage. Ana readied her weapon. Elizabeth guided the barrel down to the floor.
"Your master's dead," Elizabeth said.
"You killed him?"
There was no trace of vengeance nor hope in the question.
"His disease killed him."
The Ang nodded, "Grokiddlers."
"You knew he was sick?"
"Are you here to continue his work?"
"What sort of work did Uhkira do here?" Elizabeth asked.
She kept Ana's rifle aimed at the ground with her fingers.

"He improves."

"Improves? That's what you call it?"

Elizabeth had to hold the barrel down harder.

"What other definition is there? I was a dim witted brute before Master. Worse; I was an Ang."

"I don't understand. Aren't you still an Ang?" Elizabeth said.

"I'm Krei. My mind was a gift from Master. With a Krei's brain inside my head I am worthy of being his assistant. Of being Krakk."

"Krakk? That's your name?" Elizabeth asked.

The creature nodded.

"If you were his assistant, why'd he keep you locked up?" Ana said.

"Master sometimes needed to work alone. In those circumstances, there was no need for my presence. I think he feared I would escape after his death."

"You helped him experiment on people?" Ana said.

"Yes. And I shall assist you, should you deem me worthy."

"And if we don't?"

There was a sharp edge to Ana's words.

"Then my purpose will have expired."

"Uhkira's work will not be continuing, Krakk. But we may have another purpose for you."

"We do?" Ana asked, giving Elizabeth a sideways glance.

"He can help Querius. What Uhkira made him do is not his fault."

"I only have one purpose. A single reason for my creation. To assist in Master's work."

"Uhkira gave you life. Regardless of his intentions for you, life is a choice. Now you have to choose. Die with Uhkira's legacy, or help use serve a greater purpose," Elizabeth said.

"What purpose do you aspire to?" Krakk asked.

"Discovery," Ana said, "It's what real scientists do."

Krakk considered this for a moment, then collapsed down on one knee. He bowed his head.

"I will serve," he said.

His three eyes rolled upwards, the glittering expressiveness offering submission.

"No, you won't," Elizabeth said.

Ana pulled Elizabeth aside whispering, "Do we need his help?"

Elizabeth looked at the Ang. Thick horns and dark eyes. His scars. She was doubtful, but did not say anything.

She grabbed the electric collar at the back of his neck and tried to snap it apart. A fierce bolt surged through her arms, sending them into a painful spasm, shooting away from Krakk.

"The collar cannot be removed, Master."

"My name is Elizabeth," she told him.

Ana pushed Krakk's face up with her muzzle, turning his neck so she could get a better look at his collar. A small locking mechanism with three roll slots. He did not resist as Ana maneuvered his head.

"There's a lock on the side of the collar," she said to Elizabeth.
"626?"
"Probably."
Elizabeth remembered the bloodstains. She thumbed the code into place. The muted zaps from the collar died out and the collar peeled away.

Krakk's skin was pale beneath, wrinkled like expired fruit. Green mildew sat inside the grooves of Krakk's neck.
"How does it feel to be free?" Elizabeth asked him.
"Unusual," he said, rubbing at his throat.
"We have some samples on our ship, and we can't figure out the species. Not even the strain of the species. Think you'll be able to?"
"Master has taught me well."
"Good. But before we can do that, we need to radio our ship to come get us. You know where there's a com device?" Elizabeth asked.
"No."
"Uhkira doesn't have *anything* like that?"
Krakk looked into the darkness and scratched his scars.
"There may be something in his office."
"There was no com device in there," Elizabeth said.
"His office?"
Krakk looked doubtful.
"Yeah."
"A small room with a bookcases and single wooden desk?"
"Sounds about right."
"That's not his office. I can show you to its door," Krakk said.
"Good enough. Lead the way."

Krakk hesitated, uncomfortable with the idea of leading. There was a dull toll as he stomped on the steps of the ladder. He pulled himself out of the trapdoor and turned back for Elizabeth. For a single cold moment, she thought he was about to swing the door closed on them. He could topple the shelves over and lock them inside forever. Instead, he reached down the shaft and hauled Elizabeth out. He tried to do the same to Ana but she recoiled away, wriggling out of the tube on her stomach.
"The office is this way," Krakk said.
Every third step, he allowed the two of them to catch him before continuing through the maze. He stopped directly in front of a wall and looked back over his shoulder for guidance.
"What now?" Elizabeth said.
Krakk pressed a finger to the wall. It sunk into the concrete and a piece of the wall slid away, opening up into another room.
"Did Uhkira know you could do that?"
"Master did not show me how to access his office, though I did watch him do it. Master believed I could not learn, that I was only capable of the thoughts he had engraveded in me. He was mistaken."

"So you could be something else? Something more than Uhkira made you for?" Elizabeth said.
"And yet he chose to help Uhkira massacre and torture people," Ana said.
"What choice did he have? He only had one teacher, only saw one side of the story. Uhkira ripped out his brain and shoved a new one in to see what would happen. He's a test subject, just like everyone else."

TV monitors were arranged in a semi-circle on the back wall.
"What are they for?" Elizabeth asked.
"It's best I leave them off," Krakk said. Behind her, Ana shivered.
Elizabeth's eyes surveyed the array of buttons, drinking them in. She remembered back to when she first woke up, dumbly watching Ana fly them to safety with no idea what the switches inside the ship did. Ana had taken charge in the crisis. Their differences were vast but cosmetic. Their similarities ran deeper.

"I found the radio," Ana said.
Elizabeth took it and turned the dial to find the Victory Pearl's frequency. The radio was an old design, coiled wire spiraling out from the speaker box. Elizabeth laced her fingers through it as she spoke hopefully.
"This is Elizabeth Ranger for the Victory Pearl, do you read me? Repeat, Elizabeth Ranger for the Victory Pearl, do you read me?"
Spitting static was the only reply.
"Try this," Ana said, cupping her hand softly around Elizabeth's to rotate the dial to a different frequency, "As long as Donovan hasn't changed it, that should work."
"This is Elizabeth Ranger for the Victory Pearl, do you read me? Repeat, Eliz –"
"Elizabeth? Boy howdy!" Donovan hollered from the other end of the radio.
Elizabeth hugged Ana and let out a thick, relieved exhale.
"Send a fucking shuttle to pick us up this minute!" she laughed.
"Yes ma'am, Captain," he said, "Ana's there with you too?"
Elizabeth held the radio up to Ana's mouth.
"I'm right here Donovan," she said.
"Glad to hear it. Should I send the shuttle to pick you up where we dropped you off?"
"We're inside Uhkira's base of operations and the defenses are disabled," Elizabeth said. She leant over to the turret terminal and flicked all the switches to 'off'.
"The front door it is. Is Uhkira with you?"
"He's dead, but we've got his Ang assistant, Krakk."
Krakk looked over vacantly at the mention of his name then turned back to the blank monitors.
"Oh. Um... Okay Captain. Stand by for evac."

Ana

The wind was harsh on the roof of Uhkira's base. The shuttle landed in front of them, hot blasts from the engine warming Ana up. Roka got out, carrying heavy metal shackles in his arms.
"What are doing with those?" Elizabeth said.
"You told Donovan you had Uhkira's Ang."
"He's not our prisoner."
Elizabeth looked at Ana for support, but she kept quiet.
"It's fine," Krakk said. He stepped forward and held his arms out in surrender.
The handcuffs locked with an echo. Krakk's chained hands drooped down.
"It's for the best," Ana said to Elizabeth.
"We're supposed to be giving him a second chance."
"We are, Elizabeth. We could have left him there."

Ana and Elizabeth climbed aboard the shuttle and sat down. Krakk stood in the middle, head bowed.
"You alright?" Elizabeth asked him.
He glanced over at her, "What's the smallest room on this shuttle?"
"I guess that would be the bathroom."
"I don't like large rooms."
Krakk made his way to the bathroom.

Ana looked around. Her eyes caught Elizabeth's and she turned away. Her skin felt raw and itchy. *We escape*, Elizabeth had said. *Life is short, especially for Humans*, Rusalka had said. She thought about Sam and felt sick.
"Listen, about us..." Elizabeth said.
"If you want to forget it ever happened, I understand."
Ana kept her eyes on the floor as she spoke.
Elizabeth touched her shoulder.
"Is that what you want? You wanna be my dirty little secret?"
A mischievous grin on her face. That ragged red hair. Sam was gone. Elizabeth was here.
"If that's what you want," she said.
"Right now I think people will be more concerned with the fact that we're still breathing, so let's leave it at that for now."
Ana nodded. No words came out.

For the rest of the flight they sat side by side, staring out into the starry darkness. Ana couldn't bring herself to look at Elizabeth. She did not listen to the twitching emptiness of her hands, her body begging to be held.

"We're here," Roka shouted through to them.

Everyone was gathered in the hangar. Clearly Brack and Isoline had returned and announced their death. Now everyone was eager to hear their tale of survival. As they stepped out, Brack rushed to Elizabeth, pushing Ana aside.

"I thought you were dead," Brack said.

"We could hear you through the bracelet. You just couldn't hear us," Ana told him.

"I think we'd all be interested to know just how you managed to survive," Isoline said.

She stepped towards Brack as she spoke, slithering her arm around his neck like an expensive scarf.

"They said there was a huge explosion!" Lavell said.

"There was. Ana got me to safety inside a cave before the grenade went off," Elizabeth said.

Ana smiled and felt herself blush with pride.

"How did you two survive?" Ana asked Brack.

"I created an energy barrier," Isoline answered for him.

A what?

Ana decided not to ask.

"What happened with Uhkira?" Brack asked.

"Dead," Ana said.

A voice came from inside the shuttle, "You guys brought back a pet?"

Rusalka stuck her head out from the shuttle doors. Elizabeth turned to her, single eyebrow raised.

"Hey, if you didn't want be to look you shouldn't have left it unlocked. Which reminds me, Lavell? That second drawer on your bedside table?"

Lavell reached for the rifle at her back.

"Has never been opened," Rusalka continued with a grin.

"He's not a pet. He was Uhkira's assistant and he's going to help us," Elizabeth said.

Krakk shuffled out of the shuttle.

"An Ang? A rather dangerous and foolish choice," Isoline said.

"He has a Krei brain. Uhkira experimented on him, but he's the best chance we've got of solving Querius' mystery."

"Ah yes," Querius squirmed his way to the front of the group, "If you'd come with me, Mr...?"

"Krakk. Are you my new master?"

"You don't have a master here," Elizabeth said, "And until they figure something out I guess we just sit tight."

The group started to leave.

"One more thing," Elizabeth said.

She pulled Ana close and kissed her.

"Now you all know."

Ana's skin was hot and red. Every eyeball in the room crawled over her.

"Come on," Elizabeth said.

She grabbed her hand and dragged her through the crowd.

"Where are we going?"
"I need a drink."
They were out of the hangar now and in the elevator.
"But where are we going?"
"My room."
"Oh."

~*~

Elizabeth threw her jacket down on the bed. She took a long necked bottle out from the fridge.
"What's that?" Ana asked.
Elizabeth rooted in the cupboard and brought up two glasses.
"It's Sudince wine. Mogg picked some up for me."
She poured the liquid out. Thick and rich red.
"I don't drink," Ana reminded her.
"That's what you said last time."

~*~

Blood coursed through her veins. It flowed like lighting atoms. Elizabeth's rough fingernails scratched. She kissed hard with tender lips. Their pupils dancing a drunken waltz. Elizabeth bit and Ana electrified. The bed was soft beneath them. Elizabeth was on top. She pressed Ana's wrists down onto the sheets. Ana's fingertips groped the air, muscles tight. Elizabeth's mouth was warm. Ana closed her eyes to feel it more.

Elizabeth

A glass of wine rested on the table, red liquid shimmering in the early morning light. Elizabeth sat up. Ana's blonde hair spread like sunrise across the pillow next to her. Elizabeth looked at the glass. Then at Ana, then back at the glass. Silently, she slid out of bed. Ana did not stir. A bottle of wine sat empty on the table too. One? Was that all they had? She took a sip from the glass, recoiling from the taste and the warmth. She walked over the bathroom. Her toe caught a second wine bottle and sent it clattering against the doorframe. Loud enough to wake Ana. She rose with a long purr, stretching her back out.

Elizabeth offered the glass out to her.
"Hair of the dog?"
Ana squirmed away, hand out.
"How much did we have last night?"
"That's the second bottle I've found," Elizabeth said.
"That wasn't why we...?" Ana's voice trailed off.
Elizabeth thought for a moment.
"No."
Ana nodded.
"Good. I liked it."
Elizabeth cupped her face and pulled her close. They kissed, lips meeting sweetly.
"I understand though, if you want time. After Sam," Elizabeth said.
"I don't –"
"You talked about her a lot last night."
"Did I?" Ana's voice creaked.
"Yeah."
"She meant a lot to me."
"I understand," Elizabeth said.
"I want this, Elizabeth. I do. I just... I might not..."
Ana fumbled for words.
"We'll do it slow," Elizabeth said.
She leaned in and kissed Ana again.

Ana

They stayed in bed for the next couple of days. Ana slept cradled in Elizabeth's arms. She dreamt of Sam but did not feel guilty when Elizabeth touched her. It felt right, and good. Elizabeth could help patch her up.

She was lying on Elizabeth's arm. The jagged red hair fell across her face and tickled her nose.
"Right, sit over there," Ana said, getting up.
"I'm your Captain," Elizabeth said with a smirk, "You can't order me around."
"I'm your doctor. These are doctor's orders."
"Got me there."
Elizabeth rolled out of bed and sat in the chair Ana offered.
"I'm surprised you haven't asked how I healed you yet."
"Go ahead," Elizabeth said.
"Basically, with the new innovations in stem cell research, I was able use your intact skin to synthesize and regrow –"
"Magic. Gotcha."
"You don't want to hear it?"
"I know I asked, but I don't think I'd understand, Princess."
"Princess?" Ana repeated.
"You don't like it?"

Ana let the word take hold of her. It made her feel… special. Sam had never really made her feel that way. They were there, they were together. But she couldn't remember Sam ever making her feel wanted. The casual way Elizabeth threw the nickname out. *Princess*. It meant *I'll protect you*. It meant *I'll put you first*.

"I like it," Ana said.
"I've got good taste. But then I guess you knew that. Hey what're you doing with those?"
Ana took a pair of scissors from the bathroom.
"Giving you a haircut."
Ana snipped at the air.
"What, I'm not pretty enough for you?"
"You could be prettier," Ana smiled.
Elizabeth relaxed and leaned back in the chair.
"Did I ever tell about the time I stole a little girl's blanket?"

Elizabeth

Krakk and Querius made no progress in two weeks. Time crawls when you're waiting. She started to feel stale. She needed to move.

Each morning she eased Ana's head off her chest and trained in the gym. Forr joined her, getting accustomed to his new hand. They mostly sparred. Elizabeth was three years out of practice and Forr was working with new tools. She had enough purple welts to know it packed a heavier punch than his old fist, even if it slowed him down a little.

She was woozily getting back to her feet when Donovan called her bracelet. Forr was cursing himself for resorting to the sucker punch, too slow to deflect Elizabeth's jab to the chin.
"Received a transmission for you, Cap."
"Heading up now."
Forr pulled Elizabeth back to her feet. His grip was tight without hurting. He was getting better. The first time he had almost pulverized her bones.

Donovan spun around in his chair as Elizabeth entered the cockpit.
"Let's hear it," she said.
Donovan spun back around and started the message.
"Greetings, Ranger Elizabeth I have the information you seek."
The transmission cut out.
"That's it?" Elizabeth said.
"We also received location co-ordinates but yeah, that's it."
This nasal hiss, the grammatic clumsiness with Human names. It was a Shrook.
"Alright. Give Roka the co-ordinates."
"West said all missions had to go through him."
"West isn't stuck here going stir crazy. If this guy's got information we can't afford to pass it up," Elizabeth said.
Donovan sighed, "Who'm I calling?"
"Rusalka, if you can find her. I'm damn sure I won't be able to."
"Only two of you? Could be a trap," Donovan said.
"I know. I can smell it a mile away, but that doesn't mean the bait isn't real. I'm taking Forr and Lavell too, but I'll tell them myself."
"No flies on you, Captain. Surprised you're not taking Ana though."
"Excuse me?"
"I don't mean to be presumptuous, Cap. You've just hardly left her side recently."
"She's a doctor. Not supposed to be going out in the field unless we need her."
"Fair enough. I'll send Roka the codes down and tell him to get off his ass."
He kicked the console to swivel the chair.

Rusalka

"Okay, so both hands. Right hand on the handle, left finger keeps it steady."
"Like this?" Ana asked.
Rusalka batted the gun away.
"*Never* point a gun at someone, sweetie!"
"Sorry!"
Ana held her hands up and let the gun drop to the floor.
"And don't drop them either. It's dangerous and you could break them."
Rusalka plucked the derringer up.
"Guns can break?"
"They're not diamonds."

Their new Ang crewmate had helped Rusalka set up a firing range. A thick tank full of ballistic gel was tipped and set against the back wall. The goo gathered at the base, slowly sliding out. A foot and a half deep, it was more than enough to absorb the impact of Ana's derringer pistol.
"Like this," Rusalka said.
She stood behind Ana and guided her hands into place. Ana's fingers turned limp as Rusalka positioned them around the trigger.
"Elizabeth ever do this with you?" Rusalka asked.
"She never taught me how to shoot."
"That's not what I meant," Rusalka chuckled.

A bang and a kickback. Ana's elbows dug into Rusalka's side.
"Little warning next time," she said.
"Sorry."
"Did you at least hit what you were aiming for?"
"... I wasn't really aiming."
"Well, that's the point of practicing shooting, sweetie," Rusalka said, "Try this."
Rusalka took a coin out of her bag. She pressed it against the ballistic gel and packed it flat.
"Aim for that,"
Rusalka stepped back. Ana nodded. She shuffled her feet out and then in. She rolled her shoulders and raised the pistol.
"When you're ready, sweetie."
A bullet burst into the gel, a few inches above the coin.
"Damn."
"Just a little lower!"
Ana fired again. Rusalka's ears twinkled and the bullet hit the metal coin, pushing it back into the blue.
"I did it!"

Rusalka plunged her arm into the gel and retrieved the coin. Her bracelet gurgled inside. She pulled it out and held it to her ear.

"...zabeth wants you for a mission. Just been sent a set of co-ordinates."

"Just me?"

"She's taking Lavell and Forr too. Head down to the armoury and –"

"Not Ana?"

Rusalka looked at Ana. She was blushing, lip bitten awkwardly.

"She said Ana's our doctor. Not to be taken into the field unless strictly necessary"

Rusalka clicked her bracelet off.

"Guess I've been retired," Ana said.

"I'd keep practicing," Rusalka told her, "Just in case. And you should carry that with you at all times from now on."

"Why?"

"Because every other person around here does. And you're more than just our doctor."

Forr

Lavell cupped an apple in her palm while Forr cut segments away from it, keeping the knife steady in his repaired hand. He sliced a piece off cleanly and raised the impaled fruit to his mouth.
"There. I knew you could do it," Lavell said.
They looked up as Elizabeth walked over.
"Head down to the armory. I need you for a mission. Both of you."
Forr looked at the knife in his hand.
"I'm not ready."
"I wouldn't be taking you if I believed that. I've got a feeling this is a set up, so hand to hand might come into play. Lavell, you go in covert with Rusalka. I don't want anybody knowing you're there."
Elizabeth walked away, then looked back.
"And keep an eye on her. I'm not sure about her angle."

Forr threw the apple at a garbage can.
"Just like the old days," Lavell said.
"Except I've only got one hand," Forr said.
Lavell reached up and stroked his cheek.
"I've never known Elizabeth stand for a charity case. Have you?"

Rusalka was already at the armoury when they arrived. She sat on a weapon bench with her legs swinging casually in sweeping circles. She had a pistol strapped to each thigh and knives at her back.
"So what do you guys think about Elizabeth and Ana?" she said.
"What do you mean?" Forr said.
There didn't seem much to think about.
"I think she's on the rebound from Brack," Lavell said.
"You never said to me," Forr said.
"You wouldn't be interested."
"I won't get dragged into this," Forr said, "But Elizabeth and Brack ended three years ago."
"Not to her! To her they just broke up! To her they *never* even broke up!" Lavell said.
"Exactly. And now she's got a mission that she admits could be a trap, but doesn't want either of them watching her back?"

Rusalka took out her knife and examined her reflection in the blade.

"It's none of our business," Forr said.

Lavell bowed her head in a sulk, "We're just talking."

"How would you like it if people 'just talked' about us?" he asked.

He pulled her into a warm hug.

"You guys are a cute couple," Rusalka said, jumping down silently from the table.

"Most people have a stigma about Krei/Jahlder relationships," Lavell said.

"A lot of those people are Krei. Or Jahlder," Forr said.

"So... what's his thing look like?" Rusalka asked, glancing at Lavell from the corner of her eyes.

"I'm standing right here," Forr said.

"You offering to show me?"

Lavell started to giggle.

"Come on, Lavell. Give me some girl talk."

"Sorry. I don't kiss and tell," she said with a smile.

"Does that mean you kiss it?"

Lavell playfully pushed Rusalka away. Forr continued to fasten his battle gear. His metallic hand struggled with the latches of the armour.

~*~

Elizabeth was leaning against the shuttle, talking to Roka as they approached.

"Keep the engine running while we're in there," she told him.

"What exactly is this mission for? Donny boy wasn't exactly forthcoming with details," Rusalka said.

"That's because we don't have any. We received a transmission from a Shrook who said he has information. I don't trust him but I'm sick of sitting around waiting for answers to hit us in the face."

"Agreed. There are lots of pretty things out there, just waiting for me to steal them," Rusalka said.

"Roka's traced the co-ordinates to a space station. Me and Forr will go in and meet the Shrook, you two are gonna infiltrate the station undetected. If nothing goes wrong, don't reveal yourself."

"Oh Ranger. Where's the fun in that?" Rusalka asked, sliding by.

Rusalka and Lavell continued their hushed discussion while the engines purred into life.

They glanced up occasionally and giggled before returning to their whispers.

"What's gotten into them?" Elizabeth said.

"Don't ask," Forr said.

He stood and moved over to the window. He pressed his head against the cool glass. Elizabeth came and stood by his side.

"Something on your mind?"

He raised his hand, clenching. Unclenching. He fiddled with the transmitters on his forehead.

"Lavell did a good job," Elizabeth said.

Behind them, Lavell chuckled brightly.

"What if I can't protect her anymore?"

"How many times did you knock me on my ass while we were training?"

"You let me win."

"That sound like me?"

He stared out into the darkness of the stars.

"What about you?" he said.

"What about me?"

"You and Brack."

"There is no me and Brack," she said, staring out at the jade rocks floating through space.

"But there was," he said.

He turned to face her. Elizabeth's eyes stayed forward.

"Years ago."

"Not to you. I just want to know you're okay."

"Why are you asking me this?"

"It's like a bee in a jar," he said, "This dangerous thing inside you. And you need to crack the lid a little, give it air. But if someone else opens it for you, the bee'll just fly out. Everyone might get stung."

Elizabeth smiled and swung a right hook at Forr's shoulder.

"That's for going soft on me."

Elizabeth

The space station was a long silver tube, dark and narrow, exposed wires sealed to the wall. They travelled a ways down the inner workings until they reached a small dock.
"Remember, you two stay out of sight," Elizabeth said told Rusalka and Lavell.

The Shrook was waiting for them. He stood invasively close. Elizabeth and Forr stepped out and he had to lean back. Elizabeth walked further into the dock, leading him away so he would not see Rusalka or Lavell still inside. He was well dressed for a Shrook, wearing a scarlet gown with golden thread. He smiled, baring his honey toned teeth, thin and sharp as needles. Shorter, meaner Shrook flanked him at either side holding long, melodramatic axes crossed above his head.
"Ranger Elizabeth," he said, smile growing, "You brought a friend."
"Forr Hort."
"Oh, I know who you are. I'm a big fan of your broadcast. My, my. Your hand?"
He gawped at Forr with ghoulish curiosity.
"You said you had information?" Elizabeth pressed.
"In my office. And I consider myself a civilized gentleman, against the Shrook notion that names are decadent. You may call me Warden. Now, this way please."
Warden opened his palm to show them down a hallway. His gown draped across the floor. His footsteps floated.

The passageway had large paintings in ornate frames. Warden seemed to slow in front of certain canvases to allow Elizabeth to soak up the masterpieces in his collection. She had no appreciation for the talent. Still a treasure hunter at heart, what impressed her was rarity. There were three paintings Elizabeth herself had once searched for. She felt a tickle of respect that Warden had been able to get his hands on them. But he rushed past them. He had no idea of their value.

Warden stopped in front of a door. His sentinels stood either side. He eased the door open with his fingertips, then let it close.
"I'm afraid I don't allow firearms into my office. You may surrender your weapons here."
"My gun's like a part of my arm," Elizabeth said.
"Arms can be amputated," Warden said.
He glanced unkindly at Forr's bionic hand.
Elizabeth nodded and they both handed their weapons over.
"Now we can discuss the matter like civilized people," Warden said.

She entered and sat on a chair at the nearside of an antique desk. The back of the chair was stiff and uncomfortable. The sort of discomfort the owner would only put up with having paid an extortionate amount for the chair in the first place.
"They made these chairs on Dessar, in honour of Queen Follsie's coronation. Only ten of them were ever sent off planet, and I own four of them," Warden said,

settling down into his own uncomfortable seat.

"I can see why they stopped the line," Elizabeth said dryly.

"I must say, you've made quite a name for yourself, Ranger Elizabeth," Warden said, ignoring her comment, "The greatest treasure hunter in the galaxy."

The sleeves of the robe rode up at his elbow, revealing scrawny arms.

"I can't be that good. You never hired me."

"Your reputation contained a certain morality that didn't comply with my goals. This desk, for example?"

Elizabeth studied the carved figures for the first time. The females of different races: Human, Krei, Jahlder, Leho, Torfus, Umbra and Shrook. All kneeling with flayed backs, kissing the feet of a fat Ang that sat on a throne. The women wore collars, their leashes wrapped around the Ang's colossal fist.

"That's the sort of thing Ranger Elizabeth might object to, no?"

"Do you think this is art?" Forr asked.

"I think it's valuable."

"It's vulgar."

"I must say," Warden said, turning back to Elizabeth, "I didn't realize you'd be bringing a companion."

"Not a problem, I hope?"

"Oh, quite the opposite. I'm honoured by the presence of a broadcast star," he said, flashing a strange grin, "Though I can't say I care for that Jahlder bitch you work with."

Forr's metal fist slammed into the table.

"Don't call her that!"

His fist left a dent. Warden smirked.

"Can we cut to the chase, Warden?"

"Are you aware what the most valuable object is in this room?" Warden asked, leaning forward.

She knew how to unlock the simple riddles Warden spoke in.

"Let me guess. Your information?"

Warden smiled and leaned back, flashing the needles in his mouth.

"No, Ranger Elizabeth. The answer is you."

"Come again?"

"You have made no small amount of enemies. Men who would do things to you that would make you beg for rape."

Elizabeth felt a chill like a razor down her spine. Her face remained still.

"If I begged then it wouldn't be rape, would it?" Elizabeth asked.

Warden's face soured.

"That tongue won't be so quick once it's cut out of you. Shame. I would've liked one as beautiful as you in my collection. But alas, a buyer has already been procured."

It had all been a trap. And a damn simple one too. Elizabeth sprang across the desk and seized Warden's throat.

"Guards!" he shrieked.

Elizabeth's fingers tightened around his windpipe. The door behind them swung open, crashing against the wall. Elizabeth turned to see Warden's sentries brandishing their long axes. She had counted on Lavell and Rusalka eliminating them by now. Where were they?

A knife lunged through one of the guard's throats. A fine mist of dark blood showered the office. The other guard looked at his comrade in terror. Spit sprayed from his scream. Lavell placed her palms either side of his head and twisted, snapping his neck with ease. The Shrook thudded as he hit the floor. Rusalka still had her victim perched upright, impaled by the blade. She kicked his back, scraping him off her knife.
"You left that a little late," Elizabeth said.
"You told us not to reveal ourselves unless we had to," Lavell said, wiping the sprayed blood off her hands.

Elizabeth threw Warden back in his chair. There was a creak as it broke under the strain.
"Looks like your deal's off," she said.
"Deal?" Rusalka asked.
"There was no information. Our friend here had put me up for sale. Tell me who the buyer was and I'll spare your life."
"Do you play cards, Ranger Elizabeth?"
Warden shifted forward.
"We're not playing your game anymore."
"I'm dreadful at cards. You were my all in. And it appears I've been called."
"Just give us a name," Lavell said.
"I don't talk to vermin, you Jahlder whore."
Forr ripped Rusalka's pistol from her hip. He fired at Warden's head until the clip was empty.
"Her name is Lavell," he told the wet pulp of skull that slid down the leather.

Rusalka

The Shrook's body sagged limp, face smeared across the chair. A mess of bone and meat. Rusalka took the gun from Forr's hand. His metal fingers continued to squeeze to air.
"Don't touch my things."

An alarm started. A low and constant drone. Rusalka pushed the chair aside and the body flopped onto the floor. The blood reeked of wet earth. She leant under his desk and saw a red button.
"He set off an alarm. We need to get out of here," she said.
Elizabeth and Forr retrieved their guns from the dead guards on the way out.

"Are you alright?" Lavell asked Forr.
"He shouldn't have called you that."
"I didn't hear it," she said, tapping her translation implant.
"I did."
"Come on. Let's get back to the ship."

A company of guards greeted them wielding shotguns that looked like miniature cannons.
"Now you know why we took so long," Rusalka said.
They were quicker than the guards, sending a barrage of bullets through them before the shotguns fired. Over the bodies, they sprinted down the tunnel back to the shuttle.
"Open up!" Ranger shouted.
The shuttle door rose with obedience and the four of them dove in. The shuttle roared into life and the whole station quaked.

An orange inferno chased them, biting at the shuttle's tail.
"What set that off?" Lavell asked.
"That button wasn't an alarm, it was a self-destruct. His men were collateral," Rusalka said.
Elizabeth looked back at the explosion.
"All his treasure's been destroyed."
Rusalka wiped her knife clean, pressing the flat of the blade to her fur.
"Better they be destroyed than belong to someone else."
Roka surged out of the station and the fire quelled.

~*~

"We're gonna be stuck on that ship until Querius and Krakk figure something out," Elizabeth said.
"We don't have to be," Rusalka said.

"What do you mean?"

"Think about it. We're all treasure hunters. We've got a shuttle that will carry us far enough to acquire a better vehicle."

"You mean until we can steal another ship?" Forr asked in a disapproving brogue.

"There's none of us could claim to be kayeedar."

"My translator just bugged out," Elizabeth said.

"Mine too."

"And mine."

"We've all broken the law for our own gains," Rusalka explained.

"Write it down and I'll add it to the lexicon. Translators don't handle Umbra linguistics as well as other species' languages," Lavell said.

"We could convince the pilot to abscond with us," Rusalka said.

"How would we do that?" Elizabeth asked.

"There's only three ways to convince anyone to do anything. Money, sex, and knives through the neck."

"Which one are you suggesting?"

"I'm not fucking him."

"We're not killing Roka," Elizabeth told her.

"Fine. Offer him some of the score," Rusalka said, sheathing her curved weapon.

"We're going back to the Victory Pearl, and we're gonna wait. I hate it just as much as you do, Rusalka. But you joined us because you didn't want miss what we might find."

"This discovery that we're apparently on the brink of? It had better be monumental."

Roka came over the speakers with a crackle, "Incoming com link from Querius. Patching him through."

"Incredible, Miss Ranger. Quite incredible. This species... unseen... unheard of... remarkable!"

"You're breaking up, Querius."

"The link is fine, Captain," Krakk said, "Doctor is just excited. Our findings are unprecedented. I have compiled a report for you to peruse on your return."

The com cut out and Elizabeth looked at Rusalka with a sly grin.

"You got lucky," Rusalka said.

~*~

Querius descended on them as they left the shuttle. He was like a cawing bird, fluttering, skittering, making no sense. Krakk stood by patiently, listening to Querius fly from one subject to another. Rusalka wondered if Uhkira ever acted this way, like a giddy child when slicing open some creature's brain revealed something new about existence. She doubted it.

Krakk. Ang... Krei... the man was fascinating. She she should probably be listening.

"...which is precisely why it's so fascinating! Don't you comprehend what this means?" Querius said, eventually pausing for breath.

Rusalka turned to Krakk and he smiled. The first she had seen cross his lips.

"The DNA strand pre-dates any known species. Whoever this belongs to, they could be the oldest species in existence," Krakk said.

"Why does that matter to us?" Elizabeth asked.

"Why? Why, infinite.... Discovery... Answers..."

"Doctor is thinking of the advancement of science, but this matters not to Captain. However, something so old would be very rare. This species appears to predate even the Jahlder."

"And the Umbra?" Rusalka asked.

Krakk turned to her.

"No one knows how old the Umbra are."

Rusalka just smiled.

"Any idea where they could be?" Elizabeth said.

"I have a dossier which compiles the most likely of locations, if Captain would like to read it."

"I trust you. What's top of your list?"

"We think Purple 24, based on the spores we also found your artefact that had no link to neither Green 3 nor the rapui."

"Back to The Barley Charted?" Elizabeth said.

"That's our best guess."

"I'll tell Donovan to set a course."

Lavell

She and Forr left the hangar while the rest of them discussed the discovery. Her photographic memory replaced the static in her head. Forr grabbing Rusalka's gun. Her lion.

The elevator stopped and Forr turned for the armoury. Lavell took him by the hand and gently pulled him towards their cabin.
"I need to change out of my armour," he said.
"No, you don't."
"It's covered in blood."
"I know," Lavell said, her palm softly cradling his new hand.

They entered the bedroom. Lavell kicked the door closed with her heel then crawled onto the bed. Forr just stood there. He was not used to seeing her act this way, and he had forgotten what to do with it.
"Make love to me like I'm Krei," she said.
"I don't think –"
"I want to."
The Jahlder told ghost stories about Krei love making back on Herso.

She stripped off her armour and knelt on the bed with her back to Forr.
"Why..." he started.
"Because I love you. All of you, and I know you love all of me."
Lavell looked back over her shoulder.
"I don't want this from you," he said.
She took his hand and guided it over her scars.
"You're Krei. This is how you did it before you met me."
"My life didn't start until I met you."
Lavell's shoulder blades rolled as her back arched arched.
"My brave lion. I want you to love me like I'm Krei."
She leaned back and kissed him powerfully, inviting his flat tongue into her mouth.

His metal hand cupped her bare thigh, hoisting her close against him. She peeled herself away. She wanted him to. The Krei found combat and competition everywhere. Lavell was supposed to wrestle with Forr for dominance. But as she took him in deeper she had no interest in dominating. She wanted her lion to take her. He wrapped his arm around her neck but did not tense. Her throat was resting in the crook of his elbow. She leaned forward with obedience as he pressed his weight down and slid inside.

Soon the hurt dissolved into a pleasurable friction. She had never felt Forr move this fast before.

It left her breathless. When it was done, all she could do was lie next to him, weak and limp.
"Nisno alme quor hoo meaher," she said.
"Was that old Jahlder?" he asked.
"The kind they don't install on translators."
"What does it mean?"
"Literally it translates to; 'There is no distance which can be measured empirically which would affect my love for you.'"
"I can see why the expression died out," he said.
"The more romantic Jahlder prefer 'I will love you forever, across the stars.'"
"I didn't think there were any romantic Jahlder," Forr said.
Lavell sat up.
"There's me."
"Talanacti."
"My lion," she said, leaning in to kiss him.
He moved away, fiddling with his transmitters.
"Something wrong?" she asked.
"When I shot that Shrook... it jammed. I didn't mean to fire that many rounds."
Lavell unclipped his nodes and removed his metal hand. It didn't jam. It was fueled by thought and emotion. He fired that many because he wanted to protect her.

She kissed his forehead and tried to fall asleep. The Krei way had hurt.

~*~

The ship rocked with a violent tremor and her face fell hard against his.
"What was that?"
Forr jumped out of bed. He ran to the window, Lavell behind him. Red razor prongs poked from a pointed oval. The ship was a teardrop with guns.
"She found me," he said bitterly.
"Who?" Lavell asked, but he was already running towards the flight deck.

Forr

Donovan's hands moved across the control panel with purpose as Forr entered.
"Kinda busy right now!"
"Open a com link with the hostile ship. It'll stop shooting."
"How do you know?"
"Just do it!" Forr shouted.
But Donovan already was. He was a man who thought actions first and questions later was dumb, but no dumber than questions first and actions later.

"You're patched," he said.
Forr picked up the com mic just as Elizabeth entered the room. Her first move was for the ladders up to the cannons.
"Serpe, stop!" Forr shouted.
"Finally found you. Sorry I was a little later than my crew on Rassek."
He could hear her smirking. Elizabeth let go of the ladder and turned to him.
"What do you want?" Forr said.
"You need to come home."
"I have no home. I was exiled."
"The exile has been revoked. Welcome back to the fold."
"The Krei removed an exile?" Donovan said, "How important are you Forr?"
Forr covered the mic with his huge palm, "That depends how Krei have died since I left."
"What's that mean?"
"Forr is a Krei king," Elizabeth said.
"No, I'm not," Forr said. He uncovered the mic, "I'm not going back."
"Don't be stupid, Forr. Three Krei fleets are primed on your vessel as we speak."
"Is that a bluff?" Donovan asked, looking at the blank scanners.
"Your captain speaks too loudly," Serpe said.
"Not the captain, ma'am. Just the pilot."
"I'm the captain," Elizabeth said.
Serpe let out a cough of dry laughter, "The red haired human cunt. Your company does not befit your stature, Forr. Is your Jahlder whore there too?"
"Don't call her that."
His knuckles turned pale around the mic.
"If you came back to Excha, you could have your pick of Krei females. You could have *any* Krei female."

"Not interested, Serpe."

"Forr's too important to our mission to let him leave," Elizabeth said.

"I'd heard the Human liked to involve herself in matters in which she has no business."

"The answer's no," Forr said.

"Allow me to assist this mission, and when it is done you shall return with me to Excha. Refuse, and I blow your ship up, along with you, and the Human, and the whore."

Ships started to appear on the periphery of the radar.

"She's not bluffing," Donovan said.

"Don't call her that."

Serpe had already disconnected.

Forr thought about Lavell lying in bed, unaware of how close she had come to hateful annihilation.

"I guess I should go greet the new arrival," Elizabeth said.

"No. I'll go," Forr said.

"One thing Forr," Elizabeth said, grabbing his arm, "I don't care how many fleets she has. On this mission, she reports to me."

~*~

A ferocious itch climbed his stump, growing stronger as he descended into the hangar. Serpe's shuttle opened. The steps rolled out like a tongue from a dragon's mouth. Blue legs slinked down the steps. That azure skin had haunted Forr on Excha. Krei's born with indigo pigments were thought to be destined for greatness, but he was born grey. They must be truly desperate to seek him out.

She tossed her helmet aside.

"It's been a while."

The blonde fur across her back was thick and clean.

"You shouldn't have come," he said.

She touched his arm.

"What happened?" her voice flashed soft, "Is this your whore's work?"

"It was blown off when I was trying to save a child from your death squad. Lavell gave me my hand back."

"A Jahlder child?"

Serpe ripped the limb away from him and spat yellow phlegm. The electrodes shorted and stung as they were yanked away from his temples.

"You even smell like her. True Krei wear their wounds with pride, they don't hide behind ornaments!"

"I'm not true Krei. That's why they exiled me."

She stepped closer to him, putting a soothing pressure on his throbbing forehead.

"That's history now."

"I love Lavell," Forr said, picking up his appendage.

Serpe snatched at his throat and hoisted him against the wall.

"Don't you dare speak her name to me!"

"Why come here? Why hunt me down?"

"Hunt you down? You had a broadcast! A puppet Krei, dancing for the Jahlder whore."

"Why not kill me?"

She leaned in closer. Her breath was acrid.

"*They* want to. *I* want to save you."

"I saved myself a long time ago," Forr said.

Serpe loosened her grip.

"Our child would be a great warrior."

"*Our* child?"

She held her arm in front of him.

"You see this blue? My family deserve the Harkrak title. Return with me and give me my offspring. You owe me that."

"No."

Her hand was at his throat again.

"Refuse and I kill the whore."

The grip tightened. She could kill Lavell easily. She hated Jahlder. She would enjoy it. Forr's good hand still held his metal fist. He swung it at Serpe like a club. Her skin split open and she stepped away, letting him go.

"After I do this, you leave us alone. Both of us."

Blood wept from her cut. She smiled.

"Once I get you back to Excha, you'll never leave."

Forr reattached his bionic hand, twisting it back onto his stump. He flexed his fingers while Serpe turned away in disgust.

Ana

Ana sat up bed as Elizabeth returned.
"What was all that?"
"Another new arrival," Elizabeth said, sitting down on the bed's edge.
"Where are they going to sleep?"
"That's not really my concern right now, Ana."
Ana shuffled closer and rolled the pads of her thumbs around Elizabeth's shoulder blades, massaging.

"Sorry, Princess" Elizabeth purred, "It's just this new arrival is responsible for Rassek."
Ana's hands stopped abruptly, nails biting into the skin.
"The Jahlder colony?"
"She's here to get Forr. Let her come aboard or she'd blow up the ship. And I saw the fleet she had at her disposal. It was no empty threat."

Ana sank back into the pillow. Elizabeth handed her a t-shirt from the floor.
"Forr's making some kind of deal with her."
"Do you trust her?" Ana asked.
"Forr seemed to. Or at least he's smart enough to know that he's better off biding his time."
"Why does she need Forr?"
"I think a lot of his family are dead. Apparently he's got some important title now."
"I had a brother once. He died," Ana said.
The words just fell out of her.
"What happened?"
"Malaria. He was sickly even before I was born. It's one of the reasons I became a doctor. My parents didn't want me to."
"I've never heard you talk about your family before."
"That's because I don't like them."

Elizabeth lay down next to her.
"I never knew mine," Elizabeth said.
"West tried to find them, but the orphanage had no records. It burnt down."
"You knew I was an orphan this whole time? Why didn't you say anything?"
"It didn't seem important. I mean, not that it's *not* important, just – "
Elizabeth kissed her. Ana didn't really understand why.
"You know, I ran away when I was nine. I spent the first week just wandering around the street, hoping someone would find me and take me back. Then I realized they just weren't looking."
"I can't even imagine being homeless that young. You must have been terrified."
Ana wrapped a comforting arm around Elizabeth's shoulder.
"I never could've admitted it at the time. Every day was a fight for a loaf of bread."

"Every day? How did you survive?"

"After a while I got in good with some merchants. I'd do jobs for them, pickpocketing mostly, and they'd give me food. Once I got better, I could pickpocket enough to buy anything I couldn't just steal in the first place. If no one carried coin, I never would've made it past ten."

"And you left Earth as soon as you could?"

"Didn't you? There's so much to see, so much to do."

Ana sat up but didn't answer.

"I was 18 when I kissed my first alien," Elizabeth continued, "I'd met aliens on Earth, but I'd only ever been attracted to Human girls. This Jahlder though..."

Ana snickered, "He was Jahlder?"

"Shut up!"

Elizabeth pulled her back down onto the bed. Her hands swam up Ana's neck, tickling until she couldn't breathe for giggling.

"Borreah was his name," Elizabeth said, hands stopping, "These absorbsion panels stretched across his face like a handlebar moustache. He was the head of these really cheap mercenaries. I was just a dumb kid. The ship I stole crashed on Mars and these were the first guys I found. It would've been easier for them to kill me, but he took me under his wing. He was so rugged and exotic."

"A rugged Jahlder?"

Elizabeth tickled her again. She giggled and writhed beneath her fingertips.

"Are you gonna shut up and let me tell the story, Princess?"

"Okay! Okay!" Ana wheezed.

"I think he had a thing for naïve girls who worshipped him. I started to outgrow that, and he happened across another runaway. This one was Jahlder too. I found him in bed with her and I just lost it. It was so stupid, it wasn't like we were in love or anything."

"What did you do?"

"I pulled the girl out of bed. I think she cut her leg open, she was crying about it. It wasn't her fault, but I didn't care. Borreah actually liked it, the sick fuck. Started to kiss me, trying to take my clothes off. I kissed him back until he let his guard down, then I tied him to the bed and took off in his ship. Never looked back."

"I used to read comics about girls like you," Ana said.

"So what about you? Ever kissed an alien?" Elizabeth asked.

"I hadn't even seen an alien until around four years ago."

"None? How is that possible?"

Ana turned away.

"You already know. You must have figured it out."

Elizabeth lay a warm hand on her shoulder. Ana let out a tense sigh.

"I grew up on a Human Only colony."

"Seriously?"

"Don't judge me."
"I'm not judging, just... surprised. You hear stories about the people who live there," Elizabeth said.
"They're true. Rumours and lies about other species sprout up like weeds and blossom in the soil of ignorance. That's why I had to leave. My parents disowned me and I was cast out."
Elizabeth sat up, arm around Ana's shoulder.
"So... how many people have you kissed?" she asked.
Ana held up two fingers shyly, "Just you and Sam."
"I've got so much to teach you," she said.
"You just better hope some rugged Jahlder doesn't steal me away."

Elizabeth

Elizabeth spent the rest of the day in bed. Ana was a shy lover, meek but giving.

The next morning, she headed for the gym to meet Forr. While she waited, she hung a black waxed punching bag and circled it, dipping and ducking, peppering with jabs.

Two blue hands gripped the bag. Elizabeth took another punch. It didn't move. She looked around the bag and saw Serpe, her face tensed and joyless.
"Can I help you?" Elizabeth asked.
Serpe coiled her knuckles and swung at the bag. It ripped the hook from the ceiling, white plaster dust snowing down on them. Serpe shook it away smugly.
"Power isn't what's important in hand to hand combat. Speed is," Elizabeth said.
She swung a right hook that caught Serpe's cheek. A cheap shot, but it felt damn good.
"That's for calling me names," she said.

Serpe drove at Elizabeth with a rapid flurry. Elizabeth went on the defensive, forearms rising to block. She felt the cold wall press up against her back and landed two in quick jabs. Serpe was too fast for a third. Serpe grabbed her wrist and clenched so hard Elizabeth felt like her bones were about to burst.
"You Humans are odd creatures. Incapable of seeing defeat, even as it stares you in the face."
"We call that determination," Elizabeth said, trying to wrestle her arm free.
"I call it foolishness."
Elizabeth headbutted Serpe. The grip on her wrist fell loose. Three fast body shots and now Serpe was defending.
"The Krei fight valiantly when they know they'll win, but they're quick to retreat it the odds turn against them," Elizabeth said.
"We call that strategy."
Serpe blocked Elizabeth's punch with an elbow. The impact blasted them apart and into an unspoken truce.
"I call it cowardice."

Donovan came over the speakers, ending round two before it started.
"Captain? We have visual on Purple 24. Within shuttle range and awaiting your orders."
Keeping a cool stare on Serpe, Elizabeth raised her bracelet to her lips.
"Gather the team in the Mess Hall. I want to brief everybody before we head out."
"Yes, ma'am."
"Am I part of the team?" Serpe asked dryly.
"You volunteered to be, the way I remember. And whatever crap you have going on with Forr, once you step out of my shuttle on my mission, everything else gets put on hold."
Serpe grinned as if this amused her.

Elizabeth watched her leave. She waited in the gym a few minutes longer. She wanted the rest of them to assemble before her arrival. One of the oldest power plays in the book. Keep them waiting for the one in charge. She never would on the old Victory Pearl. But her crew was inflating. She needed to be on top.
"You got those diagrams Querius drew up?" Elizabeth asked.
"All uploaded. Ready for when you need them," Donovan replied.
She poured water out onto her warm skin. It dripped down her red hair and she shook it dry. Another moment passed. Elizabeth untied then retied her boots before heading up to the Mess Hall.

Forr and Lavell sat front and centre. Brack and Isoline were nearby in relaxed slouches, gazing at each other with dull smiles. Brack held a bushel of reju berries while Isoline nibbled them from his palm. She caught Elizabeth staring and flashed a smirk as she continued to bite. Ana loitered by the doorway. Elizabeth nodded for her to take a seat.

Serpe was the only one who had arrived armed, a long barreled rifle across her back. She stood in the centre of the room with an eerie stillness.

Elizabeth climbed on to a table to get everyone's attention. She cleared her throat to speak, but Rusalka stole into the room, late. Elizabeth waited, teeth clenched on her tongue.
"Excuse me," Rusalka said, taking a seat by Ana.
"Alright, listen up. This is what we came for. I don't know if this is endgame or just another piece of the puzzle, and I sure as hell don't understand it, but we need this fragment. There's creatures on this planet we may never have seen before. Older than any of our species."
"It would be tactically unwise to take such a large convoy into unknown territory," Serpe said.
It sounded more like an order then a suggestion.
"I'm sorry, did I miss the memo where you were put in charge of my ship?"
"You are so full of Human folly."
"We split into two groups. Querius and Krakk have narrowed the search area down to this stretch of land."
Elizabeth pushed a switch on her bracelet and Purple 24's terrain appeared.
"I'd share with you how they figured it out but I don't know myself."
"Well, basically they would – " Lavell started.
She stopped bluntly, gauging the disinterest in the room.

The strip lit up in two coloured sections, stretching in from North and South.
"Me, Ana Rusalka and Serpe will be Fireteam Alpha. We'll start East and head central. Brack, Forr, Lavell and Isoline, you guys are Fireteam Bravo.
"Shouldn't we change the names?" Isoline said.
Elizabeth thought for a second. Maybe they did sound a little stupid. But she wasn't going to admit that now.
"Forr, you take the lead. Start South and meet us central. This place is so far in The

Barely Charted we don't have any detailed maps, but going off Allke, this won't be the kind of thing that's gonna be buried in some mound of dirt. We're looking for something hallowed and revered."

"Make sure everyone has their bracelets tuned to channel three so we can communicate in the field," Lavell said.

"And did I not receive the memorandum where this vermin was put in charge?" Serpe said.

"Yeah, did I not send it to you?" Elizabeth asked.

Forr turned to Serpe, "You would do well to listen to her."

"You would have us be as the Jahlder are? You have forgotten what it means to be Krei. They are no better than insects!"

Serpe lunged at Lavell. Forr stood quickly, blocking her path. They stared at each other, dark eyes fighting dark eyes. Elizabeth pulled them apart.

"You're not surrounded by your fleet anymore. One bullet's all it would take," Elizabeth growled.

Serpe pushed her away and spat on the ground.

"Everybody head to the armoury. I'll go to the hangar and prep the pilots," Elizabeth said.

"I think you should apologize to her," Isoline told Elizabeth.

Elizabeth just glared.

Ana was looking over at Elizabeth with wide, questioning eyes. Elizabeth gave reassuring wink to let her know there was a plan.

Ana

Ana lingered in the doorway of the armoury rather than push her way through the crowd. It started to thin out. Ana ventured inside. Just as she was equipping her rifle, Rusalka dropped down from the ceiling and helped her attach her chest plate.
"Where did you go?"
"I have other friends on this ship besides you," Rusalka said.
"I don't believe you," Ana smiled.

In the hangar, Elizabeth was directing people to their shuttles. Roka would fly Bravo. Mogg was taking Ana's team. Serpe pushed everyone out of the way.
"We should use my ship. It's faster and it has more firepower."
"It won't fit us all."
"Then I could take it alone. Link up with your ground team once you have a lock on a location."
"Was I unclear? You answer to me. Get in the shuttle."
Serpe spat at her feet as she climbed the steps.

Take off was less smooth than Roka's, a metallic spluttering cough from the engine. It quietened down and silence filled the shuttle. Rusalka broke it.
"Would people here say Krakk is more Krei, or Ang?" she asked.
"That grotesque thing is no Krei. It's a monstrosity," Serpe said.
"Uhkira was the monster," Elizabeth said.
"Uhkira was a fool, a stain in the great Krei name."
"He was cruel," Ana said.
Serpe gave her a hard look. Ana felt the eyes burning her. She was determined not to show her nerves.
"I have no quarrel with that. Greatness achieved through the pain of others is no less great," Serpe said.
"You can't believe that."
"Human scientific history is bloodier than Krei. Regardless, Uhkira did not achieve greatness. I have difficulty seeing how he was even attempting it, cutting people open and seeing what happened to them... he was a curious child. His results were worthless."
"Krakk isn't Krei or Ang. He's nothing," Ana said.

Rusalka smiled passively. It gave nothing of her own opinion away.
"How do you feel, Mogg? Does Krakk's mind make him one of your people?"
"I just fly the ship."
"Don't you want to involve yourself in our philosophical deliberation?"
"I just fly."
"You're a delight."
"It's the mind that makes the man. I'd say Krakk's a Krei," Elizabeth said.
"I agree," Rusalka said with a breezy smile.

Ana touched Rusalka's soft arm.
"You saw what Uhkira was doing. You can't think that's natural."
"I never said it was natural. And if we were talking about Uhkira I'd be firmly in the 'he's a monster' camp. But Krakk's not responsible for his own creation."
"You can't manufacture a Krei." Serpe said.

The shuttle rocked and Ana fell out of her seat. Rusalka caught her by the wrist.
"Entering the atmosphere," Mogg announced belatedly.
"How come that never happened with the other pilot?" Rusalka asked.
"It's to do with the yaw, pitch and roll," Ana said.
"How do you know that?" Rusalka said.
"I'm a licensed pilot."
"Thought you were a doctor."
"I'm both."
"Are you the ship's only medic?" Serpe asked. It sounded like an insult.
"I'm the only qualified doctor."
"Then you shouldn't be here. You should remain on the ship at all times."
"Ana's a good soldier. I want her on my team," Elizabeth said.
"Human recklessness," Serpe said, turning away.
What had changed Elizabeth's mind?

The shuttle slowed as the dense, violet forest came into view.
"All right, helmets on everyone. Querius says this atmosphere could be toxic during prolonged exposure, so no risks," Elizabeth said. She pulled a thick collar over her shoulders so the helmet would lock in place over her blue jacket.
Ana tied her hair back into a bun. Rusalka just stood by the door, one leg cocked.
"You aren't gonna wear a helmet?"
"It continues to amaze me how little the rest of the Universe knows about the Umbra. I don't need a helmet because I don't breathe. We don't have respiratory systems."
"You don't breathe?" Ana asked, "How do you survive? How do you talk?"
"How do *you* talk?"
"We force air against our vocal chords. That makes them vibrate, and sound comes out."
"Most people would just say they don't know."
"But I do know," Ana said.
"Well, I don't. I haven't studied Umbra anatomy and neither has anyone I've ever met. All I know is I can stay underwater for hours, poison gas has no effect on me and I can't be strangled."
"What if someone strangled you so hard they snapped the bones in your neck?" Serpe asked.
"Let's not test that one out," Rusalka said, opening the door of the shuttle.

It was spongey underfoot as they stepped out. The light glinted along the mauve edges of the grass, a solemn glow. Overgrown leaves choked thick trunks of black bark. Elizabeth read her bracelet and pointed into the shadows.

"Lucky us," Rusalka said.
Isoline's voice came over the com link, "Ranger, this is ground team Bravo."
"I put Forr in charge of that team."
"We've landed, heading central now."
The com cut out.
"Bitch."

They walked forward into the leafy opening. A dense canopy swarmed overhead and sapped the light away. Lush grass died away into loose mud. Elizabeth turned her bracelet's torch on. Slow silence, cautious footsteps. Ana crunched down on a dead twig. Serpe turned and glared at her. She waited for an attack from the darkness, but not came. She let out a quiet sigh of relief. Her knees were quivering, threatening to buckle. The passage through the bushes was narrowing. They had to crouch now. Hard stalks clattered as they rode over their helmets.

By the time Ana pushed the last branch out of her face, Rusalka was nowhere to be seen. Elizabeth sprayed her lightbeam into every shadow but all she found was leaves, dense and dark.
"Were you holding her prisoner?" Serpe asked.
"She was here voluntarily. But I think she was having second thoughts."
"She never mentioned anything," Ana said.
"When Warden lured us to his ship... on the way back she was talking about running away to become treasure hunters again. She wanted me to come with her."
"Why didn't you?" Ana asked.
She had never asked Elizabeth why she hadn't tried to run in the first place.
"Because my place is here. With you."
Ana smiled and reached out to hold Elizabeth's hand.
"Humans are filthy beasts," Serpe turned away, disgusted.
"What, there are no lesbian Krei?" Ana asked.
"None left alive, no," Serpe said. Icicles dripped from every syllable.

The mesh of trees and thorns thinned out. In the distance, Ana could see a spire reach up and pierce the clouds. There was a deep lake in front of them. Mud scum floated on the murky water. A thick tree floated on a small island, central. Gnarled dark roots plunged down into the lake like chains.
"Well, can we all swim?" Ana asked.
"Get down!"
Elizabeth dove back onto Ana, pushing them both to the floor.
"What's wrong?" Ana whispered.
"This is why we executed your kind on Excha. Uncontrollable urges," Serpe said.
Elizabeth yanked Serpe down with them.
"Unhand me!"
Elizabeth slammed her hand against Serpe's speaker to stifle the sound.
"Look across the water," Elizabeth told her.

Ana rolled off Elizabeth and squinted across the bay.
"I see him," Serpe said.
"Me too," Ana lied.

Elizabeth

Elizabeth put her hand on the side of Ana's face and turned it subtly. There was a figure, possibly Human, wading through the water. Its eye was pressed to the scope of a sniper rifle.
"Three of us can take him out," Serpe said.
"He's got the range on us. Could pick us all off before we draw if we're not careful."
"I can take him out from here," Serpe said, raising her weapon.
Elizabeth immediately pushed the barrel down.
"We don't know this terrain. Say you take him out and he's got five friends hiding in the jungle. What then? Our only option is to get by him undetected."

Elizabeth stepped slowly into the water. She lowered herself, keeping her eyes on the Human as her face submerged. Water immediately flooded into her helmet. She could feel the wet earth clinging to her face. It stank of salt and rotten weeds. She coughed and rose up, collapsing on the mud of the bank.
"Elizabeth?" Ana said.
She fumbled with the latch of her helmet and tossed it aside. Water ran out from her nose as she struggled for breath.
"The helmets aren't waterproof," she spluttered.
"What about the atmosphere?" Ana said.
"*Prolonged* exposure," Serpe said, "We should be fine if we move quickly."
The pair of them ditched their helmets while Elizabeth rolled over, still gasping. She wiped her dirty hair out of her eyes and saw a cluster of hollow blue reeds poking up from the water. She tore three reeds out and handed one to each of them.
"Yes... that might work," Serpe said, holding the reed up to one eye.
"Mm," Ana nodded. Elizabeth could tell she had no idea.
Elizabeth blew through her reed to make sure it was clear. She clamped the reed gently between her teeth and slid into the water.

Elizabeth did her best to wave away the floating grime. She waded through the lake until the water was too blurry to see through. She surfaced. They had crossed maybe half of the lake, but the Human had not moved. He was waist deep. He suspected something. Back and forth he moved his scope. Elizabeth sank underwater again. They needed to distract him.

Submerged, Elizabeth pointed to the tree's sunken roots. Through the mistiness of the lake they looked like twisted vipers, waiting to strike. Elizabeth swam over and clawed her way up onto the small island. She reached into the water to heave Ana up then rested back against the thick tree trunk. It was wide enough to hide the three of them from view.
"What's the plan?" Serpe said.
"We need to distract him. We're going nowhere as long as he's standing there."
Ana picked up a large stone from near the tree.
"We could use this," she said.

"Hitting him with a rock would give away our position just as much as shooting him," Serpe said.

"I mean, I could throw it in the water. Give us a chance to get past while he investigates."

"Oh," Serpe said, "That might work."

Elizabeth took the stone from her and lobbed it back across the lake. The Human paddled forward, towards the splash. Elizabeth tossed another one. Closer to the Human. She wanted him to feel hunted. He moved further forward, treading water. A third stone, smaller and way off to the left, had him obsessed. He dove into the lake, swimming towards the ripples of the rock.

"Now's our chance," Elizabeth said.

They grabbed their reeds again and swam to the grassy clearing. Once her head was above water, Elizabeth spat away the reed. She looked over her shoulder at the Human standing on the opposite bank. One noise and he could convince himself he misheard something. Two noises and it might still be just an animal disturbing the calm. But three noises... three noises was an intruder. Three noises meant he was being stalked. With madness, he thrust his sniper rifle into the reeds like it was a sword cutting into the belly of a beast.

The water rolled off her jacket as they walked up into dry land. They would have to hurry through the rest of Purple 24. The atmosphere would wear them down without their helmets. Their helmets! If the Human found them –

Too late. A tribal scream came across the lake. Elizabeth turned and saw the sniper rifle rising. She ducked behind a boulder, trying to drag Ana down with her. Before she could, a bullet ripped through Ana's shoulder. She fell, writhing in pain. Elizabeth pushed her hand to the wound. Ana was trembling in shock.

"Stay with me, Princess."

But she had already fainted.

While the Human reloaded, Serpe ran for the protection of the nearby jungle. The earth moved with a shrill and savage jingle. A bear trap gobbled up Serpe's leg. Its razor teeth tore through her thick armour and thicker skin like they were made of wet paper. Below the knee, Serpe's leg was a mangled mixture of frayed metal and shredded, bloody skin. She seethed through her teeth until she passed out. Falling forward, she hit her face off one of the winding black roots. Her jaw cracked, sodden with blood.

Ana was safe behind the protection of the boulder, but Serpe was still horribly exposed. The bear trap's chain was short. Its maw clenched. Elizabeth couldn't move her. All it did was tear the trap deeper into Serpe's flesh. Surely the sniper had reloaded by now. Why hadn't a second shot come? She looked around and saw the sniper flat on his back. The shimmering hilt of a dagger stuck out from his face, rifle slowing sinking into the swamp.

Something dove out of the island tree into the lake. Within seconds a woman was on their shore. She stood over them with a second dagger in her hand. Her hair was long, dark and mangy. Mud clung to her. A shawl of dark lizardlike scales hung off her. The woman raised the dagger to Elizabeth's chin. Several more were laced into a bandolier across her chest
"What do you seek here?"
Elizabeth leaned back.
"Are you Human?" she asked.
The mud made it hard to discern the woman's species. Her eyes were a golden shade that Elizabeth had never seen before.
"Your kind might call me that."
"My kind? I'm Human too," Elizabeth said.
"You're a Paxet."
Elizabeth glanced down to the glinting knife.
"We're not here to cause trouble. It was your friend who shot at us."
"I've just thrown a knife through that man's face. Do not accuse me of friendship."
"Fair point," Elizabeth conceded.
"You should leave this place," the woman said.
Elizabeth backed away. The woman allowed it, knife remaining raised.
"Is that a warning or a threat?"
"It is advice, delivered from the tip of a blade."

Elizabeth's hand itched for her pistol. She reached for it slowly and tossed it to the ground. An offering of peace.
"We're not here to hurt anyone. We're looking for an artefact."
"So your intentions are not to harm us, but to steal from us?"
"I already have part of it. It touched it, and it burned," Elizabeth told her.
"No one survives the Fire."
"Has this happened to other people?"
"I've heard stories," the woman said, "the kind each generation tells the next. But alone, you have no hope of taking it, and your friends will die soon if they stay here."
Blood ran from the open wounds on Serpe's face. Ana's head hung limp against her chest. The woman scooped up a mound of dirt and swathed it on Serpe's cheek, pressing a long, rounded leaf until it stuck.
"That will quell any infection," the woman said.
Elizabeth nodded her thanks and offered her hand to shake.
"Elizabeth Ranger."
"Nyomee," the woman said, grabbing Elizabeth's palm and coating it in slimy muck. She wiped it clean on her thigh and called the shuttle on her bracelet.
"Mogg, we need evac. Ana and Serpe are down. They're not likely, but they will be if we don't haul ass now. Track our location, there's just about space to land."
"Roger, Ranger. ETA three minutes."

Nyomee jimmied the bear trap with a strong twig. It snapped open with a creak.
"Take me with you when you leave," she said.
The dagger had been sheathed. Her golden eyes were big and sweet.

"Why?" Elizabeth asked.

"This has become a hateful place, a shell of what it was. But more than that, if you survived the Fire, I want to be a part of your story. I know this planet and its people. I can help you."

"There's another group of us at the other end of this jungle. Hopefully they'll have better luck than we did."

"I doubt it," Nyomee said, "If the Hunters don't get them, the dinosaurs will."

"Dinosaurs?"

Nyomee nodded.

"Seriously?"

__Isoline__

Forr and Lavell were hanging from thick branches, suspended by their ankles, swaying like dead fruit. Too fast, too foolish. Brack was on his knees, hands tied together behind his head. A Human pressed the butt of his gun to Brack's forehead, stabbing it at him repeatedly.
"I don't suppose I could get you to stop that, could I?" Brack said.
The Human jabbed the gun against him once more.
"I'll take that as a no?"
The hard wooden handle of the rifle crashed down into the side of Brack's face.
"Shut up, Brack," Lavell said.
The Human looked up at her with a snarl that became a manic smile.
"You will never breach our city!" he screamed at her, "An army of thousands guard its walls!"
"Lesson well and truly learned. Set us free and we won't bother you anymore."
Another smash to the cheek was Brack's only reward for his wit.

Isoline was hidden behind shrubbery, biding her time. Thorns poked at her back, unable to breach her stiff scales. While the rest of them had rushed forward, she had evaded capture.

The Human took pleasure in their arrest. He strolled, snaking his steps around them with his rifle held in a loose, cocky grip. Isoline waited until he was in front of Brack. She pounced. The fright alone was enough to make him drop his weapon. A spinning kick sent it careening away. Isoline forced her pistol past his teeth, chipping them. Sweat rolled down his red skin. Isoline stared at him.
"You're going to untie these people. Then we're going to get on our shuttle, and leave. If you signal for your army to come and save you, my boyfriend's going to be wearing your face," she said.
"I *do* quite like my own face, though," Brack said.
"Shut up."
She shoved the pistol further down his throat. Like a steering wheel, she used it to direct him to Brack's knots, then to Forr and Lavell's. They landed with a crash. Isoline drove the Human down to his knees. She kept her gun in his mouth but swapped her hands on the grip, thrusting her free hand out to Brack.
"Call the shuttle for me."
He keyed the buttons and she moved it back to her lips.
"Roka, you can come and get us now. Can you see our location on your tracker?"
"Yep. You guys got what we came for?"
"Their city is heavily fortified. We need a new plan," Isoline said.
"I read you. Elizabeth's team came back early too."
He handed her arm back to Brack for him to disconnect the com link.

Isoline kept her pistol pushed down the Human's throat until Roka arrived.
"Stay here until you starve to death," she told him.

Lavell

Elizabeth burst into the shuttle as soon as they reached the Victory Pearl. She grabbed Lavell by the wrist and dragged her out.
"We need to get to the Med Bay. Now," Elizabeth said.
Her grip was hard enough to hurt.
"Has something happened to Ana?"
"Ana and Serpe. They both took a bad hit."
"What happened?"
"We tried to sneak past a local sniper. Almost made it, but he saw us and caught Ana in the shoulder. Serpe stepped in a goddamn bear trap. I think the atmosphere took care of the rest and they were both out cold."
"You and Rusalka okay?"
"Rusalka screwed us. Ran off as soon as we landed. I don't think she's coming back."
"She was talking about leaving," Lavell said.
"If she wanted out she just had to ask. But you don't leave in the middle of a mission."
Elizabeth's steps quickened. Lavell struggled to keep up.
"It doesn't seem like her."
"Whatever. I'm done with her," Elizabeth said, "I take it you guys hit trouble too?"
"No injuries, but Forr and myself were caught in rope traps, ended up hanging from the trees. Brack tried to free us, but he just ended up disarmed and tied up himself."
"Where was Isoline when all this happened?"
"She managed to remain undetected."
"What a surprise," Elizabeth said bitterly.
"She was the one who freed us," Lavell said.
Elizabeth made a non-committal murmur.
"Their city seems like it's impenetrable. Any ideas on what we do next?"
"We've got an ace for when we go back. Inside information."
"They took down two of your squad and you still managed to take a prisoner? That's impressive, even for you," Lavell said.
"She's not a prisoner. She came willingly."
"Another new face?"
"She saved our lives. Killed the sniper before he could reload."
"I liked the old days," Lavell said, "Just the four of us."
Those days seemed long ago now.
"The old days were just me. Then me and Brack, then me, Brack and Forr.

Then you came along. I like to make additions that have something to offer the group."

Was that really how Elizabeth felt? Were she and Forr no different from Isoline and Serpe? Did Elizabeth feel no extra loyalty or love for them?

"You've added a lot recently."

"Believe me, they weren't all my choice."

Elizabeth stopped her as they reached the Med Bay, crooking her hand inside the bend in Lavell's elbow.

"When you're done here, I want you to meet the Human from Purple 24. Leaving a closed community like that... I want you to check she's on the level."

"I'm not a lie detector. I can't turn it on and off with a switch."

"I trust your judgement," Elizabeth said. A moment passed, "And I miss the old days too."

Lavell closed the door with Ranger's last words echoing in her head. It was typical of Elizabeth to sign off with a vote of confidence just when Lavell needed it. She was little more than an ad hoc medic, only able to patch up cuts and heal broken bones. All things considered, the shoulder was a pretty good place to be shot. But a bear trap was a new one on her.

Lavell washed her hands and pulled on a set of latex gloves. They only had Human sized pairs. One finger hung limp and empty. The gloves needed to be stretched halfway down her forearm to remain tight. Ana and Serpe were lying on separate steel beds, both still covered in blood. Elizabeth had taken off Ana's chest armour and wrapped a bandage tightly around her shoulder. The gauze was already stained and seeping red. Gently, Lavell unwound the bandages. There was a large hole ripped through her skin, but slightly lower than the shoulder and off to the side. She examined it closely. A through and through. Lavell found a tube of Ana's skin knitting salve and rubbed it across the wound. She appeared in a stable condition, so Lavell replaced her bandages with a clean set and turned to Serpe, who looked in a worse way.

There was a hard crust of dirt pasted to Serpe's cheek with a leaf embedded in it. She feared it was an infected scab, but as she touched it the mud crumbled away and a clear liquid flowed out. The wounds beneath were surprisingly clean. She swabbed them with alcohol to be sure, but it looked like a simple stitch up was all they would need.

She twisted the nozzle on an anesthesia canister and pressed the mask to Serpe's mouth to ensure she would stay asleep. She took out a strand of wire thick and strong enough to hold Krei skin together. There would be some scarring to the right side of Serpe's face, but nothing too noticeable. And besides, she knew the Krei did not consider scars to be disfiguring, even if the rest of the Universe did.

As Lavell worked the needle through Serpe's dense hide, she saw her lip tugging up into a smile with the movements of the thread Serpe was like a Krei in the old Jahlder stories. It was hard to imagine Forr was ever friends with her. With the stitching finished, Lavell taped over Serpe's cheek to stop the thread from snagging or coming loose before the skin had a chance to heal over.

Next she moved onto Serpe's leg. While Elizabeth had been able to remove Ana's armour, she had no such luck with Serpe's. The prongs of the bear trap had chewed the metal. It spiked up and stabbed down. She would need to get rid of the armour to even see what she was dealing with, let alone go about fixing it. She really did prefer it when people had just been shot. Lavell pulled a cabinet closer and began opening its drawers. She didn't know what tools would help this situation, but hoped she would find one. The closest thing to a solution was a bone saw. She tested it and sent the small circular blade whirring. It seemed to be in working order. She strapped a surgical mask across her face and steadied the saw against Serpe's armour. The saw started to spin and cut through the plating from Serpe's knee down to her ankle. Sparks spat. Her hands were hot. With this part loose, she was able to pry the armour up. There was a shard lodged through her shin. She raised the fragment of armour slowly, a pulpy scraping as she lifted it free. It clanged as she dropped it into the metal tray by the side of the bed, dark blood splashing. Pressure on the wound slowed the bleeding. She wrapped them in fresh bandages. Once the blood had been washed away and the metal removed, it was nothing out of Lavell's comfort zone. It might take Serpe a while to recover full walking strength to her leg, but she would in time. The Krei were a strong, resilient people. The Jahlder had learned that much during their war, and Forr had taught her even more.

Just as Lavell was tidying the drawer of instruments, Ana woke up with a cough. She tried to sit up in the bed, wincing from the pain. Lavell eased her back down and explained what happened.
"Elizabeth," she said, "Where's Elizabeth?"
"She's fine. Get some rest, I'll tell her to come by soon," Lavell said.
"Did we find it?" Ana asked.
She pressed her arm to her injured shoulder.

"Just rest," Lavell told her, sending her to sleep with the anesthesia.

Lavell headed for the Elizabeth's quarters to update her on Ana's condition. The sound of an argument in the Mess Hall dragged her over. She heard Elizabeth's raised voice. Elizabeth was usually so cool and composed. As she walked closer, a second voice became audible. Isoline's cold tone. Quieter, but loaded with venom.

Lavell pushed the door open slowly, hoping the hinges would not creak. It turned out there was no need for caution. The two of them were grandstanding. Everyone was present. Forr was over by the counter, holding a glass of fruit juice. He flashed a smile at Lavell and she skirted around the perimeter to join him.
"Elizabeth told me about Serpe. How is she?"
"A few scars. And she'll need to recover the strength in her leg, but I know Krei. It won't take her very long."
"She's a survivor, I have to give her that much," Forr said.
"What's this all about?"
"Our new crewmate," Forr said, pointing over at a Human wearing scales, "At least, that's how it started."

The new Human sat at one of the far away tables, matted hair cast down over her face and knees curled up to protect her body. Near her, Roka and Mogg were stood in the corner, Roka's arms crossed in delight. He was enjoying the argument very openly. Mogg's face was much harder to read. The Krei were good at that. It took her years to understand the subtlety in Forr's expressions.

The only one who dared sit near the epicentre was Brack. He was at the closest table with his brow furrowed and the corner of his lip twisted down, obviously torn on who to root for.

Elizabeth

"Your argument is futile. She should not be on our ship," Isoline hissed.
"How much clearer can I make this? It's not your call!"
"Perhaps we'd all be safer if it was."
"Is that some kind of joke? I don't know how or why you took control of the second squad on Purple 24, but I'd say you're 0 for 1."
"You fared even worse, even with your years of experience," Isoline said, spitting the sarcasm out.
"They're both fine, by the way," Lavell piped up.
Elizabeth glanced over, surprised that she was even there.
"Thanks, Lavell," Elizabeth took a deep breath to soothe her tone, "Will Ana make a full recovery?"
"Flesh wound," Lavell said, nodding.
Isoline pulled Elizabeth back into the line of fire.
"We failed on Purple 24 because we didn't have a plan. You go here, we'll go there? You need a military mind for tactics. What we are undertaking here is very different to sticking your hand into a dark hole and hoping you pull something shiny out," Isoline said.
"Enough of this!" Forr shouted, "You're clearly working up to a mutiny so I'll say right now that my vote is behind Elizabeth."
"Mine too. She's our leader," Lavell said.
"And mine," Roka said.
Elizabeth turned to him, surprised by the instant show of support. He gave her a knowing nod and she offered one back.

Isoline faced Brack, who was already squirming uncomfortably.
"You don't think we should have let this unknown Human on our ship, do you?"
Brack looked at Isoline. He glanced over her shoulder at Elizabeth and Nyomee. Elizabeth hated what he had been reduced to. Once a charming warrior. Brave and witty and *one of them*. But Isoline had torn him up and pasted him back together in her own image. She had taught him how to dance and now she wanted everyone to watch.
"It's difficult to judge. We don't really know her yet."
That was not a Brack answer. He used to be decisive. Isoline slammed her hands down on the table either side of him and stared into his eyes.
"On the other hand, the two we met did try and kill us. Possibly not the wisest decision to invite the third one into the fold," he said.
"I knew you'd see sense," Isoline said.

Elizabeth grabbed Isoline by the shoulder and hauled her away from Brack. Her fist burned as it tightened, desperate to connect with Isoline's jaw. Isoline smirked, daring her. Donovan's voice came over the com speakers, interrupting their fight before it went too far. He had a knack for that. Elizabeth wasn't sure if she was grateful or annoyed.

"Hate to interrupt this girl on girl show, believe me. But we've got a bogey on our tail. Not fired yet, but it's checking out our ass and getting close enough to smell it."
"This isn't over," Elizabeth told Isoline.
"Count on it."

Elizabeth ran to the flight deck, followed by Nyomee. Lavell headed to the turrets, ready to engage if necessary.
"Any chance this is one of your people?" Elizabeth asked.
"We do have small ships, but we rarely go off world. They're mainly for supply runs to nearby planets."
"You don't think they'd track you down?"
"They all think I died years ago."
Nyomee did not look her in the eye.

They reached the flight deck and Elizabeth did not push the question further.
"They've been trying to make contact for a minute or so," Donovan said, "Thought it best to wait for you."
He handed Elizabeth the com mic.
"This is Elizabeth Ranger of the Victory Pearl. State your business."
"I've got you a souvenir."
It was Rusalka, sounding happy and relaxed.
"Forr and Lavell are in the turrets awaiting instruction. Give me one reason why I shouldn't give the order to blast you out of the sky."
"It's a really nice souvenir."
"This isn't a joke, Rusalka. We got ambushed when you left. Ana and Serpe took a hit."
A brief silence of static.
"Did they die?"
"No, they're fine," Elizabeth said.
"Then don't scare me like that. Now open up and let me aboard. Don't tempt me into running away with this all by myself."
"You owe me one hell of an explanation," Elizabeth told her.
"Oh sweetie, you can consider that debt repaid."

Elizabeth disconnected.
"I guess I'll go see what's so important," Elizabeth said as she left.
"Okay, Captain," Donovan said, swiveling in his chair.
He noticed Nyomee for the first time and his eyes lingered on her.
"Another newbie?" he asked.
Nyomee offered him a dirt covered hand and told him her name.
"What does all this *do*?" she asked, bright eyes swimming over the control panel.
Donovan started to show her. Elizabeth left them to it.

~*~

Rusalka arrived with a rough landing. Elizabeth was in her face as she stepped out.

"You don't ditch the mission," she told her, "Not ever."
Rusalka smiled sweetly.
"Now, be nice to me or you won't get your present."
Rusalka leaned into the ship and picked up a leather drawstring bag. Elizabeth stole one of the knives from her back and pressed it to Rusalka's throat as she jerked back around.
"I don't care what you've got in there. You leave me in the shit again, and I'll slit your throat."
"You have a reputation for being one of the best, deadliest thieves in the galaxy, Ranger. But I have no reputation. Think how dangerous that makes me," Rusalka said.
Elizabeth pressed the knife threateningly close. Rusalka gave her a wink. She dropped it to the floor with a clatter. Rusalka eyeballed her while she picked up the dagger with her foot, handed it to herself and slammed it back into its sheath.
"You never would have gotten my blade if we were playing for keeps."
"What have you got that was worth all of this fuss?" Elizabeth asked, tone still tense.
"Oh, trust me. This is."

Rusalka loosened the strings on her knapsack and unfurled the contents theatrically. It was a twisted, golden pipe.
"What is it?" Elizabeth asked.
"It's the scepter," Nyomee said from the doorway, "How did you get this?"
"Seems we're kindred spirits, Ranger," Rusalka said, ignoring Nyomee, "Neither of us can resist anything shiny."
Nyomee stepped forward, approaching the scepter with awed reverence. Her eyes were wide and full of fright.
"This is sealed inside Yerin's vault, behind a door of steel and stone," she said, glancing at Rusalka with the same impressed, scared look.
"I'm good."
"It is guarded by armed soldiers at all times."
"I'm very good,"
"Don't keep us in suspense, Rusalka. I know you're dying to tell us," Elizabeth said.

Rusalka

Rusalka heard two noises. The first was the twig snapping under Ana's feet. A booming crack. Second, a much quieter rustling. A creature in the distance had heard them. No one else would have noticed the sound. If she didn't act quickly, the creature might kill them all.

She dove into the thicket of leaves and crept towards the rustling. It was getting closer. She stopped. Waited. The rustling again. A nearby tree started to shake. Rusalka drew her blades. The leaves leaned forward and the creature lurched out...

It was a small bird, blue feathers, maybe about a foot high. She started to laugh.
"You scared me, you little –"
SHMMMMP!
A colossal set of scaled jaws crashed through the trees and swallowed the bird whole. Rusalka stared up at the monster as it chewed. Blue feathers floated around its serrated teeth. It towered over her. Green scales and silver claws. The beast was three times her size. It sniffed the air as she hid. It hadn't seen her. Not yet. Using one of the tree trunks as a scratching post, it scored deep into the bark. Teeth still grinding the bird to slurry, it wandered off.
"I like this planet."

She had read about Earth history, but almost all of it had been about Humans. Dinosaurs were ancient creatures that existed long before them. How was one still alive? And how did it reach The Barely Charted?

The dinosaur's stomping rang in her ears as she continued through the forest. It sounded like it was heading away from Ana and Elizabeth. They were safe.

She found a set of footsteps and decided that regrouping was not worth the effort. Krakk had said the fragment would be inside a monument. This trail could lead her right there.

The footsteps in the mud sent her in a circle. They were a guard's tracks. She slipped inside the circle and kept to the shadows. Dark trees engulfed her. Through the shadows, she reached a clearing. A spire climbed up into the clouds. A pit of fire surrounded it. In front of the flames, guards lined up in a barrier.

She skirted around the forest but could see no obvious opening. The guards were smart. There was a long, open space where the trees had been shorn away. No cover or blindspots. Ordinarily she would have waited for a weakness to present itself. They always did, in time. But the dinosaur complicated things. Even with her hearing, it had caught her out. If it found the rest of them...

The dinosaur. The solution to organisation was chaos.

Rusalka retreated into the purple trees, ears twitching. She saw another blue feathered bird. It was pecking at the ground peacefully. Silently, she twisted a vine away from a tree trunk and tied it into a lasso. She tossed it around the birds neck and tightened. It flapped its wings without a cry of complaint. The bird did not seem to care.

Rusalka tied the vine to a stick and walked deeper into the darkness. The bird bobbed at the end of the vine like bait on a fishing rod, letting out a merry chirrup.

~*~

The dinosaur was not hard to find. Rusalka followed the shattered trees and saw it slouched over, gnawing at its own claws. She stuck to the shadows and dangled the bird out. The dinosaur looked around, stood up and started to advance. Each footstep was thunder. The vine rotated slowly and the bird saw its fate. Suddenly, it began to squawk, wings flailing. Rusalka ran back the way she had came, bird screeching wildly, dinosaur chasing with earthquake footsteps.

She reached the spire and launched the fishing rod, javelin style. It landed just in front of the fire pit. The dinosaur charged for it, berserking through the guards. The ones who weren't paid enough ran. The more foolish stayed and shot at the beast, sending it into a frenzy. Its enormous snout moved like a wrecking ball, tossing three guards away. A fourth fired at the dinosaur's ankles. It bellowed, toppling forward into the fire pit. Scales aflame, it thrashed through the spire. Rusalka saw it. A long, golden tube, shaft twisted elegantly. It was perched in a glass case at the top of a stone staircase. While the dinosaur continued to rampage, Rusalka rushed through the carnage and grabbed the relic.

She snuck away, leaving the dinosaur to feast. Another set of tracks led her to small dock. One hotwire later and she was heading back for the Victory Pearl, spoils of war nestled safely in her drawstring pouch.

Elizabeth

"What happened when you first touched it?" Nyomee asked.
"That's your reaction? You heard the part about the dinosaurs, right?"
"Seriously, Rusalka. Nothing at all? It didn't burn you?" Elizabeth said.
"What exactly is this thing, Ranger? And what's inside that room in the middle of the ship? I've never known a room I couldn't break into."
"Don't worry about that. I need you to remember exactly what happened. Anything at all..."
"Ranger, nothing happened. Do you understand? See for yourself."
She slapped the scepter down into Elizabeth's palm. A blistering fire scorched her skin. She bucked down to her knees

The pain snapped away as Rusalka pulled the scepter off. Elizabeth got to her feet woozily.
"What the hell was that?" Rusalka asked.

Nyomee placed her hands either side of Elizabeth's face. She could drown in her golden eyes.
"You survived the Fire..."
Elizabeth pushed her away and ran off, weakened legs stumbling. Something had entered her mind so strangely. She rushed to her quarters and grabbed a pen from the gilded gold box on her desk. Her fingers white where they gripped her pen. When she was done, she pushed the notepad away and leaned back in her chair, breathless and sweating.

Patches of moss sprouted up across strong roots that ripped through the earth beneath them. A crooked tree stood at the foot of a hill, a building behind it at the peak. A gang of dark feathered birds sat on thin branches. They sagged under the weight.
"Is this what the scepter showed you?" Nyomee said.
She was standing in the doorway, matted hair resting against the frame, on tip toes to get a closer look at the notepad.
"You've got to stop sneaking up on people," Elizabeth said, handing her the sketch.
"Sorry. I'm used to being quiet."
Nyomee ran her fingertip across the drawing, up the curve of the hill. Mud crumbled from her nails and fell across the paper. She blew them away lightly and handed the pad back.
"Do you know where it is?"
"Nothing in our stories mentions a tree of this kind, nor where the other pieces are kept. Just that they were scattered across the universe so they could never be reassembled," Nyomee said.
"What happens when they are? Reassembled, I mean."
"The tales vary. Some say death, some say life. If a truth exists it will lie somewhere in between."

"I'm not much of a fan of poetry."

"How are you feeling? The scepter seemed to have quite an effect on you, but your friend did not appear to care."

"Rusalka? I don't think she has friends," Elizabeth said, "But I'm fine, thanks."

"Is that what happened last time? I've heard it told in our stories, but to see it was... frightening."

"Last time I was dead for three years. So this is an improvement."

Nyomee's mouth hung open.

"I'll figure out where this tree is, but first I'm going to visit Ana. Head back to the flight deck and speak to Donovan. He'll sort you out with your quarters."

~*~

She had not had the time to worry about Ana since they had returned from Purple 24, but now her mind was free to fret. It would be her fault if something happened to Ana. The thought of losing her felt jagged in her heart. She thought back to the old advice someone had once given her on Earth. *People leave their shards in you.* It was supposed to be a warning to never let anybody in. They only hurt. Elizabeth never saw it that way. If you hurt, you were alive. Her relationship with Ana was new and fresh. She wanted to soak up every moment while it was still pure.

Ana's entire right side swaddled in bandages. Elizabeth stuffed the sketch of the tree in her back pocket and sat down. A lock of blonde hair had fallen across Ana's face. Elizabeth gently brushed it away. She unfurled the gauze and padding, knowing she would be able to redress the wounds easily. With the amount of bandages she had wrapped around herself over the years, she could do it with her eyes closed.

Elizabeth laced the bandages around her hand as they came away from Ana's body. She folded them into a neat bundle and dropped them into a medical trashcan. Ana's flesh was pale, soft beneath Elizabeth's careful fingertips. The bullet hole was dark red. A trail of blood leaked down the ridges of her ribcage. The skin was knitting together well. She went over to the sink and held a sponge under the tap. Ice cold droplets ran through her fingers. She pressed it tenderly to Ana's skin and washed the bloodstains away with slow and gentle movements. When the red was gone, she toweled her skin dry and covered the bullet hole with a set of fresh bandages.

She sat by Ana's bed and waited. Precious and fragile. Elizabeth should have done a better job of protecting her. She picked up Ana's limp hand and held it fondly. She wrapped it in her own warm embrace, kissed Ana's cheek and hoped she would wake soon.

Her mind wandered back to the tree, to what it all meant. She was getting visions now? These relics had had no effect on anyone in hundreds, maybe thousands of years. Why her? Why now? There was nothing special about –

A cough. Elizabeth looked up and held Ana's hand tighter. Ana's long black lashes

fluttered like a butterfly taking flight. The dimples of her lips twitched.
"Hey there," Elizabeth said with a smile.
Ana smiled back weakly. She pressed her weight on her palms.
"Don't get up. You were shot," Elizabeth told her, gently lowering her back down.
"I remember," Ana said slowly.
Her voice was hoarse.
"It went straight through. Lavell patched you up as soon as she landed. You and Serpe."
"Serpe?"
"Got caught in a bear trap trying to avoid the same sniper that hit you."
"You...?" Ana said weakly.
"Me?"
"Are you okay?"
"Unscathed. One of the locals took out the sniper for us. We thought she could help us with the terrain of Purple 24, but Rusalka brought back the fragment anyway. Still might be worth keeping her around though, she seems to have a better idea of the mythology better than anyone, and she's already gotten us out of a jam."
"Maybe... maybe I shouldn't come anymore. I'm too much of a burden," Ana said.
I want you with me.
"Last time you saved me. This time I saved you. That's how it works."
I'll save you next time. Don't worry.
Elizabeth kissed her forehead.

Ana coughed again and Elizabeth fetched her a glass of water. She drank it slowly. Her fingers ran down the inside of the bandages, peeling them away from her skin. Elizabeth touched her hand, trying to stop her.
"The wound hasn't healed yet," Elizabeth told her.
"If I can see it, I can tell you what salve to use."
Elizabeth nodded and moved her hand away. Ana continued to unravel. She balled the bloodied strips of cloth up and tossed them to the trashcan. She placed her fingertips either side of the bullet hole, prying it apart and gritting her teeth.
"Don't," Elizabeth said.
Ana tried to roll over, reaching under the bed.
"Don't move. Just tell me what you need," Elizabeth said.
"My armour. There should be a blue vial in there. It's a stronger version of the salve I gave you for your knees. It aids the healing of Human flesh."
Elizabeth brought it over to her. There was a spectacular hole in the bodywork. Curled spines expanded away from where the sniper's bullet had penetrated. The river of blood had dried brown down the white. Elizabeth handed her the vial. Ana dabbed over the exposed tissue with a feather touch. She exhaled sharply with every cutting bite of the cold salve.
"I'm gonna redress the bullet hole, then you're can get some rest, okay?" Elizabeth said.
"Put cotton pads underneath the bandages. It'll make for less pressure so it heals faster."
Elizabeth placed two squares of cotton on Ana's skin, one above the bullet hole and

one below, and wrapped the bandages over them.

"Elizabeth?" Ana said, holding her arm as she tucked the final tail of gauze away.

"Yeah?"

"Thanks."

Elizabeth kissed her cheek warmly and told her to get some sleep.

Rusalka

Rusalka took her relic to the Krakk in the research lab.

"Where's Querius?" she asked.

"In the broadcast centre, talking to his wife."

"Querius is life bonded?"

"She doesn't like Doctor to work so much. He calls her every day. Sometimes they talk for hours."

"Really? That seems like something I would know. Why don't I know that already?"

Krakk just shrugged, not looking up from the device he was tinkering on. He held a set of tweezers between his fingers. They looked like the bones of an insect in his giant hands.

"I got you this. Figured you could work some magic with it."

Rusalka handed Krakk the scepter but her barely glanced at it before dumping it down on the desk with a bang, never letting go of his tweezers.

Rusalka rang her tongue across her teeth slowly.

"Is something wrong?" she asked.

"You should have stayed with the group. They would have kept you safe," he said.

"I keep myself safe."

His work stopped now, the tiny tweezers cast aside.

"This time. Master told me many stories of vain heroes. They all died, Rusalka. That could be you."

She put her furry hand against the hide of his chin and forced his three dark eyes to stare directly at her.

"It won't be," she said without blinking.

He gave no reply.

"I have a favour to ask," Rusalka said, "How much do you know about other species?"

"That depends. Master taught me a great deal, but I know much of it was lies."

"Like what?"

"He tells me that Jahlder are cold and calculating, but I see kindness in Lavell, love for his wife in Doctor. Humans are angry and cruel, but Captain forgave me for my work with Master, offered me a second chance. All of my biological and anatomical knowledge is correct, however."

"What did he tell you about Umbra?"

"Nothing," Krakk said.

"What do you think of us now?" Rusalka asked.

"I think they are pretty, Furball."

Rusalka turned away from him, hiding her smile.
"What about the Torfus? You've studied them?"
"Extensively. They are a unique species."
She walked over the door and softly pushed it closed.
"Tell me how the Torfus brain works."

Ana

It had been three days since they had returned from Purple 24. Yesterday she had been able to walk around the Med Bay relatively painlessly. She was ready to sleep in Elizabeth's quarters again. Elizabeth had stayed with her, napping slumped over in her chair, but had not gotten any decent rest since Purple 24. They decided to keep Serpe out for a few days to monitor her condition. While she walked, Elizabeth told Ana about the relic Rusalka had returned with, how it had affected her. The drawing, the image and how it felt inside her brain.

Ana studied the crumpled paper.
"Have you shown anyone else?"
"Nyomee was there when I drew it. She doesn't know anything about it."
"Oh," Ana said.
She hadn't met Nyomee yet. Ana didn't like that she had been in their room already.

Nyomee's knock at the door was a light and eager rapping. Ana's fears became amusement. The woman's hair was knotted straw, her skin covered in filth. Neither she nor Elizabeth had showered for three days, and still the woman's smell attacked every inch of the room. Her unshaven armpits were curled with dried sweat. Ana held her breath and thanked Nyomee for her help, and kept it held while Nyomee nodded and smiled. She exhaled with a gasp once Nyomee had left.
"She stinks," Ana said.
"Don't be mean. We might need her expertise to finish this," Elizabeth said.
"Well, if her expertise means slathering up in mud and never bathing, I think I can do without it."
"Just remember she saved your life," Elizabeth said.
Ana held the paper up.
"Have you showed West?" Ana asked.
"I thought you'd want to be there."
"Let's go now then," Ana said.

She eased her feet over the side of the bed. Another day or two of rest would not hurt. But she was getting restless, and she could tell that Elizabeth was losing patience. Her first footstep was a stumble. The second one was stronger, Elizabeth offering a shoulder.
"We don't have to do this today," Elizabeth said.
Ana could hear the words were hollow. She did not want to be Elizabeth's damsel in distress the way she was with Sam. Elizabeth had put faith in her, bringing her out into the field, and treating her with respect. She was only just realizing Sam had never offered her that.
"No. We need to get back on track," Ana said.
She pulled a t-shirt over her head, trying to hide the ache in her side from lifting her arms too high.

They walked to the central chamber. Ana pressed her eye to glass panel by the door while Elizabeth looked away. The doors hissed as the lock released. Ana tried to grab one side and haul it open but Elizabeth brushed her away.
"You don't want to open up the wound," she said.

The fizz of wires echoed around the room as they entered. Ana had almost forgotten the copper smell in the air.
"We found the second fragment on Purple 24," Elizabeth said.
I know
"It gave me a vision. I don't know what it meant."
The tree
"How did you know that?"
I see every corner of this ship. Time is of the essence. Waste no more of it here
"These things have been hidden for thousands of years. We're not up against a clock here," Elizabeth said.
You are in the base of my hourglass. You might drown in sand
Ana felt her skin chill.
Dr Yukishnov is not to go into the field with you again. It places too great a risk on the only established medical professional on board
"No dice. Ana stays with me."
She has no training. She has no value
Ana took a deep breath. Her own inadequacies, summarized so succinctly.
"I need people I trust around me. I can't put a value on that."
Elizabeth turned and headed for the exit. Ana followed, but West's voice scraped them back.
I gave you the gift of life, Miss Ranger. I do not appreciate it when my gifts are squandered

"We shouldn't have waited so long to tell him," Ana said, "You should have left me in the Med Bay."
"I needed to know you were okay. And next time we head out, you're coming with me. I don't care what he says."
No value. Maybe Sam had been right not to trust her with a gun.
"I'll go back to the Med Bay and monitor Serpe's condition."
"I'll show the tree to Querius," Elizabeth said, "He's probably our best bet for figuring it out."

She waited until Elizabeth had walked off fell against the wall. The bullet wound was still hurting more than she wanted to admit. In the Med Bay she would reapply her salve and take a dose of painkillers.

Elizabeth

Elizabeth could hear the muffled shouts from inside the research lab. Querius screaming. She slammed her shoulder into the door and burst it open.
"Ranger!" he exclaimed.
Elizabeth looked around the lab, puzzled. Querius was alone, standing at his worktable with a strange, cog operated monocle over his left eye.
"I thought I heard a struggle in here."
"Oh. I fear that was simply me," Querius said, letting out an embarrassed cough.
"You?"
He lifted the monocle over his head.
"I have an unusual work style. Believe it or not, the chaos keeps me focused. Jemsa used to enjoy it. She used to laugh and ask me if I used the technique to keep me focused during... other activities," Querius said.
He sighed, mouth curving into a smile.
"You miss her?" Elizabeth asked.
"I miss who she was. Honestly though, it is relief somewhat not to see her every day now, seeing her suffer. That thought may be shameful and selfish, but it is how I feel."
"I understand," Elizabeth said.
She could see Querius' lip beginning to tremble, his hand shake. He turned his back on Elizabeth and stared at the desk.

"Anyway," Querius said, straightening his back, "My guess would be that you came here to discuss something more important."
She took the crumpled piece of paper from her pocket and handed it to him. He lay it on the desk and wiped his hand across it from corner to corner methodically to flatten it.
"You have quite the talent, Miss Ranger."
"Before that I'd never drawn anything in my life."
"Perhaps the Human English expression of beginners luck is appropriate here then," he said, smiling and handing the paper back.
She did not take it from his hand.
"I drew it right after I touched the fragment Rusalka brought back. I wasn't even aware that I was doing it. Just looked down at the paper and there it was."
"I see," Querius said.
He brought the paper up to his eye and examined it closer.
"My memory is growling, Ranger."
"Excuse me?"
"It's a Jahlder expression. My absorbsion panels can sense something blurred. I recognize this tree, I'm sure of it. In a book, in a photograph. Somewhere. I just can't recall it. The memorial equivalent of a word on the tip of my tongue. Don't worry, I'll find it. Perhaps Krakk can help me."
"Where is Krakk anyway?" Elizabeth said.
"Working on a side project. I encouraged him to do so, I feel keeping a mind occupied

normally means it behaves when you really need it. I myself am working on a miniature turret to attach to your bracelets. I discussed the project with Lavell first and she was quite excited by the idea. I would not have continued my augmentation if the original inventor did not agree with it."

"That sounds useful. And important. Do you want me to go and find Krakk, give you an extra pair of hands?"

"Krakk was a slave his entire life. I do not wish to subject him to that once more for my own gains."

"Does he talk about it?" Elizabeth asked.

"Krakk is a pistachio, Ranger."

She suppressed a chuckle, "Is that another Jahlder expression?"

"Oh. I believed it to be Human."

"Do you maybe mean he's 'a tough nut to crack', Querius?"

"No. That doesn't quite fit," Querius said, raising a pondering hand to his chin.

"Well that pistachio thing's a new one on me."

"Some days he shares a little, some days a lot. Some days nothing at all. Maybe he would share more if I pried, but I don't like to."

"Sounds like you make quite the team. Keep me updated on your turret design, I'm sure it'll come in handy. A girl never can have too many toys."

"The upgrade itself it rather simple, it's the attaching it to the already saturated foldaway compartments on the bracelet that is proving the stumbling block. But I will find a way, Ranger. Have no fear."

"I don't doubt it. But the main focus is that tree, understand? See if Krakk can help out with your growling memory when he gets back."

"Of course, Ranger. Of course."

Querius nodded his goodbyes as Elizabeth closed the door behind her.

Ana

Serpe's condition was slowing improving. Ana spent the next few days in the Med Bay, but the nights by Elizabeth's side. She took her pain killers in secret while she worked. Her skin was still tender under Elizabeth's touch.

Ana turned off the anesthetic that had been flooding Serpe's body. After a while, her eyes opened slowly like a rusted gate. She yawned, stretching out her dried lips. Ana heard the skin around her mouth crackle. Serpe lifted her hand to her chin and ran a finger down the thick, crisscrossed stitching that held her face together.
"That's not healed yet," Ana said, moving Serpe's hand away.
Serpe stared straight at her for a moment. Ana watched her pupils dilate, adapting to the light. A good sign. Clarity returned and Serpe recognized her.
"What's the damage?"
"That facial injury for starters, but I would say you got off lightly. And I don't know if you recall, but you stepped in a bear trap."
"A bear... I don't remember that," Serpe said.
"Your leg has healed a lot better than hoped. You'll need some physiotherapy, but there shouldn't be any permanent effects."
"How long before my leg is up to full strength?"
"It's difficult to say at this point. I've been working on an injection that helps numb pain receptors while strengthening muscle damage. Pharmakon. It will help you exercise without pain so you can heal your leg faster. Once your stitches are set more I'll give you a daily shot of it."
"Give me a mirror," Serpe said.
Ana took out her compact, surprised at Serpe's vanity. Serpe held it close to her chin, studying the handiwork of the stitching.
"Impressive work, Miss Yukishnov. How long until they need undarning?" Serpe asked.
"I'd recommend four days for them to heal fully. But you needn't praise me. I was injured too. It was Lavell who treated you."
The mirror came crashing down on the side of the bed, showering sharp flakes of glass around the Med Bay.
"You let that Jahlder touch me!?"
"Technically, I was unconscious," Ana said.

Serpe hadn't heard her. She was already in a fury. Her mouth frothed as her finger tensed around the poles of the bed, rattling the frame. She swiped her hand to her chin, clawing until the stitches tore. Chunks of flesh were scratched away. Dark blood sprayed from her fingertips as she tossed the thread aside.

Ana rifled manically through the cabinet drawers. She searched for a needle with a strong enough dose to knock Serpe out. As it plunged into Serpe's neck, she almost fell over the side of the bed. Ana propped her back up and daubed a pad in antiseptic gel. She wiped it across Serpe's freshly torn open skin, washing away the blood and scabs, preparing the mangled skin to be re-stitched.

Lavell

Down in the Mess Hall, Lavell poured hard candy into a bowl. She picked out her favourite colours and ate them first. Forr was in the gym, working on his hand to hand combat. On the flight to Purple 24 Roka had mentioned he used to be a boxing coach, and Forr had since enlisted his help. Elizabeth had not been to the gym since they had returned from the last mission.

She tipped her last of the sugary sweets into her mouth. Nyomee walked by holding a tray and Lavell waved her over. The Human's golden eyes widened in distrustful surprise.
"Hello," she said cautiously.
Lavell looked down at Nyomee's plate. There were two turkey legs, bones crossed and meat glistening with grease. It looked a big meal for such a small Human.
"I thought you might want some company," Lavell said.
Nyomee picked up one of the legs and bit into the meat, tearing it from the bone. The crisp skin dropped back onto the plate in shreds.
"I'm used to isolation. It's how I lived back home," Nyomee said while chewing.
She wiped at her chin with her forearm, taking away the grease but leaving a smear of grime behind.
"Was it always that way?"
"It used to be better. Simpler."
Lavell focused her absorbsion panels as Nyomee spoke. She had told the truth, so far.
"How did it use to be?"
Nyomee took another chomp of the meat, slurping it away from the bone.
"We were a self-sufficient society. Farmed, raised livestock, things like that."
"What changed?"
"It just couldn't stay like that. Power struggles started. A harsh winter killed off a lot of people and raised tensions among the survivors."
Lavell could sense something, but she wasn't sure what.
"That's why you left?" she asked.
"Yes," Nyomee said.
Lavell's panels started to twitch, but she didn't need them to know Nyomee was lying. She was staring down at her plate, pushing the bones around with the backs of her fingers.
"There's more to it," Lavell said, leading her.
Nyomee looked up and let out a heavy sigh.

"They were the catalyst for why I had to leave."
"What happened?"
"You must understand, many people came to escape the rest of the galaxy. It was a fabled place, its existence whispered of with weak hope. I did not flee there. I was raised there, and my grandparents simply sought the peace it promised. But several people were driven there through fear. Then Yerin was invaded."
"Who invaded you? Another city?"
"We have no other cities. That's why everyone felt so secure. Until a Krei ship landed outside our walls."
"The Krei invaded Purple 24? Why were they even there?"
"As a Jahlder, it's only natural that you would associate the Krei with butchery and bloodshed. But these people were not conquerors. They were refugees."
"I don't understand," Lavell said.
"They had heard the whispers. All they wanted was to be safe. But they weren't Human, so…"
Nyomee looked down, burying chin in chest. Lavell touched her hand.
"Our leaders shot them. The unarmed, the innocent, the young. Gunned down to preserve our perfect peace. How could I be part of a society that would do that to people who only wanted safety and shelter?"
"It must have been horrible."
Her grip tightened and Nyomee recoiled.
"Sorry," Lavell said.
"I left that night."
"So why join us?"
"When Yerin was good, my people told stories of the Fire."
"The what?"
"Elizabeth Ranger touched it and lives. I was told a great person would survive the Fire, and I was taught that great people are good, at heart. I am here to aid your quest, and to redeem my own soul," Nyomee said.
"That's a very noble aim."
"Thank you for offering me your company, Lavell. I hope that next time we can choose a lighter topic for discussion."

Querius

Querius' memory continued to growl for days. He had never physically stood in the tree's presence, that much he had figured out. He continued to tinker with his turret upgrade, hoping to settle his mind. So far the answer had not come.

"Try this, Krakk," Querius said, handing him a bracelet.
Krakk strapped it around the girth of his wrist. Querius guided him over to a long glass tube, just wide enough for Krakk to fit his arm inside. There was a dense blue gel at the far end, about a foot and a half away from Krakk's fist.
"Will the ballistic gel be strong enough, Doctor?"
"The turret is only loaded with pellets, not bullets. This test is just to see if the trigger can withstand the strength of your grip. Forr's bionic limb offers the same level of pressure."

Krakk grabbed the trigger. The mini turret fired three rounds into the blue goo before it snapped under the strain.
"Fantastic!" Querius shouted as the pellets hit the ballistic gel.
"The trigger broke, Doctor," Krakk said.
"What? Oh, that can be fixed, that can be fixed. No! The tree! Ranger's fucking tree!"
"You've remembered?"
"My books! My fucking books!"

Querius frantically pushed aside the equipment on his desk until it spilled on the floor with a metallic crash.
"Your textbooks are in those drawers," Krakk said, pointing.
Querius raced over and yanked open the top drawer, flinging books aside. They landed on the ground, covers splayed and pages creased. Eventually he found the right one, slamming its bright green cover down on the desk. He skimmed the pages wildly.
"There!"
His finger tore the page as he pointed to one of the photographs. There was a mass of fine print page taking up the entire right leaf, but the left page was covered in a large, glossy picture of a tree. Its trunk was hooked over and crooked, its roots fat. They stretched down the hillside. It matched the drawing perfectly.
"Tupurs. It's a small planet not too far from the Jahlder homeworld, Herso. I once wrote a study on the small worms that inhabit its terrain. Visited the planet but never saw this tree. Read this book extensively. The page, the image, it must have gotten stuck in my memory. Rather ironic."
"Ironic?" Krakk asked, picking up the mess.
"The worms I studied. They had a nasty habit of boring into skulls, trapping themselves inside," Querius said with a smile.
"I don't understand."
"That's exactly what my memory did."
Krakk stared at him for a second.

"Should I input Tupurs's co-ordinates into the ship's computer?"

"Yes, yes, Donovan will need them. I'll radio Ranger and let her know we've found her tree."

Querius ran his finger rapidly across the text, soaking up the information once more.

"Oh no. Oh no, this won't do," Querius said.

"Doctor?"

Krakk stopped searching the grip map for Tupurs and glanced over.

"Yes, yes. I remember why I have not seen this tree now. When I visit planets I like to explore them, have the feeling that my feet have touched every blade of grass on its surface. I thought maybe this was not the case with Tupurs because I was younger, obsessed with my work. No time for leisure, back then. That is not the reason. Tupurs has a forbidden zone, a small palace guarded by marching guards. Interestingly, this is a mixed race army, a quite unusual concept for an organized security outfit. Bands of mercenaries, yes, but –"

"Interesting maybe, but worrying for Captain and her crew," Krakk interrupted.

"Hm? Oh, of course, of course. I'll be sure to notify her of the impending hostile forces."

"I've located Tupurs, Doctor. Now I need the specific location of the tree on the planet's surface."

Querius ran his hand to the bottom of the page, examining the small print.

"Oh dear. It doesn't appear to say."

"Can you figure it out?"

"I haven't done this in a long while," Querius said, laying his hands on the paper.

He was about to focus his absorbsion panels when he noticed the tear. He smoothed it down with his palm then splayed his hand across the page. His absorbsion panels drank the information in. Giddy knowledge flooded him. He lifted his hand away from the book and took a handkerchief from his pocket, blotting away beads of sweat.

"Did you find them, Doctor?"

"Yes," he said with a weak smile.

He walked over to the map and typed in the co-ordinates.

Ana

Querius rushed into their quarters. Ana grabbed the sheet and pulled it up to her neck to hide her body. Elizabeth sat up, nakedness on display.

He was rambling and Ana wasn't listening. Trapping the raised quilt with one arm, she leaned out of bed. There was a t-shirt just out of reach. She stretched but it was still too far. Her fingers tiptoed across the floor. Querius hadn't paused for breath. She kept her eyes on him as she rolled on her side and was finally able to grab it. She pressed it into Elizabeth's hands but Elizabeth shook her away.
"I'm trying to listen, Ana."
"Jahlder remember *everything* they see," Ana whispered.
Querius's voice stopped.
"Thanks for the info, Querius," Elizabeth said.
"Yes, well. I'll leave you ladies to it."
Querius turned and left, closing the door quietly.

"Do you think he heard me?" Ana asked.
"Probably not," Elizabeth said, tossing the shirt back on to the floor.
"I just didn't want him looking at you."
"Jealous?"
"That photographic memory... don't you think it's creepy?"
"Do you think Lavell's creepy?" Elizabeth asked.
"I wouldn't let her see me naked."
Elizabeth just laughed.
"So did you hear any of that, or were you too concerned with protecting my modesty?"
"Sorry for caring, I guess," Ana said.
"Aww, don't be like that Princess," Elizabeth kissed her forehead.
"You don't think that was weird? Him barging here like that?"
"He's a weird guy. Tell you what. From now on, only you see me naked. Promise."
Ana looked at her. The mischievous grin. The wry eyebrows. Her irritation melted.
"He knows where the tree is?"
"Tupurs. I'll keep the brief short tomorrow. Don't want to give people a chance to interrupt like last time."
"No. Tonight's interruption was rude enough, wasn't it?"
"You're still mad?"
Ana didn't answer.
"Let me make it up to you?"
"... How?"
Elizabeth smiled. Ana let the quilt drop away from her body.

~*~

Elizabeth had not lied about keeping it short.

"We'll travel on two shuttles but land together. We'll only split if we absolutely need to. Gives us safety in numbers. I don't want a repeat of last time."

"It only took *one* of us last time. Just, for the record," Rusalka said.

Ana shushed her.

"Tupurs forbidden zone isn't a secret, but it's got even better protection. It's low key. Everybody knows about it but nobody cares," Elizabeth said.

Serpe stumbled into the room, holding onto the doorframe for support.

"I'm coming on the mission," she said.

She placed no weight on her injured leg.

"You shouldn't be walking yet," Ana said.

"I'm not here to lie in bed bleeding."

Serpe ripped the bandage on her face. Underneath was ripped flesh and zigzag stitches.

"What happened to your stitches?" Lavell said.

"I replaced them," Ana said.

"With a hacksaw?" Forr asked.

"I tore them out. I will not be soiled by Jahlder, unlike you," Serpe said coldly. Her fiery eyes were fixed on Lavell.

"I'm really not in the mood to get involved in all this Jahlder Krei shit, but you can't walk," Elizabeth said, "I don't think we'll have any volunteers to carry you around Tupurs, so you'll have to sit this one out."

Serpe took a deep breath, seething in.

"Miss Yukishnov has an injection she can give me."

Elizabeth turned to her. Ana felt her skin glowing hot.

"That's... that's not quite what I said."

Sweat was starting to roll down Serpe's cheek. It trickled down her stitches, dripping onto the floor. Her fingers gripped tighter on the doorframe.

"A pain suppressor. That strengthens muscle. You told me it was ready."

Serpe was starting to slump against the wall.

"Is that true?" Elizabeth asked.

"For physiotherapy! It would be used in a controlled environment, for –"

"Would it work?" Elizabeth interrupted.

"It's been tested extensively. It was designed to allow injuries to heal without the restriction of a pain barrier."

"So if you gave it to Serpe, how long before she could stand up straight?"

"Almost instant."

"And run?"

"Ten minutes," Ana said.

"Go get it. The rest of you, armoury then hangar. You know the drill by now. I'll stay here and get Serpe up to speed."

Once everyone had left, Ana helped Serpe to a chair. Serpe wrapped a reluctant arm across her shoulders.
"Thank you for your faith, Captain."
Elizabeth lifted Serpe's leg up onto a stool to take the weight off, but let it crash down from an inch above.
"Let me make one thing damn clear. I don't like you. Not even a little bit. And if I suspect that you're working an angle with Forr, you'll be out the airlock without a spacesuit," Elizabeth said, "But I anyone who crawls out of bed with a broken leg so they can fight by my side is all right in my book."

Ana left to get the serum. Elizabeth and Serpe were sat in silence when she returned. When she told Serpe about the pharmakon, she'd hoped Serpe would field test it for her, although she would have preferred it not to be on such a crucial mission. It *had* been extensively tested, but only on rats.

Ana held the syringe up. A shining light glinted off the sharp tip of the needle.
"Does it have to be so big?" Serpe asked.
"Krei have the thickest skin of anyone in the galaxy. For a Human it could be half the length, maybe less," Ana said.
She ran her finger down Serpe's thigh in search a vein.
Eventually she found one just above the knee. She rubbed at the skin to make the vein pop out. Serpe looked away as Ana pierced the needle through the skin, tensing her ragged jaw.
"Do you want to hold my hand?" Elizabeth asked.
Serpe glared at her.

Ana thumbed down the plunger. Serpe gritted her teeth as the pharmakon flowed into her.
"Has it worked?" Serpe asked after a few seconds.
Elizabeth punched her in the knee.
"You feel that?"
Serpe felt down her leg, scratching at the skin.
"That's incredible," she said.
"Put your weight on it," Ana suggested.
Serpe cautiously put her foot on the floor and stood slowly, pulling herself upright against the chair.
"How long will it last?"
"I can't be sure of that. You'll use it up faster in combat, with a higher heartrate. I'll take extra doses out with us."
"I'd like a word with Forr before we depart," she said to Elizabeth.
"Make it quick."

Forr

Forr looked over as Serpe entered the hangar. She no longer propped herself against the wall. She walked tall. Her eyes found his, summoning him over.
"Give me a minute," he said to Lavell.

Serpe led Forr into a dark alcove behind her docked shuttle. The scent of leaking oil hung in the air. The shadows were cold and damp.
"Your whore lays hands on me again, and I'll kill her. It sickens me that I am weak enough to warn her."
Serpe spat on the ground.
"You hurt her and our deal is off," he said.
Her hand rose and cradled his cheek.
"Our deal? You make it sound so trivial. It's what we need."
"It's what you want!" he shouted.
Serpe slapped him, hard across the cheek she had been cradling. His metal hand rubbed his sore skin.
"An heir. A Harkrak of my blood would be worthy of the title."
"You'll get it. To keep her safe."
"That Jahlder has made you soft, but I see that you are strong. Stay on Excha. With me."
She reached for his bleeding lip but he shoved her back.
"My exile meant nothing to me. You are everything I hate about our race," he snarled.
Elizabeth stepped around the corner into the alcove.
"Whatever shit you've got going on I need you to hit the pause button until we get back," she said.

She led them back to the group and split them between the two shuttles. Lavell, Elizabeth and Ana would be on his shuttle.
"Oh, and Rusalka? I meant what I said. You abandon us again and you'll be wearing those knives on your insides."
"Well, now that your ego's been sufficiently boosted by that show, Elizabeth, I suppose we should leave."
Lavell stuck close to Forr as they climbed up the steps to the ship. She rubbed at his back, running her fingertips across the soft fur that peeked above his armour. He looked down at her and tried to force a smile, but he did not speak.
"Is everything okay?" she asked.

"It's fine."

"You can talk to me, you know."

"It's nothing," he said with a hard edge, but Lavell would not let go.

"My lion. I don't like to see you wounded."

She stroked the side of his face, the same place Serpe had slapped. The skin was still tender. Her touch stung. He winced through it and did not move away.

"You don't need to worry," he told her.

"We're a team. When you worry, I worry."

Forr kissed her forehead with dry lips.

"Serpe wants me to return to Excha after this mission."

"Why?"

"To fulfil my Harkrak duty. She wants me to pass the honour onto her family in a ceremony."

"Are you going?"

Forr ran his hand through Lavell's smooth white hair. She stared up at him.

"I told her no," Forr said, "I told I would not go back to Excha, that I was happy to see the Harkrak line disappear."

"You said that?"

"I love you. And nothing can ever make me hurt you."

A lot of things happened on Excha that made him hate himself. A lot of doubts, a lot of regrets. He had never hated himself more than right now.

Elizabeth

Elizabeth rushed over to the shuttle window.
"Roka, you see that?"
"I see her. Should I engage?"
A third ship heading for Tupurs. It looked Human in design, but other than that Elizabeth knew nothing about it. She was wary of starting fights in shadows.
"I don't mean to question your masculinity Roka, but I can see from here they've got a bigger package than we do."
"It's not all about size."
"Touch a nerve, Roka? They're faster than us too. And I'm not about to attack a stranger with two known advantages. Keep a lookout but do not fire unless fired upon. And radio Mogg to tell him the same. Isoline, Rusalka and Serpe are all on his ship with itchy trigger fingers."
"Will do," he said.
"Is there another ship out there?" Lavell asked, head resting on Forr's chest.
"Yeah. But we're not in The Barely Charted now, we're back in the Known Systems and traffic isn't gonna be uncommon. Their LZ doesn't look like its near ours so it doesn't change the mission."

Roka began his descent. There was a dense forest off to the east, one that would provide them with cover while they approached the crooked tree. Shelter not just from the guards, but from the fierce rain that rattled against the shuttle. Roka opened the shuttle door and the wind attacked. It was a bitterly cold gale, spraying icy rain against Elizabeth's blue jacket. The tails whipped around her legs as she walked down onto the wet turf. Clods of dirt swirled up in the downpour.
"Get over to those trees!" Elizabeth shouted against the whistling gust.

The world was quiet under the canopy of the forest. Stray raindrops fell through cracks in the green ceiling. The crew of Mogg's shuttle caught up to them.
"Why did you order Mogg not to fire on that ship?" Rusalka asked.
"They were bigger than us and faster than us. Those were the two main reasons. The third was the fact they were innocent and meant us no harm, clearly. But I'm not sure that one matters to you."
"Don't fool yourself that you know me, Elizabeth. I'm better than you at what you do, and if you need to give yourself a reason for that, make me into some amoral monster that you would hate to be."
"The unknown ship dropped something," Isoline said, cutting them off.
"Like what?" Ana said.
Her voice was skittish. Elizabeth needed calm.
"Quite possibly a bomb," Isoline said.
"I didn't see anything."
"No, you wouldn't have. I imagine your shuttle was blindsided to it."
"Well, anyone on Isoline's ship see anything?" Elizabeth asked.
Rusalka, Serpe and Nyomee all shook their heads. Rusalka's was curt and angry,

avoiding eye contact. Brack was the only other passenger on Mogg's shuttle. He hunched, shrinking under the weight of eyes on him.

"I... I think I might have seen something, yes."

Elizabeth's heart dropped. He was lying for her. He was pathetic, submitting to Isoline's every word. He was a man with passion in his veins but she had bled him dry.

"Where did it land?"

"Judging –" Isoline started.

Elizabeth raised her palm to stop the words dead.

"I'm asking him."

Elizabeth stepped forward, toe to toe with Brack. He tried to turn his face away, avoiding looking into her eyes.

"Where did it land, Brack?"

"I couldn't say for sure, Elizabeth."

"You're lying."

"It landed –"

Another palm stopped Isoline's answer.

"Mission continues as planned. We head east until we see a clearing."

The storm carried her hair across her face and she turned away.

"Help!"

A high-pitched shriek came through all their bracelets at once. A cacophony of static smothered the scream. Rusalka and Nyomee covered their ears.

"Who was that?" Nyomee asked.

The screaming started up again. Elizabeth flicked her com link to mute and the rest of them followed. Rusalka was leaning against one of the mossy tree trunks, doubled over, fingers rubbing at her forehead.

"It was a Human. Female, late twenties," Rusalka said.

"You can tell all that?" Ana asked.

"How could we hear it? Does the Jahlder not know how to create a closed frequency?" Serpe said.

"This is exactly why I kept it open. So we could hear a distress call that broadcasted on all frequencies. We have to rescue them, Elizabeth."

"Typical Jahlder. We have a mission. We will not desert it in aid of some Human who has fallen down a hole."

"Saving a life must come first. Your callousness is the reason the Krei will never defeat the Jahlder," Lavell said.

Serpe raised her arm to strike and Lavell cowered, eyes squeezed closed. Elizabeth's pistol pressed against the blue skin of Serpe's temple, stopping the slap.

"You do that and my respect for you drops back down to zero. I already told you I don't like you, and I tend to make rash decisions when I'm pointing a gun at people I neither like nor respect."

Serpe's hand lowered with a stiff robotic creak. Elizabeth moved her gun away slowly.

"My point remains valid. We must continue the mission," Serpe said.

"Help!" the crying came again, "Our ship crashed. We have children!"
Ana's wrist, still screaming. She jostled, flustered, to mute the calls for help.
"Children, Elizabeth! There can be no debate, we have to help them. No mission comes before that," Lavell said.
"Can you locate them remotely?" Elizabeth asked.
"The com link can track the source of the distress signal."
"This is an unacceptable tangent, Ranger. We have a mission," Serpe said.
"Tangent? We're talking about the lives of the young!" Nyomee said.
Isoline stepped in front of Nyomee, nose upturned.
"Why don't you get a wash? The lives of strangers are always expendable. That unidentified ship changes everything. This mission may very well have a time limit now."
"We're saving the kids," Elizabeth said.
"I believe that this fragment holds great importance, even if you seem to have forgotten it yourself. I will be heading onwards as planned," Isoline said.
"As will I. Mission comes first," Serpe added.
"Do what you like. Neither of you were actually invited here," Elizabeth said, turning to face the rest of the group, "Anyone who has a soul and wants to save some scared little kids, raise your hand."
Ana and Lavell's hands shot up, followed quickly by Forr and Nyomee's. A hand ballot felt trivial, but what else was she do to? Isoline was right about the time limit. It was her priorities that were wrong. Every second they wasted was a second they could have spent finding the stranded children.

Rusalka stood nonchalant with her back against a tree, cape brushed aside. She tossed one of her knives into the air and watched it turn, catching it effortlessly by the handle and pitching it upwards again.
"Rusalka?" Ana asked, hand still raised.
"Sorry sweetie. If I gave my help to everyone who asked for it, I'd own a lot less stuff by now. I suppose your moral read on me was correct, Elizabeth. Congratulations."
"Didn't doubt it for a second."
"You can't be serious," Ana said.
"She's made her decision, Ana. That just leaves you, Brack," Elizabeth said.

Again, all eyes turned to him. Again he wilted under their weight. Elizabeth was not about to lose this one. Pitying how much his spirit had been pulverized under Isoline's thumb was one thing, but the Brack Harganagan she once knew did not turn his back on suffering children. She put her hand on his shoulder, drawing him slightly away from the group, hoping it might sever Isoline's spell over him. Her soft palm ruffled its way across his sharp scales.
"Look at me, Brack," she said.
His eyes were dim, almost extinguished. Distrust was in them now, maybe even a trace of fear.
"You heard those screams, same as I did. You know we can't leave those children to die."

"Isoline has a point –"
Elizabeth clamped her hands either side of Brack's face.
"That's not how we do things. You know that. Hell you *taught* me that! Please, Brack. Please. I need you on this one."
He jerked his head away from her, his pointed skin tearing the flesh on her hands.
"I'm sorry, Elizabeth. But we came here to get that fragment, and the longer we wait the more chance we lose it. It's important."
Elizabeth crashed her head forward against his skull, drawing a slice of blood as he crumpled to his knees.

Forr dragged Elizabeth away. She put up no struggle as he guided her back.
"He says he's not coming," Elizabeth said.
Forr's hands let go of Elizabeth's arms. Now he needed to be held back, pushing Brack back to the ground as he struggled to his feet.
"Who even are you now?" Forr growled.
Brack squirmed backwards.
"You died, Elizabeth! I lost you! What was I supposed to do?"
Isoline draped her arm around his shoulders and led him away.
"We both died these past three years," Elizabeth said, "At least I had the decency to come back."

Those continuing the mission skulked away. The rest of them huddled around while Lavell tweaked her bracelet with a tiny screwdriver. A nearby tree had fallen recently, a wet stench from the torn up soil floated around them. Dirt dripped from the strong, spiraling roots like dark teardrops. Ana swabbed Brack's blood away from Elizabeth's forehead. Her head was fine but her hands were shredded. Loose thin strips of skin hung from her palms. A slow breeze snuck through the trees and stung. The fierce gale outside of the forest would be torture.
"You still got that salve?" Elizabeth asked Ana.
"Always carry a few vials."

Ana flicked a release catch and the vials popped out of her hips, fanning out like a peacock's plumage. She massaged the gel onto Elizabeth's injured palm softly. Hurting meant healing. Ana pecked Elizabeth's cheek.
"I don't need a kiss better."
"Sorry. I just thought… after Brack."
"Don't," Elizabeth told her.
Ana looked down sadly. Elizabeth kissed her forehead then turned to the group.

"Alright, we need to move quickly people. Lavell, you found them yet?"
"No exact location. The trees are interfering with the tracker. But I can give you a compass reading. Judging from the signal strength it's not far from here."
"It'll have to do," Elizabeth said, offering her wrist to Lavell.
Lavell ignored it, keying a command into her own bracelet.
"That's fine. I've sent the reading to all of our bracelets. Including the rest of them, in case they decide to turn back."

"I wouldn't count on that," Elizabeth said.

"You sure you're okay?" Forr asked her.

"If you need a moment to compose yourself, we can take the time," Ana said.

"No, we fucking can't, Ana. There are children out here dying, and we've already wasted enough time because those four assholes don't think their lives are worth anything. So we *don't* have time to take a minute so you can all hold my hand and braid my hair and tell me how Brack's not worth it anymore. Because believe me, I fucking know that! Understand?"

Ana nodded back meekly. Elizabeth saw the same haunting stare of fear she had just seen in Brack's.

"I'm sorry, Princess," Elizabeth said, tracing her fingertips through Ana's blonde hair, "I'm sorry. But we do need to find those kids soon."

Ana's lips curved up into a smile that trembled.

Their bracelets told them to head north. Nyomme scooped up water from a puddle. She rubbed it over her face and hands until they were clean. She dried them against her knees, then grabbed at a low tree branch and swung herself up on top of it. She used the branches above as rungs on a ladder.

"I can see a good distance from this height. I'll send a com back and ask them where they are."

"Good idea," Elizabeth shouted up.

Nyomee turned her com link off mute and spoke into it.

"We're coming to rescue you. Do you know where you are?"

"Help!"

Elizabeth heard the screams, even on the ground.

"Can you see anything that might help us to find you? A distinctive tree, a carved rock, anything?"

"Our ship crashed. We have children!"

Their words had an aching hopelessness.

"We'll get all of them to safety. You as well, but we need to find you. Try and –"

"Help!"

"She's hysterical. You might as well come back down, Nyomee. The woman's probably in shock," Elizabeth shouted up.

"Is anyone injured? We have medical supplies."

"Our ship crashed. We have children!"

"Leave it, Nyomee," Elizabeth hollered.

Nyomee swung back down, weaving through the branches with grace.

"Why didn't she answer me?"

"The children she's with are probably her own. She'll be in shock. She may even have a head injury. It's possible that with her hysteria and concussion she just didn't hear you, all she can do is scream the same three sentences out over and over and hope that someone hears them," Lavell said.

"We need to find them fast," Elizabeth said.

Leaves crunched underfoot as they followed the noise of the compass. The beeping grew louder and faster as they approached the signal's source. The storm faded,

carrying the smell of sweet, dark rain. The beeps were almost a continuous hum now. There was a steep slope only a few footsteps away that ran into a deep trench.
"They must have landed down there," Elizabeth said.
A small furry creature lay in the dirt. It was a marpus, a ratlike creature with long claws and a puffy tail. Its fur was a matted and mangy brown, teeth encrusted with green. Glassy eyes stared up at the sky, tiny neck twisted and broken. Shrapnel and wreckage were littered around the corpse.
"Poor little guy," Lavell said, scooping orange leaves over him.
"Maybe he fell out of the tree when the ship crashed," Forr said.
"The ugly squirrel can wait," Ana said as she started to carefully slide down the bank.
The soft mud was slippery underfoot. They all descended backwards, hands pressed against the wet earth. All except for Nyomee, who slid down as if surfing.

The path down the hill led to a winding cavern. A thick stone arch cast a black shadow inside its cold walls.
"Think they're in there?" Forr said, peering into the dark.
"Some wreckage here, but no ship," Elizabeth said.
Lavell's eyes roamed around the edge of the cave, "A ship would have to be very small to fit inside there. Hardly a trace out here."
"Maybe it wasn't a full ship. Just an escape pod," Ana said.
"Torches on," Elizabeth said, "They must be close now."
The light from her wrist cast a wide beam with a soft glow. Lavell had learned from Olivia's mistake on Allke. The torches illuminated the cave without disturbing the wildlife. Bats hung from the grooves in the grotto's roof. Their short, curved ears stretched shadows of sharp knives, but they did not murmur as the light beams flashed across them. The air was colder, the walls more damp with every step.
"Hello?" Elizabeth called into the darkness.
She strained her ear to hear a reply. There was nothing but the muted splintering of moist, rotting twigs. Then call came back. The same hopeless shouting.
"Help!"

They quickened their pace, running as they ducked under the bats.
"Our ship crashed. We have children!"
"They're very close," Lavell said.
"Can't be. Screams aren't loud enough yet."
"I feel it, Elizabeth. Very close."
Lavell moved her torch to the ground, looking for a sign of them.
"Help!" the voice said again.
"We can barely hear them, Lavell. You're off this time."
"How often does that happen?" Forr asked, "Something feels wrong, Elizabeth. They aren't answering. And why would a hysterical woman and her scared children take shelter in a cave full of bats?"
"People do strange things when they're scared. We just need to find them."
"Eek!"
Elizabeth turned around to see Ana on the floor, face smeared in a streak of dirt.

She offered a hand to help her up.
"You okay, Princess?"
Ana wiped the wet clod of muck from her cheek and looked behind her.
"I think my foot got caught on something."
Elizabeth shone her torch at Ana's feet, expecting to see a rogue root or tough rope of vine. Instead a shining glimmer reflected back her, bright enough to make her squint.
"What is that?" Ana said.
"Careful," Forr warned her.
Ana felt around its shape while Elizabeth coated it in torchlight. It was a small metal box, its surface scratched and scuffed. She picked it up slowly, blowing crumbs of dirt off. She scored around the edge, searching for a catch or lip to remove the lid.
"I can't open it," she said.

Elizabeth gestured for the box to be given to her. Ana passed it and she turned it over in her hands. Something inside rattled as she shook it.
"Help!"
The shouting was louder now.
"Did you hear that?" Elizabeth said.
"Maybe they're coming towards us," Lavell said.
Elizabeth stroked her hand across the top of the metal box and felt a ridged dome.
"Someone light this up for me?"
Ana and Lavell sent two beams across the box. In the soft glow, Elizabeth could see clearly. The ridged dome was a grille, set inside a chrome ring raised up from the metal box.
"Our ship crashed. We have children!"
Elizabeth lifted the grille to her ear. It crackled weakly.
"Is something inside?" Ana asked.
"Help!"
It screeched in Elizabeth's ear. She recoiled from the sudden noise.
"What's wrong?" Nyomee said.
"I don't understand," Ana said, staring at the box in Elizabeth's hand as it continued to beg for help.
"It's a damn radio!"
Elizabeth hurled it at the wall. The box shattered with a fizz of dying static. Overhead the bats cawed, their leathery wings flapping wildly as they collided in their desperate escape. Elizabeth felt their wet fur fly past her, their clammy wings whipping through her hair. Ana and Lavell shrieked, swatting at the passing vermin. The sprayed lightbeams from their flailing arms allowed her to see Nyomee. The girl was standing in the centre of the cave, arms spread wide and head tilted up. Eyes closed in bliss. One swooping bat became entangled in Nyomee's long messy hair, but her face remained without a trace of panic. It struggled and squawked, wings and feet kicking. Her hands moved up to her hair and delicately parted her tangled locks until the creature was free to race after its brothers. She let out a sad sigh once the bats were past, disappointed that the experience was over.

"Are they gone?" Ana asked, a tentative quake in her voice.

"You can open your eyes now," Forr told her.

She was shaking. Forr offered her his hand to hold but she could not stop herself from collapsing into his chest. Lavell rubbed a kind hand across her back.

"It's okay now. You're okay," he told her.

"None of us are okay!" Elizabeth shouted.

Elizabeth's voice echoed through the eerie silence. Ana stood to attention.

"How did this happen, Lavell?" Elizabeth asked.

"Whoever put the radio here must have set it to transmit on all frequencies. It was a trap, to lure someone here."

"But who would go to the trouble of creating a phony distress call? The signal wasn't strong enough to go off world," Forr said.

Elizabeth slammed her fist against the cave wall, leaving her hand cut and bloodied.

"Elizabeth!"

Ana rushed forward.

"They were right! They were fucking right."

"Don't do that again. You'll break your hand."

Ana poured more salve over Elizabeth's fresh cuts.

"Who were?" Lavell said.

"Isoline!" Elizabeth shouted, wincing as the salve got to work.

"The package from the ship," Forr said, "The shrapnel."

"That ship's after the fragment, and it wanted us out of the way. We have to get over there, now!"

"How did anyone know we were coming?" Ana asked.

"We can figure that out later. All that matters now is we have to get there before it's too late."

Brack

Brack's blood trickled down through his scales, dripping in front of his eyes. He had wanted to support Elizabeth. It was far nobler to save an innocent child than it was to follow orders. But he could not shake off the notion that the pursuit of the fragment was the right thing to do, regardless of what the others might think.
"What's that noise?" Serpe sniffed the crisp air.
A high-pitched buzz every few seconds. Rusalka toggled a switch on her bracelet and the noise became quieter.
"It's these," she told everyone, "They're trying to guilt us into turning back by adding the co-ordinates to our compass."
A wave of sadness hit Brack as he switched his to mute.

"We should go this way around," Isoline said.
There was a landslide blocking the obvious straight route. They could climb the grassy peak to higher ground or to delve even deeper into the undergrowth of sharp, twisted vines. Isoline was in favor of the descent. Brack agreed.
"Height in battle is always an advantage," Serpe said.
"Not if it gives away your position too early," Isoline told her.
"If only our great, benevolent dictator was here to guide us," Rusalka said airily.
"With our numbers reduced, remaining undetected is now imperative. Low ground is our only option," Isoline said.
Serpe yielded with a short nod. She had begun to favor her left leg. The effects of Ana's serum were wearing off.

They waded through the weeds, slashing at the fat stalks to strip the shrubs.
"Elizabeth would have chosen higher ground," Rusalka said.
"You had the choice to stay with her," Isoline said.
"Oh, I agree that down is the way to go. I don't like to be spotted. I'm shy."
"Is everything a joke to you?" Serpe asked as she sliced through the saplings.
"Elizabeth's problem is that she thinks being in charge of a few thieves is enough for her to play military commander," Rusalka said.
"Exactly," Isoline said.
"Finally, a thing we can agree on," Serpe said.
"What about you Brack? You must have some stories about her."
Rusalka sheathed her blade and turned to him.
"Well, of course back then, we *were* just a few thieves."
"Still. I bet it was her way or no way," Rusalka said.
His eyes made a quick dart to Isoline.
"I suppose. But then, her way did make us all very rich."
"She's a snake, Brack," Isoline said.
She spun to face him too. Wet mush of dark leaves dribbled from her blade.
"She worms her way in where she's not wanted, grabs all she can, then slithers back out. She's a snake, Brack," she repeated, "Isn't she?"
He wriggled his balance from one foot to another. Rusalka eyes. Isoline's fixed stare. He was an ant trying to avoid the fire from two different magnifying glasses, unsure where one flame ended and the other began.
"That is a rather accurate description of what we did, yes."
"She kept things from you," Rusalka told him.
"Things? What things?"
"*Material* things. She considered herself leader of your little gang. You don't think

she felt entitled to a bigger cut of the score?"
"I had my own little trove as well."
"You deserved those things, my love," Isoline said.
She stepped forward and cupped his face in one hand. The other held the knife. Her thumb snagged on the crust of dried blood as she stroked his forehead.
"Most of them are yours now."
"Ours," she told him, finger pressed to his lips.
"Every hunter has their secret hoard," Rusalka said.
"I don't think Elizabeth does. She was always more concerned with the thrill of the chase than the prize."
Isoline forced her finger against his lips again, harder this time. Vibrant eyes stern.
"She has one. And -"
The rest of her sentence was cut off by a long, drawn out scream.

They turned to see Serpe on the ground. She stabbed her knife into the dirt and pulled herself back to her feet.
"What happened?" Brack asked.
"Nothing!" she spat.
Serpe tried to push him aside, but her arm gave up and clawed at him for balance.
"Hold her up a second," Rusalka said.
She pushed her way through trees. The sound of her crinkling footsteps turned into the hard hacking of wood. She returned a few seconds later with a five-foot trunk, roots and branches trimmed away.
"What is that?" Serpe said.
"It's a crutch. Don't pretend you don't need it."
Serpe snatched it away from her and jammed it under her armpit.
"Don't slow us down," Isoline said.

Serpe

The soil was firm underfoot. She kept pace as the other three sliced through. The green shoots began to thin out. Through the veil of flora, Serpe could see that crooked tree sitting on the hilltop. Ranger had detailed it perfectly. The knots on the wood and the breeze that bent the branches back. Each leaf at their tip standing to attention in the wind.

The rest of them stooped, bodies low behind what remained of the forest. She forced herself to crouch, hand tight around the crutch. Her skin burned pale. The wood started to slice into her palm. She was foolish. Soldiers do not hinder the team. If you have to die, you don't take anyone down with you. She slid her hand down the crutch, skin slippery with blood as the jagged wood slashed at her. Agonizing pain, stretched and unrelenting. Grunts seethed through gritted teeth and flared nostrils.
"Quiet back there," Isoline told her with a glare over her shoulder.
Her cane began to tremble. She should have stayed on the ship. This was pride. Krei's poison. But that Human nurse had a serum. If they had all stayed together, all stayed on the mission, everything would have been fine. Instead… Instead…

Brack

A loud crack. A heavy thump. Isoline swiveled quickly.
"I said quiet."
Words on deaf ears. Serpe was down, stalks of grass slithering over her cheek. The makeshift crutch had shattered, scattering a swarm of wood chips.
"It would appear we are another light," Brack said.
"Focus. We can still do the attack with three. Brack, you and Rusalka take the -"
"We could barely do it with four," Rusalka interrupted.
"And what do you suggest?" Isoline asked.
Rusalka swathed herself in her cape and dove through the dark roots. Isoline's head followed her into the twisting maze of vines.
"Somebody order the pincer movement for two?" Brack asked.
Isoline withdrew her face from the shrubbery.
"Not with just two of us."
She peered over the green ridge, pulling Brack down. Through the thorns, he could see the outline of the guards around a palace. Only four of them gathered at the top of a hill. Three boulders on the steep incline. Isoline told Brack her plan and he nodded his agreement.
"The Umbra always seems to have a trick in reserve. We can only hope there is an effective one coming," Isoline said.
She locked her energy canister into her gun and allowed it to charge.

They continued along the edge of the bushes until the plants were trimmed back to their stumps. With a quick dart and roll, they made it to the first rock. Still no sign of Rusalka. There was nowhere along the hillside. He flashed his head around the rock and caught a glimpse of the guards. Only one appeared to be paying attention to his duty. If they could take him out quietly, they might just have a shot against the other three. They would need to get close. A bird cawed. The guard's eyes turned skywards. Isoline and Brack moved one boulder closer to the summit.
"I've got a plan," Brack said.
"Show me," Isoline said.

Her head tilted sideways in curiosity. He grabbed another glance at the guards. Picking up a pebble, he rapped it against the boulder in a scratching click.
"You've got his attention," Isoline said, spying around the opposite side.
Brack hit the rock against the boulder again, harder than before. The sharp noise echoed out around the empty valley. The one attentive guard, Human, started towards them, rifle clutched in a cautious grip. Brack whipped the stone through the air, sending it crashing against the next boulder up. The guard took a quick glance at the rock, then a longer stare when he realized nothing was there. Confusion made soldiers sloppy. All Brack had to do now was reel him in. He picked up another stone and began to tap it off the boulder once more. Harder and then softer, changing the pitch and volume. The guard's footsteps were less steady now. Brack switched up the pace of his tapping as the guard crept closer, slowing down to a click... click... click...

Brack allowed silence to fall. The guard stopped dead in his tracks. Brack could see his thoughts. Maybe he should head back. Maybe... clickclickclickclickclick!

He stepped into Brack's eye line. Brack grabbed him in a throttle, forcing him off the rock. A heavier click filled the air as his skull broke. Isoline swiped a knife deep across his throat. A thick waterfall of blood dripped down his skin and rolled off the leather of his uniform. Isoline cleaned the flat of her blade against a patch of the black leather then folded it away. Brack peered out to see the position of the guards still alive. They had not moved. The cannon on the hill sagged downwards sadly, like a whimpering dog. Upset that it was not being played with. A puppy now, it could still morph into a wild beast and roar.
"We're clear to reach the next boulder now," Brack said.
"Wait," Isoline said.
The wind rose.
"Now we go."

Brack propped the guard's body up against the rock and ran for the next boulder. They were close enough the smell the gunpowder caked inside the cannon. The death in the air. He looked to Isoline for guidance. Before she could signal, carnage broke. Rusalka dropped between the three guards. One of them mounted the cannon and a wild shot burst Brack's cover in a shower of stone. Isoline leapt out. Brack frantically pressed the dials on his bracelet.
"Elizabeth, it's Brack. We have a situation here! Need assistance immediately, repeat immediately!"

Ana

Elizabeth and her crew were already racing through the groves when Brack's message came.
"Brack! We're on our way now. What's happening there, anyone down?"
No answer but the static.
"Brack! Do you read me?"
Elizabeth's pace quickened. Forr kept up with her, Lavell not far behind. Nyomee travelled above them, in the treetops. Ana had already fallen a down twice. Her white body shell smeared with globs of muck. Her knees ached sore. She struggled on, breathing razor blades. Cheeks red, skin sticky with sweat.

They had been heading for Brack anyway, his position tracked on their bracelet. Brack's call was the gust at Elizabeth's back. It was a lead weight at Ana's ankles. Nothing, only static. Moments after he reported a critical situation in a distress call, his com link went dark. Nobody wanted to say anything. What could they say? Without the answers, the only option was to get there faster. The trees began to thin out and the trail diverged. There was a dark descent into some misty undergrowth. It had been savagely torn apart by a wild animal. Beyond it was a wider path that led upwards. Without looking back, Elizabeth started her ascent.

The track was steep. Ana could barely scramble up the dirt track. Without trees to swing from, Nyomee slipped back through the pack to her.
"I'm fine," Ana panted out.
Ana's blonde hair turned dark with sweat. Nyomee pushed her forward onto all fours. The shock took Ana's breath away. Dirt scratched at her skin. She looked across at Nyomee, confused. Nyomee crouched onto all fours too and bound up the hill with speed and ease. Ana took a lungful of fresh air. She couldn't match Nyomee's pace, but the method was much faster and less tiring. She caught the group at the top.

"What happened to you?" Elizabeth asked.
A cloud of dark dust clung to the wet mud across her armour and tangled in the knots of her hair. Ana gasped for breath and a shook her head for Elizabeth to move on.

From the peak, they could see the palace in the distance. Purple flashed like glitter as energy canisters were fired. While Elizabeth radioed Brack – no reply – Ana worried about Rusalka. Her heart went cold as an orange explosion flared up.

Rusalka

As rock rained down, Rusalka raced for the cannon. Without cover, Brack was horribly exposed. She could hear the bubble and hiss as the cannon coolant readied another shot. She flicked one of her knives towards the turret. It whizzed past the guard, piercing the energy tube behind. In a swirl of orange and metal, the cannon splintered into the air. Thick smoke billowed around the downpour of shrapnel.
"You owe me a new knife," Rusalka told Brack.

Isoline had killed one of the guards already. The other was on the floor, her foot pressed down on his chest.
"Mercy. Mercy!" he begged.
"Don't believe in it."
Before she pulled the trigger, a bullet came from the darkness shot through Isoline's hand. Her rifle dropped with a clatter. She did not scream as the blood sprayed from her fist. Rusalka shot the guard clean between the eyes and turned to the palace.

A group of Human women swaggered out. They pulled the forestocks back to load up their shotguns. Most wore ragged jeans, some with legs torn off at the knees. Others wore skirts, short and ripped with black tights more ladder than not. Unlaced biker boots covered their feet. Dark vests wrapped in jackets or bandoliers on their toned bodies. Hair was shorn, braided and long, often all at once. The flesh on show was marked with either muck or ink. None of them said a word. Brack approached. A fast knee crushed up between his legs and his gun was slapped away from him while he doubled over in pain.
"Hardly found shit, ladies. Move out!" a voice called.
The women shuffled back into the darkness, shotguns still aimed. There was a rattling hum behind the palace. A shuttle appeared and the women grabbed ropes that trailed from it. The ground shook as a ship blasted into the sky and soared away.

"Damn it!"
Rusalka strode over to the entrance, stepping over Brack. Her knife was lying among the wreckage of the cannon. Hilt scalding hot to the touch. She juggled it hand to hand to cool it. Loud, rapid bursts exploded behind her. Isoline firing into the sky after the ship. Rusalka disarmed her with a strong kick.
"Don't be pointless," Rusalka said, trapping the gun beneath her feet.
"I wouldn't need my gun if you hadn't destroyed the cannon."
"It was your boyfriend who was pinned back. One of us needed to do something."
Rusalka looked over at Brack as he clawed at the palace tiles.

"I'd go easy on him for a week. Make sure you use a lot of ice."

~*~

Elizabeth reached the doors of the palace, Forr and Lavell close behind. Rusalka loosened her stamp on Isoline's weapon and kicked it back to her. With a quick and offended sweep, she scooped the rifle into her hands.
"What the hell was that ship?" Elizabeth asked.
"A group of Human women beat us here. Gave Brack some rather painful swelling for his trouble," Rusalka said.
Elizabeth glanced over at Brack tenderly cupping his sensitive parts. Rusalka saw her flash a smile before her face tensed. She pointed to the smouldering cannon.
"What happened? Could've shot them down if we still had it."
Brack struggled to speak, "They had me trapped. Rusalka saved me."

"Why weren't you with us!" a voice shouted. It was weak and hoarse. Ana caught up, her face cherry.
"We're friends, aren't we sweetie?" Rusalka asked her.
Ana just stood there, blonde knotted shock flailing in the wind.
"You have to trust me."

"The cannon was not the issue, foolish as it was to destroy it," Isoline said, "If you had been here, we could have secured the base much faster. We could have kept the turret active. We could have the fragment. I don't see any children with you. I trust they were all okay?" Isoline said. Her eyebrows were raised with mocking confidence.
"It doesn't matter now," Elizabeth said.
A look of understanding grew across Isoline's thin lips.
"There weren't any children, were there?" she said.
"I'd rather make that mistake a thousand times if it meant I got to save one child."
"Spare me your speech on the iniquity of my soul, Elizabeth. Everyone else around here might fall to the floor to kiss your feet, but I'm not so blind. You made the wrong call. Be a big girl and take it. If you listened to me, we would have the fragment. You're not fit to lead this crew."
Elizabeth's hand shot out, stinging Isoline between the eyes with a closed fist. Rusalka heard the skin tear open.
"Have you ever had a thought you have not acted upon? Ever reconsidered the rashness with which you live, even for a moment? Sometimes urges, however satisfactory their payoff may be, must be suppressed for a greater good. I control mine. If I did not, each day would end with a pile of corpses."
"Is all that pretty talk supposed to make up some kind of threat? I'm earning my way onto the pile, that it?"

Isoline wiped her fingertips across her lip, flicking away the dark drops of blood.

"I could reduce you to your knees with a wink and kill you with a whisper."

"Very impressive. I'd need a gun, but luckily I'm packing," Elizabeth said. She swept her leather jacket back over her holster. The pistol grip glinted. Isoline, already holding her rifle, moved her finger to the trigger. With one hand bloodied, the barrel shook.

"Let's not do this now, ladies. We can measure them when we're back on the ship," Rusalka said.

She wiped the soot and the grime from her dagger. Confused eyes turned to her.

"I guess I'm more used to breaking up pathetic arguments between men. You're not going to shoot each other, so why not on the count of four, you shake hands. Okay? One, two, three, four."

They both turned to Rusalka with unimpressed stares.

"Well. I suppose that was to be expected."

"Where's Serpe?" Forr asked.

"That took you a while," Rusalka said.

She stepped between Elizabeth and Isoline, bumping the rifle out of the way.

"Bottom of the hill. Whatever you gave her back on the ship, I don't think it was enough."

"Any more and she wouldn't have been able to move. Not *often* enough was the problem. She should have stayed with us," Ana said.

"To save the imaginary children, you mean?" Isoline said.

Ana stared at Isoline, sweat still running down her glowing skin. Rusalka handed her a flask of water.

"I'm going back for her," Forr said.

He started down the hill and Lavell trudged after him.

Ana held the vial out to Forr as he passed by her. He took it with a nod and handed it off immediately to Lavell.

"Take this. Inject her just above where the injury is."

Elizabeth and Isoline appeared to come to a truce. Hateful glares aside, weapons had been holstered. The immediate threat of friendly fire had been extinguished.

"Who were those other people?" Nyomee asked.

"All women, all Human," Brack said.

"A tribe of some sort. Tattered clothes. Flew off with the fragment in hand. And, no doubt, grins on their faces which I fully intend to wipe off," Rusalka said.

"I plan to rip them off," Isoline snarled through teeth.

"Merely wiping them would satisfy me. Nothing was hurt but our pride,"

Rusalka said.

Isoline held her bleeding hand up, curling it into a fist to wring out blood. She opened it to reveal a hole through the flesh.

"Well, and that I suppose," Rusalka said.

"You can fix this," Isoline said, holding her hand out to Ana.

This was not a question. She ignored Isoline's hand, even nudging it out of the way.

"Tattered clothes? Did they all have strange hairstyles?" Ana said.

"All Human hair is strange to me, sweetie. Sorry."

"Humans have ghastly, ugly hair. It grows out of them like weeds," Isoline said.

Her hand was still out, waving for Ana's attention. It caught hold of the collar of her armour but lacked the strength to grip. Ana wrapped a careless bandage around it as she pressed Rusalka for more details.

"Was it strange lengths? All different? Some cut short, some braided? Did they all wear black?"

"Do you know them?" Elizabeth asked.

"That does sound like them," Brack said.

"When I lived on Earth, there were groups who thought the HO colonies were getting too soft on other species. Too tolerant."

"Seriously?" Elizabeth said.

"I believe her. Those who pursue enlightenment leave the next generation more enlightened. Those who pursue ignorance leave the next generation even more ignorant," Rusalka said.

"Something like that, I suppose. Anyway, this group broke off and formed their own territory. They would fly out to alien settlements nearby, kill a local as a warning to leave Earth alone."

"That's horrible," Elizabeth said.

"And it was only the females?" Isoline asked, rewrapping the loose strips of cloth around her hand.

"It started when a group of Torfus males snuck into the HO camp and raped a young girl. There may now be similar groups of men. Even if it began as misguided revenge, their only motivation is violence now. They called themselves the Mundus"

"We have to get back to the ship. Hope that the girls returned to Earth, and see if Querius can find some way of narrowing our search for them down," Elizabeth said.

They heard heavy footsteps behind them as Serpe appeared. She had her arm around Forr's shoulder. There was a noticeable shuffle and stumble to her walk, but Rusalka saw the strength was returning.

"I should have had a stronger dose," she growled at Ana.

Elizabeth stepped in between them and shoved Serpe away.

"You should have stayed close."

"Haven't we established that your dalliance was foolish? You are fast eroding your usefulness, Ranger," Isoline said.

Isoline turned her back. Elizabeth reached for her pistol but Ana touched her hand. Rusalka heard the soft scrape of skin on skin. Ana cradled Elizabeth's fingertips, staring with big, imploring eyes. Elizabeth relaxed her arm. Once Ana let go, she raised her bracelet to her mouth and called the two pilots for evac.

Ana

Killers and murderers are different animals. She knew Elizabeth was the former. Her line of work called for it. Ana could reconcile that. But she couldn't let her murder Isoline. As they boarded the shuttle, Elizabeth was silent. Ana hoped she would forgive her.

Elizabeth immediately walked to the window, gazing out over the plains of Tupurs as the shuttle took off. Ana wanted to join her. But every word would be the wrong one. Silence could be damaging too. A warm hand touched her.
"You did good," Rusalka said.
"What do you mean?"
"I saw. Elizabeth was going to shoot her, wasn't she?"
Ana glanced up. Elizabeth was leaning into the glass with a clenched fist. Ana hunched over into Rusalka, voice low.
"Did anyone else see?"
"I don't think so."
Ana nodded.
"Why did you stop her?" Rusalka asked.
"You just said I did good."
"But you couldn't have known I would complement you on it. I'm only curious of your reasons, sweetie."
Ana took a deep breath.
"I didn't want Elizabeth to kill an innocent person. I hope she realizes that she wouldn't have wanted to either."
"Thank you," Rusalka said, standing up.
"Thank you?"
Had she just passed a test?
"Her death would have been unjustified. The rest of this journey will be much more enjoyable now."
A mischievously mysterious grin crossed Rusalka's face. Ana's eyes returned to Elizabeth.
"You should apologize," Rusalka said.
"I was helping her."
"I know. But if you tell her that, she'll argue. If you apologize, she'll apologize too."
Ana wasn't convinced.
"Trust me," Rusalka said.

Ana's legs ached, muscles stiff as she stood. Footsteps timid. Her hand nervously climbed through her blonde hair, entangled in dirt and sweat. She reached the window but did not look out at the vast, colorful galaxy. Instead, she stared down at her feet.
"You here to tell me off?" Elizabeth asked, casting her a sideways glance.
"I shouldn't have interfered. I'm sure you knew what you were doing," Ana mumbled.

Her eyes did not rise. Elizabeth's hand touched her back, pulling her in closer.

"I'm sure it wasn't like this when you were with Brack," Ana said.

Some nihilistic urge inside her forced it out. She felt her pulse beating on the base of her skull.

"No. It wasn't," Elizabeth said simply.

Ana's stomach became a hollow steel pot.

"I'm sorry. I shouldn't have –"

"Me and Brack were too similar," Elizabeth continued, "He wouldn't have stopped me. And now he'd be trying to make me laugh. Take my mind off it."

"I don't know any jokes," Ana said.

Elizabeth kissed Ana's forehead.

"You don't have to, Princess. That's the point," Elizabeth turned to the window, "I don't know how to be a good person. I'm broken. I'll always be a killer."

"You're not a murderer," Ana said.

Elizabeth smiled. Ana rested her head on her shoulder.

Roka

Something had happened on Tupurs, but he did not care enough investigate what. Fly the shuttle. That was his detail. Nothing else. The com button started to flash.
"This is Roka. Receiving."
"Hey man, got something from West," Donovan said.
"I'll patch it through to Elizabeth."
"Not this time. He wants you to broadcast it for the whole shuttle. I'll tell Mogg to do the same."
"Whatever. We still on for tonight?"
"I need my lucky hat back, don't I?" Donovan said.
"You can need it all you want. You ain't getting it. You wanna invite the Doc again?"
"Querius? I don't know, I feel bad taking all his money."
"I don't."
"You're a bastard, Roka," Donovan said.
"All right, channel's open for West when he's ready."

Miss Ranger
West's dark voice echoed. Roka could hear Elizabeth in the main compartment.
"Look, we didn't –"
I know what happened. You failed
"We can discuss this back on the ship."
Your crew needs to hear what happens when you fail
"We'll get it back. There was a slip up, that's all."
It cost you dearly. It will cost the good doctor more
"Krakk?" Rusalka said.
The Krei who is an Ang, or the Ang who is a Krei
"I never got philosophy," Roka muttered.
No, he is a curious creature. There is intrigue in the brute. I'd like to keep him. I refer to Loslou, poor soul
"Querius is a damn good doctor. What happened on Tupurs has nothing to do with him. He found the place!"
He is good. But so is Krakk. I don't *need* two. And after you failed me, I don't *want* two
Roka felt numb. He couldn't move.
"Leave Querius out of it. It's my fault we deviated from the mission."
Yes. It is. Remember that, when you hear what comes next. You still

have value to me, but I think the doctor has outlived his
"Don't you touch him!" Elizabeth screamed.
"Ranger?" Querius' voice, confused.
"Querius, are you okay? Where are you?"
"I'm fine, I'm fine. How did the mission go? I trust you are now the proud owner of the third fragment?"
"No. I don't have time to explain, Querius. Where are you?"
"I'm in the private broadcast room. I was just talking to my wife, but the link seems to have cut out. Perhaps it got entangled with your broadcast. Once Lavell returns she can help me rewire – "
"Querius, get out of there!"
"Now, Doc!" Roka shouted.
"What's wrong? I don't underst –"
His words gave way to guttural choking noises. Heartbreaking coughs.
"Why? Nothing. And why?" he whispered.
Elizabeth kicked through the door to Roka's cockpit.
"Turn it off, Roka! Close the fucking channel!"
"I'm trying!"
His fingers prodded desperately at the buttons. They had all been disabled. They had no choice but to hear Querius die a drawn out, agonizing death.
Find the fragment. Do not fail me again
Elizabeth slumped down against the floor. Her hands slammed the wall. Rusalka walked up to her, footsteps met with a deathly glare.
"Just fucking don't, okay?" Elizabeth told her.
"You couldn't have known," Rusalka said.

Roka stared out across the stars dumbly. For a long time, the shuttle cruised the darkness without his control. After the feeling returned to his body, he opened a com link with Donovan.
"You hear that?" he asked.
"He played it through the ship too. I can't believe it."
"Look, I'm not up for cards tonight. Not after that."
"I hear you. You need a drink though. So do I. We'll pour one out for the doctor."
"Querius didn't drink," Roka told him.
"Well, if he'd heard what we just heard, he might start."

Krakk

Nothing... and why. He had seen death many times. He had never felt it before. Carrying Doctor down the hall and back to his lab, he lay him down on the small bed Querius kept by his workstation. Querius' body was light in his hands, loose as a scrap of linen. Still, a great weight dragged down on his arms. He understood the solitude Master lived in. Friends become a part of you, and you bleed when they get torn off.

Querius' hands slopped over the bed. Krakk folded them across Doctor's chest. He had never met the man locked inside the ship, Elizabeth's master, but he knew he did not want that man to tell the widow Loslou. He had spoken briefly before he murdered Querius and blamed Elizabeth, but Krakk was not fooled. The man had a choice. Querius' wife deserved to have the news broken by somebody who cared for Querius. His wife deserved to see him come home, but this was a kindness Krakk was unable to grant.

He hoped she would be angry. Everything else was new to him. Suddenly his mouth felt dry. Fingertips numb. Palms damp. He dialed the number Querius had stored. A Jahlder woman appeared on the screen. She leant in very close to the screen, white eyes squinted.
"Hello?" she said.
Krakk could not answer. His mouth was full of glue.
"I think this is the wrong connection, Ang. My communicator is always acting up. I've asked my husband to fix it, but he's got more interesting things to fix before he puts his own house right."
Her white hair was quietly pulled back into neat bun. Her panels were narrow, sloping down to her chin from the corners of her small, taut lips. She reached forward to disconnect.
"I work with Querius," Krakk coughed out.
She sat back in her chair and pursed her lips tighter.
"I have some bad -"
"Wait, you work with Querius. *You?*"
"Yes," Krakk nodded.
"You're an Ang," she said.
"I am."

The conversation had moved in a unexpected direction. He was stranded without a map.

"Has he hired an Ang to be his lackey? A thug to hand him tools when he should be holding his wife's hand? What pitiful invention is he off tinkering with now, something important enough warrant abandoning our conversation before its conclusion? I find it amazing that he tries to hide himself behind things as small as atoms when I come looking, and more amazing still that I can never find him."

"Querius is dead."

Krakk needed to get it out.

"No," the widow said, "I just spoke to him."

"I'm very sorry. We can return his body for burial."

She leaned forward, strands of her hair slipping out of place. She was shaking, trying to disguise it.

"Go and fetch him, Ang, and tell him he is being spiteful."

Krakk did not understand. He could not fetch Querius. He could not tell him anything.

"Querius is dead," he repeated.

"I want a child," the woman said softly.

"I'm not sure what -"

Querius' wife ended the com link. He stared at the black screen and swallowed down the heaviness in his throat.

Mogg

The broadcast made him sick. He sat in the kitchen, not cooking. No one had come for food. Donovan and Roka radioed to invite him for a drink in memory of Querius, but moving felt impossible.

A fist rapped on the metal shutters of the serving hatch. He ignored it. The noise only grew louder.
"I told you guys, I'm not –"
He flung the shutter open. Serpe was standing there, leaning on a crutch.
"You're the chef aren't you?"
"One of my jobs."
"So where's the food?"
Her arm shook as it gripped the cane.
"Kitchen's closed tonight. I think people have lost their appetite."
Serpe's eyes narrowed.
"A grey Krei that mourns a Jahlder. You make your ancestors weep."
"Nicest thing anyone's said to me in a long time."
"People die. The living need to eat."

That sneering blue skin. Mogg shook his head and climbed over the counter.
"You want to eat? Make your own."
She tried to block him as he walked away.
"A Jahlder is dead. On Excha there would be banquet."
"That's why I left."

Mogg pushed past her and left the Mess Hall. His legs dragged him to Querius' lab. Deep breath. He ran his hand through his fur before he knocked, feeling loose strands. Krakk peeled the door open.
"I'd like to say goodbye," Mogg said.
"There'll be a funeral tomorrow," Krakk said.
"I won't be here tomorrow"
Krakk seemed to understand. He stepped aside and allowed the door to swing inwards.

Rusalka was in the lab too, arm looped around Krakk's. She bowed her head as Mogg passed by. Krakk had done a good job. There was no trace of pain left in Querius' face. He seemed free. Mogg didn't speak, only looked. No currency was worth this. He'd left Excha in search of peace and wandered into war. After a moment of silent respect, Mogg nodded to Krakk, turned and left.

His legs were lighter now, but his head still hung heavy. This place held no hope for him now. He reached the hangar and found it deserted.

A fresh start. Elsewhere. He had done it before. You work hard, you get by. Any one of these shuttles would take him as far as he needed. *That sneering blue skin.* There was only one ship he wanted. Red as Human blood. He took a screwdriver from the tool hatch and crawled under Serpe's shuttle. Blue Krei never noticed the little things. Her door had been loose since she arrived, small buckle on the lower lip. He'd never bothered to fix it. Driver in place, he slapped down on the shaft and popped it open.

Inside, he worked the screwdriver on the control panel. It slipped loose and left wires exposed. Mogg had lost count of the amount of sharp-fighters he'd built in his life. Green to brown. Hotwired. The engine spluttered and came alive. He ran out of the shuttle and set the hangar doors on a timer. They creaked open as he clambered back inside. More fur fell out. Screwdriver tucked in his pocket, he blasted off.

Krakk

The next morning, they held a memorial for Querius. Krakk had not slept last night. Neither had Rusalka. He had no idea about the rest of them.

They stood around his desk. Krakk had prepared his body to be sent home. Rusalka's small hand wrapped tightly around his, her head near his chest. He could feel her body twitching, her fingers squeezing. Donovan and Roka spoke fondly of their card games with Querius, while Lavell told of her discussions on any manner of subjects with him. Her voice creaked with sorrow. Most of the crew muttered niceties, embarrassed they had nothing to say. Serpe declined to attend at all. Isoline's eulogy surprised Krakk the most.

She stepped forward and stood straightbacked. She took a sip from the glass in her hand, then laid it down on Querius' workbench, leaving a water ring. The eyes of the room were drawn to her.
"Querius was a dear friend of mine. The underappreciated cog in our operation, one that will be sorely missed. It is a rare event for a soul to come along whose mere presence enriches the lives of those around him. There may be those here who until his terrible death under the most unfortunate and _avoidable_ circumstances thought of him as nothing more than a scientist, technician, engineer. All three. The choice depends on your experience of the man. But those who knew him, truly and deeply knew him, will surely remember him as something far greater. And those of us who knew him so well know no shame in shedding a tear in his memory, do we?"
Rusalka gave a soft spasm in his arms and sobbed. Krakk ran a finger across her cheek to wipe away a tear but found her fur dry.
"Would anyone else like to say their words?" Isoline asked.
She walked away from Querius' desk and took another drink.
"I do." Elizabeth said.

Her expression was dark. Jaw tense underneath red hair. Shoulders taut, arms stiff by her side.
"A lot of you were on Tupurs with me, the rest of you heard what happened to Querius," she said, letting out a sigh that crumpled her.
She turned to the picture of Querius which Rusalka had placed on his desk.

"It's my fault. I killed Querius."

"Elizabeth, that's not -" Ana started.

Elizabeth raised a hand to silence her.

"It is. I know a lot of you are thinking it. Now I've said it. I'm sorry, Querius. Sorry I ever dragged you into this shit."

Elizabeth's hard stare lingered on Querius' picture a second longer. Then she turned and hurried out of the room, Ana following.

Elizabeth

"Elizabeth, wait!"
"That's what everyone thinks, Ana."
"You couldn't have known, Elizabeth. Nobody blames you."
"Everybody hates me for this, and I'm not surprised. I hate my fucking self."
"Well, I love you."
She leaned in to kiss her, but Elizabeth twisted away.
"You can't just make this go away, Ana! This is not a kiss and make up moment!"
"Most people agreed with you. Me, Forr, Lavell, Nyomee... we all came with you. We all would have made the same call. And you know why? Because it was the right call."
"If I'd listened to Isoline, Querius would be alive right now," Elizabeth said.
"And those children? In that cave?"
"They weren't real!" Elizabeth punched the wall, fist near Ana's face. Ana's eyes were locked tight as she trembled away from it.
"I should just take a shuttle and split. Mogg had it right. Start back from scratch. Fuck this key, fuck the lot of them."
An unwise plan, Miss Ranger
West's voice from a speaker behind them.
You do not know the entire truth of things. We should speak. Miss Yukishnov, you might accompany us
Elizabeth looked at Ana. She did not move her fist.
"Do you know the entire truth of things?" Elizabeth asked.
Ana did not respond.

They walked towards the central chamber. Ana pressed her eyes to the pad. This time Elizabeth stared at her, watching. The dark damp fell on them again.
"What is the entire truth? What were you talking about back there?" Elizabeth asked.
You saw what happened to the good doctor
"I didn't realize you were so willing to abuse your absolute power, but I always knew you had it."
Listen to your heart beat
Don't think about pink elephants. She couldn't *not* think about her heartbeat. She raised her hand to her chest. The rhythmic thud of blood pumping. A little faster than normal, maybe. Was that his point? Could he sense this, hear it even?
"I'm not afraid of you," she said, and felt her heart thump harder.
I wouldn't dare suggest so. This is the same racing pulse you feel before a fight, when you stalk your prey. When you take a lover to your bed. Don't listen to the speed. Listen to the beat
Elizabeth heard Ana whimper out a tear.
"I don't understand," Elizabeth said.
Ana was shuddering. A quivering hand rose up to dry her eyes. A leaf on a branch, barely hanging on.

Can't you hear it? Feel it?
"I didn't know. They didn't tell me what it was until it was too late," Ana whispered.
"What?" Elizabeth asked.
Bad-um-um. Bad-um-um. Bad-um-um
West said with methodic timing.
Elizabeth raised her hand to her chest again, pulling down the collar of her vest. And she could feel it. Bad-um-um. Bad-um-um. Bad-um-um.

There was something else. Something more. Not an extra heartbeat, not quite. The confusion and terror must have shown on her face.
It would seem that even without Miss Yukishnov's training, you're able to comprehend the situation
"What have you done to me?" Elizabeth's voice shivered.
She could feel her heart pounding faster. Every knock of that horrible extra half beat.
"I didn't know what it was, Elizabeth. You have to believe me!"
"What?"
Sweat was running down into Elizabeth's eyes now.
"It's a bomb," Ana said quietly.
Silence.
Bad-um-um.
"There's a bomb attached to your heart."
"You put a bomb inside me?"
"I didn't know what it was... I thought –"
"You're a doctor! What, you were just asked to put metal and wires and not to mention goddamn *explosives* inside a heart and you thought 'who knows, maybe it'll help'?"
"No one had ever repaired a heart before, Elizabeth. Not like yours. It wasn't even there."
"And explosives work? Who knew? Why don't you fly to the cancer wards next and see if shooting them in the fucking face cures them!"
Try to leave and the bomb will be detonated. That is all

"Elizabeth, I'm sorry," Ana said.
She placed her hand on Elizabeth's back. Elizabeth spun away and pushed her into the wall. There were thin streams of sweat dripping down her face as she held Ana up. Her fist twisted inside Ana's collar, lifting her off the ground. Ana's feet fluttered for traction, finding none.
"I'm sorry, Elizabeth."
"A bomb, Ana."
She spoke with teeth clenched, spitting the words. She dropped Ana to the floor.
"You put a bomb in me."
"I'm sorry," Ana said again.
"Look, I don't think you should sleep in my cabin tonight. I'll have Donovan make the arrangements."
"I can make my own," Ana said.

Her voice splintered as she scrambled to her feet and ran off.

Elizabeth ran her hands through her hair. She sat down with her back to the wall and hung her head. Bad-um-um. Bad-um-um. Bad-um-um. Don't think about pink elephants. She couldn't not hear her heartbeat. That extra half beat, torturing her. She could feel herself falling into it, like a black hole.

A hand extended out to help her. The hand was red and scaly, decorated with an elegant overkill of jewelry. Isoline.
"What do you want?" Elizabeth said, looking up.
"Come with me."
She didn't really want to. But her legs forced her to stand. They dragged like her boots were made of cement as she followed Isoline back to her room.

The room showed no trace of being slept in. Elizabeth remembered when she used to share a room with Brack back on the old Victory Pearl. Sheets wrinkled. Pile of books by Brack's bedside, makeshift bookmarks lodged between the pages of several. He never read one book at a time, preferring to be immersed in as many worlds as possible. There was no sign of this habit being kept up here. No ornaments. The white sheets were pristine, pulled smooth. Isoline sat down lightly on them and guided Elizabeth towards a dark leather chair.
Elizabeth remained standing, "What do you want, Isoline? I've got other things on my mind right now."
"Sit."
Elizabeth sagged into the chair.
"I'm not talking about Tupurs. I made a call, and with hindsight things could've gone down differently."
"You don't like me, do you?" Isoline asked.
"No," Elizabeth said, "And I get the impression the feeling is mutual."
"We only think about each other in relation to Brack. I'm his current beau, you were his first real love. We are natural enemies."
"I don't think about Brack that way now. I... I have Ana."
"You don't sound so sure. Do you have Ana?"
"We had a fight. I don't know anymore."
Why did she just tell Isoline that?

The hinges of the door creaked, slow and strained. Isoline walked over and pressed it closed. She twisted the bolt lock with a heavy thunk.
"What colour underwear are you wearing?" Isoline asked as she walked back to the bed.
"Blue," Elizabeth answered immediately.
What was wrong with her?
"How many days have you worn them consecutively?"
"Two."
Elizabeth answered without skipping a beat.
"How vulgar," Isoline said with a disapproving tut.

This wasn't right. Elizabeth could feel her brain pulsating. Fighting. Struggling. Dying.
"What are you doing to me!"
She stood sharply and drew her gun, aiming point blank at Isoline. The pistol could almost peck her cheek. Isoline looked at the gun, amused, and pushed her finger up against the muzzle, shushing it.
"You aren't going to shoot me. Drop the gun."
It fell from Elizabeth's grasp. Elizabeth stared at her hand. She had not felt that. Not controlled that. She swung a punch at Isoline.
"Stop."
The command was tired and simple. For a few seconds Elizabeth's arm froze, fist clenched.
"Put your arm down by your side. Haven't you figured it out yet? Everybody knows about Torfus brains, how most of our elders go insane from the strain of their very thoughts, but no one really appreciates why. Ours brains are too powerful. And once in a generation, those powerful minds breed a Torfus like me. I could make you wear that dirty underwear for the rest of your life, you realize? I could make you wear nothing but them. But I don't go in for humiliation."
"Go fuck yourself," Elizabeth said.
"You are aware that if I said that to you, you would have no choice but to do it. You are valuable to me, Ranger. You just need to learn. On your knees," Isoline said.

Elizabeth's legs buckled beneath her, landing hard on her kneecaps. Isoline stared. *The eyes. That's how she does it.* She kept her eyes firmly on the floor. A sharp grip around her chin wrestled her head upwards.
"Look at me, and *keep* looking at me," Isoline said.
The voice bubbled with irritation and rage. She strode around the room. Elizabeth's gaze followed her everywhere. Calm returned to Isoline's voice as she sat on the bed.
"That one doesn't always work, I'm afraid. But I've spent my time here slowly getting know your mind, Ranger. Not the most complex of things, but very resilient. A cockroach of a mind."
"I'm to be your toy?"
"You have no value as a plaything. You're acutely aware that I'm controlling you. It vastly diminishes my amusement. No, I have other plans for you."
"Are you controlling Brack?" Elizabeth asked.
"Silly girl," Isoline leant in close to Elizabeth's face, "Questions are my domain. Now, you want to kiss my foot, don't you?"
Elizabeth's face wrinkled in disgust, but her body was already bowing.
"Don't worry. I have no interest in you sexually, but the servitude will do you good. Something needs to break your bravado."
Elizabeth placed both her hands flat on the floor and lowered herself until her puckered lips met Isoline's foot. She was straining her neck to stop, but her mind would not listen. Her lips remained for several seconds. All the while, Elizabeth could not stop looking up. She was staring into that foul, superior cackle. The feet had a heavy, perfumery musk, like an exotic flower. Poisonous.

With a curl of her finger, Isoline ordered Elizabeth to rise.

"Pick your gun up. And don't try anything stupid. I can tear away your dignity piece by delicious piece, or I can rip it off with a flick of my wrist. I can also leave it relatively intact; the choice is entirely yours."

Elizabeth scooped the gun off the floor. It felt unfamiliar. She had her fingers curled around the handle, but none inside the trigger loop.

"A wise decision," Isoline said, noting the position of Elizabeth's hand, "I want to know about your treasure hunting."

"Stories? That's all you want? Brack can tell you stories."

"Can and does. A born storyteller with a very skilled tongue. But he's a fool. He believes sharing a bed means sharing everything. I want the stories about just you."

"You mean before I met Brack?"

"I've seen Brack's little trove. The trinkets he has kept for himself over the years. It's a modest hoard. I want yours."

"I don't have one," Elizabeth said.

"Impossible. Do not lie to me," Isoline said, squinting her eyes.

"Couldn't you just convince people to give you whatever you want with this power?"

"It would be boring. I'd have to go from place to place collecting meagre riches each time, and as you know, some people take more convincing than others."

"I don't have a secret hoard anywhere," Elizabeth said. The corner of her mouth twitched up.

"You must have sticky fingers. That's why you became a treasure hunter."

"I became a treasure hunter because I was good at it. My earliest treasure was bread. Not sure if there's any left for you but it's probably stale by now."

Elizabeth could feel Isoline's hold on her weakening.

"We'll do it the long way, if we must. Tell me everything you've ever taken. And don't lie to me. I can make you shoot yourself, remember that."

"A blanket, when I was six," Elizabeth answered, "This other girl at the orphanage had a really thick blanket. Maroon with an Aztec design. I hated her. I was freezing and she somehow had this huge warm blanket. So I stole it, one night just eased it away from her. But I didn't sleep with it, not right away. I had to hide it, so she wouldn't steal it back. I buried it outside, in a plastic bag. Every night, I lay there shivering, waiting for her to fall asleep, then when I was sure she had, I'd get the blanket out from that shallow hole. Every morning I'd rebury it before she woke up. I was warm for months before she stole it back."

Elizabeth hated Isoline then, far more than she had even as her body stooped to kiss her scaled feet.

"As touching as that little glance at early life of Elizabeth Ranger is, I was thinking of things you've taken which have some value."

"Things are worth what we say they're worth."

"No jewels?"

"Jewels are expensive and pointless. They're worthless to me."

Isoline tensed her lip.

"Tell me anything you kept for yourself during your treasure hunting career which you are still able to locate," Isoline said.

She was grating her words now.

"There's a box on my desk. Gold. I keep my pens in it."
"Only gold plated. I've seen it. What else?"
"I had a few other things like that on the Victory Pearl. Cups, paperweights, things like that. Don't know what happened to them after I died."
"Other things, then. Things that weren't kept on the ship."
"We sold enough to keep us well fed, clothed and keep the engine running. Then I let Brack and Lavell take what they wanted. Forr was like me, he didn't really care."
"I don't believe there was nothing, Elizabeth."
"Nothing? No, after big scores there was always plenty. Even after Brack and Lavell had harvested their favourites and we'd sold most on for coin. But like I said, me and Forr didn't care. So we placed the leftovers in the airlock and we spaced them. Then we ran up to the cannons and fired until it was all obliterated. Maybe once in a while a necklace or brooch got away from us, but the hell if I know where it is now."
"There's really nothing left?" Isoline asked.
Now it was Elizabeth's turn to stare hard.
"Nothing," she said truthfully.
"That can't be possible..." Isoline said quietly.
"I'm not lying to you. I can't," Elizabeth said.

Isoline's eyes flashed onto the gun.
"Then you're no use to me. I don't like to have my time wasted."
"Neither do I. Do this quickly."
"That's not how I play, Princess."
Was the nickname coincidence?
"That gun in your hand," Isoline said.
Elizabeth looked at it. She could take it apart, polish it and have it back together in a minute, but right now her fingers were afraid of it.
"You want to feel the metal on your cheek, don't you?"
The questions were commands. Her skin flinched as the cold barrel rubbed against it. She needed to loosen the fangs clamped down on her brain.
"Tell me the truth about Brack," she said.
"Don't make demands of me."
These were bonds that could not be broken by brute force. They had to be slipped out of.
"We both know where this is going. Whatever you tell me, I'm taking to the grave."
"Put your finger on the trigger," Isoline told her.
Elizabeth placed her finger through the loop gently. Her body felt disconnected, skin made of air.
"Does he actually love you? Is he aware that it's all a trick?"
Isoline didn't answer.
"Do you remind him when he forgets?"
Isoline smirked.
"I think that gun will shut you up. Put it in your mouth."
Elizabeth obeyed. Her teeth gripped down. This was how it would end. People in her line of work didn't get old.
"Taste it," Isoline ordered.

Elizabeth's tongue flopped around until it found the muzzle. Inside was rank copper. Elizabeth hoped Brack had not been demeaned like this. She was waiting for the final command. Waiting for it all to end.
"Now, pull the –ahcck!"

Two curved blades shot through Isoline's head. They impaled her eyeballs, piercing them out of their sockets. The two blue gems stared up at the ceiling, sinewy strands of bloody gristle keeping them attached, barely. The two knives were withdrawn. Isoline collapsed to the floor, mouth hanging open. As her body fell away, Elizabeth saw Rusalka behind her, wiping the blades clean against her fur. Elizabeth felt faint. Like she had just been unplugged. She stumbled back into the wall.
"How long have you been there?" Elizabeth asked, recovering her breath.
"Pretty much the whole time," Rusalka said.
She threaded her daggers back into their sheathes and spoke with nonchalance.
"Why didn't you do something!"
Blood pounded her skull.
"I killed her," Rusalka reminded her.
"Why did you wait?"
Rusalka looked at her steadily, taking the question seriously.
"To see how painfully she deserved to die."

Elizabeth glanced down at Isoline. Yellow pus oozed from her punctured eyeballs. Blood soaked worms crawled across the floor into her sockets.
"Nobody will know, Elizabeth. Not the details."
She knew it was better to survive, logically. But how weak she had become.
"How did you know?"
"Isoline attacked me the first time I met her. I got the better of her, but she convinced me to let her go. Then that energy barrier at Uhkira's. I became suspicious and had Krakk investigate Torfus brain patterns. The reason so many of them go crazy is because of how powerful their thoughts are. And very rarely, their thoughts are so powerful they're able to push them into the minds of others."
"Can they do it to other Torfus?"
"I couldn't figure out if she was controlling Brack. If she was, along the way he seemed to fall for her for real. I followed them on Tupurs to find out more, and to see what her interest was with you."
"Thanks, I guess. Did you have to be such a bitch about it though?" Elizabeth said.
Rusalka gave Elizabeth a sideways glance.
"Five seconds. You were nice to me for five seconds after I saved your life."
"Sorry. And thank you, really."
"I had to seem as if I had disdain for you, to convince Isoline into dropping hints. She's far too vain. In reality, I have a great deal of respect for you," Rusalka said.
Rusalka ran her teeth across her tongue, considering this.
"*Some* respect for you," Rusalka corrected, "Though you treat Ana terribly."
"Excuse me?"
"All that girl wants is to feel validated by you. You need to give her some affection

back, and I don't mean only in your quarters."
"You don't know what you're talking about," Elizabeth said.
"I know enough."
"You *don't*."
Elizabeth's tone drew a line under the conversation.

Isoline's body was starting to slip forward. It squeaked as her nose slid across the floor.
"What should we do with her?"
"We have to tell people what happened. Then we pack her up and send her home. No memorial, no ceremony. Just get rid of her," Elizabeth said.
"We don't need to tell them everything. We could –"
"Yes, we do," Elizabeth interrupted quickly, "Maybe leave out the feet thing."

~*~

Elizabeth and Rusalka decided to announce Isoline's death to the ship through the com speakers. At least, it felt like they decided that. Rusalka suggested it and Elizabeth, still woozy, agreed.
"Hey there, Captain," Donovan said as they entered the flight deck, "You feeling alright? You look kinda pale."
"I'm fine."
Her feet fumbled beneath her. She grabbed the back of his chair to stop herself from falling. "No one blames you, you know. For Querius, I mean."
"This isn't that," Elizabeth said, standing up straight.
"Can we borrow the broadcast mic?" Rusalka said.
Donovan handed the mic over to Elizabeth.
"Something wrong?" he asked.
"More like something's better," Elizabeth said.

Elizabeth took a deep breath and pressed the broadcast button. There was a click of static then nothing. She didn't know what to say. She felt Rusalka's hand on her back.
"Just tell them the truth, Elizabeth."
Her throat was a vacuum. Words suffocated there. She said the only thing she could think of.
"Isoline is dead."
She winced at the severity of it. This was how she broke the news to Brack? Her stomach felt heavy.
"She was going to kill me. I'll spare the details, but Isoline was able to hypnotize people. When Rusalka found me, I had my own gun in my mouth, and Isoline was about to make me pull the trigger."
Okay, that's it. Everybody knows. *I can stop talking.*
"Her remains will be sent back home. I'm not getting involved in anything messy, so we just tell people she died in the field."
Stop. *Stop.* She couldn't. She had been uncorked. No way to stop until everything

was poured out.

"I didn't like Isoline, I made no secret of that. I'm asking that you trust me, and trust Rusalka, when we say we acted in self-defense. The important thing now is we move on. Get the mission back on track."

She needed to keep everyone focused on that. *Bad-um-um.* She couldn't afford to fail.

"I'm sorry, Brack. Not for what happened. It needed to. Maybe I shouldn't have told you like this, though. Maybe I should have talked to you first. I'm sorry. I didn't mean to hurt –"

Rusalka snatched the mic out of her hand and closed the broadcast link.
"No. Don't do that," Rusalka said.
"He didn't deserve to be told like that. He was a victim too."
"Don't open the door for him. He has other friends, Elizabeth. He doesn't need you in there, not when he's vulnerable. You can't be together."
"Are you telling what I can and can't do?"
Elizabeth felt lightheadedness coming on.
"You're with Ana," Rusalka said. Slowly, as though it were a complex statement Elizabeth would not understand. Perhaps she didn't. Not in the way she once had.
"We're not together anymore," Elizabeth said.
Weren't they? Maybe her mind was still groggy, blurting out things only half thought.
Rusalka's hand crashed against Elizabeth's face, hard enough to leave a red welt. Behind them, Donovan busied himself at the command centre.
"Don't you dare hurt her."
"I know you saved my life, but you know nothing about it Rusalka!"
Elizabeth shoved her aside as she left the room.

~*~

It had been a long, hard day. The kind of day when the rest of the Universe woke up on the wrong side of its bed. Elizabeth walked back to her quarters, mind repeating a dull mantra. Please, no one be there. Please, no one be there. As if thinking it over and over again might make it happen. She couldn't deal with Ana tonight. She hadn't made up her mind yet, and didn't trust herself to decide when it was so weary.

Somehow, the mantra worked. She collapsed onto the bed. She just wanted to sleep. But her mind was cruel. Querius, Ana, Isoline, Rusalka. Querius Ana Isoline Rusalka. Querius-Ana-Isoline-Rusalka. She dug her nails into her palms. She wanted the pain, the distraction. Sleep would not come. And then slowly, suddenly, it did.

There was a knock at the door.
"Ana..." Elizabeth said.
It was dark now. She turned over in the bed and sat up. What should she say? Invite Ana in? Tell her to go away? Apologize? Argue? It didn't matter. It wasn't Ana at the door.

"Brack?" Elizabeth said.

Her body turned tight.

"Ana's not here," Brack said. Was that a question? Elizabeth couldn't tell.

"Why are you here?" Elizabeth asked.

He gave no answer. He just walked into the room. He sat down on the bed. He kissed her. Everything seemed... unfixed. Time did not flow. It jumped. Her upper lip tickled. Her fingers laced through the familiar pathways on his cheek. Chest. Hips. Suddenly pushing him away.

"You can't just do that!" she said.

She was naked in the darkness. Only his outline was illuminated. There but not there.

"What did Isoline say?"

"I don't want to talk about it."

"I wasn't in love with her, was I?" he asked.

"Which answer's less painful, anyway?" she said.

He sat back down on the bed, facing away. Head cupped between his legs. Brace position. Crash landing imminent. Watch out for falling debris.

"I love you, you know," he said. No Pin Um. Elizabeth had already deleted it.

"Don't say that."

"I do. And you know it. The way you kissed me on Karno. The way you kissed me now. There was a longing in it, Elizabeth. A nostalgic desire."

"Stop it."

He looked straight at her. Eyes aglow, sparkling.

"You and I, Elizabeth. It's always been you and I."

"Stop it! I can't do this, I'm with Ana!" Elizabeth shouted.

"She's not here. I don't know why, and forgive me but I don't care. You need someone tonight. I need someone. We need each other."

He placed his hand on her chest, feeling her heartbeat. His hand splayed out flat. That horrible rhythm, racing now. Bad-um-umbad-um-um. Bad-um-umbad-um-um. Badumumbadumum.

"I haven't felt it since you came back," he told her.

Rusalka

A tear rolled down Ana's cheek, dragging a stain of black sludge down her alabaster skin. It landed with a splash on Rusalka's fur. Her chest was already turning mangy with mascara teardrops.
"Should... should I go and see her?" Ana said.
She looked up at Rusalka, eyes red rimmed and welling. Naïve, innocent, in pain.
"Give her tonight, sweetie."

They were nestled inside Rusalka's cubbyhole. Rusalka ran her hand through Ana's hair, claws slicing through knots she snagged in.
"How would you like a game of cards? I could teach you some more."
"I didn't know it was a bomb! Nobody told me!" Ana said.
"I know, Ana. I know."
"I just, I thought they were to help restart the heart. I'd never seen a bomb before. Sam just... she told me to hand my notes over every week. When I got them back, they had been changed. I thought West was just helping me. I had no idea what he was doing!"
"You can tell Elizabeth in the morning. But she needs sleep, and so do you. Lie down. Can you do that for me?"
Rusalka offered Ana the bundle of rags to rest her head. Ana balled them up into a pile and curled up with her knees tucked into her chest. Rusalka wiped the tears from her chest and continued to caress Ana's hair.

Elizabeth

Elizabeth woke slowly. Memories of last night crashed through her sleepy haze. As Brack's hands touched her body last night they injected her with lustful bias. With the lights bright and the sheets cold, the choice was far less simple. Ana had brought her back to life, even if she had added some extra parts. Brack had ran to Isoline. Fallen for her. Death would defeat her control of the mind, but not the heart. If Brack loved her of his own free will, then he still did. Even if he hated her now, he still loved her. Love can't be switched off. And when a heart's broken it hurts more, the shards inside you, cutting with every beat. Elizabeth couldn't be with a man still carrying that around. She owed Brack honesty. But he had already gone. Things had just gotten much harder.

She splashed icy water against her face. Her eyes were cloudy. She dressed quickly and made her way to the gym.

Brack was on the treadmill, back straight. Brack always used to work out in the mornings on the old Victory Pearl. She had never seen him in here on the new ship. He glanced up and smiled at her in the mirrored walls, cooling his sprint to a gentle jog.

Sweat was bleeding into her eyebrows. Brack was down to slow footsteps and she still hadn't thought of what to say. Quick and easy; the band-aid metaphor. It seemed fitting here. That was all Brack really was. A temporary cover on a fresh wound. Not the permanent solution.

The treadmill stopped and Brack stepped off.
"Where did you go this morning?" Elizabeth said.
"You looked so peaceful."
He took a step forward. Elizabeth countered with a subtle shift backwards.
"You shouldn't have kissed me," she told him.
He grinned.
"As I recall, you kissed back dear. And then some."
He tried to caress her cheek but she batted him away. The sharp scales left a red scratch down her face.
"We can't do this," Elizabeth said. She felt prickling blood start to weep through the fresh cut.

Rusalka's voice came from behind them.
"Can I speak with you a moment?"
Elizabeth turned and Rusalka dropped down from the ceiling.
"We're busy at the moment," Brack told her.
"Yes, I can see that. I only wonder if this is preparation *to be* busy, or the aftermath of business," Rusalka said.
Each word was slow, measured.

Rusalka's hand wiped the trickle of scarlet from Elizabeth's cheek. Her fur stung in the fresh wound. Brack grabbed Rusalka's arm.
"Don't tell her," Elizabeth begged.
"She'll have to find out at some point, Elizabeth dear," Brack said.
What right did he have? He had hunted her down, lurked at her bedroom door. Taken advantage. They had both been hurting. The next morning he disappeared like smoke from a burnt out candle.

"No, she won't! It shouldn't have happened. It won't happen again."
"It was *meant* to happen, Elizabeth," he told her.
His eyes glowed with innocence. She knew that only hid the lies.
"None of this was meant to happen," she said, "I wasn't supposed to die, and you weren't supposed to fall in love with a psychopath while I was gone."
"I wasn't in love with her," he said.
His voice was small.
"You know what she did. How it worked," Brack continued, filling the painful silence.
"The hypnotism only works when she's making it work. She needed to be in the same room, thinking about you. If you weren't in love with her, how could she still have power over you when you weren't even on the same planet?" Elizabeth asked.
"She was different, more powerful..." his voice faded away, unable to hold up its own fragile weight.
"Brack..."
"That kiss, on Karno. I still loved you."
"You felt so guilty afterwards you insisted she join the mission. Or was that her power too?"
That last barb felt cruel. She was not pleased to see it pierce.

Silence danced between them. Rusalka looked at both of them but did not move. A crackle came over Elizabeth's bracelet.
"We've received a transmission," Donovan said.
Elizabeth let the words float.
"Who from?"
"I don't know. But that in itself is something interesting," Donovan said.
"Cut to it."
"We're not really in the mood for stories right now Donovan," Rusalka said.
"Yeah, I guess we're still shook up off Isoline, right?"
The silence exploded. A glass grenade between the three of them.
"Basically, anyone who's anyone is in our database, and anyone who's no-one's in there too," Donovan continued.
"And this guy isn't?"
"This *girl* isn't, no. Cap, we've got military records, civilian data, prison files... you name it, we've got it. Anyone's ever taken a photograph of you, you're on our computer."
"So she's off the grid."
"*Hiding* from the grid. For us to not have her, it has to be deliberate evasion."
"What's she want?" Elizabeth asked.

"Uhhhh, this might be a need to know basis sorta thing, Ranger."

Elizabeth looked from Rusalka to Brack, then back again. Brack stared down at the floor. The mention of Isoline's name had thrown him into the distance. He seemed unable to locate himself. Rusalka had taken out her knife and started sharpening her claws.

Keeping her eyes fixed on Rusalka, Elizabeth answered, "No more secrets. Put out a general coms, everyone gather in the Mess in fifteen minutes. We'll watch it together."

"You got it."

There was a twitch on Rusalka's face. Elizabeth couldn't be sure, but she thought it was a smile.

Forr

His bionic fist stood by the bedside, gripping the air in an empty clench. He unwound the wires and attached the nodes to his temple. He worried it onto his stump. Beside him, Lavell stirred. She purred with eyes closed.
"Are you going to the gym, my lion?"
"Roka seemed pretty shook up yesterday. Not sure he'll want to go through any drills."
"You could do them with Elizabeth, like you used to."
"I think she'll want to be alone today."
Nothing and why. He thought about it and felt sick. Lavell sat up and adjusted his nodes. The hand felt more responsive. More alive. He pulled her closer and kissed her forehead.
"I don't want to do this anymore," he said.
"Do what?"
"This."
His good hand gestured to the room.
"...Us?" Lavell asked.
"I *only* want to do us. It's the death I'm sick of."
She was staring at him.
"Never us," he said.
He kissed her again.

Lavell draped her legs over the bed, turning away from him.
"Why's Serpe still here?"
His skin turned dry. Fur stood on edge. His tongue felt rough.
"She's trying to convince me to go back to Excha."
"Are you going?"
"I already said, I'm sick of the death. Nothing could make me leave you."
She looked back over her shoulder.
"Promise?"
"I promise," he lied.
He needed to keep her safe. If he didn't give Serpe a Harkrak, she would hunt Lavell down.

She climbed out of bed and walked to the bathroom. The scars down her back shone violet.
"Why doesn't she believe you?"

Tongue rough again.

"She... I don't know. Listen, I think we should leave. Just the two of us."

Lavell leaned out of the bathroom.

"Leave?"

"Aren't you sick of all this too?"

Get the jump on Serpe. Maybe she'd never find them. It had taken her years this time. Without the broadcast show, she'd have no lead. The Krei might think him dead and give the Harkrak chair to the next in line.

A dark thought impaled him. He could kill Serpe. He would be free. They would be safe. Lavell's light voice dispelled the demons.

"We can't leave."

"Why not? We've had our adventures."

He walked into the bathroom as Lavell was brushing her teeth.

"Elizabeth would never abandon us."

Nothing and why. She was right. Elizabeth needed them now.

"After this mission then. Just the two of us."

"You're really serious, aren't you?" she said, rinsing.

Nothing and why. That could have been him. Worse, it could have been her.

"I want to retire with you."

Her fingers tugged as his fur. He stooped forward and she kissed his forehead.

She filled a vase with water from the sink. Her fingers traced the gentle petals. He could never kill Serpe. A murderer couldn't deserve to be with someone so pure.

"I think I'm ready to retire..." she said.

"We'll find a nice garden world for you. New flowers to pick every day."

Donovan came over the coms.

"Captain wants everyone in the Mess Hall in fifteen. Emergency meeting."

Elizabeth

Brack shuffled away into the furthest corner of the Mess Hall. Rusalka, normally revelling in scandal, seemed embarrassed to be there. She stalked away too, taking up position on a far away bench. Serpe radioed from the Med Bay. She would sit this one out.

Elizabeth lingered by the door, knowing Ana would pass by. She didn't know what to say to her. She didn't know what she *wanted* to say. But she needed to see her. It was masochism. She wanted to make her own heart burst.

Forr and Lavell were the first to arrive. Lavell's arm around his waist, loose and loving. Forr came closer.
"Elizabeth..."
His eyes were soft with pity.
How did he know? How *could* he know? Her head swam with guilt and regret.
"You can't blame yourself for Isoline. She was never a part of this crew, she was a saboteur."
Elizabeth didn't respond, she just stared blankly.
"Come on Forr, not now," Lavell said, pulling him away gently.

She clenched her jaw. Krakk and Nyomee walked in. Nyomee had washed herself, hair straight and sleek. The mud was gone. Elizabeth almost didn't recognize her. Nyomee waved and Elizabeth grated her teeth.

A blonde blur stepped into the hallway. Shaky footsteps, shoulders hunched. Red rings around her eyes, puffy and blotchy skin. The bloodshot crackle in her whites.
"Hi," Ana said softly.
"Ana, look we need to talk," Elizabeth told her.
Ana had one hand holding her elbow. Trying to fold herself up and disappear.
"Yeah," Ana said with a sniffle, "We're okay though, right?"
And wasn't that the question?
"Yeah," Elizabeth said, just to say something.
She reached out to brush a tear away from Ana's cheek, but her hand felt only fur. Like a spark of lightning, Rusalka appeared in between them.
"Let's sit down," she said to Ana.
She led Ana away. Turning back, she mouthe, *"Not now."*

"Everyone's here, Cap. Want me to roll it?" Donovan asked her.
"Sure."
Elizabeth ran her hand through her hair, scratching at the skull. Grey static fuzz appeared on the broadcast screen. A woman's snarling face sat in the centre. Buzz cut hair down one side. Dark lipstick parted to reveal a flash of teeth. It had changed but Elizabeth recognized it instantly. Olivia. She knew it was a recorded video, but it felt like Olivia was glaring right at her.

"Hello Elizabeth. Long time no see, huh? I know you were busy being dead or whatever, but you should know that your crew *royally* fucked me after you were gone. Like, in the ass. Sideways."

There was an audible sigh of disgust behind Elizabeth. She couldn't make out who it was.

"Anyway. We've been tracking your ship ever since you've been in our sector. I only knew it was you when I saw that dumb blue jacket. I see your tastes haven't changed too much."

Olivia paused for drama and Elizabeth felt herself flush hot.

"The point is, I have something you want. And *I* don't want it. I don't believe in this shit," she tapped a poorly stitched Mundus logo on her jacket, "I only joined them because I thought it would be fun and that I would make money. But now I'm bored. So I'll sell you this... thing, for 1000 currency. But you need to come now. Like, right now. And come alone. I'm sending the co-ordinates."

Olivia reached out and covered the lens. The screen went black.

"I don't trust her," Forr said as her face disappeared.

Elizabeth turned around sharply.

"What do you mean?"

"It has to be a trap. She gets something from this."

"Lavell. You feel anything?" Elizabeth asked.

"No, but the knowing is never that strong off a com link. But *she* was the one who abandoned us. She stole an escape pod and ran away. It's not safe to just *take* one, there are system processes, safety checks. Right, Brack?"

Brack made a noise. It might have been a 'yes'.

"The girl has no loyalty to anyone," Forr said.

"She was thrown away like garbage when she was four!" Elizabeth shouted.

Everyone leaned back, pushed away by the tidal wave of anger.

"I just think —"

"No! I don't care! Look, the last mission I went on with Olivia literally killed me, so I *know* she can be a fuck up. But you have no idea what she's been through. She has no loyalty because no one ever had more than a second's worth of loyalty to her."

"I'm... sorry, Elizabeth," he said.

Elizabeth could feel his hot breath on her face. She could smell it. She hadn't realised, but she'd walked across the room. Her finger was pressed into his chest.

"No, I'm sorry," she said.

Lavell lay her hand across Elizabeth's shoulder.

"Everything alright?"

"Yeah," Elizabeth said.

"You sure?"

"Yeah," she repeated. More conviction, "I think seeing her again just got me for a second."

Forr gave her a friendly smile and she took a step back.

"It's your call, Elizabeth. We'd follow you anywhere."

She took a deep breath.

"Look, trap or not, we need this thing. I have to go get it."

"I suppose you're right. Whatever Olivia has planned, she's already won if we don't try. Or at least, we've already lost." Lavell said.
"Not knowing what this thing even is, I trust you with it far more than I trust her," Forr admitted.

A hiss of distortion came from the speakers. A voice boomed. West. The first time he had addressed the crew since Querius. Several of them looked shaken.
Elizabeth. Take Miss Yukishnov with you
"Olivia said to go alone."
I heard
The voice cut out.

She looked over at Ana, finger looping innocently through blonde hair. Elizabeth hollowed out. Nothing left but a heartbeat. Bad-um-um. She took a glance at Brack. He stared at the wall with absent eyes.
"Should I get the shuttle ready?" Roka asked.
"Yeah. We'll be there in a minute," Elizabeth said.
He trudged out of the room.
"Well Rusalka, easy way or hard way?" Elizabeth asked.
"Pardon me?"
"We both know you're coming on this mission. Easy way is you just get in the shuttle. Hard way is you sneak along and then jump out at the worst possible time."
"You say 'jump out' as if I'm some clown. I act with grace and agility. And besides, hard way isn't *nearly* as much fun when you know about it."

~*~

The shuttle felt smaller than usual. Ana sat across from her. Elizabeth knew she had to talk first. She had no idea what would come out of her mouth.

"So I guess we should talk."
"Yeah. I guess so," Ana said.
Ana chewed her nails. A nervous mouse.
"I need to tell you something," she said.
Ana gave the hint of a nod and began to chew her fingertips.
"Last night, I... I fucked up."
"That his name?" Rusalka muttered.
Elizabeth ignored her.
"What?" Ana said softly.
A beat.
"What?" again.
Quieter.
"Brack came to my room last night. I was in a really bad place after everything."
"What happened...?"
Another beat.
"I'm so sorry. I never meant to hurt you."

"I don't understand."
But Elizabeth knew she did. She reached out her hand to console her and Ana collapsed into tears. In a sightless instant, Rusalka was by Ana's side, arms wrapping around her.
"I didn't... I didn't mean to..."
"Give her a minute Elizabeth."

Elizabeth walked over to the shuttle window. Space was dark. It swallowed her. Forehead against she glass, she forced herself not to turn around and watch Ana cry. The sobs, muffled and echoed against Rusalka, scratched through Elizabeth's skin.

The blackness outside ate her. She noticed, with a strange suddenness, that the sobbing had stopped. The silence choked her like a thick fog.
"What does this mean for us?"
Ana spoke at a careful, unsteady pace. Elizabeth turned to face her.
"We... I don't know."
"Well, what does it mean for you and Brack?"
Ana looked up on the final syllable, her voice developing a hard edge. Streams of tears and mucus shone around Ana's nose. It broke Elizabeth, to see the damage.
"There's nothing between me and Brack, Ana. I swear. This was just... me. I made a mistake."
"That doesn't make what you did any better. A mistake isn't an excuse!"
Her voice rose with a screech. Ana looked over to Rusalka and took a deep breath.
"I want to be with you, Elizabeth. But I don't want to be with someone who hurts me like this just because they're mad."
Elizabeth's mouth was dry, "I didn't do it to get back at you, Ana."
"I'd like some time to think about our future Elizabeth."
Ana's mouth. Rusalka's words.
"Okay," Elizabeth said, and swallowed hard.

~*~

"Uh, Ranger... we've got an issue."
Roka's voice smashed the silence.
"What we got?"
"We can't go as low as we'd like. Visibility's poor with this fog, and if I know anarchist, xenophobic cults they'll have surface to air missiles, probably manned by an itchy pair of hands. Or girled, anyway."
Ana pushed a parachute pack into her arms.
"Ana, I –"
"After the mission. We'll talk then," Ana said, turning her back.
"I don't want us to die mad at each other," Elizabeth said.
It was a dirty trick.
"Then it'd be a good idea for none of us to die. That's certainly my intention," Rusalka said, lacing her arms through the parachute loops.

Elizabeth tensed her jaw and strapped her own backpack on.
"Get us close to Olivia's co-ordinates and we'll make the jump, Roka," Elizabeth said, "We'll find a safe LZ and send the details for pickup."

Soon the shuttle was engulfed by moss green fog.
"This is as close as we're gonna get, but you're still looking at a half a mile walk, unless the wind's in your favour."

Elizabeth pulled a collar over her head and slotted her helmet into place. She slammed her fist into the button and the door slid open. Her jacket fluttered. She hated wearing the helmet.

Ana jumped off first, a step into open air. She twirled, legs tense and tight. The girlish clumsiness was gone from her small frame, replaced by a steely resolution.

Rusalka sped past her, leaping into the air. The tail of her cape danced as she swam through gravity. Elizabeth jumped off in a swan dive, plummeting downwards. The wind slashed against her skin. She pulled the ripcord and the breeze became softer.

She floated and landed on the marshy ground. Rusalka dangled in the bare branches of a nearby tree. Her mouth a stiff, unamused line.
"Alright, get this out of your system and then cut me down."
"Don't you always have a set of knives on you?"
"For obvious reasons, I store them away whenever I jump through space," Rusalka said, body swaying in the trees.
"Where do you store them?"
"In a separate pouch."
"And where is –"
"Stuck in the tree too, Elizabeth! I get that you're enjoying this, but do I need to remind we could be killed for even being on this planet?"
"Yeah, yeah. *Hang* on…"
"Uhh, that was terrible."

Elizabeth drew her blade from her bracelet, cut her own parachute loose and started to climb into the tree. Before she was even halfway to Rusalka, the rope snapped. Rusalka hurtled to the ground, but landed with no more than a crunching of leaves. Wide-splayed paws cushioned her fall. Elizabeth looked up at the rope. It had been cut cleanly.
"Thank you, Ana sweetie!" Rusalka shouted up into the leaves.
Ana was crouched on a thick branch. Fist rested on a bent knee.
"We ready to get going?"
"This place is too dangerous. We should travel as a group; safety in numbers," Elizabeth said.
She turned around. Rusalka had already gone.
"Great…"

Ana

Ana dropped from the trees.
"Where's Rusalka?"
Elizabeth just sighed.

They were alone together. The thought hit her like a drenching of cold water. Suddenly, with a sharp shock, then it clung to her. Every footstep was heavy. She took the lead ahead of Elizabeth, pushing stray branches aside. Tearing them apart with her hands. Elizabeth seemed unusually happy with Ana leading. Perhaps she was guilty. Good. She couldn't stand to look at Elizabeth right now.

Eventually, they came to a thicket that couldn't be hacked through. Ana's blade bounced away without so much as a chip. She sighed and kept her vision forward.
"Where now, Elizabeth?"
The sound of Elizabeth pressing buttons.
"It says straight ahead," Elizabeth told her.
Ana took a deep breath and turned around. Elizabeth wouldn't look at her, instead staring slightly beyond. Ana stepped to the left and forced her to meet her gaze.
"Well we can't go straight ahead, can we?"
"If it makes you feel better, Rusalka's probably already there."
"It doesn't," Ana said.
"How about I scout left, you go right. Whoever finds a clearing first radios the other?"
"Fine."
She had no intention of radioing Elizabeth.

Ana's hands felt their way along the grove. Thin trunks and stubby branches. They felt so small and vulnerable. But every time she attempted to force her way through, the trees snapped back, trapping her hand. Every now and then, Elizabeth radioed with messages like "No luck yet. You?"
Ana never replied.

There was no end to the trees. She saw a hole in the dirt. It seemed to twist down into a tunnel. Perhaps it passed the thicket completely. If she was really lucky, it would also block all radio communications.

She climbed down into the hole, feet feeling through the darkness. Just as her head disappeared into the pit, her foot slipped. Arm scraped against the rocks. A fierce jolt sent her end over end, blackness twisting above her. The pit was attacking her. The visor of her helmet screeched. An uppercut from a foothold sent her spiralling backwards. Her body slapped against the ground and skidded, landing in the damp. Blood seeped inside her armour. Her muscles felt like they were lined with rusty nails.

She saw her reflection in the dark water. Armour chipped, visor scuffed. Pain took over. Her eyes going blurry, she allowed the world to turn white.

Elizabeth

"Ana? Ana!"
Her eyelashes started to twitch.
"Oh thank God..."
Elizabeth scooped her arms around her. Ana mumbled noises of returning consciousness. This might be the warmest she had ever hugged Ana. It made her feel like her soul was cracked.

Ana's eyes opened fully and turned darker. Fear? Hatred? She pushed Elizabeth off.
"What are you doing here?"
"You fell."
Ana slid her visor up. The scuff marks jammed. Eventually she gave up and threw the helmet aside. Elizabeth saw her eyes clearly. Not fear or hatred. Distrust. Much harder to erase. Elizabeth unclipped her helmet and placed it aside too. Ana was still staring, brows furrowed.
"I... was following you," Elizabeth conceded.
"You still think of me as some fragile little girl, don't you?"
"No, I –"
She reached out to brush a strand of hair out of Ana's face but it was slapped away.

Elizabeth leant against the cave wall. Rough rock scratching at her skin. The moisture cooled her, flesh going numb. Ana stood and kicked at her helmet lightly.
"Why did you have to do it?"
She spoke with a quiet forcefulness.
"I... I'm not good at this," Elizabeth said.
Ana waited.
"I've never felt about someone like this before. Brack was never... it was just fun. It was different with you. It meant something. I'd never told anyone about burying my blanket before. I'd never wanted to be with someone just to *be* with them. When things stopped being perfect between us I couldn't take it. Brack was the old days. When nothing was complicated and nothing hurt. I know it was a really, *really* shitty thing to do. And honestly, if you'd done it to me, I'm not sure if I'd forgive you. But I'm hoping you're a better person than me. Because I know you are."

Ana looked up with big, wet eyes. Elizabeth saw her own desperate reflection in the welling tears.
"You thought we were perfect?" Ana asked.
Elizabeth couldn't speak. Her mouth was exhausted.
"I need a little time."
Elizabeth nodded.
Ana took a deep, unsteady inhale.
"You wanna keep the lead?" Elizabeth asked.
"I think you should take it again," Ana said.
"You're the one who found us this killer shortcut," Elizabeth said.

Ana handed Elizabeth back her helmet.
"Let's just see where it leads."

A little way through the tunnel, the cavern widened into a muddy track. Light started to pour in. Elizabeth raised her arm to block the bright glare while her eyes adjusted. A feeling of rebirth. Things needed fixing between her and Ana, but it was the first time she had known that about someone and *wanted* to fix it.

They stepped out of the cave.
"So where are we?" Ana asked.
Elizabeth took a glance around. The thicket of trees was some way behind them now. They had probably overshot Olivia's co-ordinates. No building in sight. Wherever Olivia wanted to meet, it was probably underground. Elizabeth could see her own footprints. Clay. Easy to excavate, simple to support. There could be whole city beneath them.

Her bracelet made two rapid beeps.
"What's that mean?" Ana said.
"Close. We just need to find it."
"How do you mean?"
Elizabeth knelt down and carved a circle with her finger.
"See?"
Ana stared for a second.
"Is that... a code for something?"
"It's clay. Means it's easy to dig through. She's underground somewhere."
A sharp whistle pierced the air. Elizabeth turned around to see Rusalka's paw waving in the distance, cape fluttering in the breeze. Her silhouette black against the beating orange sun.

Elizabeth and Ana jogged over. Rusalka moved a flat rock and jumped down a hole. The rock was flawlessly smooth and round. Sanded down to a clean cut circle. Too perfect. Somebody had made this. The underground city theory was looking better and better. Once upon a time, it had been on her list. She hadn't thought about that list in a long time...

~*~

An underground city. Damp smoke in the air. Walls decaying and scrawled with graffiti. A homeless person, probably human, possibly not, was curled up under a pile of rags down an alley. A group of kids were setting fire to a nearby trash can.
"Something wrong?" Rusalka asked.
"I just always wanted to see an underground city, that's all," Elizabeth sighed.
Rusalka looked left and right, appearing not to understand.
"I'll say again. Something wrong?"
"You ever seen one before?"
Rusalka laughed, "Look, it stinks. It's ugly. It's full of people more likely to kill their

own grandma than offer you a stick of gum. Sounds like every city I've ever been to, above ground or below."

"I guess I'd always thought it'd be like a utopia or something."

"You know what you get when you dig deeper underground? You just hit more shit. Everyone who makes these things think they're reinventing society, but all they're really doing is giving the undesirables another place to hide."

"Have you been to a lot of underground cities?" Ana asked.

"My old line of work sent me to these places a lot. If you're happy and successful, you stay on the surface. Only insects tunnel downwards."

Dim streetlights buzzed. Everyone wore blacks and dark greens, collars raised and hoods up. Sheltering from a storm. She was tempted to drop a coin, watch them come clambering out of the cracks... people like that disgusted her. She could've been one of them, but she rose above it. Rusalka was right. This city was just like every other she had been to. Dirty.

"I can't believe you two had sex in the firing range room," Rusalka said, turning away from them.

"How did you know that?" Ana said.

Rusalka turned back now. She wore a face-wide grin.

"I didn't. Not until you just admitted it."

Elizabeth punched Rusalka on the shoulder, but couldn't stop herself from laughing. Rusalka launched her fist into Elizabeth, collapsing into a fit of laughter herself. Ana let out a burst of nervous giggles and suddenly the three of them were weak with laughter, faces blushing red as they struggled to breathe.

Someone behind them. The laughter stopped. Elizabeth spun. One of the city's vermin snuck up on them. She had her gun pressed into its forehead. Rusalka had her knife held up to its throat. Elizabeth wondered who had reacted quicker.

"Can't imagine this was the outcome you expected," Elizabeth said.

It bared its teeth. Sharp. The cowl fell down, revealing a snout.

"It's always a Shrook," Rusalka said.

"You want him, or is he mine?"

"I mean, he didn't even take anything," Rusalka said, stroking her knife up and down his neck.

"Trying to take something doesn't bother me. It's just the being so bad at it."

"You don't mind someone trying to steal from you?"

"Not really. If they can do it, I respect them. But this guy failed hard."

"Let's compromise."

Rusalka dragged the Shrook's hand from his pocket and quickly whipped the knife across his palm, slicing a cross which oozed with blood. Rusalka kicked him away. He fell and scurried off.

"You weren't really going to kill him, were you?" Ana asked.

"Of course not," Elizabeth said.

"Maybe," Rusalka said

They replied in sync.

"Seriously?" Elizabeth turned to her.
"He was a thief. I don't like thieves."
"*I'm* a thief! *You're* a thief!"
"We steal from places, not people," Rusalka said.
She wiped her blade clean against her fur. The conversation seemed to be boring her.
"Those things in places *belonged* to people," Elizabeth reminded her.
"Look, Ranger, we disagree. That's fine. You won't change my mind, I won't change yours."
Elizabeth slotted her gun back into her holster.
"It's not always a Shrook, you know," Elizabeth said.

~*~

They kept silent as they waded through the darkness. No different from the insects now.
"This looks like the place," Elizabeth said.
Tall grey walls, rotting like diseased teeth poking out of the earth. Ridden with cracks from wayward bullets or energy fire. Windows dirty but intact. Roof rusted but without holes.
"This does *not* look like the place," Ana said, "I thought it would've been some high security... palace or something. Anyone could find it here."
"That's the point. It blends in. I like this girl. Smart," Rusalka said.
"I probably taught her this. You know, back when we were thieves."
If Rusalka heard Elizabeth, she didn't show it.

Elizabeth pushed open the door. The only light was a sickly fluorescent glow. Olivia's shadow was curved and sharp. Rounder outline of her nose and cheeks and hips with angular limbs and spiked hair. A cigarette smouldered from her lips.
"That's a filthy habit," Elizabeth said.
A dry chuckle crawled out of the silhouette.
"They're the healthy kind. The multivitamin ones they sell on Turanga. Want a hit?"
She stretched out her hand. The smoke swirled around her shadow.
"I'll take one," Rusalka said.
Olivia's shape changed. All edges. The cigarette fell to the ground. She stepped forward, crushing it as she drew her gun. The glow from the barrel cast her face in a menacing purple.
"I told you to come alone."
"Not my own boss anymore," Elizabeth said.
She raised her arms up in surrender and stepped forward. Olivia's pistol glow washed over her.
"They're cool," Elizabeth told her.
Olivia switched the gun between the three figures. Panic spreading. Even with the new haircut, Olivia was still a scared little girl who should've stayed on Earth.

She stumbled backwards, almost tripping over a stray slab of rubble as she saw

Rusalka.

"You brought an alien!"

Olivia's second hand rose to grip the gun now, both trembling.

"Don't move bitch!"

"You'd be dead before you hit the ground," Rusalka said, but made no move for her blades.

Elizabeth stepped close to Olivia, pushing her gun back down.

"She's cool, alright. Let's just get this over with."

"I *told* you to come alone," Olivia said. It sounded like she was holding back tears.

"I know you did. But I couldn't. That message you sent didn't even come to me, it came to my boss. He ordered me to bring these two along."

"Look, fuck this. You have any idea what would happen to you if the Mundus saw her? And if they saw me? I want the price doubled."

"Doubled? Come on Olivia, be reasonable."

"Reasonable? Your alien scum could get me killed. I didn't sign up for this shit."

Rusalka reached for her blade.

"Fine. Doubled. Where's the relic?"

"Transfer. Now," Olivia said.

Elizabeth took out a pouch of coin.

"Hurry up," Olivia said. Her feet tapped with impatience.

"What are you so afraid of?" Rusalka said.

"Don't," Ana said softly. It was eaten up by Olivia.

"What the fuck does it have to do with you? I don't even know what you *are*, but I already know that's the problem with your fucking species. Just keep out of it, okay? The Humans are talking."

"They'll be bleeding in a minute..." Rusalka said.

"What did you just say?"

Olivia drew her gun again and centred it on Rusalka. One blade knocked the gun out of her grip while the other whipped up under Olivia's chin.

"What about instead of doubling you pay, we half it? Doubling seems like stealing, and I don't like thieves."

Wood splintered. Running footsteps burst into the room.

"There she is!"

"Traitorous bitch!"

"She's with an alien!"

"Kill her!"

A band of Mundus ran into the room, hollering. Shooting from the hip. Elizabeth turned in a kneeslide. Seven Mundus women quickly became five as Elizabeth fired off two headshots. The rest of them scurried behind a broken staircase. Elizabeth hurried to one of the concrete columns.

"This is your fault! They followed you here!" Olivia shouted across.

"No one saw us. You really think you can sell out the Mundus and they don't retaliate?"

"There was that Shrook..." Ana whispered to Elizabeth.

"I heard that! I told you we should've just killed the Shrook!" Rusalka shouted.
"It wasn't the –"

A grenade skidded across and Elizabeth shoved Ana to safety. Olivia sprinted towards it. She took a wild swing at the grenade, booting it back. It careened off a nearby rock and looped up into the air, bursting with a blast of orange heat just as Elizabeth dove into Olivia.

Rusalka

"Ana sweetie? Are you okay?" Rusalka called out.
"Fine. It's five against two now though."
"I've been keeping count sweetie. Have you got a line on them?"
Rusalka heard the pop-crack of two shots from Ana's rifle. Both missed.
"The stairway twists around. I can't get them from here. Maybe if –"
"Do you have any sticky grenades?" Rusalka interrupted.
"My aim's not great..."
"Not what I asked."
"I have two."
"Great. Set one for 15 seconds, detonate it and hold it out."
"Are you crazy?!"
"Left hand, please."

Rusalka pulled a blue orb from her bag. A chrono shield. Umbra tech. Highly dangerous and unstable. Emergency use only. They slowed time down for the user for a limited time, but overexposure carried a long list of symptoms. The kindest was death.

The chrono sheild hatched into life. Rusalka's eyes stung, adjusting. The battlefield yells stretched and distorted. Dust froze in the air like stars in the night sky. Her feet pounded the ground, almost slipping in her new reality.

She scampered over Olivia and Elizabeth. Olivia's armour was burnt-corked. She had borne most of the blast. Shots swam past the shield slowly, the heat from the energy beams warming her fur. She twisted away from them and surged towards Ana. The sticky grenade poked out in her left hand as she tucked her knees up to her chin.
"Thank you, sweetie."

Rusalka grabbed the grenade and bounced between the rock and rubble, bounding closer as the grenade counted down. Tick. The shots were nowhere near her now. Gravel floated as time stopped. Tock. She reached the Mundus, crashing down on one of their guns. A long scream. The cheeks rippled in slowmo. Rusalka leaned away from the sprayed spit.

As her feet pushed the shotgun barrel down it went off, blasting away the face of another Mundus crouching nearby.
"Well, that was unexpected."
She slapped the grenade onto the wall then sprang away again. She deactivated the shield and landed in a heap. Legs too slow.
"Just thought you'd want to know, it was an alien who killed you! An Umbra too, and we're supposed to be filthy creatures!"

The grenade exploded with a red cloud of smoke. The room fell quiet.
"Whatever will people think of you..."

Elizabeth

Elizabeth's eyes eased open. Ana was standing over her, armour glinting in the dim glow.

"Déjà vu all over again," Elizabeth said.

Elizabeth ran her hand through her red hair. She felt for wet blood but her hand was dry.

There was an ashy shadow in the far corner. Dark powder coated the wall, charred bodies splattered. A stray arm grasped at air, fingers blackened and crisp. Bone stabbed out from ripped flesh. Chunks of organs trickled down into a red puddle.

"So, what'd I miss?" Elizabeth asked, surveying the carnage.

"Sticky grenade," Rusalka said.

"Olivia! We took out your posse! I think that makes the original deal about even!" Elizabeth shouted into the darkness.

Ana lay her hand on Elizabeth's shoulder. She pointed over in the corner. Elizabeth's eyes followed her arm. Olivia was lying perfectly flat, legs straight and arms across her chest. She looked like she was waiting for a casket.

"She... she didn't make it," Ana said.

Elizabeth walked over to Olivia and knelt down beside her.

"We've already got the fragment. It's in this bag," Rusalka told her.

Elizabeth took out some coins and tossed them on her body.

"Fair deal," she told Olivia.

"What are you doing?" Rusalka said.

"Honour amongst thieves and all that," Elizabeth said.

Rusalka handed the bag over. Black velvet. Elizabeth gently pulled it open and looked inside. Long and dark, scored with green engravings. Like a chunk of firewood crawling with moss.

Elizabeth turned her attention to Olivia again.

"We should bury her."

"She's underground now," Rusalka said dryly.

Elizabeth stared at her, arms folded.

"Fine," Rusalka relented, "There's a patch of wasteland behind here. Is that suitable?"

"Better than she'd get back on Earth I'll bet."

Lavell

"Knock, knock!"
Lavell sang as she tapped on the door to the Mess Hall. Brack was sat there, bowl in front of him, staring at the wall.
"Has he moved since Olivia's message?" Forr asked.
"Stop pushing," she chided gently.

Lavell sat down across from Brack. His eyes bore through to the wall behind her. He traced a spoon through his bowl in an infinity loop.
"That lasrell soup?" Lavell asked.
He might have nodded.
Forr swept her up in his massive arms. She gestured towards Brack with her eyes. Forr stared back blankly. A subtle stamp to the foot later, he realised.
"So, what's the deal with you and Elizabeth?" he said.
"Forr!" Lavell slapped his muscular shoulder, "What he means is, how have you been feeling?"
"But you said –"
Lavell gave a sharp look.
"You've not been yourself recently, Brack," Forr said.
He looked at her for approval.
"I'm... fine," Brack said.
He spoke low and slow, like a man learning a language.
"It must be difficult, dealing with the death of a loved one," Lavell lay her hand on Brack's.
"You must believe Elizabeth. If she says Isoline was trying to kill her, that's the truth."
"Forr!" Lavell said.
"What? *We* believe her, don't we?"
"Of course we do," Lavell said. The very question was ridiculous.
"Precisely," Forr said with a smug smile.
"That is not the point. What Forr is *trying* to say," Lavell said with a pointed stare, "Is that everything you found out about Isoline must be tough. And we're here for you. As your oldest friends, we just want to support you."
"Precisely," Forr repeated. The smile was gone.
"I'm fine," Brack said again.
He pushed his soup bowl away, stood silently, then trudged off.
"Poor guy," Forr said.
Spine stooped forward, shoulders lopped. A husk.

Forr fished through the pale liquid in Brack's bowl for the spoon. She watched his huge fingers dipping in the tiny bowl, soup sloshing up into his fur.
"What?" he said.
The spoon in slipped from his grasp and landed in the bowl with a splash. Lavell giggled as the flecks sprayed across his cheeks.
"What?"
A smile spread across his face.
"Nothing. I just like you, is all…"
"Oh yeah?"
He pulled her in closer, smothering her in a wet kiss.

Elizabeth

The sun had started to set. Darkness spread through the sky like ink dropped in the sea. She thought about Olivia, buried by two strangers and an old friend who hardly knew her at all. Mourned by no one. Black took over the horizon. How easily that could have been her, had life turned out a little differently. She took Ana's hand and squeezed it tight.
"I really am sorry, you know. For everything."
They rested their heads against each other, staring through the fogged glass of the visors into the glamorous dark. They were swallowed by the shadows.
"You hurt her, I'll break your neck!" Rusalka hollered at them.
She took this be a sign of Rusalka's forgiveness.

Elizabeth moved away and called Roka. Her whole body felt restored. Reborn from ashes.
"We ready to split?"
"Can you reach these co-ordinates?"
"Wind's died down. Should be fine to reach you now."

Roka reached them within a couple of minutes. The shuttle doors lifted open.
"We get everything we needed?" he asked.
"Indeed," Rusalka said, stepping aboard.
Ana followed her in. Elizabeth picked up a handful of dirt.
"Everything okay, Captain?" Roka asked.
Elizabeth thought about Olivia one last time and tossed the dust into the wind.

~*~

They were halfway back to the Victory Pearl when the first missile struck. Elizabeth fell to the floor, dragging Ana down.
"What's the situation, Roka?"
"Better strap in. We've got one, two... fuck. Six of 'em on our tail. Whatever you took, someone wants it back. Bad."
Elizabeth crawled to the window. She could only see five of them. A Mundus fleet. Like their ripped uniforms and shorn haircuts, the ships were random assortments. Two Torfus military crafts. One with a cannon from The Barely Charted welded to the front. The other had wings ripped as cheesecloth, patched up with sheet metal. A third looked like an ME-2, a cheap gunship with energy blasters, the fourth a smorgasbord of engine parts, cannons and fins in blue and red and green. Elizabeth was surprised it could fly at all. The fifth was the most worrying; a seemingly perfect condition Krei sharp-fighter. Probably the best mix of speed and power in the galaxy. She squinted hard but could not find the sixth.
"You sure there's six of 'em, Roka?"
"I can't see it either. But I've never known our radars be wrong."
A zap of energy surged past the window. Roka veered hard starboard.

"Can we handle them?" Elizabeth asked.
"The sharp-fighter's a concern, but the pilot doesn't seem to know what she's riding. Rest of them we can avoid easily enough, but we've got no guns."
"None?"
"We're a transport shuttle, Captain. There's sharp-fighters back in the Pearl's hangar."
A missile glanced off their tail in a violent crash.
"Call Donovan! Just let me concentrate on not getting us killed!" Roka shouted.

Elizabeth radioed and a female voice answered.
"Hello, this is the Victory Pearl."
"Nyomee? Where's Donovan?"
"He's been teaching me how to work the controls. I can't fly yet, but I can operate the com stuff."
"Where's Donovan?" Elizabeth asked, cutting her off.
"He stepped out to use the bathroom. But I can help! What do you need?"
"We've got six ships on our tail, most custom models so we don't know their full specs. One we can't even see, but it's on the radar. We'll bring the party to you but we'll need someone on the cannon. You'll also need to get our fastest sharp-fighter out there with us; they've got a Krei one that'll out-manoeuvre our cannons. And we need this all five minutes ago. Got that?"
"...Donovan's back now."
There was a static crackle of a mic being adjusted before Donovan's voice came through the com link.
"You say there's six of them, Cap?"
"You hear the rest?"
"One on the cannon and get a sharp-fighter out to you. I'll try and get this sixth bogie once you draw 'em closer. Any suggestions for who you want on the cannon?"
"Br –" Elizabeth started.
Her voice broke away.
"Forr was always a good shot. He should be able to work it, even with his new hand."
"I'll get him on it. Lead those horses to water and we'll make 'em drink."

Forr

Forr had almost finished his lasrell soup when the alarm blared. His mechanical hand was still twitchy. It squeezed Lavell's arm tight.

"You okay?"

"Still getting used to the hand," he said, focussing on uncurling the fingers from her forearm.

"You should *tell* me if it's not working," she said, reaching up to the transmitters on the side of his head.

"I'm fine, my pact," he said.

His good hand gently brushed her away.

Nyomee's voice came over the coms.

"Forr? Could you come up to the cockpit?"

He looked up at the speaker, then across at Lavell.

"Why was it Nyomee?"

"Donovan's been teaching her to fly."

"How do you know that?"

"I pay attention," she giggled, "Come on."

~*~

They hurried up to the flight deck. Not fast enough to beat Serpe.

"How are you out of the Med Bay?"

"You've forgotten what it means to be Krei," she said.

"Leave him alone," Lavell said.

"Does that thing follow you everywhere?"

"Elizabeth's busy getting shot at, if you're done?" Nyomee piped up.

"Shot at?" Forr said.

"Mm-hmm. Got what she needed from Olivia but the Mundus sent a six ships after them. She needs somebody on our cannon, and she needs that someone to be you, Forr."

"Me?"

Forr stared down at his bionic hand.

"You'll be fine, my lion."

"They can only see five ships, too. Sixth one must have a camo shield or something," Donovan said

Forr tensed, relaxed and then tensed his hand again.

"Cap wants someone in a separate shuttle too. They've got a Krei sharp-fighter that'll probably be too quick for the cannons, even with the big guy at the helm."

"My shuttle could have defeated them, but the grey traitor stole it."

"Lavell's our best pilot," Forr said.

Their fighting days were supposed to be over. Now he was volunteering her to be his co-gunner.

"The Jahlder? Preposterous. She won't be a good enough shot to catch a Krei sharp-fighter," Serpe said.

"You've never seen me shoot."

"I've seen Jahlder."

"Ladies, ladies," Donovan said, stepping between them, "Our best fighter's a two person. Looks like we've got ourselves a new dream team."

Lavell laced her fingers together, stretching them out. She chewed on her lower lip. Her eyes narrowed. He leant down and kissed her forehead.

"Be careful, my pact."

"You be careful, my lion. I'll be brave."

~*~

He climbed the ladder up to the cannons quickly, more aware than ever of his hand. Every grip on the rungs echoed through the hollow tube. Roka's shuttle was just appearing as Forr wrapped his hands around the trigger sticks. His thumb twitched on the bionic hand.

The ships tailed Roka's shuttle like streamers. Forr sent a powerful energy blast right through the centre and they scattered. His eyes scanned shuttles. Five. Damn. The sixth was still hiding. An ME-2 had spun furthest from the group, disoriented. A second shot sent it spiralling down in a surge of smoke. Forr switched the ammo from energy to bullets and sent a fine spray at another shuttle, this one a range of colours and parts. Enough left wounds in the side and the shuttle peeled away from Roka. But it remained in flight. Forr tried to centre on it again but his bionic hand swerved too far.

"Damn it!"

Another shuttle joined the fray. Lavell and Serpe's sharp-fighter. Forr abandoned the multicoloured shuttle and focussed on protecting them. Donovan was right. Bullets or energy, he couldn't get close to the Krei sharp-fighter. Lavell veered high and away, dragging the sharp-fighter with her. It was smart flying, leading the enemy's best shuttle away and into a dog fight.

The wounded shuttle was still flying, but it was slow. Carefully, he found it. He switched back to energy ammo and fired. A twitching delay in his bionic hand. Still quick enough to catch its rear in an explosion of purple. Ignoring the sixth and the Krei sharp-fighter, he was down to two. Both were adapted Torfus fighters. Neither should cause an issue.

The fighters turned their attentions away from Roka and stared down the Victory Pearl. Rats before an elephant. Capable of fright, but no real damage. One of the fighters had cannon from The Barely Charted on the front. The cannon jerked up and spat an energy bolt out. Donovan swerved sharply and Forr lost his aim. His bionic hand couldn't stay steady.
"Let me know if you're going to do that again, Donovan!"

One of the transmitters on his head had come loose. His fingers moved slower. The shuttle's cannon glowed red. He let go of the triggers and fiddled with the transmitter. He glanced at the cannon again. Still red. Still in cooldown. Still safe. He reattached the transmitter and tried to move his metallic fingers. They weren't in sync. The cannon dimmed from red to pink. Getting ready to fire.
"Keep us steady, Donovan!" he hollered down the pipe.
He yanked the transmitter clean away and his hand fell loose and limp. He felt for the pulse in his temple and tried to reattach the transmitter. Cannon now pink to purple. Locked and loaded. His hand jolted to life, reflexes returning at light speed. It caught the fighter in its crosshairs and tore the cannon from its roof. The cannon crashed into the second Torfus shuttle, crumpling its nose. Both ships turned and scarpered.
"You tell me you meant that and you're lyin' you sonofabitch!" Donovan called up.
"Let's find that ghost ship! I'm feeling lucky!"
Forr let out a huge roar and sent a flurry of bullets out, hoping for the telltale flaring on the camo shield. None came.

Roka's shuttle dipped out of view as it reached the Victory Pearl. Forr watched Lavell climb. Krei ships were determined even without a Krei pilot. The bloodthirsty breath from a generation of Krei was soaked into the metal of that sharp-fighter. Lust for death flowed through the circuitry. And right now, it was gaining on Lavell.

Lavell

Lavell sent their sharp-fighter careening down and away as the Krei shuttle bit at their ankles.

"*Static*! I had them in my sights!"

"And we were in theirs…"

"Coward."

Lavell continued with her plan. The Krei sharp-fighters were fast and durable, but their streamlined design gave them reduced visibility. If she could roll away into a blind spot, Serpe would only need two or three good shots. She had told Serpe all this, of course, and had even received a curt nod of agreement. This apparent agreement did not limit Serpe's complaints.

Lavell feigned dipping then rose swiftly. The pilot read her and surged upwards too. She cursed her own cleverness. Continuing with the dip would've given Serpe a shot. A quick barrel roll gave her room to manoeuvre again. The shuttle rattled as Serpe fired off a clean shot the Krei ship's wing.

"Didn't think we had enough room for that," Lavell said.

"A Jahlder wouldn't."

Lavell ignored her. She felt a tingling in the back of her neck. Like she was trying to *know* something.

Smoke billowed from the Krei wing. Minimal, cosmetic. Still, the smoke would reduce their visibility even further. The smart choice – the *right* choice – was to lead it around and see if it could handle turning with a damaged wing. But her hands weren't interested in the right choice. Her fingers gripped tight, starting to burn. She drove forward, through the dark clouds, Kamikaze-style. Shrouding her ship in smoke, she left the other shuttle sightless. They were inches away as the black vapour parted. Close enough to see the dust around the boltheads. She yanked the wheel, hoping her reactions were quick enough. She wasn't brave enough to look. They caught the edge of the ship, metal kissing metal. Lavell opened her eyes just in time. A second energy wave obliterated the Krei sharp-fighters nose. Gracelessly, the shuttle spiralled downwards, spewing sparks.

"We could have died you *static* Jahlder *static*!" Serpe shouted.

"We didn't though," she said.

Perhaps she had raised Serpe's view of the Jahlder with her aggressive, Krei-like tactics.

"The risk was not worth the reward. We were doing just fine without your foolishness."

A sparkling hit the corner of Lavell's eye. The dissolving fizzle of a camo shield. The sixth ship. She recognized it instantly. A Jahlder fleetmaster. The knowing. It was trying to warn her. Lavell kept the engines at full blast and hoped she could somehow do enough to avoid the fleetmaster's two cannons.

A vermillion fireball engulfed one of the fleetmaster's turrets. Dark smoke swallowed them again. Forr. The Victory Pearl's cannons would be enough. All she had to do was stay safe. All she had to do was stay hidden. All...

The smoke dissipated. A lightning bolt of energy plucked them from the sky. The engines failed. Steering shot. She looked down at the planet below them. There was nothing left to do. Just wait for the right moment to eject.
"Take this!" Lavell screamed, tossing one of the parachute bags over her head.
A hand slithered in front of her eyeline, heading for the eject button. She batted it away.
"It's too soon!"
Lavell waited another half second then slammed her fist into the button.

The chill of space flooded through, ice chips scraping across her skin. She kept her eyes closed until the beeping on her bracelet told her it was time. She pulled the ripcord and her whole body went limp. She thought about picking flowers. Watching the wind carry their petals. She felt like one of those small, curled, pink petals. No thoughts, no fears. Only the journey.

The ground beneath her was a rich, blood red. She took a stumble as the parachute lowered her, running as the chute's trapped air pulled her along. Yellow and orange weeds crushed under her feet, pale juices seeping out. She unclipped the parachute and keyed in a quick message to the Victory Pearl.

Lavell turned to look for Serpe. She landed about a hundred yards behind her in a combat roll. Lavell waved but got no response.
"I've sent the ship our co-ordinates!" she shouted as she made her way over.
Serpe removed her helmet to reply.
"I've already sent them."
"Maybe they'll find us twice as fast now?"

Serpe turned away. There were yellow and orange weeds under Serpe's feet too.

Lavell took off her helmet.

"I have nothing to say to you, Jahlder."

"My name is Lavell."

Forr's words moving through her.

Serpe turned to face her.

"Jahlder are all the same. You are puny, weak-willed and presumptuous. Forr will have to bathe long in the rivers of Excha to remove your stain."

"He said isn't going with you."

"He lied."

"I'm his talanacti," Lavell said. She took care to pronounce the word correctly.

Serpe's eyes narrowed.

"Fairy stories. He knows his duty."

"Forr doesn't care about that stuff."

"It's beyond your Jahlder comprehension, but all Krei are born with a compulsion to their duty. Forr will not fail in the face of his. He has been many shameful things in his life, but he is not a failure."

"Forr has nothing to be ashamed of."

"He has you."

"He's already told you he's not going back with you. Why are you still here?"

Serpe's smile grew wider. Like her face had taken a blow from a sharp axe.

"Forr always did struggle with the hard truth. Oh, I must remember to thank him for handing me this serrated blade to rip through your heart. Forr will return to me to Excha and we will sire a Harkrak heir. Together."

Rage bubbled inside her.

"You're lying! Forr would never do... that with you!" Lavell said.

"The only reason he left all those years ago was because he couldn't take the pain of my miscarriage."

Lavell's voice jammed in her throat.

"All those years, all those nights you shared: he was using you to get over me."

"That's not true," Lavell said.

She felt herself trembling, vibrating. White hot wrath.

"You were a passing distraction, a salve to soothe his wounds. And when your lion *static* me, he shall have no thoughts of you!"

Lavell leapt forward. Her fist hammered down on the Krei's face. One, two, three. Blood started to leak through Serpe's thick skin. Sharp fingers clawed at Lavell's cheek. Serpe hissed as the warm blood oozed out of Lavell. Wind slashed at the fresh wound. Lavell's hand fumbled on the earth. Her fingers scratched the dirt until her palm felt rough rock. She grabbed it and swiped across Serpe's face. The hissing stopped.

Lavell rolled off Serpe and stared up at the stars. Forr... Serpe... Could it really be true? Their life together had been beautiful, but had it all been a painting? A masterpiece hanging in the background of his real life. She couldn't believe it, she couldn't –

Serpe's pistol clicked. She turned away from the stars. They were the last thoughts she had before a bullet carved through her skull.

Elizabeth

Roka drove their shuttle into the Victory Pearl's hangar. West's voice boomed over the intercom.
Connect the fragments, Elizabeth. Time is dripping down. We are running out of air
Elizabeth removed it from the bag. It glowed warm. Nothing else happened.
"I guess we should get this to –"
She was cut off by her bracelet beeping.
"That's weird."
"What?" Ana asked.
Elizabeth held up her bracelet.
"It's a bunch of numbers from Lavell. No idea what it means."
Rusalka glanced quickly.
"They're co-ordinates."
"I know that. Why's she sending them?"
Rusalka turned to look out of the hangar window. The realisation caught Elizabeth in the stomach.
"Think she got hit?" Elizabeth asked, but she already knew.
"It's pretty near where we are. No other reason to send you a message like that."

Elizabeth pulled the door open. Roka was eating a miha fruit, spinning it in his fingers as he took quick little bites.
"We need to head back out to these co-ordinates. Now."
Roka stripped the miha down to the core in two large bites. He chewed rapidly and took the bracelet she offered out.
"Right now? I need to refuel first."
Running out of air. Querius. It was a threat. But she could not abandon Lavell.
"You don't need to come. Just tell me which shuttle will get me there fastest."
"There's a sharp-fighter around here somewhere..."
As she looked out of the shuttle, Forr kicked down the hangar doors.

Forr

"We need to go and get her!"
He had spent enough time tinkering down here to know there were three shuttles that would get them there quickly.
"This one, Elizabeth! Let's hurry!"
She beat him there and jumped into one of the backseats.
"We'll get her, big guy."
Forr readied the engines. It felt like old times. Except in old times, Elizabeth would never let anyone else drive.
"Buckled up?" he asked.
"Ready when you are."
Forr took off as Ana hit the button for the hangar shutters. He jetted out and dove through the debris.

Forr steered through the smoke and the wreckage. The Jahlder fleetmaster smouldered next to them. He was too slow. If he had shot faster, he could have disabled the cannons before it got a shot off at Lavell. His grip was clumsy as it took them in for a rough landing.

"I make it like, 50 yards? I don't see her though," Elizabeth said.
Forr checked his bracelet then nodded.
"Maybe they found a bunker."
They. It wasn't just Lavell he was looking for. Part of him hoped they would patch up their differences alone. Work out a solution so he could stay with Lavell. This part of him had been cultivated by Lavell; she had grown him into a better person. His Krei core knew they would wait it out in stony silence.

They ran over to Lavell's co-ordinates. Forr knelt down and ran his hand over the footprints in the dust.
"She must have gone looking for Serpe."
"Serpe was here too?"
Forr was already following Lavell's trail. He explained the battle as they walked. The fleetmaster's cannons. His slow hand.

They reached a discarded parachute, edges stained red. Forr ran his fingers along the trim. He heard Elizabeth gasp. All the missions he had ever been on with Elizabeth, he had never heard her gasp.

"Oh fuck, Forr. Get over here."

He abandoned the parachute and sprinted over. His bones turned to water. He clasped both hands to his head. Elizabeth stood with her hand trembling over her lips. Lavell lay limp. She looked less than lifeless. Knees splayed and buckled. Back bent backwards. Glassy eyes staring up at the stars. The hole in her forehead was clogged with blood. Her mouth hung softly. Next to her, Serpe was flat on her back, limps sharper. Angular like roadkill. Her face was ripped open, mottled with blood rivers that pooled in her fur. He collapsed to his knees and held Lavell's head close. The warm liquid soaked him. His heart hurt. His lungs ached. He screamed and did not stop. Elizabeth put her hand on his head and his voice crumbled into a dry squeak. Staring deep to Lavell's eyes, he kissed each cheek. The sour tang of spilled blood. His mighty fingers rolled her eyelids closed.

"I'm sorry, Forr. We'll take them back to the ship and make sure she gets a real burial."

"Leave Serpe."

In the silence, he felt so small. He was looking up at the stars, trying to share Lavell's last sights, when Elizabeth eventually broke it.

"Looks like Serpe fell and hit her head off that rock. Then she... shot Lavell? Why would she do that?"

Forr knew what had happened. He knew the moment he saw them. *This is what it must be like to be Jahlder.* To know. Without question, without reason, without the power to change things. It was a terribly painful power. He did not envy those who had to live their lives this way. Serpe had told her. His past... his future. He wondered how much she had told her. He wondered if she had died hating him.

Elizabeth

Elizabeth had to turn away. The jewel of a bullet hole between the eyes of one of her dearest friends was already too hard. But she knew Forr's pain was greater. It cast her in the role of nursemaid. She wasn't strong enough to help. She felt shame in her stomach.

Forr's weeping continued to pour into her ear as she walked away.
"Donovan," she spoke into her bracelet, "It's not good. When you come to pick us up...." her words faltered, "Come with a box."
Donovan spluttered on the other end. Elizabeth had never had to recover a body before. She had only heard Borreah do it in her gang days. Something in her brain must have dug out the memory.
"...How many?" Donovan asked eventually.
Elizabeth thought about what Forr had said. She thought about Lavell. Flowers. Bullet hole. Oozing blood. Serpe.
"Just the one."
"I hate to ask, but who didn't make it?"
"Neither. But we're only bringing Lavell back."

Elizabeth sank to the ground and stared up at the darkening skies. Her fingers traced mazes in the dirt, every one doubling back on themselves until the earth was just a mass of scrawls. Her fist slammed the ground, drawing up a cloud of dust. She should never have gone back to that temple. Never touched that shield. Never gotten her friends killed. She looked up. The slow moving clouds rolling on with time. She should never have bought maps to The Barely Charted.

Her mind went back further. Never should have met Lavell? Never should have left Earth? No. Despair would not fuel self-pity. Lavell's blood was on her hands. But this quest needed to be completed. This was bigger than any of them. She didn't know what West knew, or what he wanted. But she needed to find out. Lavell's death would not be for nothing.

Elizabeth's knees shook as she walked back to Forr. Lavell's head lay across his lap. From a distance they looked peaceful. But she could smell the blood.

Elizabeth touched Forr's back. He looked down and seemed to realise all over again. Colour leaked away from his face.
"I've called Donovan. We'll make sure Lavell has honour in death."
Forr nodded. He moved her as if she was only napping. It made Elizabeth's heart sting. Forr walked to the discarded parachute. Without saying a word, he dragged it back and ceremoniously set it over Serpe's corpse. He circled around it, making sure her whole body was covered. Then he stood by Elizabeth's side. She nodded like she understood. She did not.

They waited for the shuttle to come. Then, with Roka's help, they picked up Lavell and set her gently in her coffin. Forr tore a fistful of flowers from the dirt and softly lay them down beside her.

None of them had words good enough. The short shuttle ride back took place in a shared, respectful silence, heavy with regret.

Ana

As Elizabeth and Forr raced over to a shuttle, Ana opened the hangar shutters. The shuttle flew past and the jetstream threw her against the wall.

Rusalka closed the door and offered her a hand.
"You need to be careful with her," Rusalka said.
Ana stood straight and closed the shuttles.
"I can look after myself," she said seriously.
"I just don't want her taking adv –"
"I *said* I can look after myself, didn't I?"
Rusalka smirked.
"So what happened underground?"
Ana didn't feel like telling her, so she didn't. She shrugged her shoulders and told Rusalka not to worry about it. Surprisingly, this was enough. With a gentle leap into the shadows, Rusalka was gone.

The only sound was Roka at the far end of the hangar. Rattling metal, dripping oil, whirring tools. The mechanical symphony relaxed her. With the blackness outside, she felt strangely calm. Like maybe things we're getting better. Maybe, finally, things were good. Once this was all over, she and Elizabeth could tour the stars, without a worry or quest.

A sudden clatter. Roka dropped his tools. Ana turned and saw him staring, slack jawed. She followed his wide open eyes to the sound of scraping footsteps. Brack was walking towards her. Walking was the wrong word. It was too... civilised. Naked and bleeding. His right leg gave a little hop, left leg trailing behind. A sick and rotten sludge in its wake. His arms swayed like reeds in a storm. Eyes shuttered slowly, slowly, slowly closed. They popped open, bright and aware, then started to close again. Slowly, slowly, slowly.

Blood dripped down his face. An aimless arm pawed at the wound. It only smeared blood further across his lips.
"Brack? Is everything okay?"
He looked at her, recognising his name the way a dog would. Ana approached cautiously. She felt for her weapon but did not draw. He stopped. Sniffed the air. Eyes no longer sagging slowly closed. They burned through Ana. He clobbered her aside and she fell backwards. The gun tipped out of her holster and skidded across the floor.

He reached one of the heavy shuttles and struggled with the door. It was like he had never seen one before.
"What are you doing, Brack?"
He climbed into the shuttle at stared at her dead on. Eyes slowly closing again.
"She told me to."

He slammed the door. The engine screamed into life. Ana banged on the windows, fists rattling the glass.

Behind her, she heard Roka running.

Brack's shuttle roared louder. Roka slapped the shutter release.

"What are you –"

The words were blown away as Brack took off. The shuttle caught the floor as it flew through the shutters and careened out of control.

"Why did you do that!"

She ran over to see Brack's shuttle sinking deeper into the dark ocean of space.

"He would've crashed into the door! What was I supposed to do?"

The explosion could've killed all three of them.

"What did he say to you?" Roka asked.

"What?"

Ana could still see the speck of him. Bobbing peacefully as the black ooze dragged him down.

"He turned and looked right at you. What did he say?"

"She told me to."

A heartbeat of silence.

"Elizabeth?" Roka asked.

Another heartbeat.

"Isoline?" Ana offered.

Ana didn't care what it meant. All she cared about was how she was going to explain it to Elizabeth. Donovan's voice came through Roka's bracelet.

"You still down in the hangar?"

"Yeah."

His voice was hardly there.

"We need you to head down and meet Elizabeth. They haven't exactly got good news."

Ana grabbed Roka's wrist.

"What do you mean?"

"Ana? It's probably a good job you're there. Elizabeth will need you when she gets back."

There was a crackle of static as he searched for the right words.

"Need me for what, Donovan? Tell me!"

"They found Lavell and Serpe, but there were already dead. I don't know any details but it sounds like something nasty. They aren't even brining Serpe back."

"Dead?"

"'Fraid so. They're heading out now, inbound pretty soon."

"And the rain never stops," Roka said.

~*~

Ana sat in the cavern of the hangar, rocking slightly. Brack's last words haunted her. The room was cold. The shadows spooked her, spiking off the shuttles. She chewed her nails and waited for Elizabeth.

Eventually, Elizabeth returned. Her shuttle landed where Brack's had taken off. She watched Elizabeth leap over her shuttle's nose, directing Forr and Roka as they wheeled out a coffin. That black box made her sick. One of the trolley wheels snagged on the floor. Elizabeth kicked the shuttle in frustration and sunk down onto one knee. She pinched her nose, trying to stop the tears. Ana lay a hand on her back. Elizabeth looked up at her, eyes red rimmed.
"Donovan told me what happened. It's…"
She couldn't find her words.
Elizabeth supplied them.
"Fucking shit."
"Yeah. That."
The wheels squeaked as Forr gently wheeled the trolley.
"Sorry, Forr. Let me help," Elizabeth said.
"No, it's alright. I have to perform some rites. I'll call you when her body is ready."
"I still need to figure out how to say goodbye."
"So do I," Forr said.
Elizabeth tossed her arms around Ana's shoulders. *Brack. How am I supposed to tell her about Brack?*

Ana soothed her, the crying quietening.
"What should we do now?"
Elizabeth leaned out of the hug and shook her head. Her eyes were watering.
"We need to get the fragment to Krakk," Elizabeth said.
"Elizabeth, I don't think we need to…"
"I need to, Ana. This has to be *for* something."

Elizabeth strode through the ship with purpose. Ana struggled to keep up. Krakk was hunched over the desk. It seemed like he was acting out a small scene, using screws as his cast.
"…charmed life…"
Elizabeth coughed. He straightened up, embarrassed.
"Oh. Hello, Captain."
One of the screws rolled onto the floor with a tinkling ring.

Elizabeth handed the fragment over. He took the other two connected fragments and tried to slot the third onto it. A flash of green appeared along the shaft. The whole thing glowed, then it shattered into pieces.
Krakk stared at the mess of black pebbles on the floor, "This may take some time."

~*~

"I need a drink," Elizabeth said as they left the lab, "You coming?"
"I don't…." Ana started.

"You can't really say that anymore."
Elizabeth led Ana to her quarters. Maybe it would give her the courage to tell Elizabeth about Brack. It would probably soften the blow for Elizabeth too.

Elizabeth kicked a chair away from her desk and gestured for Ana to take a seat. Glass chinked as she took a bottle from the cupboard. The liquid inside was a rich, golden brown. It looked much stronger than the Sudince wine they drank last time.
"What's that?"
"This?" Elizabeth took out two glasses and filled them halfway, "This is *whiskey*. It's from Earth. You've never had whiskey before?"
"They had vodka in my colony. But I never liked that."
"That's because vodka is made from stale potatoes. *This* is a real drink."
Elizabeth carried both drinks to her desk. Her other hand kept hold of the bottle as she slumped down into the seat opposite.
"To Lavell," Elizabeth said, raising her glass, "Hell of a Jahlder, hell of a friend."
Elizabeth raised the glass to Ana's and clinked it. She drained the glass in one and refilled. Ana sniffed the liquid. It smelled like burning wood. She took a sip. The whiskey scorched her tongue. It felt like it stripped the enamel off her teeth. She would finish this glass to not insult Lavell's memory, then she would stop.

Three glasses later, Ana was feeling braver. The drink no longer burned her tongue. Now it was a cosy fireplace heat. Elizabeth reeled off stories. The time Lavell wandered off from a battle with Ang mercenaries to pick a bunch of particularly beautiful flowers, or how Lavell blushed the first time Elizabeth caught her and Forr kissing. Elizabeth filled their drinks up, the golden brown liquid sloshing up the sides.
"Listen, Elizabeth," Ana said, taking a deep, warm sip, "I've got something to tell you."
"Fire away," Elizabeth said.
Her eyes looked blurry. Ana couldn't tell if it was Elizabeth's eyes moving or her own.
"You know Brack?"
Elizabeth put her hand up to stop her. She drained the glass again then spoke.
"You don't need to worry about that. It was a dumb fucking thing, but it meant nothing. I was mad and I made a mistake. Forgive me?"
"No, no, it's not that," Ana said, drinking down her own glass, "There's something about him."
Elizabeth set down her glass and put her hands either side of Ana's face.
"You know carsken?"
Ana nodded, though she didn't know where Elizabeth was going. Carsken were small vermin found on Rassek. They were like armadillos mixed with snakes, their long bodies covered in tough plating.
"I always thought my heart was like that. Coiled up tight. Protected. Brack never got in. He was like water. He soaked it, ran all over it, but he never got through. And you came along like a shard of glass. When I found out what you did, I tried to curl shut again."
"People leave their shards in you, right?" Ana said.

Elizabeth half nodded.

"Those shreds let Brack drip back in. But I promise that won't happen anymore."

Elizabeth leaned forward. Ana let her kiss her. Elizabeth's tongue tasted acrid.

"Brack left. He got in a shuttle and left."

Ana blurted it out. No other way to say it. If alcohol was supposed be a salve, Elizabeth was soaked in it now.

Elizabeth's pupils stopped dancing. She said nothing, so Ana explained.

She explained how he'd walked.

How he looked.

Slowly, slowly, slowly, closed.

She told me to.

And for a long while Elizabeth continued to say nothing. Then her head drooped. Ana saw her gulp down a lump in her throat before looking up. Still in silence, Elizabeth poured herself another glass and raised it up. Ana clinked her empty glass against Elizabeth's.

"You know, he was dead the minute he met her," Elizabeth said bitterly.

Ana stood to leave, but Elizabeth touched her thigh.

"Listen... would you sleep here tonight?"

Ana nodded. They climbed into bed. Ana wrapped her arms around Elizabeth's stomach and felt her curl up tight.

Forr

Forr wheeled Lavell's coffin into their workspace. *His* workspace. He couldn't bring himself to open it. His bionic hand touched the clasps. She was still alive in his hand. Her pulse intermingled with his own.

There was a knock at the door. A short melody. The way Lavell used to knock. His head jolted up but it was only Rusalka. He nodded for her to enter. She moved much slower than she usually did, more tentative.

Rusalka went to sit in Lavell's chair. Then she stopped and just stood by the workstation. Something on his face must have given away his panic.
"I thought you might want some company," she said.
Forr's eyes moved up from the workbench. They rolled past two unfinished bracelet augmentations Lavell would never complete. Rusalka rubbed her elbow awkwardly.
"I'd like to tell you a story, if that's okay?"
Forr nodded. It was a long time before she spoke again.
"I've been you before. I've been here. And all the kind words and the smiles and the hugs, they don't count for anything. People just use you to get their sadness out, and you're expected to soak it all up."
Forr's hand fell away from the coffin lid.
"Other than Elizabeth and Brack, I don't think anyone will miss her."
He meant it as a complement. They were cast-offs, beloved only by their own.
"I'm not trying to give you advice. Maybe this is me getting my own sadness out. I've never told this story before. I haven't always been such a loner. Well, I have. But I used to be alone *with* somebody. Koller. We knew each other since we were children. Smart. Brave. Kind. His fur was dark and coarse and oh god I loved him. One of those real ink loves."
"Ink loves?"
"Translators never pick up Umbra expressions. It's a love that's like ink. From the moment it touches you, it stains. And you can never wash it off. Koller was my ink love. We used to do what you used to do. You'd probably think we were less moral, but we'd argue we were more. Koller loved Human lore, Human literature. You ever hear the story of Robin Hood?"
Forr nodded, "Elizabeth told me it once. Rob the rich, feed the poor."
"Koller loved that story. So that was what we did. We stole from people who were

corrupt, and gave the takings to people who deserved it. But of course, we were two poor Umbra from a city in the gutter. We deserved a lot of it."

Rusalka's face started to brighten. She paused to enjoy the memory.

"Then he died. Far too young. And I was left all alone. He didn't bleed out on the battlefield like a fable. He had a muscle wasting disease. He called it cancer. It wasn't that, but he said he liked how things sounded in Human English. It was a language made for writers. By the end, it was all he talked in. Made me turn my translator off to hear it. Cancer. Cancel. There's a poetry in that. But all the damn poetry in the world couldn't save him. The cancer ate him. The hardest thing was how everyone told me I was brave. We're the same in a lot of ways, you and I. Emotion isn't expected of us. But the bravest thing I ever did was let myself cry. The strongest I've ever felt was when I was curled up in a closet, tears streaming down my face. I know Krei can't cry but –"

"We shed our fur during trauma, which I suppose is our version of crying. I didn't know Umbra cried either. I thought it was a Human and Torfus trait."

"My species is very private. What I'm trying to say to you is, you need to get through this *your* way. Not the way other people expect you to. It was a lot of pressure on me so I want you to know... I *need* you to know... it's okay. Not being okay is okay."

She took a breath and composed herself.

"I'm not going to tell you it gets better. But it does change. The pain becomes something else. I miss Koller every day. I look around and it's like there's no more green in the world. That's the closest I can get to describing it. Like I can remember that there used to be another colour, but I just can't see it. It doesn't exist anymore. It's different, and it'll always be different. But it can still be good."

Rusalka turned towards the door. Forr reached out across the workbench, his bionic hand looping around her wrist.

"Wait. Will you stay with me while I open the casket?"

Rusalka gently twisted her fingers loose.

"No. And you'll thank me for that later."

He felt a lock of fur fall loose.

Rusalka

Rusalka tensed her spine as she left Forr's room. Toes curled. She needed to keep her body tight. If she didn't, everything might burst out.

She entered the lab without knocking. Krakk was crouched down, picking up black discs from the floor. He held one up to his eye, noted down the details then laid it down carefully on the desk. There was a rhythmic beauty to it. She watched him do this three times; each time placing the disc in a different place on the desk. The lab table was half covered in the black discs but the floor was still barely visible. Rusalka stepped further into the lab, her foot hitting one of the discs with a light scrape.
"Hello?" Krakk said, turning around.
The moment Rusalka tried to respond, her body became limp. She coughed out a sob and covered her face in her hands.
"Furball?"
He left the black discs where they lay and enveloped her in his huge arms. The discs scattered and rolled as he stepped through them. He didn't say a word. He just held her.

She told Krakk everything. Koller. Cancer. Cancel. And more. How she sometimes turned her translator off when she spoke to Ana because her accent sounded like Koller's. How she couldn't listen to Elizabeth's blunt accent butcher the language. How she was tired of just being alone.
"You're not alone, Rus. Not here."
"You're a good friend, Krakk."
She reached up and kissed his cheek. Her lips left a wet mark on his leathery skin.

"So what's happening here?" Rusalka said.
She wiped away a tear.
"This happened when Elizabeth tried to reconnect the fragments. I'm hoping I can rearrange them so it can be useful again."
"Do you mind if I watch?"
Krakk pulled a chair close.
"This may take a while."
Rusalka used the back of her hand to dry her eyes.
"I've got the time."

Elizabeth

The burst of an airhorn.
Then,
The lab, Elizabeth. Now
And an airhorn again.
Elizabeth jolted out of bed. She threw on some clothes from the floor and headed for the lab as Ana started to stir.

Her jacket slapped against her legs with each footstep. The message repeating until Elizabeth reached the lab. West's voice like cogs grinding.
"What you got?" Elizabeth said.
She didn't notice Rusalka perched sweetly on the lab table.
"I think you owe him a thank you. Do you realise how long Krakk's been fixing this?"
"It's not entirely fixed yet," Krakk said.
Elizabeth's eyes moved over the green symbols glowing on the key's shaft. Her translator did not melt the letters into recognisable shapes.
"My translator's not picking it up either," Rusalka said.
"Krakk? Yours any better?"
Krakk tapped his temple.
"I don't have any translator."
"Seriously? How can you understand me?"
"I speak 7 Human languages. 43 in total. Master wanted to push the limits of my mind."
"He even speaks three strains of Umbra," Rusalka added, "I don't even know any Umbra who can do that."
"So we've got nothing?"

All that blood on their hands. Her hands. Elizabeth slammed her fist into the bench and the key trembled. Rusalka jumped off the table.
"You'll break it!"
"Caution is advised around the key, Captain. I do not know if I could reassemble it again."
She took a step back.
"It's just... we're no closer than we were three years ago when I was dead."

Elizabeth felt her heart beat. Bad-um-um. It had gone beyond keeping West happy. This was about finishing what she had started. The Fire. The tree. She needed answers.
"Not quite back where we started, Captain," Krakk said, "I can't read this, but I have seen these letters before. Nyomee often reads books with these symbols."
"Then let's get her down here."

~*~

Nyomee strolled into the room. Elizabeth cracked her knuckles
"Elizabeth... you put it all together."
"*Krakk* put it together," Rusalka said.
"Can you read it?" Elizabeth asked.
Nyomee tapped the key's shaft. The air disappeared from the room. Elizabeth's skin turned to ice.
"This doesn't make any sense to me," she said.
Elizabeth punched the wall.
"Waaaaait," Nyomee said.
Her syllables stretched out. She rolled it slowly with the flat of her palm. Suddenly, she grabbed the shaft and twisted hard. There was a loud, echoing snap, like rocks breaking.
"What are you..." Elizabeth started, but her voice fell away. A piece of the key swung from a hidden hinge. A green beam shot out and Nyomee aimed it at the wall. A set of numbers. Co-ordinates.
"You're lucky that worked," Rusalka said.
"Guess that's where this all ends."
Elizabeth reached for the key but Rusalka put her hand across to block it.
"Wait a second, Elizabeth. These aren't The Barely Charted. They're Uncharted."
"It's just like The Barely Charted with a bit more anarchy."
"You've not been this dark before. These are in the Presso system."
"Presso?"
"Do you ever watch the news?" Rusalka asked.
"I'm not sure a solar flare 500 years ago counts as news, Furball," Krakk said, "It's called System 42 now."
"Still never heard of it. But I'm not afraid of 500 year old ghosts."
Head to System 42. Now
As West's voice invaded the lab, something knocked at the door with a heavy clunk. Forr was standing there, Ana by his side.
"It's time to say goodbye to Lavell," he said.
Now, Elizabeth

~*~

Forr lead them down to his workstation.
"Did you get any sleep last night?" she asked.
He shook his head. Roka and Donovan caught up to them.
You are wasting time Elizabeth
She drew her gun and popped off two shots. One splintered the camera, the second smashed the com speakerbox. Nyomee screamed, cowering into Donovan's arms.
"Elizabeth! Calm down!" Ana said.
They were props. I see everywhere on this ship. I *am* everywhere on this ship. System 42. Now
"See this."
She raised her middle finger into the air. Rusalka grabbed her hand and shoved it down.

"We're going to a funeral."
Elizabeth looked up at Forr. He did not return her gaze. She felt her throat tighten and her lip start to shake. Suddenly she was pressed to Ana's shoulder.
"I'm sorry," she mumbled through the blonde.
Ana rubbed her back. Forr touched her arm warmly.
"Let's go see her," he said.

They reached the workstation. West broke their silence.
System 42
"Ignore it," Ana said.
Forr turned the handle but the door would not open.
"Jammed?" Krakk asked.
"He's picking the wrong damn day for this shit," Elizabeth said.
She stomped up to the door and tried to kick through it. Her boot buckled the metal, crumpling the door off its hinges. She pushed it open and saw Lavell, lying peacefully. Forr had left no trace of her wounds. The edges of her casket were decorated with petals.

Elizabeth went to step inside but Rusalka dragged her back.
"Get down!"
A fireball ate the room. Prongs of yellow and orange crawled across the floor. Petals withered to ashes. One of the fiery tongues vomited a blaze. The whole room was burning. Thick smoke spat out from the hellish heat. The coffin cracked and Lavell's body rolled out, swallowed by the inferno.

Forr collapsed against the wall, wailing. The orange flames danced in Rusalka's dark eyes.
"How did you know?"
"I heard it. West must have self-destruct failsafes everywhere."
"Why would he do that?" Ana asked.

Forr stumbled to his feet and raced into the fire.
"Forr stop!"
Somebody shouted.
Somebody else screamed.
Elizabeth wanted to rip her own her own heart out.

Krakk followed Forr into the flames. More shouts. More screams. The fire crackled. Krakk pulled him through smoke, dragging him along by his huge hands. The fur across his back was blackened and singed. The smell of burnt hair clogged the air.

Elizabeth ran away.

She was breathing acid. Her blood was crushed glass. Badumumumumumum it would not stop. She ran until her legs howled and found herself back in the lab. Those green numbers glowed. Nothing was worth all this. She ripped the key from

its stand and threw it against the wall.
"Elizabeth, no!"
It shattered with a bright blast.

And she felt herself burst.

~*~

Darkness crackled around her. Her head screamed. Knees bleeding. She heaved herself to her feet and looked around. The key, still intact, glowed in front of her. She picked it up and felt nothing. Stuffing it into her pocket, she flicked the torch on her bracelet. It barely made a dent in the dark. She had no idea where she was. There was nothing to even recognize. Elizabeth turned, torch out. A body lay on the floor behind her. Lying on its front, knees curled up. Face covered by a blonde sunset. Elizabeth ran over and brushed the hair aside.
"Ana? Ana!"
She was breathing but unconscious.

Elizabeth
West's voice crawled out of the black distance. It sounded lower. No com link. He was *here*.
"You blew up Lavell, you bastard!"
She was already dead. She was a distraction
"She was my friend."
She ran towards the voice, gun drawn.
I can explain all
Her gun dropped at the sight of him. Her running slowed to a walk. The man was made of mist.

She walked closer still. Her light beam washed over West. The ghost of a shadow. His legs dissolved in the air, the outline of his arms extending outwards always.
"What are you?"
Human, once. The last one to survive the Fire
"The Fire? You touched the fragment?"
It treated me kinder than it treated you. Or crueler, with a long view
"I've never liked your riddles."
Do you remember the dinosaurs?
Never a straight answer.
"I didn't see 'em on Purple 24."
On earth
"What are you talking about? Humans weren't alive then."
Time does not exist for me. Ever since I touched the fragment, I have started to fade
Elizabeth stepped closer. So close the light soaked through him.
"Are you a ghost?"
His hand appeared and grabbed her arm. The cold fingers chilled her skin, even

through her jacket. He smiled with chipped teeth. She tore her arm away from him.
"How are you doing that?"
If I explained, you would only say 'Magic. Gotcha.'
They were props. I am this ship. He had seen everything.
"Try me."
You only survived the fragment's burn because of the Muslatron in your blood, the shield you wore. I only survived because I was wearing a chrono shield
"They're illegal."
You were stealing when it bit you
Elizabeth walked around him, trying to figure it out. His neck turned 360. Eyes never left her as she crept in the darkness. His eyes dripped down his cheek, melting in their corners.
I did not mention the dinosaurs to tell you riddles. The extinction event was caused by the key
"How do know that?"
Time. I see all
"So how does this end?"
I know the future. Every future. The journey differs but they all end the same. A new race rises. Strong and bloody. They do not stop until the rest of existence is wiped out. They are young now. Vulnerable. Another extinction event will save us all
"You want to murder an entire species?"
To save the rest of us. You need to get to System 42. Now
"Where are we now?"
I am everywhere. You are nowhere
"Why me? If you knew all this, why didn't you do anything?"
You think yourself special? Some sort of chosen one? The key locks into DNA. You were the first to touch it and survive since me. That activated the fragments, extinguished the Fire. Nobody else can feel it as long as you live
"But you live. It still got me."
I fade. Death has already happened to me
Elizabeth took the fragment out. Heavy and cold.
"So what do I do at these co-ordinates?"
There will be a fourth fragment. Connect them and you will control destiny. You can destroy this new race
"You still didn't tell me why you never completed this."
I was close, once. I began to fade slowly. I could see versions of time, but could still control my own timeline. Could still walk. But I took too long. Once the fragments are activated, there is a limited window. You wasted three years. Your window will close soon
"Then why were the fragments on different planets? And why did we have to search if you already knew where they were?"
I failed because of traitors. They were scattered after I died. In different futures, to different places. They alter time, allow creatures long dead to rise. Searching every possibility would take generations
Elizabeth held the fragment in her palm. It was a weight that could crush worlds.

"Who are these people? This race of destroyers?"

Different futures give them different names. In the end, it does not matter

"You're sure about this?"

As sure as the sun sets in the West

"They haven't done anything to us..."

But they have! In every conceivable future, they bathe in our blood. They drink to our deaths and rip the flesh from our bones

"I won't exterminate a whole people for future crimes."

Future. Past. Present. You do not understand time. These monsters will wash the galaxy clean of anyone but themselves

She looked down at the key.

"No."

West's hand surged forward. Fingers around her throat. His bones cracked like icicles. She felt the frost scrape her neck as she floundered for air. Her vision blurred. Her windpipe strained. She almost passed out when he tossed her aside.

Do not waste this! You hold salvation in your hands. Selfishness cannot stop you

Slowly, she sucked in air.

"Selfishness?"

You will not bloody your hands to save the world entire?

"They've done nothing wrong! If we need to fight them, we will. But I will not kill babies in their beds because I fear the man they may become."

West's hands disappeared. When she saw them again, they held a small, metal box.

Go to System 42. Set off the extinction event

Elizabeth shook her head. Words hurt in her bruised throat.

Go. Or I will detonate Miss Yukishov's bomb

Elizabeth felt her chest.

Bad-um-um.

She gasped for air.

"Do it."

West held the detonator up in a grand gesture.

"I'm a killer," Elizabeth said, "But not a murderer."

The world went dark.

Ana

Her world was dark. She fumbled in the void and climbed to her feet. Her sides ached. She felt ripped open.

In the distance, she heard a guttural choking noises. With hands splayed out, feeling the empty black, she approached.
"No."
Do not waste this!
Choke.
Elizabeth. West was hurting her. Ana felt her sides. Her hands touched wet blood, but no gun. She slid he hand down the small of her back and removed her derringer. *You should carry that with you at all times from now on.*

While Elizabeth and West argued, she lurked in the shadows. Their words submerged her. They were absurd, unintelligible. Then her own name.
Miss. Yukishnov
The heartbomb.
"Do it."
Don't. Please don't.
"But not a murderer."
Elizabeth spat Ana's words out.

Ana would only get one shot. Her practise with Rusalka...

She aimed for Elizabeth's heart and pulled the trigger. The bullet blasted through her back and shattered the bomb, severing the explosives. Blue leather, torn. A jetstream of red. Elizabeth crumpled to her knees, spraying blood. The key landed with a hollow thunk. A green sphere grabbed them both and threw them into silence.

Elizabeth

Elizabeth woke slowly. Her fingers crawled across the chest. Tubes and bandages. A sarcophagus of plastic vines. Wet. Warm. A hand guided her down.
"Rest."
A needle stabbed her neck.

~*~

Waking was harder this time. Elizabeth felt her skin again. Colder. Dry. Rough. Scar tissue. A ragged red explosion from her chest.
"Good morning."
It was Ana.
Elizabeth tried to speak but only vomited. Red rose out of her, splashing down Ana's white front.
"Sorry," she said weakly.
Ana giggled.
"Don't worry about it."
She handed Elizabeth a water flask and a metal pan. Elizabeth squirted the water into her mouth and spat. More red sloshed around the metal.
"What happened?"
"I... disarmed the bomb," Ana said.
Elizabeth pressed her palm flat against her scars. Ba-Dum. Pause. Ba-Dum.
"How?"
Ana bit her lip gently.
"I shot it."
"You shot me through the heart?"
"Then I fixed it."
Elizabeth took another drink and spat pink.
"How?"
"I'm a doctor."
"No, I mean... how anything? What happened. Where's West?"

There was a hubbub behind her. She turned and saw Rusalka and Krakk.
"You're awake," Krakk said.
"I've got to hand it to you. It takes guts, dying twice," Rusalka said.
"She didn't really die," Ana said.
They rushed forward. Ana tried to push them back.
"Give her some space."

"What did he say to you?" Rusalka asked.
"Didn't I say don't harass her with questions when she wakes up?" Ana said.
"I'm in a question mood myself. How did all this happen Ana? How are we back here?" Elizabeth looked around, "...This is the Victory Pearl, right?"
"It has changed a little, the past seven years," Rusalka said.

"Seven years?"
"That's not funny, Rusalka," Ana told her, "It's only been a few weeks."

Forr appeared at the door.
"Any progress?"
"Just a little," Elizabeth said.
He rushed in, Roka following.
"Never could've forgiven you if you'd left me here with these guys," he said.
"Not leaving anytime soon. Anyway, Ana? What's going on?"
"Right. When you threw that... thing the first time, I was sent there with you."
"I saw. I tried to wake you."
"Where was that place?"
"I don't think it was anywhere..." Elizabeth said.
"When I shot you, dropping that thing set it off again. We ended up back here and I started patching you up."
"Why isn't he making us all suffocate? Why not blow the ship?"
"He was nearest the key when you dropped it. Maybe it killed him."
"So what did he say?" Rusalka said.
Elizabeth drooped her legs out of the bed. She moved, unsteady, with Ana's hand at her back. Elizabeth walked to the window and stared out at the deep purple distance. Death on the horizon.
"He wanted me to destroy a planet. I don't think the key will work anymore. Apparently there was a time limit."
"So, it's all over?" Forr said.

Another commotion behind her. She saw Donovan and Nyomee's dark reflection in the window pain. Nyomee ran for her. Her hair was clean and smelled like oranges. Donovan shook her hand once Nyomee let her go.
"Knew you'd come back to us."

Elizabeth's eyes rolled over her crew. Ana. Rusalka. Forr. Krakk. Donovan. Nyomee. Roka. This mission had been full of heartache, but that was life. That would've happened to her anywhere. *So, it's all over.* A rebirth.
"Where to, Captain?" Donovan asked.
Elizabeth looked out at the stars and smiled.